**SHE WAS A TEMPTATION
A SAINT WOULD HAVE TROUBLE RESISTING.
AND HE WAS NO SAINT.**

"You have no idea what kind of danger you're in now that I've found you."

"You wouldn't hurt me." She knew that as surely as she knew her next breath would be filled with the heady scent of man and leather and desert and rain that all mixed together to become Kane.

"I can hurt you in ways you can't even imagine."

She shook her head. "You're wrong, Kane. Why are you so hard on yourself? I trust you."

She wanted to be with him and love him, more than she'd ever thought possible. This was right. She knew it in her heart.

She was Kane Carrington's woman and somehow she knew she always would be.

Books by Teresa Southwick

Winter Bride
Reckless Destiny

Published by HarperPaperbacks

Reckless Destiny

TERESA SOUTHWICK

HarperPaperbacks
A Division of HarperCollins Publishers

HarperPaperbacks   *A Division of* HarperCollins*Publishers*
10 East 53rd Street, New York, N.Y. 10022

Copyright © 1995 by Teresa Southwick
All rights reserved. No part of this book may be used or reproduced in any manner whatsoever without written permission of the publisher, except in the case of brief quotations embodied in critical articles and reviews. For information address HarperCollins*Publishers,*
10 East 53rd Street, New York, N.Y. 10022.

Cover illustration by Jean Monti

First printing: November 1995

Printed in the United States of America

HarperPaperbacks, HarperMonogram, and colophon are trademarks of HarperCollins*Publishers*

❖ 10 9 8 7 6 5 4 3 2 1

With thanks to Stephanie Westphal
for putting a finer point on the writing,
Barbara Joel for helping me
find the emotion in my characters,
and Barbara Ankrum for always asking why.

Reckless Destiny

1

Arizona Territory, September 1883

Cady Tanner blew out the oil lamp on the table by the window and resigned herself to another sleepless night in the little pitch-black adobe. Even more than September's stifling heat, worry about her brother Jack kept her awake. Where could he be? She'd sent word weeks ago that she was coming. This was her seventh night alone in his cabin, and with each passing day her apprehension grew. What if Jack hadn't received her telegram? What if something had happened to him?

The canvas floor was rough against her feet as she felt her way to the cot pushed against the wall. Compared to her own intricately carved bed frame and fine linen sheets at home in New York, it was simple. In fact, if it hadn't been for the Tanner family photograph on the table, she would have thought the army detail she'd asked to bring her here had left her in the wrong spot. Mama would never have agreed to let her come if she'd known Jack lived in such a primitive place.

Cady didn't care. Her life back east was more stifling than the heat in Arizona Territory. She was glad to be away from her parents' social restraints, no matter how uncivilized the frontier might be. Soon she would realize her dream to be a teacher. Even more exciting, she'd be using the skills she'd learned where they were needed most.

At the women's college she'd attended, she'd discovered that the West desperately needed teachers. That was all she'd had to hear to make up her mind. Eager for adventure, she'd packed her things and said goodbye to her family. The trip had been long and tiring, but she'd finally arrived. Everything would be perfect if only Jack—

Without warning, the wooden door slammed open.

"Who's there?" The deep voice was more growl than anything else.

Cady's heart thudded against her ribs. A man's figure was silhouetted in the doorway. She could see the barrel of a rifle. She hadn't heard any noise, any warning of his approach: no footsteps, no horse, nothing. She took several steps before she realized there was no place to run.

Two years ago, in 1881, when she'd first visited the Territory, she'd stayed either in town or in a private railroad car. Help had been close by in case of trouble. This time Cady was alone. Papa had warned her about the dangers she would face, but Mama had said that Jack would be there to protect her.

At this moment, she wished with all her heart and soul that she'd listened to Papa.

As she slowly retreated, the backs of her legs touched the cot. She cried out, then caught her breath as she nearly tumbled.

"Hold still," the man snapped. "Start talkin' before I blow a hole in you big enough to drive a wagon through."

A lump in her throat expanded until she wasn't sure she could get any words out, but she knew she'd be dead if she didn't.

"Don't shoot, please, sir. I'm C-Cady Tanner. This cabin belongs to my brother Jack."

The rifle barrel lowered toward the floor. "Cady? What in the name of God are *you* doing here?"

"Jack?" She peered into the darkness, toward the voice, familiar now without the growl. "It *is* you, isn't it?"

"Sure is. Stay put while I light the lantern."

"All right." Her legs were still shaking too badly to move anyway.

She heard the scrape of boots across the canvas floor. As her brother moved toward the table, the odors of horse, leather, and smoke mixed with the scent of the lilac soap she'd used to wash up before bed. With the scratch of a match the lantern glowed to life, illuminating his tall form. He turned, and in spite of the dusty black hat and forbidding dark mustache, she recognized her brother.

"Jack," she whispered. "You nearly scared the life out of me!"

"Cady." The name was spoken in the gentle tone he used only for her.

She threw herself into his arms. "Oh, Jack!" she said, her voice muffled against his soft cotton shirt.

He hugged her tightly and rested his cheek against the top of her head. His whiskers caught in her hair. The last time they'd been together, she'd teased him for shaving twice a day to keep his face smooth for all the ladies who drifted in and out of his life. The new mustache was only one of the changes in him. He was broader through the chest and the muscles in his back were more defined, as if he did hard physical labor every day. This was not the same man she'd known three years ago in New York. But it didn't matter. He was still her brother Jack and she was glad he was safe.

He gripped her upper arms. Calluses on his fingers pulled at the fibers in her nightgown. He had never worked with his hands when he'd been employed by their older brother in his railroad company. What kind of life did Jack lead now?

He set her away from him. "Tell me what the hell you're doing here before I paddle your backside."

She shook her head disapprovingly. "I'll be sure to tell Mother that you haven't stopped swearing."

He pulled on her braid. "I see *you* haven't stopped being a pigtailed, pigheaded little brat."

She laughed. "You always had a way with words. Is that why you greet your guests with a gun?" She tossed her long braid over her shoulder.

His expression darkened. "Out here, yes. You learn to shoot first and ask questions later."

"I'm very glad you didn't shoot. Where have you been, Jack? I've been here a week, getting more frantic every day. I even went to the fort, and the young officer I spoke to said he'd alert the daily patrols to watch for you."

"Cady, for God's sake. Why didn't you let me know you were coming? You've got to quit being so impulsive. Dammit, I almost killed you!"

"But you didn't. God knows you've threatened often enough to do me bodily harm." She planted her hands on her hips and glared at him. "For your information, Jackson Tanner, I did say I was coming. I sent a telegram weeks ago."

"Which I never got. I've been away. Did it ever occur to you to wait for a reply?"

"It's not my fault you spend so much time looking at rocks in the mountains."

"It's called prospecting."

"Whatever. Aren't you even a little bit glad to see me?"

"Sure, I'm glad to see you. Lord, you've grown up. Some man might just look at you twice now." He studied her, and a tender expression slipped into his dark eyes. "But I wish I'd known you were coming. I'm only going to be here long enough to gather supplies. Then I'm going back up into the Superstition Mountains."

"Why do you have to leave?"

"I just learned there's a canyon up there filled with gold. Only the Apaches know where, but they don't mine it. Something about being disrespectful to their gods. I plan to find that canyon."

"If they don't mine it, I can't imagine they'd be too happy about you doing it. Sounds dangerous. Maybe you shouldn't—"

"I have to." He leaned against the table by the window. Outside, a half-moon cast an eerie glow on the desert. "We can have a short visit, then I'll take you down to Phoenix and put you on a train for home."

"I'm not leaving. I have a job to do here."

"A job?" He snorted. "You can't stay in Arizona. It isn't safe for a woman by herself."

Well, she wouldn't go back and let her father run her life. He meant well, but it was time to stand on her own two feet. "I'm not a little girl anymore. Don't tell me what to do. I'm sick to death of men ordering me around." Anger made her cheeks burn. "First Papa, and now you."

Another man had told her what to do once, two years before. She remembered that time as if it were yesterday. She'd come to visit their older brother, Jeff, while he was building a bridge for the railroad. On a night with the moon so big and yellow she could hardly believe it was the same one she saw at home, and the stars so bright they sparkled like diamonds on blue velvet, she'd kissed a dashing army officer. She'd kissed him until her knees turned to butter and she could hardly breathe. She'd kissed him and knew she'd follow him to the ends of the earth and back if he asked.

When that same man had told her to go home because she wasn't cut out for life in the Territory, he'd hurt her terribly. In one evening, she'd given her heart away and had it returned in pieces.

Now she'd come back, eager to take charge of her own destiny. No one was going to tell her what to do ever again.

"I didn't accept a teaching position at Fort McDowell and come all this way just to turn around and go back," she said.

His eyebrows lifted. "So you're a teacher now? In her letters, Mother said you were studying, but I didn't know it was official."

"Well, it is and I'm here to work."

"If you had waited for me to respond to your telegram, I could have saved you the trouble."

"If I had waited to hear from you, someone else might have taken the job."

He snorted. "Not likely. The last teacher was an enlisted man who showed up for school drunk after only a week. After that, he was relieved of his duties. The funny thing is, he'd never touched a drop of liquor before, and as far as I know he's been sober as a judge since."

"You told me about him in your last letter, and that's why I'm here. It's clear the man didn't want to be a teacher. I do. And it suddenly came to me where my training would best serve."

"Remind me to be more careful what I put in my letters from now on." There was a teasing light in his eyes. This was more like the Jack she remembered.

"I will." She fanned her hand in front of her face, trying to create some air to cool her.

"Let's sit on the porch," he said. "This time of night it's more comfortable out there."

She nodded and reached for her cotton duster on the end of the bed.

"What do you need that for?"

"Because a lady always dresses modestly."

"This isn't the East." He grinned. "There's no one for miles around to see you." It was good to see him smile, even if it was at her expense.

They walked out on the porch, and a lovely breeze dried the moisture on her flushed face. The half-moon revealed the dark shape of mountains in the distance. Cactus and scrub and sand filled the desert floor in between. She could feel the warmth of the wind as she sat on the step. With her back against one of the cotton-wood poles holding up the roof, she studied her brother.

He leaned his shoulder on the support across from her. The pose was casual, but she sensed uneasiness churning below the surface. That had always been in him, but it was sharper now and edged with a fervor she didn't understand.

"How'd you talk Mother into letting you come?" His lips thinned. "She does know where you are this time, doesn't she?"

"Of course. She agreed quite readily to this plan for two reasons." She took a deep breath. "Number one, you're here."

"I knew it. She expects me to nursemaid you."

"That's not true. I'm perfectly capable of looking after myself."

"Let's put that aside for a minute," he said. "What's the second reason?"

She hesitated. This was the hard part. "The scandal."

He went completely still, then carefully looked her over, stopping at her abdomen. "Could you be a shade more specific?"

"I'm not in the family way," she said. "Although I was engaged to be married. Did you know that?"

He shook his head. "Who?"

"His name is Lieutenant Will Hardesty. He's in the army, stationed near the teaching college I attended in Baltimore."

His gaze darted to her left hand. She held it up and wiggled her naked ring finger. "Nothing there."

"What happened?" he asked.

"I couldn't go through with it."

"Why?"

"A lot of reasons that don't matter now. I just knew it wasn't fair to him."

"Could it have anything to do with that captain you met when you ran away from school two years ago, the one Mother told me about? She never did mention his name."

"And I can't remember it." The lie tasted bitter, but she was pleased that her voice sounded carefree and almost normal. She was surprised that Jack had mentioned her brief encounter with Captain Kane Carrington. She'd tried hard to forget him, including almost marrying someone she didn't love. But maybe she owed him thanks for one thing.

She thought she had left school for good, two years ago, but that was before Kane told her in effect that she was useless. His assumption that she was a pampered rich girl sent her home eager to gain some skills. She'd realized it wasn't the studying she hated as much as the exclusive, snobbish school she'd been sent to. She had no tolerance for those who judged people by how much money they had or how high up they were in the social order. So she'd simply enrolled in the best women's teaching college she could find.

If Kane hadn't pushed her away, she might never have found what she really wanted. She'd also never have hurt that poor young lieutenant. That was why she planned to avoid affairs of the heart and put all her energy into teaching—the reason she'd come to the Territory in the first place.

"So you left your intended standing at the altar."

"Not quite, but very nearly." She sighed. "Then your letter came, and I knew where my training would do the most good."

"So it really is my fault you're here."

"Mother was angry—not at me," she added quickly. "She encouraged me not to go through with the vows if I had the slightest doubt. But there was a lot of gossip. She would have agreed to almost anything to get me away from 'all those narrow-minded biddies.' Her words, not mine."

"Sounds like her."

"So I sent you a telegram and here I am. Easy as pie."

"I wish Mother hadn't let you do it."

"I had to, Jack. I couldn't sit there like a bump on a pickle and wait for life to come to me. I have to find my own way. They told us at school that teachers are scarce in the Arizona Territory. It's a patriotic duty to go west."

"What's that got to do with you?"

"I'm here to settle the frontier."

He looked at her for a second and then threw his head back and roared with laughter. "Do you plan to settle it single-handed? Or can anyone help?"

"You know what I mean."

"Yes." His mouth thinned to a grim line. "That's why I can't let you stay."

"Give me one good reason," she cried.

"I can give you more than that. For starters, you'll need a man to watch out for you, and I'm away prospecting most of the time."

"I already told you, I can take care of myself."

"Maybe where it's civilized, but not here. A teaching certificate won't protect you from a band of renegade Indians. Or flood. Or insects. Or disease."

"I know you're just being protective, and I love you for it. But the fact is, even if you were here all the time, you can't keep me safe from those things. And Fort McDowell is only two miles away."

"That won't do you any good if I'm not here and the Apaches decide to pay you a visit."

Cady had to think fast. She knew when Jack made up his mind about something it stayed made up. He would take her bodily to the train in Phoenix if he decided that was best.

"What if I live at the fort while you're away? Would you object to my staying then?"

He was quiet for a long moment. "I would feel better if you were under the army's protection while I'm away. Major Wexler is a good man. He'll see that you're safe." He glared at her. "If you listen to him and do what he says, maybe—"

"Thank you!" She jumped into his arms. "You won't regret this, Jack."

"See that I don't." He set her down and his eyes narrowed. "You know if there's no room for you there, you're going home."

"There must be somewhere for me to stay."

"You really have grown up." His expression told her

he was anything but happy about it. "There's such a shortage of women out here, something tells me those soldiers would find a place for you if they had to build it special. Maybe this isn't such a good idea."

"Too late. Everything's settled." She patted his arm as she headed back inside. "It's all going to work out fine. You'll see."

Kane Carrington reined in his horse at the top of a rise. He pushed his campaign hat back and ran his forearm across his sweaty brow. Only eight in the morning and already hot. He scanned the desert from left to right and shook his head. He'd been stationed all over the Arizona Territory, and almost everywhere he went the landscape was the same. He hadn't figured out yet why the barren desert and jagged, spectacular red mountains appealed to him. He only knew there was something about their rugged beauty that drew him.

He'd just come back from a two-week patrol the day before. Most of Company C thought he was crazy to get back in the saddle and ride for pleasure, but he needed to. At least while his mind was occupied with controlling his mount, he didn't have time to think.

As Kane scanned the horizon again, a dust cloud to the right caught his attention. At first he thought the wind had raised it; then he realized it was moving along the road to the fort, traveling steadily and fast. As the cloud moved closer, he could see the dust was kicked up by a horse and buckboard. Something was wrong. The vehicle was moving too fast for that rutted road. If there was a driver, he wasn't in control.

Kane settled his hat low on his forehead, tied his kerchief over his nose and mouth, and nudged his horse forward to intercept the runaway. Caution battled his need for haste as he guided the animal through the scrub, watching for snake holes, rocks, or hidden gullies that could cause fatal injury. As soon as they reached the road, ten lengths behind the wagon, he urged the animal forward at full speed. Dust swirled around him, and he bent his head to protect his eyes from the worst of it.

In a matter of minutes, he edged alongside the runaway vehicle and kept pace for several seconds. There *was* a driver; the woman was holding onto the seat for dear life. He saw that the reins had fallen and were being kicked around by the horse's hooves. He could try to turn the animal off the road, but the scrub was high and might do more harm than good. He only had one choice.

"Whoa, there," he called to the lathered horse as he grabbed the harness.

The animal was tiring, and with very little effort Kane slowed it down. When the wagon was completely stopped, he turned his attention to the driver.

He couldn't tell her age, but she was a slender little thing. Her hat, an impractical concoction, had slipped down over her eyes. She didn't even know enough to wear a wide brim hat to keep the sun off her head and face. With both hands gripping the wagon seat during the wild ride, she hadn't been able to push the thing out of her eyes.

"Are you all right, ma'am?"

She sat very still for several seconds, seeming to catch her breath. Tentatively, she released one hand, then the other. She removed a long pin from the crown of her hat and pulled it free. Golden-brown hair spilled around her shoulders. The strands rested over her breasts and skimmed her waist—a very trim waist.

She pushed the mass away from her face and shook her hair back before looking at him. Her green eyes, familiar eyes, widened. Something caught and squeezed in his chest. Cady? Cady Tanner? It couldn't be! But there she was, even more beautiful than the last time he'd seen her.

He'd been deliberately cruel to her that night. He hoped she had gotten over his harshness quickly. It had taken him a long time to get used to the idea that he would never see her again. Even now, he could hardly believe she was here.

She raised one hand, palm facing him. "Don't come near me," she said fiercely. She pointed the hatpin at him and jabbed the air with it. After glancing over her shoulder, she looked at him without batting an eye. "Jack's coming any minute now. He's got a gun. He'll blow a hole in you big enough to drive a wagon through."

Apparently she hadn't forgotten or forgiven him for what he'd said to her the last time they'd been together.

"Jack?" He blinked. "What's wrong with you? Put that stupid thing down."

"So you can rob me? Without even a fight? I don't think so. If you come near me, I'll do as much damage as I can. It won't be easy to have your way with *me*."

"Have my way—what the hell are you talking about?" He studied her cheeks, red from the heat. His saddle creaked as he leaned toward her. "I think the sun's cooked more than your face."

"You stay away from me." She slid back from him and held the pin like a saber. "Can't even show your face, can you, you coward!"

Show his face? He lifted a hand to his chin. The kerchief! And he was out of uniform. She probably thought he was a bandit. He pulled the square of material down and watched her eyes grow big with recognition.

"Kane?" She stared at him and lowered the hatpin so slowly he wondered if she was still planning to use it now that she recognized him. "Good Lord, I can't believe it's you."

She remembered. He was more pleased than he should be. His heart was pounding like a drum beating cadence for parade march. What was she doing here? Why was she alone? She could have been killed if he hadn't gotten to her.

A knot of fear pulled tight in his gut before he got angry. "Are you all right?"

"Fine, thanks to you." An appreciative look softened her eyes for a second. Then she blinked, and the sudden uncertainty told him she didn't want to be grateful to him.

"What happened? Did something spook the horse?" He dismounted, picked up the fallen reins, and handed them to her.

"I'm not sure. All I did was lift these against the horse's rump." She raised her hands to show him.

"Don't!" He grabbed her arm, then took the leather strips and wrapped them around the brake. "I think they're safer there."

"All that bouncing made me ache in places I didn't even know I had." She stood, stretched, and rubbed the small of her back.

Kane swallowed hard as her white cotton blouse pulled across her breasts. Even dusty and disheveled, she was more beautiful than the image of her he'd carried with him for the last two years.

"Let me help you down, Cady."

She nodded. "I think I'd like solid ground beneath my feet."

He put his hands around her small waist, and she rested her gloved fingers on his shoulders. He lifted her and set her on her feet in front of him. She started to crumple as if her legs wouldn't hold her, and he caught her against him to steady her.

She looked up and their eyes met. A sizzle of awareness sliced through him. He was no longer standing in the middle of an Arizona desert with the sun beating down. Instead, it was the night of the reception at Fort Mohave and they were bathed in moonlight. She was dressed in some shimmering green gown that matched her eyes and rustled when she moved.

He stared at her mouth, the same full lips he had kissed until he thought he'd go crazy from wanting her. He ached to know if she still tasted as sweet now as she had then. That night, when she had tried to convince him that he needed her, she was closer to the truth than she knew, so he had told her she wasn't cut out for his kind of life. He had deliberately hurt her because he could never have her.

After all this time, she still got to him.

"Are you sure you're all right?" he asked.

"My legs are a bit wobbly is all," she said, with a shaky little laugh.

She was trying to act as if her close call was nothing out of the ordinary, but he could see she was pale and trembling. He couldn't help admiring her nerve; most women would have collapsed in tears. God, he was glad to see her! He didn't want to be, but he couldn't help it.

"You can let me go now," she said, pushing away from him.

"What?" He looked down and saw her hands on his chest.

"I'm fine. You can let go of me."

He shook his head to clear it and took a quick step back. "Sorry." As he moved away, the familiar emptiness swallowed the warmth he'd felt from having her in his arms again.

The road vibrated with pounding hooves, and Kane looked up to see a rider coming. Dust drifted around them as the man yanked on the reins, forcing his horse to a skidding stop. As agile and quick as a cat, he swung out of the saddle. From the anxious look on his face, Kane concluded that Cady hadn't been bluffing when she said someone named Jack was coming.

The man strode over to her and took her arm possessively. Intensity radiated from him like waves of heat from the desert floor. "Are you all right?"

"Fine." She pointed in Kane's direction. "He stopped the horse."

"Much obliged for your help," the man said, turning to him without releasing his protective grip on Cady.

His air of possessiveness told Kane that Jack must be her husband.

Something caught in his chest. He gritted his teeth, torn between relief that she was unavailable and unreasonable anger at the thought of her in the arms of another man.

Funny. Every time images of Cady had stolen into his mind, unbidden and unwanted, he'd always thought of her as a single woman. It made sense that she would have married. She was beautiful, intelligent, and spirited. Men would swarm around her like bees to honey.

"Glad I was around to help," he said. "Next time don't let her drive by herself."

If she were *his* wife, Kane thought, she wouldn't go gallivanting in dangerous territory alone and unprotected.

The other man's eyes turned dark and dangerous. "If you knew Cady, you'd know she doesn't do what she's told, no matter who does the telling." He turned to her. "I told you to wait for me. You don't know how to drive a horse and wagon, do you?"

"No, and I didn't try to," she said with a shrug. "You know how restless I get. I was curious." She leaned over to unwind the reins. "All I did was lift them like this—"

"Don't!" Both men hollered at once and she dropped her hand.

Jack glared at her. "Of all the reckless, hare-brained stunts. In the time it took me to saddle my horse, you could have been killed. I ought to take you over my knee."

Kane took a step forward. "Now hold on."

Jack slid his hostile gaze in Kane's direction. "Look, mister, I'm thankful for your help. But she's my responsibility and I'd be obliged if you'd butt out."

"That's awfully rude." Cady tossed Kane an apologetic look. "Don't mind Jack. He always gets like a wounded bear when he's afraid for someone he cares about."

"I don't need you to defend me." Jack sounded a lot like the wounded bear she'd accused him of being.

Kane could understand his anger. A woman like Cady would inspire fierce emotion in any man. He didn't really blame Jack, but he wouldn't stand by and let him mistreat Cady, even if she was his wife.

"No matter what she's done, you have no call to bully her that way." Kane met Jack's gaze and saw a dangerous glint kindle in his black eyes. He was feeling dangerous himself.

Cady jammed her hands on her hips and lifted her determined little chin. "Don't you pick on Jack. He's not a bully. He takes awfully good care of me."

So that's how it was. What would it be like to have a woman like Cady defend him? He would never know.

"I was just trying to help." Kane held his hands up in surrender. "Far be it from me to interfere between husband and wife."

"Wife?" Jack stepped away as if he'd just found out Cady had the plague.

"Husband?" An amused glitter stole into Cady's green eyes.

"Isn't that why you're here? To join him"—he lifted his chin at Jack—"your husband?"

She laughed. "We aren't married. Jack's my brother."

2

"Your brother?" Kane glanced from Cady to Jack, who was standing beside her.

Cady could tell by the way Kane's dark brows pulled together that he was trying to see some resemblance between them. It would be a miracle if he could find it. They looked nothing alike. She had their mother's green eyes and thick brown hair streaked with blond. Jack looked like Papa, tall, with dark hair and eyes black as coal. Cady compared Kane to her brother, something she found herself doing with every man she met. Kane was one of the few she didn't find lacking.

Both had dashing good looks and were tall, several inches over six feet. Kane's eyes sometimes seemed more hazel than light brown. Red and gold mixed together in his thick wavy hair, keeping it from being as dark as Jack's. The officer's mouth turned up slightly at the corners whether he was smiling or not, giving him a deceptively cheerful expression.

The two men looked very different, but she sensed one thing they shared. Beneath the surface, both of them carried a dangerous intensity. Cady wondered if it was life in the Territory that had made them this way. If so, did it change the women who dared challenge it?

"Yes, Jack's my brother. I can't believe you thought I was married to him."

An oddly pleased look crossed Kane's face, and she wondered why he should care. He'd been in uniform when they had last seen each other, the night he'd broken her heart. Now he wore a white cotton shirt with the long sleeves rolled to his elbows, revealing tanned forearms. Dark trousers covered his well-muscled legs. The only hint of his profession was the gold-trimmed campaign hat he'd pushed to the back of his head. Without the brim's shadow she could see his straight nose, lean cheeks, and square jaw. A holstered pistol strapped low on his hip told her he was ready for danger. Kane had been handsome as sin in his uniform; to Cady's dismay he was just as good-looking in civilian clothes.

Jack lifted his hat and blotted the sweat on his brow with his forearm. "I don't think the assumption that I'm your husband is so far-fetched. Why, a woman would be lucky—"

She snorted in a most unladylike manner. "I'll need to have a nice long chat with any woman who looks twice at you."

Kane shuffled his boots in the dust and cleared his throat. "What are you doing back in the Territory, Cady?"

"You know him?" Jack asked.

"Captain Kane Carrington. We met two years ago when I ran away from school." Cady glanced from her brother to Kane. "Kane, my brother, Jackson Tanner."

"Is this the captain I heard about?" Jack's eyes narrowed. "I thought you met him at Fort Mohave."

"I did." She hoped Jack wouldn't pick this moment to get protective and wind up embarrassing her instead. She turned to Kane. "What brings you to Fort McDowell?"

"I was transferred here a year ago." He extended his hand to Jack. "Glad to meet you, Tanner. I got to know your brother, Jeff, when Cady and I met. If you're anything like him, we'll get along fine."

"Jeff and I are nothing alike," Jack said in a hard voice. "Except that wc both care about Cady and don't take it kindly when she's hurt."

Cady's gaze slid back and forth as the two men eyed each other like wary mountain cats. When Jack finally accepted the other man's hand, she released a huge breath.

"So Jack's not your husband." Kane looked at her. "Who *is* the lucky man who's brought you out west, Cady? Maybe I know him."

"I don't have a husband. And I don't know why you persist in trying to give me one. I don't ever want to get married."

Kane blinked and a strange expression flickered across his face. Cady wondered if he was remembering the last time they were together. In trying to convince him that he needed her, she'd stopped just short of asking him to marry her. He had told her she couldn't even start a cook fire and had no business in the Territory.

A heated blush, one part anger and two parts mortification, slipped up her neck and into her cheeks. No wonder he had such a funny expression on his face. She had completely changed her tune since that night under the Arizona stars. It had been two long years. She'd almost forgotten what a fool she'd made of herself.

Then another thought struck her, and her eyes opened wider. Surely he didn't think . . . ?

"I'm not here because of you, that's for sure, captain. Why, I didn't even know where you were."

"The idea never crossed my mind."

"Well, you've got some idea you can't shake loose of. What is it?"

"It never occurred to me that you'd leave the comforts of home again for Arizona Territory. I'm curious about why you're here. A short visit with your brother?"

Jack started to chuckle. "Tell him what you told me, Cady."

"I told you the children at Fort McDowell need a teacher."

"No, the other part," Jack said.

"What part?" Kane asked.

"She's here to settle the frontier."

Kane started to laugh. Cady felt her cheeks grow hotter. This was only one of the many reasons why she never wanted to tie herself to a man. They were all insensitive, inconsiderate, ill-mannered oafs. She frowned at the two of them.

When Kane stopped chuckling he looked down at her, and a serious expression replaced any trace of amusement. "Go back home where you belong and marry the banker's son who's pining away for you."

"About the boy back home." Jack cleared his throat. "She has a small problem. My little sister was sent here to protect her from the tongues that started to wag when she left her intended at the altar." Jack stuck his hands in his trouser pockets. "And he wasn't a banker. He was an army lieutenant."

Cady glared at him. "I don't ever remember you being this talkative before, Jackson Tanner. Maybe you should spend more time with people instead of with your rocks up in the mountains."

"Maybe you're right." Jack grinned. Then he looked at

Kane. "Actually, I'm glad I ran into you, Carrington. Cady has a teaching job at the fort. I was taking her there now."

"Oh?"

Jack crossed his arms over his chest and tucked his fingertips beneath his arms. "I just came down from the mountains for supplies. I can't keep an eye on my sister, and she won't go home."

"What does that have to do with me?"

"The army got her out here to teach, so she's the army's problem—your problem."

"I see."

"No, I don't think you do," Cady said. "I'm not anyone's problem. You and Jack can stand here and discuss it all day if you've a mind to; I'm going to the fort. My agreement is with Major Wexler. I trust he's more reasonable than either of you."

Kane pulled his dark blue campaign hat low on his forehead and shaded his expression. But not before his tight-lipped look told her the last thing in the world he wanted was her at Fort McDowell.

"Oh, what's the use?" She turned away from both of them in disgust and walked back to the buckboard.

"Where are you going?" Kane called after her.

She hated that, after all this time, the deep tones of his voice still had the power to stir butterflies in her stomach. Ignoring him seemed the best thing to do.

"Cady, not one more step," Jack said.

She brushed her long hair from her eyes as she looked over her shoulder at the two angry men staring at her. Disregarding both of them seemed even better than disregarding one. Without a word, she kept walking. She stopped in front of the horse and buckboard, lifted the hem of her calico dress, and prepared to climb up.

Behind her she heard the crunch of boots in the sand and rocks. She sighed and turned to face them.

Kane rested his hands on his narrow hips. "You can't go traipsing through Indian country by yourself."

"You have no right to tell me what to do. First Papa, then Jack, and now you. You have no right."

"I have every right. I'm responsible for keeping the peace. Before you can settle the frontier, I have to make sure it's safe. If you go running around without an escort, you're apt to stir up a whole pile of trouble. Trouble puts my men in danger. That makes you my responsibility."

Cady shaded her eyes with her hand as she studied him, and when her hostile expression softened he knew he'd gotten through to her.

"When you put it like that, captain, I'd be obliged for your company to Fort McDowell."

"That's a relief," Jack said behind them. "I leave her in good hands, then."

"Leave?" she asked. "Aren't you coming to the fort with us?"

He shook his head. "No need now."

"Where are you going?"

"Into town for supplies."

"Will I see you again before you head back up into the mountains?"

He looked down at his boots. "No."

"Then this is good-bye?"

Kane saw the regret on the other man's face and heard the soft edge of censure and sadness in Cady's voice.

A soldier understood all too well how hard it was to say good-bye. He'd done it all his life. Sooner or later he would also have to say good-bye to Cady. He knew what it had cost him the first time. He didn't want to think about a second.

As Cady walked over to him, Jack fingered the thin leather reins in his hand. "I'll be back before you know it."

She stood on tiptoe and hugged him. "Take care of yourself, Jack."

"You too." He pulled her close for a quick embrace. Then he gripped her upper arms and set her away. "I'll see you."

He looked at Kane. "Take care of her for me, Carrington."

"Nothing will happen to her while she's under the army's protection. You have my word."

Jack nodded, then mounted up, waved once, and rode away. With her hand shading her eyes from the sun, Cady watched him until all that remained was a cloud of dust.

Kane stood close enough behind her to smell the scent of flowers she wore, mixed with sand and heat. The fragrance instantly brought back the memory of her in his arms. She had moved him more than he'd thought any woman could, but he refused to subject her to the rigors, hardship, and isolation of army life. He'd tried marriage once and had failed. Getting mixed up with a woman again, especially a pampered eastern woman like Cady, would only be asking for trouble.

He looked down at her as she watched her brother ride away. Strands of her hair fluttered in the wind. Lifting a hand he started to touch it, then curled his fingers into his palm.

"We need to go, Cady."

She turned at the sound of his voice, and he saw the sheen of unshed tears in her green eyes. "Do you think he'll be all right? Do you think I'll see him again?"

Kane glanced into the distance. "Your brother strikes me as a man who can take care of himself. My guess is he'll be fine. He'll turn up when you least expect him."

"I'm sure you're right." She sighed. "I have this bad habit of worrying about my family. Especially Jack."

"Something tells me they worry about you too." Kane still couldn't get over the coincidence of her showing up at Fort McDowell. "Why are you here?"

"Like I said before, it's not because of you. It's because Jack's here. I was determined to come west and teach. My parents were afraid something would happen to me."

"With good reason," Kane said. "You'd have been better off staying in the East. This is dangerous country. Why didn't you find a teaching job close to home?"

"What's best for me is not your judgment to make." She looked him square in the eye. She was a little thing and had to tilt her head back to do it, but that didn't faze her. "I made up my mind to go west—somewhere."

"Why?"

"Because I want to make a difference. I want both my brothers to be as proud of me as I am of them. Jeff is building railroads that link the country from coast to coast. Jack could have had a job with him, something safe in an office. He's looking to find his own fortune instead of choosing the easy way. Just because I'm a woman doesn't mean I don't have dreams too."

"But why here?"

"Because Jack is here, and that will ease my family's concern. There's no need to tell them he's prospecting and cause them to worry."

"There's nothing for them to be concerned about. I promised I'd look out for you, and I always keep my word."

She snorted in the same way she had earlier, in a way he knew would make the headmistress of any exclusive eastern ladies' academy cringe. But she didn't say a word as she turned away and headed for the buckboard again.

"Now don't try to drive that thing, not after what just happened. I'll take you to the fort."

"All right," she said.

As he tied his horse to the back of the rig, Kane watched her lift her skirt to scramble up, giving him a tantalizing view of her slender ankles and calves. Tempting as that was, he realized she'd rather flaunt convention than wait for his help. Just as well. He didn't trust himself to touch her without revealing how much she affected him.

It took some doing, and she was breathing faster by the time she finally climbed in, but she did it herself and sat down. He moved up beside her and unwrapped the reins from around the brake.

Cady looked at him. "Will you show me how to drive?"

Kane studied Cady's determined expression. "Yes." Her eyes opened wide. "Don't look so surprised. You seem bent on staying out here, and I promised your brother I'd watch out for you. Aside from the fact that I don't particularly want to tangle with Jack, I take my responsibilities seriously. The more you know, the better you can take care of yourself."

And if she could take care of herself, he wouldn't have to keep an eye on her.

"Major Wexler seems very nice," Cady said.

They had left the commanding officer a few minutes before to drive to her quarters. She lifted her long hair from her neck, trying to catch a possible breeze and cool herself, but there was no relief from the heat. She climbed out of the buckboard, anxious to go inside.

"He's a good man." Kane jumped down and went to the rear of the wagon. "This is where you'll be staying," he said and started to lift her trunk. "What have you got in here, rocks?"

"That's Jack's specialty. I brought books."

"All the better to settle the frontier with." He smiled. "If there's an Indian attack, you can throw books at them."

"I'm here to teach." She glanced at the revolver strapped to his hip. "Guns are your tools, books are mine." She remembered the short interview in Major Wexler's office and the obvious respect and admiration between Kane and his commanding officer. She had the impression that Kane handled a lot of responsibility at the fort, yet he'd been genuinely surprised when he recognized her after stopping the buckboard. Wouldn't he have known she was coming?"

"May I ask you something, captain?" When he nodded, she continued. "Didn't you know a teacher was coming"

"I knew."

"But you assumed I was here to meet my husband."

"I was aware that the major had arranged for a teacher. He never told me who the person was."

"If you had known it was me, what—"

Just then, she heard someone call out Kane's name followed by the sound of running footsteps. A red-headed boy of about twelve raced over and stopped beside the buckboard. "I'll give you a hand with that, captain," he said breathlessly.

Kane smiled. "Thanks, R. J. Hasn't anyone told you it's too hot to run around like that?"

"No, sir," the boy said. "Where ya been? I looked all over. Howdy, ma'am." Without giving Cady a chance to reply, he looked back at Kane. "You promised to show me how to clean a revolver."

Cady watched the boy help Kane and didn't miss the hero worship on his freckled face.

"Sorry, R. J., I forgot. Something came up. Can we do it later?"

"Sure thing, captain."

The two of them took her luggage through the last door of a long low adobe building. Each set of quarters was separated by a wall, creating small pockets of privacy for the families. She looked around the fort. In front of the boardwalk, a ditch that Kane called an acequia flowed with clear water from the Verde River to supply the post. On the other side of the acequia was a row of cottonwoods and then a large open space that Kane had told her was the parade ground.

She turned and crossed a board spread over the water and stepped up onto a wooden sidewalk beneath a ramada. This awning of brush supported by cottonwood poles was a welcome relief from the noon sun. Hanging from one of the poles was a large pottery urn with a dipper poking from the top. She took a long drink of water and found it surprisingly cool.

Before stepping inside, she looked around one more time. Fort McDowell consisted of a series of adobe buildings, offices, quarters, kitchens, a livery, and a post trader. Yet, surrounded by miles of flat barren desert, Cady knew a feeling of insignificance. She felt very small indeed and at the mercy of man and nature. In the distance, four mountain peaks loomed, the only landmark on the horizon. It brought her a measure of comfort that the mountains were there, something to break the monotony of the desert.

Cady walked inside and waited several seconds for her eyes to adjust after the bright sunlight outside.

Kane and R. J. were sweating and making terrible noises as they shoved her trunk to the foot of an iron cot that was covered only by a sheet.

The boy straightened and looked curiously from her to Kane. "I sure hope this is your sister, captain."

"Sister?" Kane whirled. "Whatever gave you that idea?"

He made it sound as if being related to her was on a par with being scalped, Cady thought. She had a good mind to throw her books at *him* instead of at marauding Indians.

"If she's not your sister, she must be the teacher my pa said was comin'." The youngster's bright blue eyes stared at her with the most hostile expression she'd ever seen.

"She *is* the new teacher. I'm moving out and she'll be staying here in my room."

"What in tarnation for?"

"Because there's nowhere else for her." Kane smiled. "I can see I'd better make introductions. Miss Cady Tanner, I'd like you to meet R. J.—Reynolds John Wexler, Junior."

Cady nodded to him. "It's a pleasure to meet you, Reynolds. I take it your father is the fort commander?"

"Uh-huh." A suspicious look stole over his freckled face. "Are you all the way from New York, ma'am?"

"Indeed she is, R. J." Kane grinned. "And don't think she'll be as easy to get rid of as Sergeant Cramer."

"No, sir." But there was a look in R. J. Wexler's eyes that sent a shiver down Cady's spine.

In spite of it, she smiled at the boy. "I think we're going to be good friends, Reynolds. What do you think?"

"Yes'm." The boy stared daggers at her. "Shoulda known right off Kane didn't marry you. He wouldn't marry no teacher."

"Any teacher," she corrected. "In case you're concerned, let me assure you that I have no intention of marrying anyone. I also plan to be here for a very long time."

Cady didn't think it was possible, but R. J.'s expression turned even more contrary. When she lifted her gaze to Kane, his look was not unlike the boy's. Why would it bother Kane to have her there? She wasn't going to have any direct dealings with him.

"Are you sure about that, ma'am? There's wild Indians in these parts. It's a mite dangerous."

"So I've heard. But Captain Carrington has assured me that he'll look out for me."

The boy's eyes grew round, as if he couldn't believe his hero would do that. "It's godawful hot, too. Bet it doesn't get hot like this in New York."

"No, it doesn't. But I'll get used to it."

"And we got nothin' but wind and dust. My ma hates that. Can't keep nothin' clean. The grit even gets in the biscuits 'cause ya can't keep it out of the flour."

She swallowed a smile and looked at him as gravely as he was staring at her. "I have two brothers. I'm not easily discouraged or frightened." She took a step toward him. "Reynolds, nothing you can say or do will keep me from being your teacher."

"Yes'm." He swallowed hard. "Captain, I'll be back in a couple minutes." Without further warning or explanation, the boy raced from the room.

A feeling of apprehension scratched at the edge of Cady's tenuous composure. Get rid of her as easily as Sergeant Cramer? She remembered Jack's letter describing the enlisted man who was dismissed for arriving at school drunk. He'd never been known to touch liquor before or since. That wouldn't happen to her. She was a trained teacher. And she never touched spirits.

As she looked around the room, she realized that these were indeed Kane's quarters.

"Captain Carrington, I can't take your bed—I mean your room." Her face burned at the implication of that one word. "There must be somewhere else I can go. Maybe where you're moving?"

"I'm sure the enlisted men would think they'd died and gone to heaven if you moved in with them, but something tells me your brother wouldn't approve."

Her face flushed hotter. She only hoped he didn't notice. "Isn't there another single woman who's willing to share a room?"

"Cady, for God's sake, this is a military outpost, not a women's dormitory."

"A simple no would have sufficed, captain."

"You *do* have another choice."

"What?"

"I can take you down to the train in Phoenix and send you back home."

"Why is everyone trying to get rid of me? All I want to do is what I'm trained for, just as you're doing."

"Women are a liability out here, especially high-maintenance women," he said, looking her up and down.

"What does that mean?"

"That you need protection and a lot of other things no one has time for. Survival takes up each waking minute and every ounce of energy you've got."

"Are you saying I'm not strong enough?"

"I'm just saying—"

"Exactly what you told me two years ago, that I'm not cut out for life in the Territory. You were wrong then and you're wrong now. You don't have the least notion what kind of staying power I've got."

"I think I have a pretty good idea."

Cady refused to discuss it further. Going home was no choice at all. If it took the rest of her life, she'd prove to this know-it-all captain that she could survive here very nicely.

"Apparently, responsibility for my welfare weighs heavily on you, captain. Maybe there's a solution that would suit us both. Jack's going back to the mountains. I'll just stay in his cabin and out of your hair." She took a handkerchief from her reticule and blotted her forehead. There wasn't even a hint of air inside to relieve the oppressive heat.

"If Jack wanted you to stay in his cabin, he wouldn't have been bringing you to the fort. He obviously felt, and I agree, that it's not safe for you to live there alone."

Kane watched her mull this over. Her face was very red. With her high-necked white cotton blouse, full skirt, and petticoats, she was not dressed for comfort. She had a lot to learn.

"So my only choice is to stay here." She looked around his spartan room.

He supposed it was plain compared to what she was accustomed to. With its white window shades and unadorned adobe walls, a woman would find it barren.

"It's not much," he said, "but I call it home."

"I hope you didn't think I was being critical. I'm merely trying to think of a solution that will not inconvenience you."

It was too late for that. As soon as he'd seen her again he'd been inconvenienced. All the feelings he thought he'd put aside forever when she went back east two years ago came rushing back.

When she waved her lace-edged handkerchief in front of her flushed face again, he grew concerned. "Are you all right, Cady?"

"Fine." She tucked the square of cotton into the cuff of her long sleeve and looked at him. "I didn't mean to appear ungrateful. Thank you for your consideration. I'd be happy to stay here."

At that moment R. J. came through the open door, carefully holding a hardtack box.

"I have something for you, ma'am." He held out the box; then, after she took it, he stuck his hands in his pockets.

A wary smile turned up the corners of Cady's full mouth. "Why, thank you, Reynolds. What is it?"

Kane had a bad feeling. The kid was a notorious troublemaker and had practically single-handedly "persuaded" Sergeant Cramer that he had no career as a teacher. If R. J. behaved true to form, God knew what the boy would do to convince Cady that a school closer to home would suit her better.

She lifted the lid and shrieked. Kane heard rattles and saw the open mouth and the fangs of the snake as she tossed the box to the floor. He reached for his gun and almost at the same moment realized the sidewinder was already dead and stuffed. The rattling sound was coming from R. J.'s pocket.

He looked at Cady and knew from her pale face and the way her eyes rolled back that she was about to faint. He caught her just before she hit the floor.

"What the hell did you do that for?"

"I heard you talkin' to her. You don't want her here any more than I do." R. J. grinned at him. "Maybe now she'll go back where she came from."

Kane easily lifted Cady's limp form into his arms. He spoke through clenched jaws. "If Miss Tanner is hurt, you'll wish *you* had someplace else to go."

3

Kane carried Cady to the iron cot, placed her gently on the sheet, and sat down beside her. Bright pink color covered her cheeks, and perspiration glistened on her forehead.

He glanced over his shoulder at the boy. "Take the basin on the dresser and get me some water." When R. J. hesitated, he glared at him. "That's an order!"

The boy promptly did as he was told.

Kane turned back to Cady. He couldn't think what else to do, so he unbuttoned her blouse, just to the point where her lacy chemise showed. Her chest rose and fell slowly. If anything happened to her, he'd personally discipline that pain in the ass, and he didn't care that he *was* the commanding officer's kid. When he got through with R. J. Wexler, he wouldn't sit down for a week.

"R. J., where the hell's that water?" he yelled.

"Coming!"

Kane took off his hat and waved it over the small, still figure, trying to get some air moving.

As soon as R. J. carried in the basin, water sloshing over the sides, and set it down beside the bed, Kane took his handkerchief, dipped it in the lukewarm water, and drew the wet rag over her face and neck. Cady moaned softly. Her long gold-tipped lashes fluttered, then lifted.

"Cady?" Kane took her cold hand between his and rubbed some warmth into it.

"What happened?" she whispered.

"You fainted." He glanced at the boy standing beside him. "Get her some water to drink."

He turned back as a puzzled expression puckered the smooth skin between her delicately arched brows. "Fainted? Me? Impossible. I've never fainted in my life."

"You probably never opened a hardtack box with a snake in it before."

"Snake?" Her eyes widened and she started to sit up.

Kane put his hands beneath her arms to help her. His palms brushed the sides of her breasts, and the awareness he'd felt while lifting her from the buckboard earlier fanned into flame. He automatically tamped it down. He remembered his feelings when he'd first met her. He'd managed to put them aside then; this time he wouldn't allow himself to feel anything. Marriage had taught him that women were treacherous and dishonest. It was a mistake he wouldn't make again.

R. J. appeared with a dipperful of water from an olla hanging outside under the ramada.

"Here's some water." Kane held the scoop to her mouth while she drank.

He couldn't take his eyes from her throat. The slender column moved delicately as she swallowed. He wondered how she would taste if he touched his lips to the spot where her pulse beat so rapidly. He pushed the thought away, but not before anger took hold. It sorely tested his temper that his response to her was the same as two years ago. No, not the same. Stronger.

She stopped drinking, and a drop of water clung to her bottom lip. Her tongue darted out and licked it away. His gut tightened a notch at the unconsciously sensual movement. If he was going to avoid another mistake, he'd have to stay out of her way. Sooner or later she'd realize Fort McDowell was no place for a lone woman. She was here to teach, but she was the one who was in for a lesson. Until she learned it, he needed to steer clear of her.

She smiled sheepishly. "Thank you."

"Feeling better?"

"Yes, thanks." Cady stared at the stuffed snake near the foot of the bed, then at R. J., who was watching her. "I remember now."

"Miss Tanner, ma'am, I never woulda showed you that snake if I'da known he'd scare you like that."

"He didn't frighten me."

"Then why did you faint? If you don't mind my askin'."

"Of course I don't mind. It was the heat."

The kid snorted. Kane was about to tell him something about being respectful to a lady when she moved.

She slid to the side of the iron cot and her calico skirt caught beneath her hip, hiking the material above her knee. At the glimpse of her thigh, the coiled tension in his belly wound tighter.

Cady wasn't special, he reminded himself. Any pretty woman would have caused him to react this way.

He stood and held out his hand to help her up so the skirt would cover that damned good-looking leg. She swayed slightly and his arm instantly circled her waist to steady her. With her pulled up against him, he felt the heat of her body and her soft breast pressed to his chest.

After a few seconds, Cady looked up at him. Her eyes were as green as the Virginia hills after a spring shower.

"I'm fine now. The dizziness is gone." She stepped away and fixed her gaze on R. J. "So you think I fainted at the sight of that snake?"

The boy managed to suppress an impish grin. "No, ma'am."

She walked over to the stuffed critter, bent down, and touched it. The slight shaking of her hand was the only sign of her nervousness, the only indication of how much courage it took for her to get that close.

"That little dizzy spell had nothing to do with this." She carefully picked up the snake with two fingers. "I assure you, I'm just not accustomed to the heat."

"Yes'm," he said, his cocky expression changing to surprise as she gripped it behind the head and turned the face toward her.

"He's quite a handsome fellow, isn't he?" She touched one of the fangs.

"Jumpin' Jehoshaphat, ma'am! You shouldn't touch—"

"He can't hurt me, Reynolds. He's dead." She looked at the fang again. "Isn't this where the poison comes from?"

"Yes'm."

"I heard a rattling sound. How—?"

R. J. stuck his hand in his pocket and produced the rattles, a two-inch-long series of horny cup-shaped rings.

She held her hand out, and the boy placed the rattles in her palm. Turning it over, she studied the segments intently. "Is it true you can tell a snake's age by the number of rattles?"

R. J. shrugged.

Kane grinned. He couldn't help respecting the way Cady was dealing with this hellion.

"I think you should find out. If you're going to give him away, the least you can do is know something about him."

"I know something about him," Kane said.

"Oh?" Cady looked up, a spark of genuine interest lighting her green eyes.

"The rattles are sections of unshed skin. Sidewinders shed three or four times a year, and the end rattles tend to break off. So the answer is no. There's no way to tell their age by the number of rattles."

"Thank you, captain. That was very informative."

"Miss Tanner, ma'am, can I have my—"

"How did you come to have this little fellow in your possession, Reynolds? Did you catch him yourself?"

"No'm."

Kane chuckled. "Tell her, R. J."

He shuffled his feet uncomfortably. "John Eagle caught him."

"I see," she said. "Is he a friend of yours?"

"No'm. He's an Indian."

"Does that mean you can't be friends? It shouldn't, you know." She glanced at Kane and one corner of her full mouth lifted for an instant, the only sign of her amusement.

"We was friends 'fore. . . ." He glared at the snake in her hands. Then he crossed his arms over his chest and looked away.

"Something tells me you don't want to talk about it. Maybe another time you'll tell me the story of this fellow's capture. Who stuffed him?"

"John Eagle's father."

"Well, I'm very anxious to meet John Eagle and his father. They sound like intelligent and skillful people."

"Yes'm," he mumbled. "Now can I have my snake back?"

She gasped in what Kane knew was phony surprise. "But, Reynolds, isn't this a gift?"

"Well, ma'am—" The boy shifted from one foot to the other.

"Because if you didn't mean for me to keep him, I'd have to assume you put him in that hardtack box to deliberately frighten me."

"Yes'm." His eyes widened. "'I mean, no'm."

"And I can't imagine any son of Major Wexler's being so unchivalrous, can you?"

"No'm," he said, looking at his boots. Kane was pretty sure R. J. had no idea what "unchivalrous" meant.

"But it would be unladylike of me to take your gift and not give you something in return."

She placed the stuffed snake on the dresser beside the water pitcher and went to the trunk at the foot of the bed. After rummaging through it, she pulled out a book.

She walked over to the boy and held it out to him. "From the expression on your face, young man, one would think I was handing you a *live* snake."

"No'm," he said, taking the volume from her. He studied the spine. "*The Adven—Adventur—*"

"*Adventures,*" she prompted.

He looked at her, then back down at the book. "*Adventures of Tom Sawyer.*"

"By Mark Twain. I think you'll like it. And I believe this makes us even," she said, lifting an eyebrow.

"Yes'm." He looked out the door. "As much as I'd like to stay and listen to more about this here book, I think my ma's callin'. I gotta go now." He started backing out of the room. "Bye, sir."

"So long, R. J."

"Let me know how you enjoy the book," Cady said. "I'll see you in school the day after tomorrow."

When the boy was gone, Kane started to laugh. "I can't believe it."

"What?" she asked.

"You have R. J. Wexler running home to his ma."

She shrugged as if it was nothing special. "Miss Agnes Biddle always said, 'When the little scoundrels are bigger and stronger than you, outsmart them and get their attention with the unexpected.'"

He chuckled again, not just at what she'd done but at the mimicked voice of her mentor. "Apparently Miss Agnes was right. It worked on R. J."

"Miss Agnes would also say, 'Don't turn your back on the scheming little darlings.' Now I know what she meant. Somehow I think I haven't yet seen the best of Reynolds J. Wexler's fertile imagination."

"He's just high-spirited. Nothing to be concerned about."

"Why does he dislike John Eagle?"

"The two used to be inseparable. Until the day they came back with that snake." Kane stared thoughtfully at the door. "If he wants you to know, he'll tell you. But don't worry about R. J. He's a little wild, and it takes him awhile to trust. But he wouldn't hurt a fly."

"Or a snake?" she asked, smiling up at him.

He grinned back. "Or a snake."

As the fresh beauty of that smiling face slammed him in the gut, his amusement faded. When she smiled, her small turned-up nose wrinkled. He could tell, if she continued to wear her little hat, that freckles would soon march across her cheeks. The beginnings of small dots were already evident. What the hell was he doing? He had things to do, responsibilities to take care of, a desk piled with government paperwork.

"I have to go. I hope you'll be comfortable here. If there's anything I can do—"

"There is something."

"I'll take care of it." He glanced around the barren room, and his gaze came to rest on the snake perched on the dresser. He walked over and picked it up. "I'll get rid of this for you."

She moved beside him, took the creature from him, and stroked its body behind the head. "That's not the something I was referring to. I've grown rather attached to him. I have two brothers, captain; I'm accustomed to things popping up when I least expect them. Why do you refuse to believe I fainted because of the heat? I'll be perfectly fine."

"Whatever you say. So if it's not the snake, what's the something you need?"

She bit her lip nervously. "I started to ask you something before, outside, just as Reynolds joined us."

He frowned. "What was that?"

"If you *had* known I was the teacher the major had hired, what would you have done?"

"Nothing." He shrugged. "I'm a soldier. I follow orders." He walked to the door and set his hat low on his forehead, shading his eyes and face. "If you need anything, remember, Major Wexler told you not to hesitate to ask."

Her mouth pulled tight. "I think we settled everything in his office. School starts day after tomorrow, nine-thirty in the morning, in the mess hall. He said you would get the word out to everyone?"

He nodded. "I'll take care of it."

"Thank you, captain. You've been very kind."

"Not kind. Like I said, I was just following orders."

"And I've kept you far too long. I'm sure you need to go do some ordering of your own. Don't give me another thought."

If only he *could* put her out of his mind that easily. If he had known she was the teacher the major had hired, he would have put in for a transfer. A good soldier knew when to pull back for the safety of all concerned.

"Good morning, children. I'm Miss Tanner, your new teacher. Welcome to the first day of school at Fort McDowell."

Cady swallowed hard as she stared back at five pairs of eyes. Three girls and two boys sat on hard wooden benches behind long tables in the mess hall. The odors of beans and bacon hung in the still air. Shouted orders drifted in from the parade ground outside.

Cady studied the girls, who were neatly dressed in cotton and calico, their hair pulled back in braids or done up with ribbons. Red, sweaty faces on the boys told her they had raced across the parade ground to get to school on time. R. J. Wexler, who she suspected would do anything to avoid school, was nowhere in sight. She couldn't teach him if he wasn't there. But three girls and two boys waited for her to fill their heads with wisdom and knowledge. And she had no idea what in the world she was going to say to them. Why had she ever thought she could do this?

She struggled to control the butterflies in her stomach. This was her first real class, and she so wanted to do a good job. If that wasn't enough to deal with, it was only nine-thirty in the morning and she was already tired. Between nervous tension and the heat that never went away, even during the night, she hadn't slept well.

That shouldn't matter, she told herself. She was a trained teacher. Miss Biddle had said Cady was one of her best students. Kane had seemed impressed with the way she'd handled young Wexler and the snake. But that had happened in the presence of a big, strong, intimidating man. The scene could have turned out differently in a classroom full of the boy's friends. She had to admit it: She was relieved that he wasn't among the five children staring at her.

First things first, Miss Agnes always said. She'd better learn the names of her students and stop thinking of them as strangers.

"I think we should introduce ourselves." Cady smiled at a little blond girl on her far right. Plump, golden ringlets framed her small face. "Why don't we start with you?"

"My name is Polly Chase." Her light-blue eyes lowered shyly.

"How old are you, Polly?"

"Nine."

"Thank you. Next?"

"I'm Martha Halleck," replied a little girl with brown eyes and mahogany-colored hair in two neat braids. "I'm eleven."

"Emily Stanton," said the third girl, her black hair pulled back with a satin ribbon from her heart-shaped face. She was a beautiful child, with lovely dark blue eyes. "I'm twelve and my pa is the quartermaster."

"Thank you, Emily. Next?" Cady prompted the boy sitting beside her.

"Bart Grimes." Straight brown hair fell over his forehead and almost obscured his hazel eyes. "I'm thirteen, and you're a lot prettier than Sergeant Cramer, ma'am."

"That's very kind of you, Bart."

Cady looked at the last student, sitting apart from

the others. His poker-straight blue-black hair, black-as-coal eyes, and bronze skin identified him immediately as an Indian.

"And you are?" she asked.

"John Eagle."

So this was the stalwart young man who had caught the snake and earned Reynolds J. Wexler's undying hostility.

"How old are you, John?"

"Fourteen."

He was two years older than Reynolds, and polite enough, but Cady sensed that he wouldn't impart information about himself easily. She hadn't expected to have an Indian in her class. She wondered if she should be frightened. He was bigger than she was, well on his way to manhood.

She thought about the things she'd read about Indian attacks, but in Jack's letters he'd said only good things about the ones he'd met.

She studied John's emotionless face and decided there was nothing to fear from John Eagle. Besides, her job was to teach; age and the color of a person's skin were of no consequence to her.

She clasped her hands together. "All right, let's get started. We have a lot to do. Before I can begin teaching you, I need to determine what skills you've already mastered."

"Miss Tanner?" It was Bart Grimes. "John Eagle can camp out in the desert without supplies and live off the land."

Cady bit her lip to hide her amusement. "Thank you, Bart. That's wonderful, and perhaps John Eagle can teach us to do the same. But that isn't exactly the kind of skill I was talking about."

"I was afraid it wasn't," the youngster said.

"Why afraid?"

"You're gonna put me back in first grade 'cause my reading's not so good."

"I don't intend to run my school that way. Why did you think I would?"

"'Cause that's what they did when I stayed with my ma's folks back east. Pa moves around a lot with the army. Sometimes I go to school, most times not. I was way bigger'n all those snot-nosed little snobs."

"I see. Although it isn't very nice to call other people names."

Cady sympathized with the boy. Not so very long ago, she'd also run into prejudice from narrow-minded, pretentious people.

"Well, Bart, don't worry. As you can see, there aren't enough of you to separate into grades. I just want to see what you already know and we'll proceed from there. All right?"

"Yes'm." He smiled.

"I saw more children in the fort. Do you know why they're not here this morning?" Cady asked.

"Don't have to be here if our folks don't make us," Polly said.

"Did your folks make you come here this morning?"

The little girl looked at her fingers. "Only a little, ma'am."

Emily raised her hand. "I heard some of 'em say they didn't want to waste the time if you were going to get drunk and have to be let go. Like Sergeant Cramer," she added.

"I see." Cady glanced at each child in turn. "I'm not a drinking woman, and I have no intention of leaving for any reason. Is that clear?"

Five heads nodded.

"Let's get to work then."

The next two hours passed quietly with the children working on the tests she had prepared to gauge their level of education. Cady was just about to announce a break for lunch when there was a disturbance at the door behind her.

"Let me go!" It was a youngster's voice.

Captain Carrington came striding into the room holding Reynolds J. Wexler by the arm. He sat the boy down beside John Eagle, went around the long table, and stood next to Cady. Kane smelled of dust, leather, and shaving soap. The masculine scents worked their way inside her and stole her breath until she could scarcely think straight. This was all she needed in front of her first class, on her very first day of school.

"What's the problem, captain?" she asked in her best imitation of Miss Agnes Biddle.

"R. J. forgot about school and went riding instead. He's sorry about being late."

"Am not."

Kane shot him a look. "If you have any trouble with him, let me know."

"Thank you, captain. I'm certain that won't be necessary. I can handle Reynolds."

Kane nodded slightly. He clasped his hands behind him and took a step back. Oh, God, he was staying. Everything she'd ever learned seemed to go straight out of her head. She couldn't deal with him *and* a hostile truant.

"Don't let me keep you, captain."

"You're not. Forget I'm here."

It would be a miracle if she could do that, the way her heart was pounding. But she had to try.

Cady looked at the redheaded boy. "I'm glad you could join us."

He sent the captain a scathing look. "Didn't have no choice."

"Any choice," she automatically corrected.

He rolled his eyes, then for the first time, he glanced at the Indian boy to his left. "I ain't sittin' next to no redskin."

Without looking in the other boy's direction, John Eagle said, "The color of Indian skin is better than white skin like a woman's and hair the color of carrots."

R. J. pounded one fist on the table and stood up. "I ain't sittin' near no stinkin' Indian."

"*Any* Indian—" Cady broke off. "Sit down, Reynolds."

John Eagle turned an outwardly calm gaze on the other boy, but his black eyes smoldered. "Anyone who wets himself at the sight of a snake has no business talking about smell."

"That's a lie. Take it back!"

John faced R. J. and shook his head. "It's the truth."

R. J. made a fist and socked the other boy. John grabbed him and they were locked in combat, each trying to free a hand to get in a punch.

Kane moved forward and she put a hand on his arm. "I'll take care of this."

"You?"

"Yes. Me."

He looked at the wrestling boys. "All right. Handle it."

She took a step forward and slapped her palms on the table. "That's quite enough!" Cady said, in her sternest voice.

The two ignored her. She rushed around the table and tried to separate them, but they acted as if she weren't there.

"Stop this instant!" she cried, trying again to use words. What other weapon did she have? The idea of force was ludicrous; both of them were bigger than she was.

When they continued to fight, she tried again to pull them apart. That didn't work, so she tried to push herself in between them. Reynolds made a fist and drew his arm back. With the agility of a cat, John Eagle ducked the punch and it hit Cady square in the left eye.

Pain exploded in her cheekbone, and her vision filled with bright yellow and orange spots.

"Jumpin' Jehoshaphat, ma'am!"

She fought dizziness as she staggered to the bench behind her and sat. Boots scraped on the canvas floor and a big body moved between her and the boys.

"No man ever hits a woman." Kane's voice echoed loudly in the mess hall. Then he was on one knee beside her. "Are you all right?"

With a hand to her throbbing cheek, she managed to open her uninjured eye. "Fine."

There was a sound behind him. Kane jumped to his feet. "If either of you moves a muscle, I'll throw you both in the guardhouse." He glared at each boy in turn. "I just might anyhow."

Amazingly enough they stood quietly, although still breathing hard from the exertion of the fight. Reynolds rubbed a hand under his nose, and his white sleeve came away streaked with blood. Cady rose from the bench and, with her good eye, looked at the rest of her students, who had watched the whole scene with avid interest.

She was so angry her hands shook. She needed to clear the classroom before the rest of her students witnessed another scene, one she was about to start. How dare Kane step in when she'd asked him not to!

"Children, you're dismissed for lunch. I'll see you back here at one-thirty." They stood and raced from the room. John Eagle and R. J. Wexler started to follow.

Kane held up his hand. "Halt."

They did, instantly. How did he do that, Cady wondered?

Standing tall, with his arms crossed over his chest, the captain speared each of them with a look. "Go wait in my office."

"Halt, you two." Cady touched his upper arm. The wide muscle beneath her palm told her how he had managed to pull the boys apart. She envied him his size and strength. "This is my responsibility and I'll handle it."

Ignoring her, the two boys continued to march out of the room.

She looked at the empty doorway, then up at Kane, and pulled her hand away. "I can't believe what just happened."

"I figure to give those two a lecture they won't soon forget. Sit down and let me have a look at that eye." He tried to lead her to the bench, but she pulled her arm from his grasp.

"How dare—"

"Simmer down. I'll take care of it. How's the eye?"

"Forget the eye. Why did you interfere in my classroom?"

"Why did I—?" He stopped, stunned, and stared at her for a moment. "Those two were trying to kill each other."

"Don't be ridiculous. Besides, from nine-thirty to twelve and one-thirty to three-thirty, this is *my* schoolroom. If my students are trying to kill each other, I will deal with it."

He pointed to her eye. "What if they kill you?"

Without hesitation she replied, "Then feel free to step in and restore order."

"I'm sorry, but I can't stand by and watch someone hit a woman."

"I'm not a woman." Heat blossomed in her cheeks as his brows lifted. "I mean to *them.* I'm their teacher. Besides, Reynolds didn't mean to hit me."

"That's no excuse. You're a woman, no mistake about that. And in about thirty minutes, you're gonna have one hell of a black eye. I plan to make those two sorry for what they did so it never happens again."

"It's up to me to discipline them. Don't you see? When you stepped in, you undermined my authority. If I can't maintain order, no one can learn."

"Looked to me like you were learning a thing or two about a right hook."

"This isn't a joking matter." She tried to glare at him, but it wasn't easy with only one good eye.

"I'm not laughing."

"I want to be the best teacher I can be. If you step in every time there's a problem, the children will not learn to respect me." She laced her fingers together in front of her. "If you hadn't been here, I would have had to handle it, wouldn't I?"

"I suppose. But I *was* here. I couldn't let them hurt you—or each other."

She touched her cheek. "It's nothing."

"I think the post surgeon should take a look."

"That's not necessary. I'll just put some water on it."

"Are you sure you don't want the doctor?"

"I'm sure."

"All right." He started to walk away, then turned back to her. "One thing: Never try to stop a fight until it's over."

"I'll keep that in mind, captain, in case you don't happen to be here the next time," she said wryly.

"I nearly forgot. The reason I happened to be here this time was because I had something to tell you."

"What?"

"There's going to be a reception in your honor given by the officers' wives."

"How lovely." She smiled and winced at the stab of pain in her cheekbone. "When is it?"

"Saturday."

"Day after tomorrow. That soon?" She cupped her cheek with her hand and wondered if she dared hope there would be no swelling or discoloration.

"Out here, folks are always looking for a reason to have a party. There's not much else to do." His gaze intensified as he studied her. "You might want to wear purple to match the color your eye will be by then."

"Emily Stanton said some of the children are waiting to see if I'll get drunk and have to be let go the way Sergeant Cramer was. You don't suppose this reception could wait until I've convinced everyone that I'm staying?"

"Those ladies want to have a party. Do you want me to tell them it's postponed?"

And start off on the wrong foot with everyone? Cady shook her head. "Wouldn't be neighborly. I'll be there. And I'll look forward to it."

"All right, then. I'll stop by for you at seven."

"That's not necessary. I can see myself there. You must have more important things to do."

"It's my duty."

"More orders?" she asked.

"Mrs. Wexler asked me to escort you."

"Ah," she said. "Do you always follow orders?"

"That's what a good soldier does."

"And you're a good soldier?"

One corner of his mouth lifted. "The army's been good to me."

"I see. Well, then, I'll be ready at seven. I wouldn't want you to disobey orders on my account."

"Cady, it's not like that."

"Never mind, captain, it's not important. But there is the matter of those two boys in your office who need to have a good talking to."

He nodded. "There is that. I'll go speak to them now." She started to say something, and he held up his hand. "You can have your turn when I'm finished."

"That's not what I was going to say. I get the feeling you have a special interest in Master Wexler."

"R. J.'s father is away from the fort a lot, dealing with the Indian agent. His mother can't seem to handle him, and I've gotten in the habit of filling in." Kane's eyes narrowed for a moment and the muscle in his cheek contracted. "I'm in charge when the commanding officer is gone. Keeping order here is my responsibility. The soldiers are my concern, their dependents are my concern, and you're my concern."

"All right, talk to them. But from now on, captain, I'll thank you to stay out of my classroom."

"I can't do that." He grinned at her. "This is the only building on the post big enough for a social gathering."

"This is where the reception will be?"

He nodded.

Her first day of teaching—a disastrous day, she added—just got worse. In two days, she had to meet the parents of her students. No doubt she'd have a black eye. And Kane Carrington would be her escort. If only Miss Agnes had taught her about men. Cady had a feeling she could go to school for the rest of her life and still not understand this one.

4

Two days after the disturbance in her classroom, Cady waited for Kane to take her to the reception. She was nervous as a long-tailed cat in a room full of rocking chairs. It was because she was meeting the parents of her students, some of them for the first time, she told herself. But, nonetheless, it would be a room full of people, most of them strangers.

Except Kane.

Tension and excitement rippled through her. Was *he* the reason she was so on edge? He was part of it. But the whys didn't matter; she had to pull herself together. As she tried to harness the butterflies in her stomach, she leaned back against the pine dresser in her living quarters. The place was small, but it had everything she needed, including a fireplace on the wall opposite the door that she used for cooking her meals.

She hoped the evening would cool off some. She was nervous enough without worrying about fainting from the heat. "It *might* have pushed me to the edge of my endurance, but it was definitely the heat that sent me into a swoon," she told herself.

But that was in the past. For tonight, she was wearing her long-sleeved white cotton dress trimmed with pink rosettes at the neck and cuffs. Her hair was woven into two braids and pinned in a sort of circle on the back of her head. Wisps of curls that refused to stay back tickled her forehead and temples. She patted her hair and decided it was neat and dignified.

She figured she was as ready for the reception as she would ever be, except for checking her face in a mirror. She'd been afraid to look, hoping her eye had improved from that morning when it had been a vivid black and blue on the upper lid and just below, too. No matter what dress she wore, or how sedately she arranged her hair, it was difficult to look dignified with a black eye.

"Purple would be more accurate," she said, braving a look in her hand mirror. For her last birthday, her twenty-first, Jack had sent her the intricately carved silver mirror. She had loved to use it, until now. She touched her temple and winced. "Oh, Lord. Still puffy and purple." How could she face meeting everyone looking like this? What would they think? She was afraid she already knew. They'd think Miss Cady Tanner couldn't keep order in a classroom.

Annoyance coursed through her again as she remembered Kane's part. She wasn't sure what she was more angry about, the fact that he was escorting her tonight because he'd been ordered to, or that he had interfered in her classroom and possibly undermined her authority irreparably.

The whole incident had surely confirmed Kane's suspicions that she had no business here at Fort McDowell. Or anywhere else in the Arizona Territory, for that matter. Did the other people here at the fort share his opinion? she wondered. If they did, would they tell her to her face? If so, she didn't think she could bear to see Kane's smirk of satisfaction.

She walked to the table beside the fireplace where she kept her cooking supplies. One person didn't need a lot, and from the fort sutler she'd purchased an iron frying pan, a coffeepot, and two plates with two sets of eating utensils, just in case she had company. Beside that she'd arranged her staples: spices, sugar, flour, and coffee.

Opening the canvas bag of flour, she dipped in two fingers and pulled them out, the tips covered with white. She patted a small amount on her upper eyelid, and blended the rest on the purple stain just beneath.

She held up her mirror again, blotted off the excess, and smoothed it as best she could. It was better, but it wouldn't hold up to intense scrutiny.

There was a knock. Her stomach jumped nervously as she glanced at the door and imagined the tall captain on the other side. Then she looked back at her reflection. "This is it, Cady. Remember what Father always says: If you can't dazzle them with perfection, fool them with charm. Shoulders back, chin up. Confidence. And for God's sake stop talking to yourself."

She walked over to the door and opened it. Kane stood on the wooden walkway under the ramada. He looked so handsome, she was the one dazzled. At the sight of him in his dark blue uniform trimmed with gold, which emphasized his masculine good looks, her heart beat wildly in her chest and she was rendered speechless. Now she was mute as well as one-eyed.

He looked down at her and almost smiled. "Good evening, Cady."

His gaze traveled from the top of her head to the tips of her toes. An expression of what she thought might be approval creased his eyes and turned up the corners of his mouth.

"Hello, captain," she said softly.

Then his gaze rested on her face and he frowned. It seemed he couldn't even look at her without getting irritated. Her heart fell and she tried desperately to keep her disappointment from showing.

He removed his campaign hat and held it in one hand. "How's the eye?" he asked.

"It's fine," she lied.

He lifted a dark brow speculatively. "Probably looks worse than it feels."

"I hardly know it's there."

"Did you let the doc see it?" He moved closer.

He was close enough for her to smell the soap he'd used on his square, freshly shaved jaw, near enough to feel the heat of his body. She wondered if he could hear her heart pounding.

She shook her head. "Completely unnecessary. If you had a black eye would you bother the doctor?" He hesitated. "I didn't think so. By tomorrow it will be practically good as new."

He leaned closer and lifted his hand to touch the corner of her eye. "Are you sure?"

She'd known the flour covering wouldn't hold up to intense observation, but she hadn't expected the inspection to be from Kane. She held her breath as he gently probed the swelling. Her legs trembled and she felt as wobbly as a newborn colt. Stop it! she told herself. Don't let him do this to you again.

She ducked away from his big gentle hand and stepped back. "I'm perfectly fine, Kane."

He shrugged as if to say it was none of his business. But Cady noticed a look, dark and intense. If she didn't know better, she'd have thought he was concerned about her.

"Are you ready to go?" he asked.

"Yes."

In the doorway, he stepped aside to let her pass. When she was outside, beneath the overhang, he pulled the door closed and moved to stand on her other side, between her and the parade ground beyond. When he offered her his arm, she hesitated before putting her shaking hand in the crook of his elbow.

This was a protective gesture on his part, a gentleman's action, something she was certain he would have done for any woman. Nevertheless, her pulse raced faster. As angry as she was with him for interfering with her job, she'd have thought his nearness wouldn't affect her at all. Yet here she was, nervous as a schoolgirl with her first beau.

"It will go away," she said under her breath.

Kane looked down at her. "What?"

"Nothing."

The night was surprisingly pleasant, and she was much more comfortable now that she was out of her quarters. The sun was just going down behind the mountains in the distance, bathing the desert in colors of gold, red, and orange. A breeze, with the barest hint of coolness in it, lifted the hair from her forehead.

As they strolled toward the mess hall, a dog barked from across the parade ground. Passing the stables, the soft nicker of horses drifted toward them.

Cady risked a sidelong glance at Kane. His profile could have been carved from the rocks that made up the mountains in the distance. Why had she never noticed the creases that ran from his well-shaped nose to his mouth? Probably because most of the time she was too busy being mad at him. She sensed his tension now and wondered if it had anything to do with being her escort tonight. Just because he always followed orders didn't mean he agreed with them or even liked them. No doubt he didn't want to be with her any more than she wanted him there. Another adjustment she'd learn to make: In the army, one had to make the best of any situation one found oneself in.

Since he didn't seem inclined to talk, she broke the silence.

"Kane, what did you say to Reynolds and John Eagle in your office after the fight?"

"Why do you ask? Have they caused a problem in school?" He looked at her sharply.

She shook her head. "Quite the opposite. They were model students yesterday. That's why I wondered what you said."

Before they crossed the narrow dirt road to the mess hall on the other side, he stopped her. She heard the clip-clop of hooves and the creak of a saddle, and the odor of an approaching horse drifted to them. They waited while a soldier on his roan passed by. As he did, the soldier saluted. "Captain." He nodded at Cady. "Ma'am."

Kane returned the salute and they continued walking. "I restricted the boys to the post for a month." His expression turned grim when he glanced over his shoulder at the horse soldier, then down at her. "That means no riding. As an outlet for their energy, I also gave them a list of chores to do every day after school."

"Oh, my."

"What's wrong?"

"Nothing, except they're going to be very busy. My punishment was standards. Reynolds has to write two hundred times 'I will not start a fight.'"

His forehead creased in confusion. "Why not 'I will not fight?'"

"There are times when you can't avoid it. I was more lenient with John. He contributed to the situation, but he didn't start the fight. He has to write one hundred times 'I will think before I speak.'"

"Why?" he asked. She stumbled over a rock, and he slowed and steadied her before strolling on again.

"He deliberately provoked Reynolds with what he said. I wanted to teach them to choose their battles wisely. There's a time to walk away and a time to stand firm."

"You do have brothers, don't you?"

"I do indeed." She smiled fondly. "My father always told them, Don't start anything. But by God if anyone else does, you damn well better finish it."

He looked down at her, obviously surprised by her swearing. "Cady Tanner, what would Miss Biddle say?"

She smiled. "She'd ask me if I quoted accurately."

He laughed. "Your father makes a lot of sense." Then he sobered. "I only hope R. J. learns something from this. It's going to be a long month for him without his horse."

"The best-learned lessons are the most painful ones. Reynolds won't soon forget this, and perhaps the next time he's tempted to fight he'll think twice."

"Well, maybe."

In the distance, she saw the guards at the fort's perimeter and wondered again why there was no wall around the group of buildings that comprised Fort McDowell. The sight of the soldiers cradling rifles in their arms like babies was becoming familiar to her— and a constant reminder that danger lurked beyond the scattering of adobe buildings.

"What about John Eagle?" she asked. "I didn't expect to have an Indian in my class, not that it's a problem. But he stands apart from the rest. I just wondered why."

"The Apaches don't trust the whites. And they have good reason."

"Then why is he here at the fort, going to a white man's school?"

"His father is an army scout, probably the best we have. It's his wish that John learn our ways as well as his own. He can see changes coming that will affect the Indian way of life. He wants his son to be prepared for both worlds."

"How does John feel about it?"

Kane shrugged. "He doesn't say much. But Indians are taught to respect their parents and elders. He'll do whatever he's told."

"Tell me about the boys' friendship. I gather they were close?"

"Inseparable. Where one was, you knew you'd find the other."

"So the hostilities started when John caught the snake and Reynolds—" She stopped, trying to think of a delicate way to say it.

"Embarrassed himself?" Kane asked with a smile in his voice.

"That must have been awful for him."

"He was mad as a rained-on rooster when the story circulated all over the post. He blamed John."

"But you just said John Eagle doesn't talk much. Why would he humiliate his friend?"

"He wouldn't. This post is like a small town. Someone, probably one of the enlisted men, saw the two boys come back with the snake and noticed the condition R. J. was in and put two and two together. The story spread like wildfire. R. J. had to blame someone, and he was jealous of John because he caught the snake."

She shook her head. "That's such a shame. Isn't there some way to get them to make up?"

"I've tried. Nathan Eagle even stuffed the snake for him. R. J. refuses."

They approached the mess hall. As the sun sank, the shadows grew darker and deeper and the lights inside seemed brighter. Laughter and the sound of voices drifted toward them.

Cady stopped and took a deep breath. "Why don't you go on in? I think I'll watch the sun set. It's spectacular here, far more brilliant than back home."

In spite of what her father had always told her, she didn't feel very charming or confident at the moment.

"If you need a minute, I'll wait with you."

She saw in his expression that he understood. She hated that he could read her so easily when she thought she was hiding her feelings. He was being very considerate. Then she remembered; he was following orders. She couldn't let herself believe that he was being solicitous. She was nothing more than a duty.

"Do you always follow orders to the letter, captain? I think I can get to the mess hall now. It's not necessary for you to accompany me inside."

"It would be unchivalrous of me to let you walk in by yourself."

"Then let's get it over with." She pulled her shoulders back.

Officers, a few of their wives, and enlisted men were gathered inside the mess hall. When Cady and Kane entered, everyone in the room stopped talking and looked in their direction. Kane felt a shiver run through Cady but she lifted her chin and appeared calm and serene, in spite of her purple eye.

She was nothing but contradictions: fiery and spitting mad one minute, soft and insecure the next. She kept him off balance, and that disturbed him.

That and the way she filled out her dress. The white material trimmed with tiny pink roses made her look like just about the daintiest, most feminine woman he'd ever seen. She smelled like roses too. In the middle of the Arizona desert, he couldn't help thinking about a green meadow filled with flowers.

It also reminded him that he had the responsibility of protecting her. The way the men were staring at her told him it wouldn't be an easy task.

His commanding officer's wife hurried over to them.

"Good evening, Mrs. Wexler," Kane said, greeting the plump, brown-haired woman politely. He held his hand out toward Cady. "May I present Miss Tanner."

"Oh, my dear." Mrs. Wexler pressed a palm to her ample bodice and stared in horror at Cady's eye. "I can't believe my son did that. His father will discipline him severely, I assure you."

"He didn't mean to do it. I was trying to separate the two boys, and a wild punch caught me."

Kane cleared his throat. "I've already taken care of punishment detail. He and John Eagle will chop enough wood to keep Miss Tanner supplied for weeks."

"That's one of the chores you gave them?" Cady asked, a speculative look in her green eyes. "Are they required to do this together?"

"It is," he answered, "and they are."

She nodded approvingly.

"I don't know what we'd do without Captain Carrington," Mrs. Wexler said. "With my husband gone so much on army business, and a high-spirited boy to deal with, I'd be at my wits end without him."

"He's very capable," Cady answered.

There was an edge to her voice that Kane knew meant she was still anything but happy about his involvement in the fight.

The woman smiled at Cady. "When R. J.'s not chopping wood, he'll get to know his room a lot better, Miss Tanner."

"My first name is Cady, Mrs. Wexler."

"We're not formal out here, except maybe Captain Carrington, who does everything by the book." She smiled at Kane. "Call me Betsy."

"I'd like that," Cady said.

The other woman frowned as she looked at Cady's eye. "It looks terribly painful, dear."

Cady shook her head. "It's nothing. I'm more concerned about your confidence in my ability to keep order in the classroom. I assure you nothing like that will happen again."

Major Wexler joined them. "Indeed it won't. My son is learning the error of his ways."

"So I heard," Cady said.

The major nodded. "Losing his riding privileges will hurt the boy more than anything and teach him a lesson he won't soon forget."

"It would me," Cady said, nodding in understanding.

"Do you ride, Miss Tanner?" the major asked.

"I do, sir. And I've missed it."

"My son is confined to the fort, and his horse is going to need exercise." The major looked thoughtful. "Would you be interested in riding Prince, Miss Tanner?"

"Oh, yes, sir," she said, without a moment's hesitation or deliberation. "May I?"

Just what he needed, Kane thought. She was enough trouble inside the fort. Now she was planning to go gallivanting around in the desert.

"I have no objections." Major Wexler looked at Kane. "Do you, captain?"

"No, sir. Not if she stays within sight of the fort."

The other man nodded. "I agree. Some of the young Indians on the reservation are feeling their oats, getting restless. Geronimo's escapades are stirring them up too.

But if you stay close by, there's no reason why you shouldn't be safe."

"Thank you, major. I'll look forward to the exercise." She smiled at him and then at Kane.

To everyone else, her expression appeared sweet and innocent. Kane saw a triumphant look that told him she discounted all his warnings. Damnation. This would feed her starry-eyed optimism and convince her she'd done the right thing in coming out west. But that would change. Idealism wouldn't be enough when loneliness and boredom set in.

The oil lanterns hanging on the walls around the room picked out the gold in Cady's hair and set it to gleaming. Kane's gut twisted at the thought of her beautiful hair on the end of an Apache war lance. "Just a word of caution. Stay alert."

"I'll do that, captain," she said, raising her voice over the other conversations nearby.

"Betsy, let's take Miss Tanner around and introduce her." The major took his wife's elbow. "There are a few men who have been waiting anxiously." He grinned at Kane. "You'll excuse us, captain?"

"Of course."

His teeth set, Kane watched Cady as she moved across the room, smiling sweetly and shaking hands as introductions were made. It irritated the hell out of him that every other man there was watching her too. The straight line of her back and her slender waist made his hand itch to curl possessively around her. Her golden brown hair was tightly braided and pinned up on her head, and he had the most insane impulse to unweave those controlled strands and run his fingers through the mass until it was wild and free.

Damn it to hell! He knew each man there was thinking the same thing.

The realization made him crazy. Cady seemed to captivate every man she spoke with, but that didn't surprise him. She was a fascinating mixture of eager young girl and sophisticated lady. With every last ounce of his being he wished she were a fat horse-faced hag. That would make his promise to Jack and to himself much easier to honor.

He was distracted for a few moments by laughter on the other side of the room. When he looked back, Cady had disappeared. Good Lord, keeping an eye on her was like trying to harness a hummingbird. It took him a minute to find her in the corner, surrounded by six blue uniforms. One man brought her a plate piled with food. Another brought her something to drink. All of them were laughing and preening, each trying to get her undivided attention. The worst of it was, he felt the same way. He wanted to walk out, so as not to have to watch her with them. If only he hadn't given his word. If only Betsy Wexler hadn't suggested he be her escort. If only he could drag Cady off, away from the openly hungry stares of all those men. If only he were a different kind of man, the marrying kind. He shook the thought away.

After everyone had eaten, several soldiers picked up musical instruments and in seconds the sounds of fiddle, harmonica, and guitar blended together and filled the room. The long tables and benches were pushed back against the walls to make room for dancing. As the strains of "Dixie" set their toes to tapping, men grabbed their wives and took them out into the middle of the room to dance.

Lieutenant Carlton held his palm out to Cady and she placed her fingers into it, giving him a brilliant smile. Never in his life had Kane wanted to hit a man as badly as he did now. If he wasn't careful, he'd be writing five hundred times, "I will not start a fight."

He turned away and walked to the punch bowl. It wasn't often he regretted that liquor was banned from the post, but this was one of those times. As he filled a cup with the pungent, sweet-smelling liquid, an enlisted man came up beside him.

"Evenin', captain."

"Harrison," Kane said, nodding.

"Nice party, ain't it?"

"Yes." He took a sip from his glass, wishing again that it was something strong enough to burn from his mind the memory of Cady flirting with another man.

"Miss Tanner's a right friendly lady."

"Is she?"

"Yes, sir. And smart, too. Said she's gonna start some kind of meetin' so's we can get together and read."

"Literary society?"

The man's palomino-colored brows drew together in thought. "Yes, sir, I b'lieve that's what she called it."

"That sounds interesting, Harrison."

Next thing he knew, she'd have his men knitting horse blankets.

"Yes, sir. I told her I wasn't much on readin', but she said that's what she's here for, to teach. She don't give a hoot if she's learnin' a grown man."

"Doesn't she?"

"No, sir." The soldier glanced anxiously over his shoulder. "Nice chattin' with ya, cap'n. I'm gonna go now and wait in line. See if I can snare me a dance with the schoolmarm."

"Yes, you do that, Harrison."

Kane took another sip and watched Cady as she danced every dance. The room got hotter by the second and stuffy with the smells of heat and perfume and lantern oil. The more he thought about her giving reading lessons to grown men, the madder he got. Did she really think these men wanted to learn to read? Didn't she understand that they'd do anything in order to be alone with her? They didn't care about book learning. They wanted *her*. And they'd do whatever they could to have her.

This turn of thought disturbed him. Ever since his father died and he joined the army, his duty and the orders Cady had challenged him about had always come first. As he'd been promoted and given more responsibility, his soldiers' safety and welfare had been his primary concern. He'd never once thought about beating the tar out of one of them—at least, not over a woman.

He pulled his pocket watch out, flicked it open, and checked the time. Ten o'clock. For the last three hours he'd stood and watched her. When he looked up, he met her gaze from across the room. She turned and said something to the man beside her. His expression went from puppy-dog eager to the sorriest-looking excuse for a soldier Kane had ever seen.

Cady crossed the room. "I saw you looking at your watch, Kane. Are you ready to go?"

He'd been ready three hours ago.

"Are you?" He studied her. Her undamaged eye paled in comparison to the purple one, and it was hard to tell if he saw shadows of fatigue beneath it. But he thought he did. "You look tired."

"I am, a little."

"Doesn't surprise me."

"What does that mean?"

"Nothing." He realized there was a sharp edge to his tone he hadn't intended to put there.

"Oh, for pity's sake. Tell me what's eating you."

"Nothing." He shrugged as casually as he could. "Just that with all that dancing, you're bound to be tired."

When she slid him a questioning look, he realized his tone was still a little sharper than he'd intended.

"If you're ready," she said, "I'll just say good evening to the major and his wife."

"I'm ready."

He watched her go. When she joined him again, the other men looked envious. He also saw what he could only describe as hunger in their expressions. He didn't blame them. He'd reacted the same way to Cady at first. He'd managed to control his feelings. It was a damn good thing he'd been the one to escort her tonight. She had nothing to fear from him.

But then he remembered the violence that had flashed through his mind as he'd watched the men dance with her. Maybe it was him she should stay away from.

Outside her quarters, Cady pressed her back to one of the cottonwood poles holding up the ramada. A pleasant breeze sent the smell of mesquite and desert sand to her as it cooled her cheeks. She looked up at the night sky and sighed. The sight was breathtaking: stars twinkled brilliantly on a midnight-blue background.

Kane stood beside her, his arm nearly brushing her shoulder, so close she could feel the heat of his body. For half a second, the masculine scent of him pulled at her, urging her closer. She swayed toward him, then stopped herself. She'd made a fool of herself once over him. She wouldn't again.

He didn't seem inclined to leave, but she could feel the tension between them.

"You haven't said a word since we left the reception. Is something bothering you, Kane?"

"No." He pushed his campaign hat back, and she

could see his face in the moonlight. His mouth tightened, and she knew he wasn't being honest with her.

"Something's wrong. Out with it, captain. That's an
order."

He looked at her sharply. "Would you like to tell *me*
about this literary society you're planning?"

"You heard about that?" She was very excited about
the way the men had received her idea. "I proposed the
concept of reading books and meeting once a week to
discuss them. All the people I met tonight were terribly
enthusiastic."

"Were these people all men?" His voice was thick
with sarcasm.

His attitude confused her. What if they were men?
"Men and women both were excited about the idea. I
get the feeling that boredom can be a problem here.
Everyone needs activities to keep busy. I expected the
women to be receptive to the idea. But even the men
seemed eager to read—or to learn to read if they can't."

"You don't get it, do you?" His eyes were dark with
intensity. "Those men would read dress patterns if it
meant they could get close to you."

"Fiddlesticks."

"Cady." He stared at the sky for a moment as if he
was trying to control his temper. "They're not looking to
books to fix their discontent. They're looking to you."

"Well, I *can* help. I can read books and recommend
ones I think they'd like. We can talk about them—"

"Cady, they don't want books, they don't want to read,
and what they want to do doesn't require discussion."

She gasped and felt her cheeks burn. "If you're saying what I think you're saying, you're wrong. Why
would any of them want me?"

He let out a long breath. "For one thing, you're single. Not that it matters to some," he muttered.

"I see."

Cady wasn't sure if she should feel flattered. Probably not. He made it sound like anything in skirts would turn a man's head here.

"I don't think you do." He folded his arms over his chest. "Have you looked in a mirror lately? You're a beautiful woman."

The compliment surprised her. She touched her eye. "This isn't very attractive."

"Doesn't matter. Makes a man want to protect you."

"I don't need protecting. But that's beside the point. I'm afraid I don't see the problem."

"Then I'll spell it out for you. The literary society is a bad idea."

"But why?"

"You're going to have men swarming around, and you're the only single female for miles. That's trouble in my book."

"I still don't see why."

"Then I'll explain."

Kane moved toward her, and she retreated until the adobe wall stopped her, the rough surface pulling at the material of her dress. He pressed close until their bodies touched from chest to thigh. She felt his warmth and breathed in the scent that was his alone. She felt his heart pounding, as rapid and wild as her own. Her knees felt soft as taffy left out in the sun.

"What are you doing, captain?" she asked breathlessly.

"Not all lessons are learned in the schoolroom."

He placed his palms on the wall beside her shoulders, trapping her in his sweet prison. He lowered his mouth until their lips were barely an inch apart. His breath fanned her face.

"What would you do if one of the men wanted

private tutoring?" he asked huskily. His breathing was ragged and uneven.

"I—I'm not sure what you're asking."

"What if he kissed you like this?" He moved his mouth a fraction closer.

"Stop." She pressed her palms flat to his chest and pushed firmly. She couldn't let him go on. She wouldn't be able to resist him if he did. Beneath her hands he was broad and muscled. She didn't have the strength to keep him from what he wanted. But she had to try.

"What if I don't?"

"You know I have brothers. They showed me what to do." She took a deep breath. "Don't make me prove I can."

His body relaxed and she slipped beneath his forearm, away from him. With his arms still braced, he lowered his head, taking deep breaths as if trying to compose himself.

"Are you ordering me not to organize a literary society?"

He straightened and shifted uncomfortably. The danger she saw in his expression made her want to back away.

"No. But when it blows up in your face, don't say I didn't warn you."

"I'll think about what you said. But I know you're wrong." She was tired and confused. She wanted to be alone. "If you'll excuse me, captain, I believe I'll retire now. I'm getting up early to ride tomorrow."

"Are you going by yourself?"

"Yes." She saw disapproval flicker across his face.

"I still don't like it."

She had left home because all her life her father and brothers had been telling her what to do. Now Kane was doing the same thing, only worse. Not only was he ordering her around, he was sticking his nose where it didn't belong.

She straightened her shoulders. "I think it's me you don't like, captain. Why is that?"

"Don't be ridiculous."

"Ridiculous?" She touched her still tender cheek and eye. "You think I'm incompetent in the classroom, don't you?"

"Cady, I—"

"You think I'm not cut out to be a teacher, don't you?"

"I never said—"

"You think I don't belong here, isn't that—"

He took a half step toward her and put one finger over her lips. "May I talk now?"

Her heart raced, not from fear—well, maybe just a little. But mostly because she couldn't think when he was this close.

"Are you ready to listen to what I have to say?" he asked.

She was still for a second and met his gaze, then nodded. He pulled his hand away from her mouth.

"Actually, I don't need to hear what's on your mind," she said. "You've made it pretty clear that you think I don't belong here."

"It's not you, Cady. No woman does."

"That's not your decision to make. Miss Biddle says—"

His hazel eyes flashed with anger. "Dammit, don't quote your spinster teacher to me. She has no idea what it's like out here in the Territory."

"How do you know?"

"I know. She sits in her comfortable parlor drinking tea and filling young women's heads with pretty dreams and romantic notions that are nowhere near the truth.

She fires them up and sends them west, completely unprepared for what life is really like."

"So tell me what it's really like."

"Dangerous." His gaze lowered to her mouth, then he looked past her to the parade ground. "If the snakes, scorpions, and poisonous spiders don't get you, the ants and the unbearable heat can make you wish they had. If that doesn't drive you crazy or kill you, the Indians will."

"I'm not afraid."

"Then you're a fool."

"Am I?" she asked, narrowing her eyes.

"Women are a liability out here." He lifted his hat and ran his fingers through his hair. "You need comforts and conversation with other women. The army discourages men from bringing their families along. When they do come, there's no such thing as putting down roots. Soldiers move constantly from fort to fort."

"Don't you see, Kane? That's why I want to start the literary society."

"To settle the frontier?" he asked dryly.

"To bring some culture—"

"It won't work. We can't offer you the niceties you had back east."

"Just what do you think I did?"

"Chamber music. Landscape painting," he said.

"I can't believe what a dreadful opinion you have of me." She put her hands on her hips.

"You're too damned naive for your own good. Don't you realize half the men on this post can't even read?" A muscle in his cheek contracted as if something had suddenly made him even angrier.

"That's why I'm here," she said softly.

"You did make it clear it wasn't because of me." He laughed, but there was no humor in it.

"I've come to teach, believe it or not, like it or not. The frontier is where I'm needed most."

"This land will break you. Arizona's not for amateurs."

She glared at him. "What makes you think you know what will or will not break me?"

"I've seen it happen."

The raw emotion in his tone caught her attention, and her anger evaporated. She recognized his pain and sensed that he was going to tell her what had caused it.

With a deceptively casual movement, she leaned back against the pole bracing the overhang. Every part of her tensed, every sense sharpened.

"Tell me, Kane. Who did you see broken?"

"I knew a woman once, born and raised out here. She married a soldier, and when he was away for weeks at a time on patrol, she turned to another man for . . . what she needed." He stopped and laughed, a sound so full of bitterness it chilled her in spite of the warm breeze.

She almost didn't want to know, but her curiosity got the better of her. "Who was this woman?"

"My wife."

5

"Your wife?" Cady stood upright, at attention, away from the cottonwood pole.

Kane heard the astonishment in her voice. He'd intended to shock her, but now he took no pleasure in it.

"Yes."

"And she was . . . unfaithful? How can you be so calm about it?" Her small body seemed to vibrate with outrage.

"It's ancient history. Doesn't matter anymore."

"Well, it should." Her righteous anger surprised him. "That was a despicable thing to do."

"Let it go, Cady." The woman had paid a high price for her sins. "Army life, *my* life, drove her to it. What happened to her was my fault."

"Fiddlesticks. It's a hard life, I'm learning well enough, but that's no reason to turn to another man. Not when she had you—" She stopped suddenly and turned her back to him. The line of her shoulders went rigid.

"Don't pity me, Cady."

"I don't. It's just that the woman obviously had no sense." She shook her head. "And you call *me* a fool."

At first he couldn't believe that she'd take his part. Then he realized that no matter what she said about this being a hard life, she still had stars in her eyes where the reality of the frontier was concerned. Time would show her how hard it was to carve out an existence in this godforsaken land. Then she would leave like Annie.

If only he didn't feel such gut-churning temptation for Cady. She'd rekindled the ache she'd created the first time he saw her, only now it was even stronger.

"You *are* a fool if you think you can make a difference out here," he said, deliberately cruel.

She whirled and stared up at him. "I get the feeling, captain, that you're hoping I'll fail. Is that why you brought Reynolds to school the first day and then stayed? Were you hoping I'd fall on my face?"

"I stayed because I know R. J.'s temper. I had a suspicion there would be trouble."

"How does it feel to be right?" she asked. An edge of irritation cut her voice.

It was partly true that he'd been watching to see if she could stand up to R. J. Was he hoping she'd fail? Maybe.

In the shadows, he couldn't make out the bruises around her injured eye, he could only see how beautiful she was, standing there in the moonlight. His gaze dropped to her mouth and her full lips. If he didn't know their touch and texture from a long-ago memory that still haunted him, maybe he wouldn't be tempted. But, God help him, he *was* tempted.

Pressure built inside him, and he looked up at the sky until he could regain control. The stars twinkled and glittered gaily, just like Cady. Tonight at the reception she had sparkled until every man in that room had been dazzled.

Including himself.

He didn't want other men looking at her. The primitive feelings shook him; he would bloody the first man who even made a move to do the things to her that he was thinking about. He wanted to hold her, touch her, kiss her. He wanted to know if she tasted as sweet and innocent as she had two years ago.

He folded his arms over his chest. "I take no satisfaction in being right about the fight."

"It doesn't matter anyway. The parents I met this evening didn't seem to care. They were genuinely happy that I'm here. And they all knew what had happened. Apparently they don't doubt my abilities the way you do." She stepped around him and opened her door. "Nothing you can say or do will sway me, captain. I'm staying. That's final."

She went inside, slamming the door shut.

He stared long after the door stopped vibrating, then smiled. He never knew what to expect from her. "Good night, Cady," he whispered.

He should have been relieved that she'd slammed the door in his face. Half a minute more and he would have kissed her senseless. Her spirit and fire made her even more beautiful than that night at Fort Mohave when she'd been dressed like a princess in the green satin dress that matched her eyes.

He stepped out from under the ramada and crossed the plank over the acequia on his way to the enlisted men's quarters. He was hot and tired and irritable. He hoped like hell no one got in his way.

It would be another uneasy night for him, just like all the others since Cady Tanner had turned up. What had he done to deserve this? To have her this close and know he didn't dare touch her. He thought of Annie. Maybe he'd done something after all.

Cady was his hell to pay.

He resigned himself to many more sleepless nights, until she gave in to the inevitable and went back where she belonged.

The morning after the reception, Cady reined her horse in at the top of a rise. She looked around quickly and, in the distance, spotted the fort. Good. It was barely in sight, she couldn't make out the sentries around the perimeter, but she knew they were there, alert, watching, holding their rifles.

She had taken the major's warning to heart but couldn't resist giving her restless mount his head. When she'd felt him tiring, she'd turned back the way she'd come, relieved to see the fort soon and know she hadn't gone too far.

She was in high spirits this morning. The wind in her face and the smell of mesquite and sage exhilarated her. Above her, a cactus wren flew and jabbered. She knew how he felt, understood his sense of liberation. She felt free and alive.

She settled her big black hat more securely over her hair and pushed the floppy brim up so she could see where she was going. As her horse walked slowly toward the fort, she thought about her conversation with Kane the night before. It had upset her, at first, because he was trying to get rid of her. Then she'd realized that he did want her gone, but not for the reason she'd thought. After learning of his unfortunate marriage, she thought he wouldn't want anything to do with a woman ever again. That's when it hit her, like a lightning bolt.

He wanted her to leave because he *liked* her!

If he didn't, he wouldn't have bothered to tell her to go back to where she came from. He wouldn't bother with her at all. And he wouldn't care whether she stayed or not.

In some way, she mattered to him.

That made all the difference. The next time she saw him she planned to test her theory, though she wasn't quite sure how. But he didn't hate her. The knowledge of that made her smile.

For the last two years, whenever she remembered the way she'd thrown herself at him, she wanted to crawl in a hole. She'd been childish and impulsive. If he'd called her a fool then, she would agree with him. Now he called her foolhardy for wanting to make a difference. That's where he was wrong, and someday she'd make him admit it.

But that wasn't the part of their talk that had kept her awake. It was what he'd said just before calling her a fool.

She patted her horse's neck with a gloved hand. "Is he still married, Prince? I never asked him. If he is, where is his wife?"

He hadn't said what happened to her. He had turned the conversation away from himself and told Cady she was wasting her time here in Arizona. That had goaded her into anger, and she had stalked inside without knowing what had become of his wife. As far as Cady knew, he might still be married to the disloyal little tart.

The wind picked up, strong and fragrant with the scent of creosote bushes, and pressed her cotton shirt against her, molding it to her breasts. The wide brim of her hat fluttered and flapped low over her forehead. Prince dipped his head and shook it, rattling his bridle and snorting loudly. Thoughtfully, she patted his neck again.

She had better find out if Kane still had a wife or she could wind up looking like a bigger fool than he already thought she was.

She turned her face to the sun, letting the warmth seep into her skin. The morning was still comfortable, but it was beginning to heat up. She had decided to take her ride early, before it got too uncomfortable.

To her left, she saw dust from another rider and figured someone else had had the same idea. She waved and saw a responding gesture. As the rider approached, she saw it was a man in uniform. When he was closer, she recognized Kane. As he wheeled his horse up beside hers, the animal shook its head restlessly.

"Good morning," she said, giving him a big smile.

He nodded. "Morning. You're up bright and early."

The sound of his deep voice washed over her, raising gooseflesh on her arms. Her saddle creaked as she shifted. He looked wonderful on a horse, she thought. Straight and tall, strong and sure. She searched for something to say.

"I couldn't sleep." Would he know it was because of him? His expression didn't change. "I figured I might as well get up and ride Prince." She patted the animal's neck. "He really needed the exercise."

"I saw you let him have his head." A grudging note of admiration wrapped around his words. "You ride well."

A ripple of pleasure skittered down her spine. "Thanks. I love riding. Jack taught me. He used to let me tag along with him when I was a little girl."

He folded his hands on the pommel of his saddle. There was a bemused expression on his face, but he didn't say anything.

"What is it, captain? I took your advice. I'm wearing a hat." She pointed to the low-crowned black felt covering her hair.

"Looks a little big."

"There's just no pleasing you. The other one was too small; this one's too big." She smiled. "Actually it doesn't stay on unless I stuff my hair up underneath. It's Jack's. He gave it to me when I was eleven, after I begged and pleaded."

"Do you always get what you want, Cady Tanner?"

She thought about his question. He should know better than anyone that things didn't always go her way. If they did, he'd have listened two years ago when she tried to convince him he needed her.

"My father always said, When you want something, go after it with everything you've got."

"What if things don't work out the way you hoped?"

"Then he'd say, Sometimes you get the bear and sometimes the bear gets you."

He chuckled. "Did it make you feel better?"

"It made me laugh. So, yes, I guess it did."

They stared off into the distance for a few moments without talking. A tumbleweed skipped and rolled across the desert floor, propelled by the wind. The only thing Cady could think about was his wife. She was bursting with curiosity, but that wasn't the sort of thing she could just blurt out.

"You said you were watching me ride. Why didn't you join me?"

"After you slammed the door in my face last night? I wasn't sure you wouldn't shoot me today."

"Oh, that." She tipped her head slightly. "You should know something about me. I'm quick to anger, and just as quick to get over it."

His eyes were in shadow, but the corners of his mouth turned up. "I'll remember that."

She bit her lower lip. Beneath her the horse shifted restlessly. "Easy, boy," she said, smoothing her gloved hand over his neck. She looked at Kane. "I guess he's tired of standing. I'm going to walk him around for a while and cool him off before I take him back."

"Good idea."

Nervously, she cleared her throat. It was now or never. She might as well see if her theory was correct. "You probably have a hundred orders to give at the fort, but I'll ask anyway. Would you care to join me if I promise not to shoot you? I don't have a gun, and even if I did, I wouldn't know how to use it."

Kane scanned the desert around the fort, and his expression turned grim. "I *will* join you because I *do* have a gun and I know how to use it. In spite of what Major Wexler said, it's not safe for you to be out riding alone."

A feeling started in the pit of her stomach, something like a warm glow. He was concerned about her safety. Would he bother if he disliked her? Common sense told her no. He could have made an excuse and left.

But that pesky common sense she prided herself on also told her he was first, last, and always a soldier. He would make certain any woman was safe. Had he agreed to join her because he wanted to be with her or because she was a female alone? Did he only feel obligated to do his duty as an officer and a gentleman?

Instinct—or maybe wishful thinking—told her he had joined her because he wanted to ride with her.

A grin built inside her, but she didn't let it show. He had just passed the first test. Now she had to find out if he was still married.

Side by side, they rode in silence for a while. Finally, Kane looked over at her. "What's on your mind?"

She thought about denying his question and decided not to. "A lot of things."

"Want to talk about anything in particular?"

"I'm afraid to bring up unpleasant memories for you."

"Why don't you let me decide."

"All right." She stared straight ahead as she rolled gently from side to side with the horse's gait. "Are you still married?" From the corner of her eye, she saw the muscle in his cheek jerk.

"No," he said simply.

"Is that all you're going to say?"

"Yes."

"Then I won't ask any more questions."

"Good."

"About your wife, that is."

One corner of his mouth lifted. "So that's not all you had on your mind."

"No."

"Is it something else that will bring up unpleasant memories?"

"Only for me, I think."

His horse danced sideways, restless and high-strung. Kane pulled in the reins and skillfully used his body to keep his seat. The corded muscles in his thighs rippled and stretched against the material of his uniform pants. She swallowed at the sudden tightness in her throat.

"Easy, Soldier Boy." He met her gaze. "Sorry. He's a little skittish. Independent. Doesn't like to be told what to do. Not unlike someone I know."

She smiled. "I've been that way all my life."

"What makes you think I was talking about you?" He grinned.

She blinked. "Weren't you?"

"I meant R. J. Soldier doesn't get along with him. I think it's Prince's scent that's setting him off."

Finally, the animal calmed and they moved forward again. Kane sat a horse as if he were born to it. His powerful masculinity set her pulse to racing as if she were flying across the desert, low on her horse's back, with the wind blowing her hair out behind her. Kane was big and strong and he made her feel safe. It would be so easy to let herself rely on him.

That tripped warning bells in her head.

She had come west to prove she could take care of herself. She wanted to make her own decisions and live life the way she chose. Was she playing with fire here? If she persevered in her quest to see how Kane felt, would she get burned?

"So what is this unpleasant thing you've been thinking about?" he asked.

She tipped her head back and looked at the sky as her lips pressed tightly together.

"You don't have to tell me if you'd rather not," he added.

"No." She glanced at him then straight ahead. "I think I need to get it off my chest." She fixed her gaze on Prince's ears as they flicked back and forth. "I want to apologize to you for the way I behaved that night at Fort Mohave. It was inexcusable."

"Fort Mohave?" His horse pranced uneasily as Kane reflexively jerked the reins. "I don't recall that you have anything to be sorry about."

"I threw myself at you like a foolish schoolgirl."

"You *were* a schoolgirl."

"Still, it was immature and unladylike. I'm sorry."

Kane was surprised at her confession. If she thought she had something to be ashamed of, she was wrong. He had been ill-mannered and just this side of rude, but he had pushed her away for her own good.

He glanced at her now, sitting straight in the saddle, the reins loosely held in her hands. The wind blew the floppy brim of her hat off her forehead, revealing the smooth skin of her face. Freckles stretched across her cheeks. A thoughtful expression clouded her eyes, and he noticed her shiner was less visible this morning.

In her white cotton blouse and split riding skirt, no one would mistake her for a rich eastern lady. But there was no doubt she was all woman. The scent of lilacs filled his head and once again he had the impression of a lush meadow bursting with pink-purple flowers. A gust of wind pushed the material of her bodice against her, outlining the fullness of her breasts and emphasizing the narrowness of her waist. As she competently controlled her horse, the shape of her slender thighs and calves was evident even through the thickness of her skirt.

He couldn't get the image of those legs wrapped around his waist out of his mind. This vision had kept him awake into the early morning hours. Even now, his breathing quickened at the sight, sound, and smell of her. He shook his head, trying to push the forbidden images away.

"My own behavior was nothing to be proud of."

"You were a perfect gentleman."

There was almost a tinge of regret in her voice.

Cady took a deep breath. "I think what stirred my temper that night two years ago was your comment that someone who couldn't start a cook fire had no business in the Territory," she said, quoting his own words.

"I haven't changed my opinion."

"I didn't expect you had, given the fact that you never miss an opportunity to tell me I don't belong here."

"I haven't changed my opinion about that, either. But you're the one who keeps bringing it up."

She looked over at him and, in the shadow of her big black hat, her eyes flashed. It was the only evidence of

the hair-trigger temper she'd showed him the previous
evening when she'd slammed the door in his face. He'd
never met a woman who kept him so off balance.

"Then let's put the issue to rest once and for all."

"How do you propose to do that?"

"What if I prove to you I *can* start a cook fire and
even make supper over it? Will you take back what you
said? Will that convince you that I can take care of
myself out here?"

"Depends on how tasty the supper is."

"I didn't say it has to be good, just that I can make it.
If I were cooking in my mother's kitchen back home, I
couldn't guarantee to satisfy your taste. But I'll tell you
this: You won't starve."

He was starving now. He wanted her with a hunger
that seemed to get bigger every time he saw her. He was
crazy, probably been out in the sun too long, a voice
inside him insisted. He silenced it.

"How can I resist?"

"All right, then. How about tonight. Sunday supper?
Say, six o'clock?"

This might be the biggest mistake of his life, Kane
thought, but he didn't have it in him to say no.

"I'll be there."

Reynolds J. Wexler, Jr., quietly climbed out of his bedroom window and settled the checkerboard more
securely under his arm. He glanced to the left and the
right to make sure no one saw him leave his room. John
Eagle had taught him how to move without being
heard. The thought of his former friend made him feel
empty inside.

He wished John had never caught that old snake.
Maybe if he hadn't they'd still . . . shoot, what was the

use of thinking on that? He was just glad John had showed him how to be quiet when he didn't want no one to hear him. Like now. It wouldn't be dark for a while yet and he had to be careful to stay to the shadows.

His mother had confined him to his room. But when his father was gone, which was most of the time, she fell asleep soon after supper. She was snorin' away now. Kane had punished him too but didn't know what his ma had said about not comin' out until he could be a civilized gentleman. And Kane wouldn't care if he did know, R. J. told himself. This was their checkers night. What could be more important than that?

R. J. knew he would be lucky this time. In their weekly Sunday evening checker game, R. J. usually came out the loser. As much as he hated losing, he liked it that Kane didn't let him win. That made him feel good. If he couldn't win fair and square, he didn't want to win at all. But he was feeling lucky tonight. He would beat the pants off the captain for sure this time, he just knew he would.

He turned the corner of the long row of adobe buildings and skidded to a stop. "Jumpin' Jehoshaphat!"

Kane was standing beneath the ramada, and that old maid schoolmarm was smilin' up at him all sweet and big-eyed. R. J. backed up and peeked around the corner, keeping himself hidden.

It made R. J. plumb sick to his stomach. He still couldn't figure why in blue blazes Kane had given up his quarters to that ol' teacher. Officers didn't do that for nobody. They always took the best for themselves, otherwise what was the good of outrankin' someone else?

Didn't make any sense at all. And why in tarnation was he visiting her? Something terrible crossed his mind and his eyes widened as that empty feeling in his stomach got bigger. Was Kane courtin' Miss Tanner?

R. J. cautiously leaned around the corner and stared at the captain. Even from this side view, he could tell Kane wasn't smilin'. Not by a long shot. And he had a funny look on his face like he was mad as all get out.

His sweaty palms caused the checkerboard to slip, and R. J. slid his hand down his wool trousers. Then he settled the game more firmly against his side. He wasn't sweatin' because he was nervous after sneakin' out and all. It was from writin' all those dang standards she'd given him. Not to mention the blisters he had from choppin' wood. No wonder he couldn't even hang on to the gosh-darn board.

Worst of all, he missed Prince somethin' fierce. He missed racin' Bart Grimes across the parade ground. He missed the feelin' he got when he and Prince beat the tar outa everyone. He stuck his head out and peeked carefully around the corner of the building, just in time to see Kane go inside. It appeared he was gonna miss his weekly checkers game, too.

And it was all *her* fault.

R. J. was tempted to tell her to go to blazes, only Kane would wallop him good if he did. The way the captain had looked while she was holding her face, R. J. had been sure he was gonna get whacked for blacking her eye, even though he hadn't meant to.

He waited for a long time, hoping Kane would come out. But he never did. Didn't he remember they always played checkers on Sunday night?

Why in tarnation would Kane rather see that ol' Miss Tanner than play checkers? She must be holding something over his head or Kane wouldn't be caught dead that close to her.

"Jumpin' Jehoshaphat! Maybe he's tryin' to get her to let up on the standards." R. J. grinned. Yeah, that must be it.

He waited, staying until the sun went down, but Kane didn't come out. He would've watched all night, but he had to go to the necessary. He turned away, shaking his head.

The captain wasn't like his pa; he always kept his word. He *never* missed a checkers night, unless he was away on patrol. So it had to be that ol' schoolmarm's fault. It was just one more in the long list of gripes R. J. had against her. The list was getting longer all the time. He'd pay her back someday, too.

"Just see if I don't," he grumbled.

Kane glanced around his former quarters while Cady put his hat on the dresser. Everything looked different, definitely smelled different—better. Feminine articles were scattered around the room. A silver brush and mirror rested on the dresser with ribbons beside them, dresses hung on hooks on the wall to his right, pages from a ladies' magazine were tacked up on the wall to the left of the fireplace.

This room felt more like a home after a few days of Cady's presence than it ever had while he'd lived there. In fact, she'd put his hat on the dresser because her beat-up floppy black one was already on the peg by the door where he used to keep his.

"I see you've made yourself at home," he said, taking a deep breath.

She looked around, then up at him. The smooth skin between her brows puckered slightly. "I hope that's all right."

"Of course."

Her scent was womanly and soft and tempting. He shut his eyes for a second. He couldn't let his feelings loose. If he did, he'd never be in control again.

He should never have come. If he had the sense the good Lord gave a rock, he'd turn right around and walk out that door.

"I'm glad you approve. I thought pictures would brighten the walls up a bit," she said. Her shoes scraped on the canvas floor as she walked to the dresser.

He stared at the provocative sway of her full cotton skirts as she moved away from him. His gaze moved to the curve of her back and her hair, twisted up into a braid. He wanted to see it down, loose around her shoulders, tousled as if . . . Stop, he told himself.

He returned his attention to Cady. Behind her on the dresser, his hat rested between a black velvet ribbon and the stuffed snake. On the left corner was a photograph.

"Who's in the picture?" he asked.

He moved beside her to see the tintype and recognized her two brothers, Jeff and Jack. The older man and woman he took to be her parents. He studied Cady's likeness. The unsmiling image didn't do her justice. It didn't capture the sparkle that lighted her green eyes or the mischievous smile he had learned to be wary of.

"A handsome family," he said.

She stood beside him and he heard her sigh. "If I didn't get lonesome for my parents, there's nothing about that life I'd miss."

Her shoulder brushed his arm. The touch sent awareness stampeding through him. He put the frame back on the dresser and moved away from her. That was the first thing he'd done right since accepting her invitation. Maybe the tide of this battle was turning in his favor.

She stared at the photo for a moment, then looked up at him. She was pretty and fresh, and the sight of her was better than anything he could think of. He was in real trouble here. He searched for something to say to break the spell she was weaving.

"How's your eye, Cady?"

"Good as new."

He studied her. The swelling was gone, and there was barely a hint of purple left on her upper lid. Above her cheek, the discoloration could have been a smudge of dirt or just the evidence of a lack of sleep. An unfamiliar, protective feeling surged within him, and he started to reach out and touch her. Just in time, he curled his fingers into his palm.

He looked around the room again, anything to divert his attention. Anything to gain the upper hand. For the first time he noticed the rough table and two benches in the center of the room. That was new. On the surface, two places were set for dinner.

He pointed to the roughly fashioned boards. "Where did this come from?"

"Lieutenant Carlton was kind enough to make it for me this morning. I needed a place to work. And eat," she said with a laugh. "Now all I lack is a decent tablecloth."

"Hope he managed to pull his detail in between making furniture for you," he grumbled.

Upper hand, hell. He didn't like the idea of his men doing things for her. It wasn't jealousy, he told himself. Just that army business came first. What the men did on their own time was one thing, but Carlton had whipped this up pretty darn quick. He didn't want the man's work suffering because he was smitten with Cady.

The odor of something that smelled mighty tasty drifted toward him. "What's cooking?" Then a thought struck him. "How will I know you didn't get someone else to start that cook fire for you?"

She grinned at him. "I had a feeling you'd say that. Dinner is ready, and I banked the fire so I could restart it when you got here."

It was already too hot in here for him without a fire. But he'd agreed to let her prove herself.

He ran one finger around the high neck of his uniform. "Let's see."

She walked over to the fireplace, which was nothing more than a small square made out of rocks set in the wall with a chimney to keep the smoke out. She stooped, and her skirts billowed around her.

After pulling a match from a container, Cady struck it on one of the stones next to her carefully arranged kindling topped with small pieces of wood. The shavings caught and she blew on the tiny flame until it burned brightly. She waited and at just the right moment she reached for a large chunk of wood. When she struggled with it for a few seconds, he moved beside her and lifted it from her hands.

She looked up at him, a warning in her eyes. "You saw me start the fire."

"I never said you didn't." He set the piece of wood on her fire. "Remind me to tell R. J. to chop your wood smaller."

He looked at her and knew he should get the hell away from her, as far and as fast as he could. But he didn't. He just held out his hand to help her to her feet. She hesitated only for a moment before placing her fingers in his palm.

A pleased, triumphant expression turned up the corners of her mouth and danced in her eyes. "Well?" She lifted one brow expectantly.

"What?"

"I think you owe me an apology. I *can* start a cook fire."

Behind her in the fireplace, the wood hissed and crackled as it shifted and tumbled forward, confirming her achievement.

He bowed slightly. "Miss Tanner, my apologies for ever doubting your ability."

"Accepted," she said with a smile. "Do you take back the part about my having no business in the Territory?"

Kane recalled his words, the ones that had sent her away with tears in her eyes. He shifted his feet. "I'm sorry about that night. I never meant to hurt you."

She clasped her hands together at her waist. Her cheeks flushed a becoming shade of pink. "I'm not going to tell you I wasn't hurt. But in time I realized I was merely infatuated and you were right."

He blinked. "I was?"

"Not in what you said. I *can* take care of myself here. But we barely knew each other." She took a deep breath. "I had no idea what I wanted to do with my life. If you had taken advantage of my youth, I never would have gone back to school and found out I wanted to teach."

"Glad I could help." If he'd been so right then, why did it feel so wrong now?

"Can we put that unfortunate incident behind us and be friends?" she asked.

He should be relieved that it was only friendship she wanted, but, dammit, he wasn't. Let her be friends with Betsy Wexler or Lieutenant Carlton, who made her furniture. He moved in front of her until only a few inches separated them. The warmth and fragrance from her body intoxicated him.

"Friends?" she said, holding out her hand. "We have a bargain then?"

Her eyes glowed, big and beautiful and fringed by thick dark lashes. Her full lips parted slightly, setting loose a wild yearning within him. What would her mouth feel like against his own? In that instant, tasting the honeyed softness of her lips seemed the most important thing in the world.

He took her hand, wrapping his big palm around her small, delicate fingers. He pulled her against him and settled her hand around his neck. For an instant, he stared into her startled eyes. Then he lowered his head and touched his mouth to hers.

The contact was sweet, soft. She felt so good, so warm, so real after what seemed an eternity of memories. A blaze started in his belly; her lips were the spark that set him off. He'd been alone for such a long time, he was like bone-dry kindling laid out and ready to catch.

He knew it; he didn't care. Until that moment he hadn't known how hungry he'd been for her.

He circled her waist with one arm and, with his other hand, pressed the back of her head to make the pressure of their mouths more firm. She made a soft sound in her throat, part sigh, part moan.

Cady thought her heart would fly from her chest when Kane held her so close. The tension she'd felt in him when he'd pulled her into his arms, against his hard, muscled body, frightened her.

This was not the teasing, flirtatious man who'd kissed her two years ago. That man had disappeared and in his place was this fierce dark stranger. But his lips were warm and firm, soft and gentle, so different from the way they looked when he was angry with her.

The tip of his tongue slowly stroked the outline of her mouth, and the sensation was so exquisite she would have slipped to her knees if he hadn't been holding her so tightly.

She hadn't let anyone kiss her since Kane, not even Will, her fiancé; she hadn't wanted to. And now she only wanted to think about the joy of Kane's touch, the rapture of his kiss, the sheer happiness of being in the warmth of his arms again after a lifetime of waiting.

With firm persuasiveness, his tongue coaxed her lips apart, then slipped inside her mouth. He caressed the moist interior until desire crested through her on waves of pure pleasure.

Cady pulled her mouth from his and stared into the silent intensity of his face. His jaw was tautly flexed, his eyes darkened. Shadings of emotion crossed his face, some of them unreadable.

Some, but not all.

Caring, she understood because it touched a core in her female soul. Needing, she knew because it pulled a string in her woman's heart. Wanting, she recognized, because she'd never wanted a man the way she did now. She'd been a girl the last time he kissed her. She was a woman now.

As her gaze slid back and forth across the tension concealed in the angles and contours of his lean cheeks, she saw another emotion. It was a moment before she recognized it, for she'd never known it before. But finally, when she understood what was inside her, she was able to give a name to what she saw in Kane's face: hunger.

The force of it scared her, made her shy away. When she pushed against his chest, Kane dropped his arms and let her go. She backed away from him.

Lord, but it was warm. Even the air blowing in the open door didn't help. Heat seemed to be all around her. The touch of his mouth on hers had been more wonderful than anything she'd ever known. But she needed to sort out her feelings. She backed up another step.

He ran a hand through his thick hair. "So we have a bargain?"

"Bargain?" she repeated. What bargain? Her chest was rising and falling so fast, she couldn't catch her breath. Time and thought were broken down to before the kiss and after. She couldn't remember anything before, only the sensations that raced through her after. She couldn't think straight.

His breathing was ragged, the sound of it filling the space between them. When he rubbed his forehead, his hand shook slightly. "Didn't we agree to forget the past and be friends?" He twisted the last word with a sarcastic edge that she didn't understand.

"Friends. Yes. We definitely agreed."

She sounded like an idiot, repeating everything he said. But it was so hot, she couldn't think. She took a deep breath. Something smelled strange. She sniffed again. It was almost like . . .

"Cady!" He lunged toward her.

She automatically went backward a step.

"Behind you!" he yelled, grabbing her and pulling her away from the fireplace.

Before she could turn to see what had alarmed him, she felt Kane wrenching her to the door.

6

"What are you doing?" Cady cried, trying to tug out of his grasp. "Have you lost your mind?"

There was no time to explain. Fear clawed at Kane's belly as he pulled her outside onto the wooden walkway. He stepped onto the four-foot-wide plank covering the acequia. Then he picked her up and dropped her into the three feet of water flowing through it. She landed on her rear end, not quite submerging. Smoke from the doused fire rose between them, along with the smell of burned material, making him cough. He was pretty sure he'd caught the fire in time, that the cloth had just smoldered and not burned her.

"Are you hurt?" He took a deep breath and let it out slowly as he hunkered down beside her.

"Hurt?" She sat up, pushing her dripping hair from her eyes. She stared up at him in complete bewilderment, then down at her soaked blouse. "No, I'm not hurt. Ask me if I'm wet." She shook her hands and water flew off. "Are you crazy? Why in heaven's name did you—"

The door to the quarters beside Cady's opened. With a lantern held high in his hand, Lieutenant Brewster stood there in his uniform pants with his suspenders coming up over the top part of his union suit. He saluted when he saw Kane. Then his gaze slid to Cady sitting in the water, and his brows rose. "Everything all right, captain?" he asked.

"An accident. Nothing serious."

"Anythin' I can do?"

"No, she'll be all right." *This* time, Kane thought.

"Good evenin', then, captain. Ma'am." He nodded as politely at Cady as if they were passing each other on the street.

"'Night, Brew," Kane said. The other man disappeared inside and they were alone again.

He reached out to her. "Let me give you a hand."

She ignored his offer of help. Instead, she cupped her hands, scooped up water, and tossed it at him. There was no time to duck, and moisture dripped from his hair and down his face. He swiped at it and scowled.

"That's the thanks I get for saving your life?"

"What are you talking about?"

"Dammit, your dress was on fire."

Her eyes widened, then her brows pulled together in a frown. "Sure it was."

He held his hand out. "If you get up out of there, I'll prove it."

She hesitated a moment, then put her fingers in his palm. "Just don't get any ideas about pushing me in there again."

"I wouldn't dream of it." He shook the drops of moisture from his hair.

She gripped his fingers and, as he helped her stand, he heard the water suck at her clothes. Awkwardly, she stepped from the ditch, her skirts clinging wetly to her.

"Are you all right?" he asked again.

"I'm perfectly fine."

He studied her in the moonlight. A pleasantly temperate breeze blew and the acequia water was lukewarm. Still, she was soaked from head to toe, and if she stayed out here long enough, she risked a chill.

"Shouldn't you go inside and change?"

"Yes, thanks to you."

He encircled her waist and helped her up the steps. Her movements were slow, hampered by her heavy water-soaked clothing. When he had her inside, a dark wet pool grew on the canvas at her feet as water dripped from her garments.

Her gaze moved to the fireplace and the log that had rolled forward and caught her dress on fire. Turning from the waist she looked at the back, studying her scorched hem. Then she looked at him and he saw that she realized she could have been badly hurt. What would have happened if he hadn't been there? Of course, if he hadn't been there she wouldn't have backed into the fireplace.

"Now do you believe me?" he asked fiercely.

"Kane, I'm sorry. I—I didn't know." Her lips trembled as she tried to smile. "Thank you."

He didn't know what to say. Her wet blouse made the material practically transparent. It was plastered to her chest, outlining her rounded breasts. Anxiety, longing, and desire mingled together and twisted through him.

"Are you—" The worry spilled into his throat until it scalded him. He swallowed it down and tried again. "Are you burned anywhere?"

She shook her head. "I don't think so. I don't feel anything but soaking wet."

"Let me check." He led her to the dresser where the lantern rested and moved it forward. "Lift up your skirt."

Her eyes grew round with shock. "Lift my—? I think not. I don't feel any pain anywhere."

"If you're in shock, you wouldn't feel anything. Let me see if you're hurt."

She shook her head stubbornly. "It wouldn't be proper."

"Not where you come from. But out here you let go of propriety to survive. Modesty won't do you a damn bit of good if you're burned and don't take care of it. If infection sets in—"

"All right. You've made your point."

She turned her back and did as he'd asked. The vision of her slender legs, encased in stockings, slammed him in the gut like an unexpected punch. The lacy femininity of her undergarments mesmerized him, made him ache to know the softness beneath the material. He wanted to go away as far and as fast as he could.

But he had to know for sure that she wasn't hurt. With her hem hiked up, he could see that her petticoats and pantaloons were not singed. He let out a long relieved breath.

"It's only the bottom of your skirt that burned. You're fine."

"I told you." She continued to hold her skirt up, as if the weight and wetness was easier that way. "I need to change my clothes. Would you mind turning around?"

"Cady, I think I should go."

"But we haven't eaten yet."

That didn't matter; he couldn't stay. He'd found out two things tonight.

The first was why he'd silenced his better judgment to accept her dinner invitation. It was simply the need to be with a woman. He was a man—a normal red-blooded man. Out here in the middle of nowhere, feminine companionship wasn't easy to come by. It was only natural that he'd want to be with a woman like Cady. Standing there wet, wide-eyed, bedraggled, beautiful, innocent as a newborn lamb, she was a temptation a saint would have trouble resisting. He was no saint.

"Cady, I think it would be best if I leave."

"What about dinner?"

Food was the last thing on his mind. He pushed the damp hair off his forehead. "I'm not hungry."

He remembered the smoke creeping up the back of her dress and realized she could have been hurt or killed. He wanted to hold her, comfort her, touch her. If he laid a hand on her, he knew he couldn't stop there.

"You're not worried about what people will think, are you?" She made a noise that sounded suspiciously like a snort. "Don't be so priggish. We agreed to be friends. Jack trusts you. Why you're like a—"

"Don't say it," he growled. "I'm not your brother."

What he felt for her right now was far from brotherly affection—or friendship. It would be so much easier if he *could* feel that way. All this had started because she'd wanted to prove something to him. She'd done it. She'd shown him he couldn't be alone with her. Not if he was going to keep his word to her brother.

And, more important, his promise to himself.

"It's time I left and let you change."

"Well, at least one good thing came out of all this. I told you I could make a cook fire, and I did," she said, lifting her chin a fraction.

"Sure. You said you could cook, too." His mouth thinned to a grim line. "And you almost did: yourself. What the hell were you thinking—"

"Me?" Her skirt started to slip and she gathered it in front of her. "You think it was *my* fault that I backed into the fire?"

He looked around. "There's only you and me here, and I was two feet away when you went up in flames."

"You're exaggerating." She tightened her grip on her skirts and drips of water plopped on the canvas-covered floor in a steady rhythm. "You want to know what I was thinking? Well, I'll tell you. I wasn't thinking at all. And that's your fault."

"Mine?" He touched his chest with a finger. "Good God, woman, you're blaming this on me?"

"If you hadn't kissed me, I would have been able to think straight. Why did you do that? Kiss me, I mean," she said, her voice softening.

"Damned if I know."

But he did know. That was the second thing he'd found out tonight. He cared about Cady Tanner.

The question now was what to do about it.

They both stood in front of the dresser. She moved a step closer to him and gripped her skirts more securely. Water squeezed from the material and splashed on his boots. She glanced down, then at him, and her chin jutted forward stubbornly.

"You just can't admit you were wrong, can you? Two years ago you said I had no business in the Territory because I couldn't start a fire. Well, Mr. high-and-mighty army captain, I can."

"Damn right! And you nearly killed yourself in it."

They were practically nose to nose, or would have been if he didn't have to look down at her. Goddammit, after all this, as angry as he was, he wanted to pull her against him and kiss her again. The memory of her curves beneath that wet material was seared in his brain.

"A woman like you stays back east where she belongs, Cady. I don't care what you said about coming to Arizona to teach. I think you're here to prove something.

And it has nothing to do with starting a fire. I want to know what it is."

A startled look grew in Cady's green eyes as a new thought occurred to her. But she only said, "You're absolutely right. Since I was a little girl, everyone has been telling me what to do. I want a chance to live my own life. I need to prove that I can take care of myself."

"And you've done a wonderful job of it." He glanced from her hair, plastered to her head, to her skirts, wadded up in her arms, to her wet pantaloons and shoes.

Fury flashed in her eyes. "I think you're right, Kane. It *is* time for you to leave." Her voice was calm, but he heard a slight tremble in it. She turned her back on him and squeezed some more water from her skirt. "I'm sorry about dinner."

"Forget it." He reached around her to grab his hat from the dresser. In spite of his good intentions to leave, he still wanted to take her in his arms. "Good night, Cady."

He walked to the door and opened it, hesitating, · waiting. She didn't say anything so he walked out into the night. He'd known it was a mistake to accept her dinner invitation; he'd gone in spite of his better judgment. It wasn't a total loss. He'd learned an important lesson.

He hadn't wanted just any female company. He'd wanted her.

He shook his head. Even if he could let Cady into his heart, he could never ask her to share his life. It was too dangerous. Far better for both of them if he stayed away from her. He put his hat on and pulled it low. Tonight he'd kissed Cady Tanner because he couldn't help himself.

˙ He wouldn't make the same mistake again.

*   *   *

After Kane left, Cady stared at the closed door. "He was right," she whispered. "I did have another reason for coming here."

What she had told him was true enough; she did want to live her own life. But he'd made her realize there was more to it than that.

She didn't know why she hadn't seen it sooner. Her mother, her father, Jack—her whole family had asked why she was so set on going all the way to Arizona Territory.

Cady had told them all that she needed to be her own woman. She had said she wanted to teach, in a place where she could really and truly make a difference. She had sworn she was going because Miss Biddle had fired her up with the knowledge that the frontier wouldn't be settled until more women went west. She had said those things and had believed them with all her heart.

But she hadn't known the truth until Kane had kissed her. She had never forgotten him, and deep down inside there was a part of her that had wanted to see him again.

"I'm here because of you, Kane," she said to the empty room.

The scent of him, his shaving soap and the masculine odor that was his alone, still lingered. Cady wanted to pull it close and hold it tight.

It was clear to her now. She hadn't even known where Kane was or if he was still in the Territory. But she'd been restless and discontented ever since she'd left him two years before. She'd even become engaged to an army officer, in the hope of finding someone like Kane.

Kane had kissed her!

She sighed, then took in a deep breath. There was another smell in the room, the acrid stench of burned cloth. Not only had he kissed her, he had saved her life.

She'd been so shaken by the power of the moment, she'd backed into the fire. What a silly fool she must look to him.

At least one good thing had come out of the disastrous evening. She finally understood her obsession to return to Arizona. And what good had it done her? She had found Kane. He had kissed her. It had flustered her so, she had set herself on fire, convincing him that she was a complete ninny.

She looked down at her skirt, stained brown from the ditch water and beginning to stiffen as it dried. "I've lost him for sure this time."

She laughed, but there was no humor in the sound. All she heard was her heart breaking. "You really are a fool, Cady Elizabeth Tanner. How can you lose what you never had in the first place?"

The irony of the timing didn't escape her. She'd realized she returned to the Territory because of Kane one day after she discovered that a woman had once betrayed him. Why would he want anything to do with a female ever again?

And even if he changed his mind, why would he want *her*?

She looked at the table set for two. Tears pricked her eyes. She rubbed them hard with her fists. "Don't you dare cry. He made you cry once before; don't you dare let him do it again. You don't need him or anyone else. You're a teacher. You can take care of yourself."

She stripped off her clothes, every dirty, wet stitch. Then she poured some water from the pitcher on the dresser into the wash basin and scrubbed until she felt clean again.

After putting on her cotton nightgown, she cleared off the table and set aside the rabbit stew she had cooked. It was dry and burned. Even if it had looked appetizing, she wasn't hungry. She set her oil lantern on the table and sat on her rough bench to prepare the next day's lessons.

"I've got work to do," she said to herself. "I don't have time for a man or for feeling sorry for myself."

Tomorrow was a new day, a day filled with the satisfying challenge of children and teaching and work. It would be enough, she told herself.

R. J. Wexler leaned back against the adobe wall behind the mess hall. It had been four weeks since that old teacher had come. He pressed his lips together as he thought about not being able to ride Prince. Now it was another Monday morning, and the prospect of five whole days of school before Saturday rolled around again weighed on him considerably.

The desert stretched out in front of him. With the sun on the other side of the building to his right, a shadow stretched almost clear over to the next row of adobes that housed his pa's office. He stayed in that shadow and kept his eyes open. Most of the soldiers were over at the parade ground and wouldn't notice him back here, but he couldn't be too careful.

It was almost time to report for school. He had a surprise for the teacher this morning. She had it coming after what she'd done to him.

After almost four weeks of restriction and chores, he was mighty sick of choppin' wood. *She* was out on his horse nearly every day, which made him mad as a skilletful of rattlers. He looked at his hand and saw the splinters as he flexed his fingers, noting the bump on his middle one, probably stained white forever from writing with chalk.

He poked his head around the building and saw Martha and Polly step up onto the boardwalk. Their footsteps clunked on the planks and dulled as they disappeared inside. He could hear Miss Tanner saying good morning to them, friendly as could be. Didn't seem like the girls ever had no punishments.

R. J. was sick of the smell of chalk dust and sawdust and every other kind of dust.

The only good thing was, he hadn't seen Kane and the schoolmarm together since the night he'd dumped her in the water ditch. R. J. smiled. He'd give up his brand-new birthday pistol and the gold nugget his pa had brought back from the Superstition Mountains if he could have seen that. He'd bet everything he held dear that Kane didn't want her there at the fort any more than he did. The bad thing was, ever since that same night, Kane had been as ornery as a bear just woke up from his winter nap and hungry as all get out. Hadn't had time for nobody or nothin', not even checkers.

From his back pocket, R. J. pulled out the cigar he'd filched from his pa. He wouldn't miss just one. Then he turned it end over end, trying to figure out which to bite off the way the men did.

"Eenie, meenie, minie, moe," he said and, taking his best shot, bit off an end. His eyes bugged out as the bitter taste of the tobacco burnt his tongue, and he spit the piece into the sand.

"Jumpin' Jehoshaphat!" he said, still spitting.

When he finally got the taste of the cigar out of his mouth, he pulled a match from his pocket and scraped it on the bottom of his boot the way he'd seen Sergeant Brewster do. Nothing happened. He tried again. Same thing.

"Dang it," he mumbled. Looking around, he spotted a rock and dragged the match on it until it sizzled into flame.

He grinned triumphantly and touched it to one end of the cheroot. Putting his mouth around it, he puffed a couple of times and watched the lighted end glow red. He needed to get this thing goin' good, so's it wouldn't go out. He sucked in real hard. A big strong pull of cigar smoke filled his mouth and burned his throat. He started to cough. Covering his mouth with his hand, he tried to hush up the sound. He couldn't seem to get rid of the bitter, burning taste. His stomach didn't feel too good either.

"Dang it," he said again, spitting into the sand.

When he finally controlled the spasms, he peeked around the building again to see if anyone had heard. Two soldiers walked by deep in conversation, and a lady with her laundry basket overflowing. No one seemed to pay him any mind.

"Almost ready," he said, fishing in his pocket for the rest of his supplies. "This oughta scare the tar outa that ol' schoolmarm. Maybe she'll get the hint that me and Kane don't want her here."

Cady glanced up from her seat at the end of the table when she noticed a body block the light in the doorway. The children, ten in all now, were already in their places working on the sums she'd given them. The sound of chalk scratching on slates stopped when R. J. swaggered into the room.

"Good morning," she said.

"Mornin', ma'am." His voice sounded raspy.

She studied him more carefully and thought he looked a little pale. "Are you feeling all right, Reynolds?

You sound hoarse. Are you coming down with something?"

"No, ma'am." He coughed.

"Are you sure? Perhaps you should go home and stay in bed, just in case."

"It's just chalk dust that makes me cough. I'm fine. Truly."

He sat down beside Bart Grimes. Across the table, John Eagle stared at him watchfully. She looked at Reynolds again and saw something in his blue eyes that gave her a little shiver. There was no reason to be nervous, she told herself. Lately, he'd been as good as gold.

"All right, then." She stood up and handed him a slate and a piece of chalk. "Bart, show Reynolds what you're doing. Not your answers, please, just the problems."

"Yes'm," Bart said.

The two boys bent their heads, one light brown, the other bright red, and industriously started on the task she'd set. As the scratching began again on the slates, she tried to shake off the feeling of apprehension. She was being silly and foolish.

Foolish.

There was that word again. It was the only way to describe her behavior around Kane. She couldn't seem to get him out of her mind. Not only couldn't she stop thinking about him, she was counting the days since she'd been in his arms. It seemed like forever, but only three weeks had gone by. When she saw him, he was always polite but distant. And he always made some excuse about something he had to take care of. Was he really too busy to talk?

Sometimes, though, she seemed to feel his eyes on her, watching her. Then she reminded herself that it was strictly duty. He'd promised Jack.

She'd casually inquired about Kane once, and Betsy Wexler had told her that he was up to his ears in work. The Indians were acting up, and there were precautions to think about. Cady hadn't seen him much, but she'd thought about him plenty.

Now that she understood why it had been so important to her to come back to Arizona, she still wasn't sure what to do about it. Only one thing was clear to her. After setting herself on fire in front of him, she had to be dignified and in control the next time he was anywhere near.

"Miss Tanner?"

"Hm?" Cady lifted her chin from her hand and looked at Martha Halleck. The child's voice had roused her from her woolgathering, and she realized it was quiet in the room. Her students had stopped writing on their slates and all of them were looking at her expectantly. "What is it?"

"We've finished."

"Yes, I see." She stood up. "I'll just walk around the room and check your work."

She stopped first beside Polly Chase and looked at her sums. "Good. They're all correct except one," she said. "What's five plus nine?"

The child thought for a minute, then counted on her fingers. "Fourteen?"

"That's right." Cady pushed the child's blond bangs from her forehead to get a better look at her blue eyes. "If you practice and memorize your sums, you won't need to use your fingers."

"Yes, ma'am."

She rounded the table and stood beside John Eagle. He was beyond sums and working on his multiplication tables. Without a word, he held his slate out. She checked his answers.

"Nice work, John. Every problem is correct."

He nodded but didn't say anything, although she thought she saw a flicker of satisfaction in his black eyes. She looked across the table at Reynolds.

"Let's see what you've done," she said.

He squirmed on the hard bench. "These were awful hard, ma'am. I didn't exactly finish 'em."

She held her hand out across the table. "Let me see your work. We'll see where you're having trouble." She stared into his face. For some reason, his expression made her look closer. She couldn't say why exactly, just that he seemed tense, expectant. Finally, she shook her head slightly and looked down. His slate was blank. "Reynolds, you haven't put any answers down. Or any problems either."

He glanced at the door. "Yes'm, I know. I don't—"

A loud pop sounded from outside.

Cady darted a look out the doorway. "What was that?"

"Sounded like a shot," Bart Grimes offered.

She set the boy's slate on the table. Fear skittered through her as she remembered what Mrs. Wexler had said about Indian trouble. "You must be mistake—"

There was another explosion, and two more right after. Outside, there were shouts and several soldiers ran by the mess hall with rifles in their hands.

"Is it Indians?" Polly Chase asked, her blue eyes big as moons.

Cady moved beside the child and bent down. "Don't be alarmed. I'm sure it's not."

Several more bursts of explosion filled the air and then the sound of a bugle call.

"It's Injuns, all right," Bart said, jumping to his feet.

Cady's heart pounded. The children were her responsibility to keep safe. There was gunfire. She couldn't let any of the boys or girls outside.

"Everyone down on the floor." She glanced at the open window behind her and felt her chest pull tight when she realized how vulnerable they were. "Reynolds, John, Bart, turn these tables over and everyone get behind them. I'm going to see what's happening out there."

The boys remained motionless as Reynolds stood up and put a hand out to stop her. "Miss Tanner, ma'am, you stay inside with the young'uns. Wouldn't want nothin' t'happen to ya." He cocked a thumb toward his chest. "I'll go see what's goin' on."

"No!" Cady took a deep breath and studied the boy. Bravery in such a young man brought a lump to her throat. He was just a child. And he was in her care. She couldn't allow him to go outside and possibly be hit by a stray bullet.

"That's very gallant of you, Reynolds." She shook her head. "But I want you to stay here with the others. I'll go."

Outside, she heard a staccato series of explosions. They sounded very close. In the distance, she heard more shouts from the soldiers. Had someone been hurt? Where was Kane? Was he all right? She wished she knew what was going on.

Stories she'd read in eastern newspapers of Indian massacres flashed through her mind. The details had been recounted in grisly detail and made her shiver. What if the Indians got past the soldiers and into the fort? How could she defend the children? She looked at them, still standing motionless.

"Turn those tables over," she shouted. "Now! And I want everyone"—she looked at Reynolds—"and I mean everyone, down behind them."

She saw John Eagle and Bart move to follow orders as she turned away.

Glancing around the mess hall, she searched franti-
cally for something to use as a weapon. This was nothing but a big open room with oblong tables and wooden
benches. All the food was prepared in other buildings,
and the men gathered here only to eat. About the best
she could hope for was a dull knife or fork. She'd be
better off throwing books to hold off the Indians. Kane
had teased her about doing just that the very first day
she'd arrived. Where was he?

She and Reynolds started for the door at the same
time. She stopped and grabbed a handful of his cotton
sleeve.

"Where do you think you're going?"

"Outside to help," he answered, trying to pull out of
her grasp.

"No, you stay put. I need you to keep the younger
children calm."

He stood to his full height. From the gleam in his
eye, she knew he took satisfaction from the fact that she
had to look up slightly to him.

"I'm a man, Miss Tanner. A man doesn't hide with a
bunch of little kids."

"I'm in charge here. And you're not a man yet."

"Old enough."

She was scared and angry and in no mood to argue.
"If you don't get down behind those tables with the
others this instant, you'll be writing 'I will obey my
teacher' until your hand falls off!"

He didn't move or say a word. She took hold of his
earlobe.

"Hey!" he hollered. "Ow! Let go!"

She pulled him closer until she could see the fine
reddish-gold hair on his chin that he would be taking a
straight-edge to in a year or so, and spoke through gritted teeth. "Move, mister, behind those tables with the

others, before this ear comes to rest on your shoulder. Do you understand?"

"Yes'm," he said meekly. He turned and, with one hand on the edge, leaped over the table and crouched down beside Bart Grimes.

She stared at them and at the open window behind. "On second thought, Reynolds, there *is* something you can do."

"Yes'm?"

"Stand guard at the window." She thought for a minute. "But stay down and keep your head out of the way."

He nodded and crouched down beside it.

"Bart and John, watch the younger ones."

The two boys nodded and she ran onto the board-walk outside. The sun was bright, and it took her several seconds for her eyes to adjust. Then she saw Kane, standing just outside the door, pistol drawn, every muscle tensed, senses alert as he stared into the distance. Cady's heart jumped a little at the sight of him. Then she followed his gaze and saw soldiers ringing the perimeter of the fort, all of them in identical poses, one knee in the sand, rifles raised and sighting an invisible enemy.

She moved beside him and put her hand on his arm. "What is it, Indians?"

"I'm not sure." He barely shook his head as a bemused expression crossed his face.

"We heard shots. They sounded like they were right outside the mess hall," she said.

"They weren't like any gunshots I ever heard before." Kane sounded puzzled.

"Then what was it?"

"I can't say, but I intend to find out." He looked down at her, and his mouth softened a little. "You stay inside. I'm taking a patrol out to—"

"You're going out there?" she asked, fear making her heart pound until she thought it might jump into her throat. "You can't."

He didn't give her any indication what he was thinking. "I have to."

"But why?"

"Because it's what a soldier does. You keep telling me not to interfere with you and the job you came here to do. Now it's my turn." He took her upper arm and started to turn her back toward the mess hall. "Go back inside with the children."

"But, Kane—"

"You'll be safe there."

"I'm not concerned about me. I'm worried about you."

The crunch of boots turned their attention to the enlisted man walking toward them. "Captain?"

Kane dropped his hand from her arm. "What is it, White?"

"I found something, sir, behind the mess hall." He stopped in front of them and saluted Kane.

In the soldier's palm, Cady saw what looked like a half-smoked cigar with a singed string attached to it and blackened, exploded firecrackers at the other end.

A muscle jerked convulsively in the captain's cheek as he raised his eyes to the other man. "I think you just found our Indians, private."

7

Kane saw the fear still clouding Cady's wide-eyed gaze. The effects of it lingered in her pale cheeks, and her mouth looked pinched and tight. If he was right, the whole thing was a practical joke aimed at her. Anger smoldered inside him, but he tamped it down as the other man handed him the remains of the cigar and the firecrackers.

They had burned recently; he could still smell the lingering odors of sulfur, gunpowder, and tobacco smoke.

"Private, spread word that the danger's passed."

"Yes, sir. Anything else?" The soldier looked at him impassively.

Kane shook his head. "That's all. Dismissed."

"Yes, sir." The man saluted, turned on his heel, and walked away.

"When I get my hands on that little hellion—"

"Who?" Cady asked. "What are you talking about?"

As he looked down at her, the fury he'd been fighting flared a little brighter. Part of it was directed at the redheaded scoundrel who had deceived everyone into thinking the fort was being attacked. Mostly, he was mad at himself and the feelings he couldn't seem to control. In a time of danger, he hadn't thought about signaling the call to arms or guarding the perimeter or taking cover.

His first thought had been protecting Cady.

"I'm going to wring his scrawny little neck." Kane tried to rein in his temper.

"Who?" Cady shaded her eyes with her hand as she continued to stare up at him. "What is it, captain?"

"R. J.'s been up to mischief again." A muscle jerked in his cheek as he gritted his teeth.

"Does this mean you don't have to lead a patrol out after the Indians?"

He saw worry in her eyes and his breath caught for a second when he thought it might be for him. Then he realized he must be wrong. She'd never been through an Indian attack. She would naturally be afraid.

"My only mission is to pursue and punish the miserable little scamp responsible for putting this military post on alert for no good reason."

"How can you be so sure it was Reynolds?"

"Look at this cigar." In his open palm, he pointed out the distinctive square cut on the end. "There's only one person around here who smokes cheroots. They come all the way from San Francisco."

"You can't mean the boy smokes those things."

"His father does. It would be easy enough for him to get one. Come to think of it, he probably did smoke it to get it going enough to set off the firecrackers."

"So that's why he looked so pale when he came to school. And why his voice was hoarse."

As word spread of the false alarm Kane watched the soldiers around the perimeter slowly stand and look one last time into the distance for any hint of trouble. They shook their heads, wondering what was going on, then went about their business.

Kane lifted his hat and, with his forearm, brushed away the sweat trickling into his eyes. "He's in a lot of trouble this time," he said, as he settled his hat low on his forehead.

Cady put her hands on her hips and stared at the doorway of the mess hall. "This explains why he was so anxious to come out during the danger and see what was going on. It's easy to be brave when you know there's nothing to be afraid of."

"I have a hunch that wasn't the only thing he had in mind."

"Why do you think he did it?"

"To get even with you."

She placed a hand on her breast. "Me?"

Kane noticed that the hand still shading her eyes was shaking. She had been scared, but she hadn't lost her head. He admired that. He would bet his captain's bars that the prank had been intended to pay her back. He knew how much R. J.'s pride had suffered over the snake and how much he hated Cady for the punishment she had given him. The boy had to learn he couldn't pull stunts like that. Kane would make R. J. Wexler wish he'd never been born.

He stared at the mess hall door. Beyond it, in the shadowed interior, some of the children were starting to move around. "I think R. J. had a lot of reasons for what he did. But since you arrived, you've made him toe the line. My guess is that revenge is at the top of his list."

She watched soldiers walking by in twos and threes, back to their normal duties. A few women with their babies had come outside and were talking excitedly. She looked back at him.

"I can't believe he'd do that."

He nodded grimly. "Believe it."

He walked her over to the doorway and poked his head in. Some of the tables were turned on their sides, but the children who had been crouched behind them were standing up. R. J. slouched lazily beside the window with a knowing grin on his face. Before Kane could go in and grab the boy by the collar, Cady spoke up beside him in the doorway.

"Everything is all right, children. There are no Indians. It was a false alarm. Boys, will you turn the tables upright, please? We'll get back to work in just a few moments." She observed the activity for a few seconds, then nodded with satisfaction as her orders were being carried out.

She slipped back outside and Kane followed to be sure she was really all right. She leaned her back against the adobe wall. He noticed the remains of anger, fear, and what he thought might be a sense of violation swirling in her eyes. But when she glanced up at him, he saw wariness too. That expression, he knew, was for him.

"What's wrong?" he asked.

"I'm sorry about turning the tables over. I didn't know what else to do, and I figured we should at least have some protection. Reynolds was our lookout. Isn't that a laugh?"

Kane glanced inside the mess hall. R. J. was standing with his back to the window and his arms crossed over his chest, a cocky stance. Some guard. He'd known there was nothing to watch for. It was time for the kid to have some of that brashness worked out of him.

He stepped through the doorway and called out. "Wexler!"

R. J. started, then stood up straight. "Yes, sir?"

"I want to see you in my office. Pronto."

The boy's face paled, but he nodded and walked toward Kane, hesitating when he was an arm's length away. "Something wrong, Kane?"

"It's Captain Carrington. And we'll discuss it in my office. That's an order."

R. J. nodded and moved forward without another word. Kane stepped aside to let him pass, but he didn't miss the irritated look meant for Cady as the boy brushed past her and on his way.

Kane looked at Cady. "You did exactly what I would have done in your place."

She went completely still, as if his words amazed her. "I did?"

He nodded. "But you should have stayed inside."

"I had to see if you—I mean, I couldn't stand not knowing what was happening."

"Curiosity could get you killed." He heard the edge of irritation in his own voice. She looked startled, but he wasn't about to explain that, when he'd first heard the noise, getting to her had been all he could think about.

His initial reaction should have been to protect his men. Ever since the day he'd joined up, the army had been the most important thing to him, like family. But instead of protecting his command as he'd been trained, he'd gone to Cady.

He'd known from the first moment he laid eyes on her that she'd be trouble. It didn't improve his disposition any to know he'd been proved right.

"I'll try to control my curiosity from now on," she said.

"It's advice that might just save your life one day. Next time, take cover and stay put. For God's sake, keep your head down or you're liable to get it shot off."

"But—"

"No buts. Just do as you're told, Cady. Follow orders."

"Yes, sir, captain." She straightened, stiff as a fire-place poker, pulled her shoulders back, and saluted. Her exaggerated military stance pushed her soft, rounded breasts against the material of her blouse. No soldier he'd ever seen filled out his clothes in quite that appealing way.

In spite of his annoyance, he couldn't help smiling. "You wouldn't make a very good soldier."

"What are you grinning at? And what makes you so sure I wouldn't make a good soldier?" Irritation flashed in her green eyes.

He wanted to say because she wouldn't fit the uniform. He decided against it. "You question every order you're given. A good soldier doesn't do that."

"It's good to ask questions."

"If you're a student"—he looked at her intensely—"or a teacher. But a soldier needs to obey without question. Someone's life could depend on him."

"You mean you do what someone else tells you even if you think it's wrong or there might be a better way?"

"That's exactly what I mean."

She nodded emphatically. "Then you're absolutely right. I wouldn't make a good soldier."

Or a soldier's wife. He shook his head, wondering where that thought had come from. He pushed it away as fast as it had popped into his mind.

"This discussion is getting us nowhere," he said.

"Truer words were never spoken. Isn't that a wonder? We agree about something." She took a deep breath. "Stimulating as this conversation is, captain, I need to get back to the children."

"And I need to come up with a suitable punishment for R. J., something that will make him think twice before pulling a dangerous stunt like this again." He tried to gauge her reaction to his words. "This is an army problem. What he did could have caused serious harm to everyone here in the fort."

"You're absolutely right."

"If anyone had panicked or shot without thinking, someone could have gotten hurt."

"I couldn't agree more."

"He needs to have a lesson he won't forget."

"Without a doubt," she said.

He realized she wasn't arguing, just agreeing as he blew off steam. She looked up at him, her big green eyes wide and beautiful, with only a small amount of her recent irritation with him still evident.

"What's wrong, captain?"

"I expected you'd want to deal with him."

"Why? This is an army problem." She turned and went inside.

Kane rubbed the back of his neck. Just when he thought he had her figured out, she surprised him again. She was probably just about the most ornery, interesting, keep-a-man-on-his-toes female he'd ever met. That was the most annoying thing of all.

Ten minutes later Kane looked at R. J. Wexler, lounging in his office, and got mad all over again. What the kid had done was serious. But Kane knew his anger was bigger, hotter, harder, because of Cady. Not just because the prank was directed at her, although the thought of it made him want to wring R. J.'s neck. But it brought home to him what he'd known since Jack Tanner dumped his beautiful little sister in Kane's lap: She was trouble.

R. J. sat on the simple wooden chair in front of the desk. "Kane, what's the—"

"Stand up straight," he said, grinding out every word through gritted teeth.

The kid jumped at his harsh tone, and his blue eyes grew round. He put his hands in his pockets and lowered his gaze.

"Pull your shoulders back, chest out. Act like a man." Kane slapped his palms on the crisscross of white scratches that marred the top of his desk. "Look me in the eye."

The boy's gaze snapped up. Beads of sweat gathered on his upper lip. "Wh-what's wrong, Kane?"

"I told you before, it's Captain Carrington to you."

So he'd decided to play dumb instead of owning up to what he did. Kane was disappointed in him. Whatever mischief R. J. had done in the past, he'd always admitted his part in it.

He took a deep, calming breath. "I'll give you one more chance to come clean. Did you set those firecrackers to go off outside Miss Tanner's schoolroom?"

Something flickered in the kid's eyes, but he shook his head. "Don't know nothin' about it."

Kane showed him what was left of the cigar and the small explosives. "Have you ever seen this before?"

"You gotta let me—"

"Yes or no." Kane gave him a stern look. He hoped R. J. would do the right thing.

The boy's shoulders slumped and all the starch seemed to go out of him. "Yes. I seen it before."

Kane nodded approvingly. He was still mad as hell about what the boy had done, but it would have been a lot worse if R. J. had kept up the lie. "I'm glad you decided to tell the truth. Why did you set off the firecrackers? Were you trying to scare Miss Tanner?"

"It was easy. She's a tenderfoot, not like the rest of us." R. J. relaxed and rubbed a knuckle across the freckles on his nose. "It was pretty funny the way she—"

Kane surged to his feet, furious at the way the boy

mentioned Cady in that offhand manner. He knew the kid understood the intensity of his anger when R. J. tipped his head back, stared up, and blinked his eyes. His Adam's apple bobbed up and then down as he swallowed hard and then backed up two steps. It was a good thing he moved out of reach. Kane knew if he touched him right now, he'd be hard put to keep himself from blistering the boy's backside. Although R. J. deserved it, that was his father's place.

He pointed at the boy. "You're in a lot of trouble, mister."

"Are ya gonna wallop me?"

"No." The kid let out a relieved breath and Kane grinned without humor. "What I have in mind is worse than a licking. For the next four weeks, whenever you're not in Miss Tanner's schoolroom, you'll be digging an outhouse."

"You can't make me do that!" he cried defensively. "My pa—"

"Your father would agree with me. He's the commanding officer. He's in charge of everything that happens at this fort." Kane leaned forward slightly. "Someone could have been injured or killed because of your damn shenanigans. What do you think that would do to his reputation, not to mention his career?"

"I was just funnin'."

"Your 'fun' could've killed someone. Because of your sh—" He took a deep breath. "Because of what you did, I think it's an appropriate punishment detail." R. J. opened his mouth to protest. "Get a shovel from the stable. Lieutenant Brewster will show you where to start digging."

"But school's still in," he protested, his voice going up a few notches until it cracked.

"I don't think Miss Tanner wants to see your sorry

hide any more than I do. Now git. I don't want to hear another word out of you."

R. J. stomped across the room, turned and glared one last time, then opened the door and slammed it as he left.

Good riddance, Kane thought. Punishment detail should work the orneriness out of him and teach him a lesson. Maybe now the kid would stay out of trouble.

Cady sat on the step outside her quarters and savored the warm breeze that lifted the curls from her forehead. In the distance, she could hear the lovely, mournful sound of the bugler blowing taps, the signal for barracks lights to be extinguished. In the weeks she'd been here, she'd learned that everyone who lived within the boundaries of Fort McDowell lived, ate, and slept by the bugle.

Reveille meant sunrise, when the lieutenant buckled on belt and sword and received the report of the company of soldiers lined up on the parade ground. She'd learned the various drill calls, recalls, and the beautiful stable call for the cavalry. Today, for the first time, she'd heard the call to arms, when the soldiers had raced from every direction for their rifles and formed a line around the outside of the fort.

Her stomach jumped a little when she remembered her fears that Indians would come bursting into the schoolroom. What disturbed her now was her feeling of helplessness to protect the children in her care.

"I have to do something," she whispered to herself. "I don't ever want to feel that way again."

What would Miss Biddle say in a situation like this? Cady wondered.

"Forewarned is forearmed," she said into the night.

She could hear the feisty little woman's voice in her head and smiled to herself. This wasn't exactly what

Miss Agnes had meant, but it gave her an idea all the same. Especially the forearmed part.

She sighed. If only she could arm her heart against Kane. It seemed her luck with him was destined to be bad. She hadn't been alone with him for three weeks, not since the night he'd kissed her. Today was the first time, and they had discussed Reynolds Wexler and how to keep her head from being blown off. At least she hadn't set herself on fire or let a horse run away with her. She had done everything she could think of to keep control of the situation.

Still, she never seemed to be able to do anything right as far as he was concerned. Some instinct told her he was finding fault on purpose. She wasn't sure why; it didn't matter. Except that she was trying so hard to fit in, and she thought she was doing pretty well until he'd told her that curiosity might get her killed.

He thought she was wrong to go outside? She didn't care. She'd do the same thing all over again. She'd been worried sick that something had happened to him, and not knowing was torture. But every time she tried to express concern for him, he shut her out.

No matter the danger to herself, she couldn't have stayed in that schoolroom this morning wondering if he was dead or alive, hurt or hovering at death's door. She was raised in a family where taking care of the people you love comes first. Protecting them was as natural as breathing.

Somehow, she felt Kane didn't understand that. For him, the army came first. She wondered if he had always been that way, or just since his wife's betrayal. Would she ever know? He didn't seem likely to tell her. Whenever the subject came up, she got nothing but yes-and-no answers.

Today's Indian attack had been a false alarm, but the fear had been very real. She knew that under certain circumstances the state of her heart could be far less important than the condition of her hide.

She made up her mind to do two things. First, she intended to have a talk with Reynolds Wexler and find out exactly what was on his mind. Kane had handled him today, but if they were to avoid more incidents in the future, she had to find a way to reach him.

Second, she planned to ask Kane for a favor. He'd no doubt laugh at her, but she had to try. If he refused to do as she asked, she would find another man to help her.

The following afternoon Cady trudged up the rise behind the livery stable where Reynolds was working. Earlier, in school, the children had been buzzing about his punishment—digging a new outhouse. Kane had certainly come up with something that would make the boy think twice before pulling another stunt.

It was a beautiful day, the sky cloudless and clear blue. The wind kept her comfortable as far as the heat was concerned, but it blew her skirts against her as she walked, tangling them around her legs. Her hair wasn't pinned up, although the sides were pulled away from her face and tied with a ribbon at the crown of her head. Still, long strands whipped across her face and she finally gathered it in one hand and held it at her nape. When she was several feet away, she heard the boy mutter something just before he jammed the shovel into the hard ground.

"Were you talking to me?" she asked.

He leaned on his shovel and looked at her. "Nope."

"I heard you. Let's be honest with each other, Reynolds, shall we?"

"All right. But you asked for it. I said it would serve you right if ya tripped over a rock, you old bat."

Cady couldn't have been more shocked if he'd given

her another black eye. She was surprised at the vehemence of his words, although after learning that the firecrackers were meant to frighten her, she didn't know why it should. She wasn't angry so much as curious about why he hated her so much.

"Why do you dislike me?" she asked.

"Who said I—"

"Stop it. You don't want me here and you haven't from the first day we met. When you gave me the snake you were trying to frighten me away, and yesterday with the firecrackers you were doing the same thing. Why?"

"Because you're a teacher."

She shook her head. "There's more to it than that. I want to know what it is."

His sullen blue gaze fixed on her for a few seconds before he spoke. "Kane's sweet on you."

This time, Cady felt as if she'd been run over by a train, but she managed to pull herself together. "I think you must be mistaken about that."

"I'm not. And I'll tell you why. When he thought there'd be Injun trouble, he hightailed it to the schoolroom right off. He was waitin' there when you came runnin' out like a scared jackrabbit."

"For the sake of argument, let's assume you're right about his—regard—for me. I still don't understand what that has to do with you."

He let out a huge sigh as if to say she was dumb as a post. "If Kane wasn't sweet on you, my punishment woulda been a whole lot easier. If you hadn't come here to teach 'n' all, I never would have set those firecrackers off in the first place."

"Were you trying to scare me into leaving the fort altogether?"

Anger flashed across his face. "Dang female. 'Course that's what I was doin'."

"But why? What have I done to make you hate me so much?"

"You're here. That's enough."

Cady wasn't satisfied with that answer. He had taken a dislike to her from the moment he had seen her with Kane. Maybe that was it. Perhaps he had a huge case of hero worship and resented anyone that the captain spent time with. That was a laugh. Kane went out of his way to avoid her.

"I want you to be more specific, Reynolds."

He rubbed a knuckle under his nose and left a streak of dirt on his upper lip. "People call me R. J. I hate being called Reynolds."

"All right. What else?"

He looked at the ground for a second; then his grip on the shovel tightened until his fingers turned white.

"Ya don't really want me t'say. Won't do no good."

"On the contrary. I think we need to clear the air."

"Just remember, you asked for it. Nothin's the same since you came. I hate readin', I hate writin', I hate school. Ya got no business ridin' Prince. And—I hate you."

She went from shock to anger. Her heart was pounding. She couldn't remember ever being this furious at a child. He was a spoiled, spiteful, willful, indulged boy and she was glad Kane was making him dig an outhouse. But she bit her tongue to avoid sinking to his level and telling him what she thought of him.

"Go on," she said with false calm.

"Yesterday, you yanked on my ear in front of the whole class. I've had a bellyful of you, more'n a body should have to take." He turned away and shoved the tool into the hard ground. "And since you came, Kane ain't got time for me."

"Doesn't have time—"

"Quit correctin' ever' dang thing I say!"

"Why, you little—" She stopped and counted to ten, trying to think what Miss Biddle would do. She hated to admit it, but Kane was right. An old maid teacher who sat in her cozy eastern parlor wouldn't have any idea how to deal with a boy in Arizona Territory who had been allowed to run wild most of his life.

She took a few calming breaths, trying to conceal her anger. In her mind she repeated over and over: *I am the adult. I am the teacher. I will remain rational and reasonable no matter what.*

Finally she asked, "Why didn't you come to school today?"

"I didn't come to school because Kane said you wouldn't want to see my sorry hide any more than he did." He whirled around. "Besides, the sooner I get started on diggin' this here outhouse, the sooner it'll be done. The captain said when I wasn't in school, I was t'be diggin'. Those were his exact words."

"He would be angry if he knew you didn't come this morning."

"You gonna run and tattle to him?"

Cady wasn't proud of it, but the truth was she'd been relieved when he stayed away. Still, one thing Miss Biddle said that made sense anytime, whatever godforsaken place you taught in, was to make the best of a bad situation. In spite of her anger at his behavior, he was still a child and she felt the need to reach him.

"No, I'm not going to tell him you weren't there. That's none of his business. It's my responsibility, and I will take care of it. You know, in a way I need to thank you for what you did yesterday."

"Ya do?"

"Yes. It taught me a good lesson, a fairly painless one. Now I can take steps to be prepared in case there ever is real trouble."

"Ya can?"

She nodded. The wind swirled around them and blew dust in her face. She coughed and blinked it away. "I'm on my way to talk to the captain now. If I explain that in a strange way you did me a favor, maybe he'll go a little easier on you."

"No! Don't want no"—his eyes met hers, challenging her to correct his slip—"special treatment."

"All right."

She brushed the long strands of hair from her eyes and looked down the rise toward the parade ground. Soldiers moved around on their work details. R. J. stared longingly at them, and she knew he'd rather be talking to any one of them than her. That bothered her more than she wanted to admit. She wanted him to like her, but after what he'd told her, she realized she might never win his friendship. Still, she was his teacher and she had a job to do.

"R. J."—Cady saw the surprised look when she used his initials instead of the hated first name—"I'll make a deal with you. I won't say anything to the captain. In return, you be in school tomorrow morning. Agreed?"

"I'll think on it." He pushed his boot against the shovel as he tried to break the rock-hard ground.

Apparently that was the best she could hope for. She sighed as she walked down the hill toward Kane's office.

Lieutenant McKenzie Thorne stood staring out the captain's window while Kane sat at his desk. He watched the pretty schoolteacher walk down the rise where she'd been talking to the Wexler kid. Soon as Mac rode in, Private Halladay over at the stable told him about the false alarm the kid had triggered. Halladay was still mad enough to take a chunk out of someone's behind for getting called to arms for no good reason. Mac hoped the men had performed well. Worry gnawed at him. It could be a drill for things to come.

The fort looked mighty good to him. He wished he didn't have to go to the hog ranch outside the fort for what he wanted: whiskey and a woman, not necessarily in that order. He watched the teacher again and wondered about her. His gut told him she wasn't that kind of woman. Too bad. She was real easy on the eyes. He wondered how she'd take the news about her brother being in hot water up to his armpits.

He looked at his commanding officer. Kane Carrington was a little too by-the-book for Mac's taste. When you were dealing with Apaches, you had to match them trick for trick. Carrington was too straightforward to be a first-rate Indian fighter. But he was a good man all the same, fair with his own men and the Indians too. That was better than most.

"We got trouble, Kane."

The other man's face turned grim and the lines beside his mouth deepened. "Spit it out."

Mac wished he could keep it to himself, as if not saying the words would make it not so. Suddenly he was too tired to stand. He'd been on the trail for a month, and now that he had four walls around him again he could let his guard down. Just for a while.

He lowered himself into the chair in front of Kane's desk. "Cuchillo and his brother Alchise left the reservation. They split up. Between them they have twenty-six warriors."

"We heard. Wexler's at the reservation now, trying to calm the rest of the Apaches down until we can catch up with the renegades."

"That's not the worst. Jack Tanner killed Alchise when his band attacked a mining camp up in the

Superstitions. Tanner shot him in self-defense and saved another prospector—named Gallagher, I think. Cuchillo is on a rampage to avenge his brother. We've talked to a few survivors of his raids. He won't rest until he's got Tanner upside down over his death fire."

"Damn."

A muscle worked in Kane's jaw and Mac could pretty well guess what he was thinking. Should he tell Tanner's sister? If it was up to Mac, he'd tell her what the hell was goin' on. No point in trying to keep the worst from her. Nine times out of ten it happened. She should be prepared. Out here, everyone's survival depended on being ready for anything.

There was a knock on the door, a delicate tap. Mac knew who it was, and he could tell by the frown lines between Kane's eyes that he did too.

"Come in," he called.

Mac turned in his chair, rested one ankle on his other knee, and pushed his hat back. Dust from the crown drifted around him. Cady Tanner opened the door and stepped inside.

"I'm sorry. I didn't mean to interrupt anything. If I'd known someone was here—" She put her hand on the door and backed up a step. "I'll come back later."

Mac crossed his arms over his chest and let his gaze travel over her from the top of her head to the tips of her toes. Yup, real easy on the eyes. He glanced at Kane, who was watching him watch her. A look jumped into the captain's eyes warning Mac away from her. Funny thing was, Mac could swear that the other man didn't even know it was there.

So that's how it was. He looked from one to the other and sighed, grateful there was no woman who made *him* look mad enough to chew nails when another man looked at her. Never would be, and that was a fact.

Truth was, he felt sorry for Kane. The pretty schoolteacher was a distraction he didn't need right now. With Indians on the rampage, he should have a clear head.

Kane stared at Mac, warning him not to say anything. Then he stood up. "Come in, Miss Tanner."

She closed the door and moved into the room, her skirts swishing like a whisper of wind. Mac got a whiff of flowers that floated from her. She smelled almost as pretty as she looked. He slid a gaze to his dusty trousers. He knew he smelled as bad as hell on housecleaning day and looked a whole lot worse. He'd been to perdition and back, so it made sense. But in a lady's presence, it made him damned uncomfortable.

Mac hadn't planned to, but when she stood beside him, he got to his feet. He towered over her, she was such a small thing. Couldn't help feeling a pull at his insides, something that made him want to keep her from harm.

"I don't believe we've been formally introduced, ma'am." He took his hat off and curled the floppy brim as he held it in both hands.

"No, I'm sure we haven't." She smiled and held out her hand. "Cady Tanner. And you are?"

"McKenzie Thorne." He freed his right hand from his hat and brushed it down the side of his wool trousers. Some good that did. He spent so much time in the saddle, it would take a lifetime of washing to get the trail dust off of him and his clothes.

He looked at her small clean hand and then at his own, streaked with dirt and grease. He sent her a lazy grin that he knew would make Kane's blood boil. "Sorry, miss. I'll have to owe you a proper hello till after I've had a chance to clean up."

"That's all right, Mr.—"

"It's lieutenant. But just call me Mac. Unlike the captain here, I'm not much on formality."

She shot Kane a look that said she'd come to words with the captain about his straight and narrow ways.

When Mac glanced at Kane, a dark look smoldered in the other man's eyes. Mac felt a grin scratching inside him, but he didn't let it out. Still, he couldn't resist having a little fun at the expense of his commanding officer. He'd like to see Kane turn loose of his starched-collar control.

"Miss Cady, ma'am, after I get a hot meal and a bath and a shave, I'd be honored to make your acquaintance a bit better."

"I'd like that too, Mac."

"Cady." Kane's voice was full of buckshot and ready to let fly. When the muscle in his cheek quit twitching, he went on. "Was there something you wanted?"

"Yes. I have a favor to ask you."

Mac had a feeling this was a good time for him to leave. "I'll let you two talk." He put his hat on and looked at his commanding officer, then down at Cady. "I can hardly wait to clean up. Just got back from the Superstition—" As soon as the word was out, he wanted it back.

Cady's chin jerked up, and her eyes glittered with sudden keen interest. "The Superstition Mountains? My brother Jack is prospecting there. Do you know him? Did you see him? Is he all right?"

Mac darted a look at Kane and saw the other man shake his head. It was a small movement, and if he hadn't been waiting for it, Mac knew he might have missed it. But the captain was reminding him to keep Tanner's trouble to himself. And now that he saw the lady, he understood Kane's instinct to protect her. If she knew her brother was up to his ass in alligators, there'd be the devil to pay.

"No, ma'am. I don't know your brother. I came by way of Thompson's Canyon."

She glanced from him to Kane, concern puckering the smooth skin of her brow. He could have kicked himself for saying anything about the Superstitions.

"Is Jack in some kind of trouble?"

The two men exchanged another communication that said keep it quiet. Mac cleared his throat and met her gaze. He grinned with what he hoped was a look that would put her at ease. "Nothin's wrong, ma'am," he said. *That we can't handle,* he silently added.

"I'm so relieved," she said on a long breath.

"What's the favor you wanted?" Kane asked, obviously trying to distract her.

"Time for me to go," Mac said.

"You don't have to. This isn't private."

Cady turned to Kane and pulled herself up to her full height, which was less than considerable. Her shoulders went back, her spine straightened stiff as the barrel of his rifle, and her eyes spit challenge until Mac almost felt sorry for Kane.

She took a deep breath. "Captain, I'd like you to teach me how to use a gun."

8

"I really think I should know how to handle a weapon. Please," Cady added politely.

Kane couldn't help smiling. She was trying to be tough as a rawhide thong, but she just couldn't quite turn her back on good breeding.

He wanted to say no. He didn't want her anywhere near a weapon, not by herself. They were dangerous even in experienced hands. He studied her delicate intertwined fingers. A woman like her should have a man to take care of her and protect her. She shouldn't have to know how to use a gun.

"Kane, I promise I'll do everything you tell me. In spite of what you think of me, I learn fast and I'll be careful."

He finally nodded. "All right, I'll teach you how to shoot a pistol."

The only indication that his answer had surprised her was a slight widening of her eyes and an almost imperceptible lift of her chin.

The determined look on her face had convinced him she would do it on her own. That would be more dangerous. She could shoot herself or someone else. Someone she didn't mean to, that is.

"What about a rifle?" she asked.

"One step at a time." He held his hands up as if to slow her down. "If the army does its job, you won't need a rifle. If we don't, a pistol for your own protection is the weapon of choice."

He glanced at Mac Thorne, still standing beside her, watching her with a gleam in his eye. It was obvious he found her spunk appealing. He was showing far more than casual interest. Kane didn't like it, not one damn bit. He had a good mind to send the man back out on patrol. It made perfect sense for a number of reasons.

No one knew where the Apaches would strike next. But Mac had a knack for figuring out what the Indians would do and more courage than common sense. It was a dangerous combination, but he managed to get the job done. He was valuable to have around.

As long as he wasn't around Cady.

That would be another good reason to give him traveling orders: to get him away from her. Kane had spent a lot of time with McKenzie Thorne, and it didn't take much to see that the ladies liked him. The way Cady looked at him told him she could be susceptible to Mac's charm. Kane wondered if he should warn her and keep her from getting hurt. Mac Thorne *would* hurt her, there was no doubt. He wasn't the settling-down kind any more than Kane was. But until Mac and his men rested up, he couldn't send them back out. For the thousandth time he wished that Jack Tanner had not gone off and left a pretty little sister in his care.

Still, he was glad Tanner hadn't taken her along to the Superstitions. With Indians on the rampage, Kane wanted her at the fort. Jack had managed to get himself in a pile of trouble. Kane would do everything in his power to see that it didn't touch Cady.

That was the other reason he'd agreed to teach her to shoot. And this was the more important of the two. Mac's information about the renegade Apaches convinced him that she should know everything she could to take care of herself. He wouldn't rest easy until the Indians were back on the reservation and peace was restored.

Mac spun his hat through his hands. "Miss Cady, Captain Carrington looks busy. But I've got some time. I'd be happy to show you how to shoot. If you wouldn't mind, that is."

Kane's gut clenched with rage. What the hell was Mac Thorne up to?

Cady glanced from one man to the other. "I don't have any objection—"

"I'm not that busy," Kane said sharply.

Kane was angry—at her, for being so easily taken in, and at himself. He wanted to grab Mac by the shirtfront and tell him in no uncertain terms that Cady had asked *him* first. He felt as if he were still in short pants and sweet on a girl for the first time. He glared at Mac. It was a warning, as loud and clear as Kane could make it, and the only one Mac would get. If the other man was as smart as he thought, he'd steer clear of Cady Tanner.

"Guess when you get cleaned up, lieutenant, you'll be on your own," Kane said.

The other man grinned back, a look that said he knew Kane was telling him to stay away from Cady. That devil smile also told him Mac was glad that *he* didn't jump at the swish of a petticoat.

Finally Mac said, "Another time then, Miss Cady. I'm sure there *will* be another time."

"As a matter of fact, tonight is the first meeting of Fort McDowell's newly organized literary society. I'd be pleased if you could be there."

"I'd like that, ma'am." Mac shot Kane a challenging glance.

Kane gritted his teeth. He'd trust McKenzie to watch his back in a fight, but when it came to a woman—this woman—he wouldn't trust him as far as he could throw him. He told himself his determination to keep her away from Mac was only to keep her safe. And that included safe from unwanted romantic attention. But was it unwanted? The way she was smiling at Mac would give any man ideas.

"Literary society doesn't sound like something you'd take to, Mac."

"I've been eating dust and slapping leather with my—" He glanced at Cady and stopped. "I've been gone a long time. The prospect of a book and the company of a pretty lady is mighty appealing."

"Why, thank you, lieutenant." She smiled and Kane felt an emotion pull tight and hard in his gut. He was uneasy when he realized the most accurate name he could give it was jealousy.

"Why have you been gone so long, lieutenant? Is there some trouble?" she asked.

"Cady, I'll have Halladay saddle our horses. We'll go out a little way from the perimeter to shoot so we don't disturb the fort and cause another false alarm. Meet me back here in thirty minutes."

"Yes, sir." She stood up straight and saluted smartly.

The sound of Mac Thorne's laughter filled the office. He walked to the door and opened it. "I'll see you tonight, Cady."

"Seven-thirty. In the mess hall."

"I'll be there, ma'am. Captain," he said, looking at

Kane with a cocky grin. He nodded and walked out the door.

Long ago Kane had given up trying to get Mac Thorne to salute a superior officer. He'd never thought it was worth the aggravation. Today he wasn't so sure. "If he didn't have such a nose for Indian fighting—" He ran his fingers through his hair. "If he keeps sticking that nose in where it doesn't belong, he's liable to get it bloodied."

"Something wrong?"

"Nothing I can't handle." He stared at her. "I gave you thirty minutes to get ready. You're down to twenty-eight."

"Yes, sir," she said again. She turned and walked out quickly.

Kane sighed. If this shooting lesson went the way her demonstration of starting a fire had gone, one of them could end up dead. If they both survived, he figured he'd probably kill Mac Thorne at the literary society meeting.

Cady followed Kane's example and reined Prince in beside Soldier Boy. They'd gone only about a mile. Her saddle creaked as she turned to make sure she could still see the fort. She nodded her head, satisfied that if there was trouble they could get back easily. On her daily rides, she'd gotten in the habit of checking her distance from home.

Funny, she'd only been at Fort McDowell a month and was already thinking of it as home. The unique beauty of the desert fascinated her. The Arizona sky was beautiful, looking darker blue than she'd ever seen it because of the way the vivid red rocks butted up on the horizon. Glancing around, she recognized the ocotillo cactus that Halladay had pointed out and, in the distance, Indian paintbrush and paloverde trees. The heat wasn't nearly as bad now as when she'd arrived. It was late afternoon and the air was cool and comfortable.

She noticed a reddish-brown prairie dog poke its head up from a small hillock that covered its burrow. A jackrabbit rustled the mesquite nearby as it hopped away. These creatures were furry and harmless. But she remembered the warnings Halladay had patiently given her about deadly gila monsters, snakes, scorpions, and spiders. Kane had her in such a hurry to meet him, she'd almost forgotten to shake out her boots to dislodge any unwanted creatures the way she'd been shown.

Kane dismounted and turned to help her down. After she eased her leg over the pommel, he put his hands around her waist. In spite of his riding gauntlets and the heavy material of her split skirt, she felt the contact through to her skin. A shiver of awareness went through her.

"You're not cold, are you?" he asked, looking at her strangely.

"No."

She stiffened, trying to keep her body from betraying her. She cared about him, but he'd made it clear that he didn't return her regard. With little effort, he lifted her down and her heart beat wildly. She took a step back, out of his reach, afraid he could feel her reaction to him. If she couldn't keep Kane from knowing he affected her, she would make a fool of herself in front of him again. She'd rather fall into a prickly-pear cactus.

Cady raised her gaze to his face. Beneath the shadow of his campaign hat, his dark eyes held an intensity that made her breath catch. His mouth still turned up slightly at the corners, but the tension in his arms told her he wasn't amused. His square jaw and the hard planes of his face gave him an air of seriousness that made her uneasy. Again she wondered what he'd been talking about with Mac when she'd interrupted them. Ever since leaving Kane's office, she'd had a bad feeling. The look that had passed between the two men had not escaped her notice. And Kane had agreed to her favor far more easily than she'd expected.

Kane had hardly said two words to her since they'd left the fort. He was angry about something; instinct told her whatever had put the scowl on his face was directly related to her. Every few minutes he'd look at her as if she'd ripped the epaulets from his dress uniform and ground them under her heel.

He stood beside her, scanning the desert for a place to shoot. A pleasant breeze stirred the yuccas and creosote bushes around them. The scent of sage and juniper mixed with something else that she recognized as bay rum. Cady glanced sharply at his face. She didn't remember smelling this when she'd been in his office just a short time ago. The room was very small. If he'd been wearing it, wouldn't she have noticed? Was it possible that he'd put it on after she'd left? For her?

The thought stirred a fluttery sensation in her stomach. He stood so close that her shoulder brushed his upper arm, sending ripples through her that settled in her breasts. The last time he'd been this close, he'd kissed her.

Cady tried to control her racing pulse. She was here to learn how to shoot, and that was serious business. She was the student; he was the teacher. If she didn't pull herself together quickly, she wouldn't be able to hold a gun, let alone shoot it without hurting herself.

She stepped away from him. "Let's get to it, captain."

He nodded, then pointed to a six-foot saguaro cactus with bushes around it and a big rock to the left.

"Over there. You'll have something to shoot at." He started walking toward it.

"That rock's pretty big. Maybe I can hit it."

He stopped, turned, and looked down at her sharply. "Don't ever aim at a rock. The ricochet could be deadly."

Cady's chin came up. "I was joking."

"Guns are serious. If you don't treat them with respect, you could wind up dead."

"I'm sorry. It won't happen again."

He moved toward the cactus, and stopped when he was about twenty feet away. "Rule number one, don't point a gun at anything or anyone unless you're prepared to fire."

She thought about that and decided it made good sense. "What's rule number two?"

"Always check your weapon to see if it's loaded."

He lifted the leather flap on his gunbelt and pulled his pistol out. "This is the grip and this is the barrel." He indicated the handle and the long thin part of the gun. "Hold it by the grip. The barrel is where the bullets come out."

Her eyes narrowed. "I'm not an idiot."

"I never said you were."

"You think just because I set my dress on fire that I can't—"

"This is an army issue Colt Forty-five." He held the pistol away from him. When he flicked something, she could see a small round hole. "This is the chamber. You put a cartridge in there and turn the cylinder. Put another one in and turn it. Keep doing that until all six chambers are full."

She looked at him and sighed. It seemed the stalwart captain was brave enough to face a band of Indians, but he'd changed the subject abruptly so he wouldn't have to talk about that night. If she knew what was good for her, she'd forget it too. Maybe someday the memory of their kiss would lose its power over her. But right now—

"Cady? Are you listening?"

"Of course." She pointed to the circular part. "That's the cylinder. The chamber inside there is where the bullets—I mean, cartridges—go."

She stood beside him, so close that she could feel the bunching and releasing of the muscles in his upper arm as he checked the gun. The scent of man, of Kane, filled her head and trailed down inside her.

The clink of bullets dropping into his hand brought her back to the present.

"This is how they go in." He pushed a bullet into each hole in the chamber and snapped it closed. He worked efficiently and confidently. She could hardly breathe with him beside her. How could she possibly learn anything?

Kane handed the gun to her. With a deep swallow, she took it. "It's heavy."

He nodded. "Hold it and aim at that cactus over there."

She did as he instructed. The weight seemed considerably more as she extended her arm; the barrel lowered as if it had a mind of its own even as she worked to keep it steady on target.

Kane watched her efforts, then moved behind her. "Let's try something."

"What?" she asked. Her voice had a breathless quality; she wondered if he noticed.

He put his arms around her. With his front pressed close to her back, she felt the solid wall of his chest, the contour of muscle that flexed as he put his hands on her upper arms. She could hardly draw a steady breath. Yet he was all business. She found that extremely irritating.

He moved his hands up and down her arms. "Loosen up."

"I am loose."

"You're stretched tight as a fiddle string. You won't be able to hit anything like that."

She took a deep breath and closed her eyes for a second. When she looked again, she was calmer. "I'm ready now."

"Open your left hand and turn your palm up," he said, taking hold of her wrist and turning it.

She did as he instructed, then asked, "Now what?"

"Put your right hand into your left palm. With your elbow braced against your body, you should be able to keep your gun hand steady."

She found he was right. She was able to keep it still. "What next?"

He dropped his arms, but she could still feel the warmth of his body. "Put your finger on the trigger and squeeze gently."

She did and a deafening explosion roared through the air, echoing toward the mountains. The gun barrel jerked to the right, and the concussion of the weapon sent her backward into him. Her arm ached all the way to her shoulder, and she would have landed on her backside in the dirt if his arms hadn't come around her. Several seconds passed before the sound of the gunshot died away.

It took longer than that before she breathed normally again and her heart stopped pounding. Her ears rang and she wasn't sure she'd ever hear right again. But there was nothing wrong with her sense of smell. The acrid stench of gunpowder filled her nostrils.

Nothing wrong with her sense of touch either. Those

strong arms sent heat coursing through her. Liquid desire melted within her and flowed into her belly.

She shook her head. "Oh, my!"

"Are you all right?" His deep voice vibrated in his chest, against her back, and she felt it between her shoulder blades.

She nodded. "I just didn't expect it to be so loud. Did I hit anything?"

"No. But I didn't expect you to. Not at first."

"May I shoot again?"

"That's what we're here for. This time, squeeze the trigger."

"I thought I did."

"You jerked it. When you do that, the bullet will go the way your wrist does." With his arms still around her, he lifted her arm again. "Here, let me show you. Pull back slowly. Feel the slack in the trigger?"

She nodded.

"When the slack's gone, squeeze gently. It's a subtle motion. When the gun goes off, it should be a surprise."

"A surprise?" She dropped her gun hand and turned toward him, out of the circle of his embrace. "How can it be a surprise? You just said rule number one is don't point a gun at anyone you don't intend to shoot. So if I point it, why in heaven's name would it be a surprise?"

"Cady Tanner, everything you do is a surprise." He took her shoulders and turned her around, putting his arms around her the way they'd been before. But she felt a chuckle vibrate through him. "Besides, it's just an expression."

She grinned, but in her best Miss Biddle voice she said, "Captain, need I remind you that guns are serious? If you don't treat them with respect you could wind up dead."

"You've got five more shots. Surprise me." There was a smile in his voice.

She took aim and fired. Trying to remember everything he'd told her, she braced one hand in the other to keep her hand steady. Her first three shots went wide of where she aimed. The fourth and fifth bullets did not go exactly where she'd meant them to, but at least she hit the cactus, making the saguaro needles fly.

"I did it!" she cried, turning toward him. "Did you see that? I shot the cactus!"

He nodded with satisfaction and smiled. "You're a quick student."

"Do you think I need more practice?"

He shook his head. "That's enough for today. Ammunition is scarce. I think you could handle a pistol if you had to."

The edge to his voice when he said it made the hair on the back of her neck stand up. Something was going on. She could feel it.

"Kane, may I ask you a question?" She handed him the empty gun, grip first.

"Of course." He opened the chamber and reloaded the pistol.

"What were you and Lieutenant Thorne discussing when I came in your office today?"

Kane looked down at her, taking her measure, assessing the keen intelligence shining in her eyes. If he lied to her, she would know it. He had to give just enough of the truth to keep her satisfied without letting her know about the danger Jack was in.

He put his pistol in his holster and folded the leather flap over it. "Mac was filling me in on what's happening with the Indians."

"What is it?"

"Twenty-six warriors escaped from the San Carlos reservation. They're raiding ranches, stages, and every white settlement they can find."

"But why?" Her eyes darkened with worry. "What do they want?"

"Ammunition and guns."

"When they take what they want, what do they do with the people?"

He wanted to spare her, but he had to be as truthful as possible. "Some of them are killed or wounded, others escape, some are taken prisoner."

"Oh, dear God." She caught her full bottom lip between her teeth. "So that's what you meant when you said if the soldiers do their job, I won't need a rifle. If they don't—" She stopped and swallowed.

"There's nothing to be afraid of, Cady. If there's an attack, and that's a big *if,* the Apaches won't get past my men. Besides, Indians aren't stupid. A small band is not likely to attack a U.S. fort where they'll be out-manned and outgunned."

"But what if they do? What if they get past the guards?"

"They won't."

"But Kane, you said I'd need a pistol if they did."

He didn't even want to think it, let alone put it into words. He'd seen what the Indians did to their victims, men and women. His insides twisted. He'd die before he'd let them get near Cady. He turned away and started walking toward the horses. "It's time we got back. The sun will be going down soon."

Behind him, her boots crunched in the sand as she hurried after him. When he was beside the animals, he felt her hand on his arm, small and warm and surprisingly strong.

"Don't you walk away. And don't think you can keep things from me. All my life everyone has been trying to protect me, and I'm sick of it. Tell me, Kane. I have a right to know. If the Indians come, what should I do?"

"I'm going to give you a gun. Like any good soldier, you will learn to clean and care for it. After that you will master loading and shooting. If the Indians get past me, you take that gun and put it to your head and squeeze the trigger."

Her eyes widened in horror and her lips trembled. "What are you—"

"You'd be better off dead than letting them get their hands on you."

She gasped and tried to step back, but he gripped her arms to stop her. "Kill myself? Surely you can't mean that."

"I do mean it." He stared intensely into her eyes. He couldn't stand the thought of her being hurt.

"You promised Jack you'd—" She stopped and pressed her lips tightly together.

"And I'll do everything I can to keep my promise. But if anyone gets this close to you, it means I'm dead." He took a deep breath. "Don't let them have you, Cady. Don't let them touch you."

Tension had been building within him since the moment Cady had walked into his office. Maybe it was the way Mac Thorne had watched her; maybe it was the danger always hovering close by in the desert. Maybe it was knowing renegade Indians were out there and no one knew where they'd strike next. Or maybe it was just that she was so damn desirable he couldn't keep his hands off her. Whatever it was, Kane couldn't stop himself from kissing her.

Her eyes widened in surprise as he lowered his mouth to hers. A sound of protest was trapped on her lips, but he only felt it for a moment before a sigh replaced it.

That small sound freed some primal need he'd buried deep inside. He wrapped his arms around her and pulled her against him. She was so sweet and small and delicate. He could feel her soft breasts burning into his chest as she settled her arms around him. The feel of her hands on his back set his heart pounding.

The wind stirred the fragrance of sage and mesquite. Beside them the horses snorted and pawed the ground, kicking up dust. Overhead a cactus wren called out in monotonous, low-pitched notes. When Cady opened her lips to him, the sounds of the world disappeared and he could only smell, and feel, and taste this woman.

He slipped his tongue into the honeyed recess of her mouth, savoring the sweetness there. A throbbing ache centered in his loins as he grew hard from wanting her. He pressed against the juncture of her thighs, instinctively seeking to ease the pressure. Did the intimacy shock her? he wondered.

She arched upward to make the contact between them more firm. God, she was a hell of a woman. He couldn't help admiring her spirit, her willingness to challenge everything and everyone. Including him— including this.

He wanted her. He'd denied it, but he couldn't any longer. As her full soft mouth moved beneath his, he knew he wanted her in his bed, with the sheets twisted around their naked bodies as he made love to her until his name was on her lips as she cried out her release.

She strained and rubbed against him until the ache inside him cut clear through to his backbone. He pulled his mouth from hers and trailed kisses over her cheek and delicate jaw, then behind her ear and down her neck. He heard her quick intake of breath and smiled to himself. So the proper little schoolteacher had a passionate spot just at the soft hollow below her earlobe.

His flash of satisfaction vanished in the next instant when she stood on tiptoe and started nibbling his neck in the same spot where he'd just kissed her. He groaned low in his throat and curled his hands into the material of her blouse. He heard her shallow, rapid breathing. It pleased him to know she was affected by him, just as he was by her.

The next moment there was a rustling in the bushes beside them, and the horses started snorting and restlessly pawing the ground. He lifted his head and cursed himself for letting his guard down.

He looked into Cady's heavy-lidded eyes. Her lips were moist and slightly swollen from his kiss. The ache inside him grew. It made him want her more; it would be so easy to forget himself. But he'd been a soldier far too long to ignore his instincts. The sounds around them, the horses' flaring nostrils and nervousness, could be because they were anxious to go home. Or because they sensed some danger he couldn't. That brought him back down to earth, hard.

He might want Cady. But he could never have her—not here, not now, not ever. Not after what had happened to Annie.

"We have to get back." He pulled her arms from around his neck.

"Not yet," she whispered. She swayed toward him. "Just one more minute."

"No." He gripped her upper arms, not painfully, just enough to get through to her. "Something's spooking the horses. We have to go. Now."

A flicker of apprehension went through her and he knew she was remembering what he'd said about not being taken alive. He wanted to tell her again to go home where she'd be safe. From the Indians. From him. He'd said it too many times already and she refused to listen. There was no reason to believe she would now. He could think of only one thing to do. As soon as they got back to the fort, he planned to take care of it.

Kane took her arm and led her over to Prince. She turned toward the animal and put one boot in the stirrup while he put his hands around her waist and lifted her into the saddle.

He swung up on his own horse. With just enough knee pressure, Soldier Boy leaped forward. Cady's mount followed, and they cantered, back to the fort, side by side.

They stopped by the stable and dismounted. Kane took the reins from her hand and looped them over the pole fence enclosing the corral.

Cady looked up at him, biting the corner of her lip as she seemed to study him. Finally she took a deep breath. "Are you coming to the literary society meeting tonight?"

He didn't want to. But he knew every man who wasn't on duty would be going. He nodded. "I'll be there."

She smiled, which made him want to kiss her again. "I'll see you later, then."

He touched the brim of his hat, turned away, and headed for his office. There was a pile of paperwork. One thing, especially, couldn't wait.

9

Kane was still trying to decide whether or not to sign the paper in his hands when a knock sounded on his door. He looked up, surprised that shadows had overtaken his office. It must be well after six o'clock. Before he could call out "Come in," the door opened and Mac Thorne did just that.

Mac's hair was slightly damp and the dark stubble was missing from his face. The smell of shaving soap and cologne followed him into the room.

"What can I do for you?" Kane asked him. Funny that he'd show up just now. He'd been thinking a lot about the other man and what the paper in his hands might mean to him.

Mac slipped his hands into the pockets of his wool uniform pants. "What makes you think I want something? Can't I just be neighborly?"

"You've never been before. Why start now?"

Mac pulled one hand out of his pocket and held it palm down about even with his chin. "The reason stands about this high and has the prettiest green eyes I ever saw."

Kane couldn't prevent the irritation that instantly flashed through him, although he'd rather be staked out over an anthill in the desert heat than let the other man see his reaction. Besides, Kane reminded himself, he had no hold on her.

"If you're looking to be neighborly to Cady, why come here? She's over in the officers' quarters."

"You're saying you don't care if I call on her?"

Care? Of course he cared.

"I have no say in who she sees or doesn't see. If you're trying to make me jealous, you're wasting your time."

"I don't play those games, especially with a friend. I'm trying to find out if you're interested in the lady or not. I don't horn in on another man's territory."

"Cady's free to see whoever she chooses." Just to make sure he didn't stand in her way, Kane signed the paper he'd just finished writing and handed the document over to the other man. "This affects you."

Mac took it and read the words. He looked up, surprised. "You're requesting a transfer?"

Kane nodded.

"Why?" His eyes narrowed. "Especially now with Apache trouble brewing. You're needed here more than ever."

"You'd make a fine second-in-command, Mac."

He shook his head and backed up a step as if Kane were carrying a contagious disease. "You know how I feel about this. I don't give orders. Why, I can hardly follow them."

"You could if you'd let yourself forget. What happened wasn't your fault."

"That's ancient history."

Kane nodded. "All right. It's not up to me anyway. First the transfer has to go through. Then it's out of my hands."

"This is because of Cady, isn't it?" Mac folded his arms over his chest. "What happened while you were teaching her to shoot?"

"Nothing."

The other man's blue eyes widened and he moved closer to the desk. "You just said she's free to see whoever she wants, but you never said how you felt. You're in love with her, aren't you?"

"That's the most ridiculous thing I ever heard."

"I don't think so." Mac's eyes glittered as if he'd found a missing puzzle piece. "You're in love with her. But you still blame yourself for what happened to Annie. You won't get—"

"I don't want to talk about this."

"The least you can do is tell Cady, so she'll understand. She's in love with you too."

"Dammit, Thorne. I said I don't want to talk about this, with you or anyone else. It's my business and no one else's. It's over."

Mac straightened. "Right. And I'm the president of the United States. I'll tell you one thing."

"I don't want to hear it."

"You're going to, whether you like it or not. If I were in your shoes, I'd tell her about her brother."

"Then I'm glad you're not in my shoes."

"She has a right to know he's in danger."

"Not in my opinion."

"You're protecting her. You still want me to swallow the lie that you're not in love with her?"

"I don't care what you swallow. About two fingers of arsenic sounds pretty good right now."

"Then you have no objection if I go to the literary society meeting tonight?"

"None. Although I should warn you that Cady Tanner is trouble with a capital T."

Mac grinned, apparently unmoved by the warning. "No objection if I walk the lady home?"

"No." The thought of Cady with another man forced Kane to use every ounce of his self-control to keep from grabbing Mac and ordering him to stay away from her.

"What if I should stand out in the moonlight with her a spell? What if I get the feelin' she wouldn't mind a good-night kiss? What if she was to invite me in?"

"You lay one hand on her and I'll—" Kane stood up so fast, his wooden chair flipped over backwards.

"You'll what?" Mac smiled. His expression said he'd set Kane up and pushed until he got exactly this reaction.

"I thought you didn't play games."

"This isn't a game. Someone has to get through to you."

Kane took a deep breath, then let it out. With an effort, he resisted the urge to wipe that grin off Mac's face. He'd never felt such a murderous fury, especially over a woman.

"There's the door, Mac. I suggest you get the hell out before I do something I'll regret."

"Looks like bein' neighborly could be hard on the constitution. You sure you want that transfer?"

"Positive."

"You're makin' a mistake."

"Maybe. It won't be the first."

Mac stared at him, then nodded and left him alone.

Kane sat down and ran his hand through his hair. He wasn't in love with Cady. He wasn't capable of loving any woman. The sooner he left Fort McDowell and Cady Tanner, the better for both of them.

*   *   *

In the mess hall, Cady had asked several of the enlisted men to move the wooden tables and benches against the walls to make room for everyone. She arranged her books on one of the tables and was ready far earlier than she had planned. After pacing in her room, she'd decided to set up rather than wear out the canvas floor. She wanted so much for the literary society to be a success. It was important to prove to Kane that she could make a difference.

But she couldn't help worrying. What if no one came? What if they came and didn't like the books she'd brought with her?

She remembered what Kane had said: Folks out here don't need much of a reason to get together. He'd said the men would read dress patterns if it meant they could be close to her. Surely he was wrong about that. If they came, it wasn't because of her. It was because they craved some diversion in their lives. She told herself that this meeting would break up the monotony for everyone. They might be stuck in the desert, in the middle of nowhere, but books could take them away, even if just for a little while.

At the thought of Kane, her heart skipped like a stone over a pond. His kiss earlier had certainly made her forget herself. She remembered how he'd pressed his lips to the hollow beneath her ear, making her knees weak and her pulse pound. It was the most wonderful feeling she'd ever known. If he hadn't insisted they leave, she'd still be out there with him.

He had promised he would be here tonight.

She could hardly wait to see him. Maybe that was why she'd set everything up so early. The sooner she got things going, the sooner she'd see Kane again.

Her heart dropped to her toes at the sound of boots scraping on the canvas floor. Hoping it was Kane and that she'd have a chance to be alone with him before the others arrived, she turned.

As she recognized Lieutenant Thorne, she couldn't hide her disappointment. "Oh, it's you."

One dark brow lifted. "Yes, ma'am. Doesn't take a genius to see you were expecting someone else."

"I'm sorry. I didn't mean for it to come out like that. I'm expecting a lot of people tonight. At least I hope they'll come," she amended.

"They'll be here. Don't fret about that." He picked up an ornately bound volume of *Romeo and Juliet* and flipped through it. He stared at her and his mouth tightened before he slammed the book shut and said, "A bloody waste, if you ask me."

"You've read the play?" She had the feeling the waste he was talking about had nothing to do with Shakespeare's tragedy.

"Yes, I've read it." The dark look disappeared and a flirtatious expression replaced it. "Does it surprise you that I'd read Shakespeare?"

"Frankly, yes. Kane told me you've got an instinct for tracking Indians and anticipating what they'll do next."

"Never judge a book by its cover, Miss Tanner," he said. "Just because a man enjoys a good book doesn't mean he can't hold his own with the Apaches."

"I'll remember that," she said, laughing. She sobered quickly when she remembered that Indians were the reason she'd been out in the desert with Kane to learn how to shoot a gun.

"You're very quiet all of a sudden. Something wrong?"

"Not exactly. Just a feeling I have." She recalled the look Mac had shared with Kane in his office. The silent communication, she was certain, meant they were keeping something from her. "If I ask you a question, will you tell me the truth?"

"Depends on whether or not it's fit for a lady's ears."

"This is nothing like that. I want to know what you and Kane were talking about when I went to his office this afternoon." He shuffled his feet and started to say something. "Don't put me off. I know it was about Jack."

"Now, Miss Cady," he drawled, "what makes you think that?"

"You mentioned you'd just returned from the Superstitions, and that's where my brother is. If it wasn't bad news and didn't involve him, there would be no reason to protect me. Call it woman's intuition if you want, but I feel it. There's something wrong. Tell me what it is."

He stared at her for a long time, so long she thought he wasn't going to answer. Finally, he nodded. "Right from the first I thought you should know. I told the captain straight out: if Jack was related to me, I'd want to know about it."

"Is he hurt?" she asked anxiously.

"No, at least not that I know of. And maybe the trouble won't find him."

"Don't play games with me, Mac. Just tell me what's going on."

"There was an Indian raid on a miner's camp up in the Superstitions." He put his hand up to stop her when she opened her mouth to ask if Jack was all right. "He's fine. No need to go all pale like that. Another miner was wounded, though. Jack saved him."

A feeling of familial pride swelled in her chest. "That's my brother. But if the miner's alive and Jack's not hurt, what—"

"He had to kill an Indian to save that miner. Jack doesn't know the one he killed was Alchise, Cuchillo's brother. That Indian is one mean son of a—" He stopped and cleared his throat. "He's ruthless, and he's got no love for the white man."

She pressed her palm to her chest and felt her heart pound. "That means—?"

Mac nodded grimly. "Cuchillo has sworn to kill the man who killed his brother, if it takes the rest of his life."

Cady gasped and swayed toward him. He gripped her upper arms to steady her. "You all right?"

"I'm fine. Does Jack know about this personal vendetta?"

"No. The Indians were split into two bands. We only found out from survivors of Cuchillo's raiding party." His gaze turned dark as if those memories belonged in a hell he couldn't forget.

"Oh, God."

Mac squeezed her arms, not painfully but enough to get her attention. "I've never met your brother, but I hear he's a man who can take care of himself."

"Not if he doesn't know there's danger. Why did Kane want to keep this from me?"

"I'm not sure. But look at it this way. Your brother's come face-to-face with Indians before, Cady. He knows better than anyone about trouble and how to take care of it."

"But he should be warned that Cuchillo has vowed to kill him. He'd be more careful." She started to pull out of his grip.

"Where are you going?" He held her fast.

"I'm going to talk to Kane."

He nodded to the table of books behind her. "But you've got this shindig starting pretty quick."

She looked up at him. "Will you greet everyone when they get here? Just tell them to browse through the books. If they see anything they like, they're welcome to take it and read it."

"Me?" He pointed to his chest. "You want me to run a literary meeting?"

"I won't be long. In fact I'll probably be back before anyone gets here. Please?"

He let out a big breath. "I never could resist a pretty lady."

"Thank you, Mac."

He pointed to her in mock anger. "If you're not back by the time this place fills up—"

Before he could finish, she stood on tiptoe and kissed his cheek. "I'll be back before you miss me. I promise."

Kane had put off the inevitable long enough and was ready to go to the literary society meeting. Just as he was reaching for his hat, Cady stormed into his office without knocking. She slammed the door and marched over to him like a woman with a mission.

She jammed her hands on her hips and glared at him so fiercely he was glad there was a desk between them.

"Why didn't you tell me Jack was in trouble?"

"How did you find out?"

"That's not important. I had a right to know."

"Mac told you, didn't he? I thought I could trust him to keep his mouth shut."

"It doesn't matter who told me. The point is, I know. And—"

"Isn't it about time for your literary society meeting to start?" That was pretty important and might distract her.

"Lieutenant Thorne is in charge until I get there."

"Mac?" He grinned. The thought of the hardened Indian fighter cheerfully pointing out books and pouring punch was as likely as Cady Tanner running a hog ranch.

"Yes, Mac. Now quit trying to sidetrack me. I've come to talk to you about a matter of life and death."

She'd seen through his flanking maneuver. Now what was he going to do? Stall her.

"Last time you were here you wanted me to teach you how to use a gun."

"And you did." The lanterns mounted on the walls around the room highlighted the pink that suddenly covered her high cheekbones. Was she remembering what had happened after he'd shown her the basic points of the pistol?

As long as he lived, he wouldn't forget holding Cady Tanner in his arms, smack in the middle of the desert. With blue sky above and the smell of sage and sand around them, he'd kissed her senseless. It was the dumbest thing he'd ever done, and by far the most exhilarating. At least this time when he kissed her, they had been out in the open and she couldn't back into the fire. He, on the other hand, was still burning.

But bedding Cady would be the worst thing he could do.

Standing behind his desk, Kane folded his arms over his chest. "So what is this life-and-death matter, rifle practice? Hand-to-hand self-defense? Explosives? I think R. J. could help you there."

"I demand that you send out a patrol to warn Jack that Cuchillo has sworn to kill him."

He wasn't sure what he'd expected her to say, but that wasn't it. "I can't order my men to put their lives on the line for the sake of one or two people who may or may not be in danger."

Her green eyes filled with hurt and anger. "Can't or won't?" she asked, her voice filled with contempt. "Would you go? Or are you afraid?"

He was afraid, but not of the Indians. He'd faced death so often it was like an old friend. He welcomed the challenge because that was what an army officer did. But

Cady Tanner could harm him far more than the Apaches. The look in her eyes made him want to do whatever she asked, for her sake. But he didn't have the manpower or supplies to send a patrol into the Superstitions to warn one man. It would be stupid and suicidal. He had to think of the men in his command first. He couldn't believe he was giving her harebrained suggestion even this much consideration. Sighing, he offered a compromise.

"Mac is taking a patrol out tomorrow. I'll tell him to make sure Jack gets the word. That's the best I can do."

"Is Lieutenant Thorne going into the Superstition Mountains?"

"No. He's heading in the other direction."

"Then how will Jack get the warning?"

"Mac will pass the word. It spreads fast out here. Besides, Jack's guard will be up."

"Can you guarantee that? He doesn't know it's personal with Cuchillo. Someone has to tell him so he'll come out of the mountains until Cuchillo is caught."

"I'm sorry, Cady."

It nearly killed him to refuse, but Cady's request was based on emotion, something an army officer couldn't afford. He couldn't put his command in unnecessary danger for the welfare of one man.

So it didn't make sense that he felt like a snake.

He shook his head again. "Jack knew the danger when he went up there. He accepted it. I can't endanger my men—"

"I see." Her chin lifted slightly. "Then I'll go and warn him."

"Like hell you will!" For the first time since she'd walked in, he wanted to move around his desk and shake her. If he knew it would make her see reason, he'd shake her till her teeth rattled.

As if she could read his mind, she took a small step

back, but her voice was steady when she spoke. "There's no need to swear, captain."

"The hell there isn't!" He took a deep breath and tried to still his thundering heart and the blood roaring in his ears. "What kind of a harebrained idea is that? Why don't you just wave a flag for Cuchillo and holler 'Come and get me!' at the top of your lungs?"

"It's not harebrained. I will study and prepare properly for the journey. I already know how to use a gun, thanks to you."

"And you think that will keep you safe from a band of bloodthirsty Apaches bent on revenge?" His hands curled into fists.

"Planning is the key," she said.

He could almost hear her precious Miss Biddle spouting that platitude. If anything happened to Cady because that stupid woman had filled her head full of romantic bull. . . .

"Planning, my backside. You will not go out there on your own to warn your brother."

"Then send one of your men with me. Brewster would go."

"You could bat your big green eyes at any man on this post, and he'd drop everything to help you. But they won't disobey my orders."

"What about one of the scouts? I bet Nathan Eagle would be able to find Jack."

"I'll bust any man who helps you down to private. And if he already is one, I'll see he never makes it to corporal. Is that what you want?"

She bit the corner of her lip and shook her head. Then she nodded resolutely. "You leave me no choice. I'll go by myself."

"You can't be serious."

He saw the stubborn, contrary gleam in Cady's eye

and knew there was nothing he could say to keep her from going out there on her own. That didn't mean his hands were tied. There was one thing he could do. And if it was the only way he could stop her, he would do it in a heartbeat.

He walked around the desk and stopped in front of her. "I'll give you thirty seconds to change your mind about this."

"I don't need any time. I'm not changing my mind. Jack is my brother. Tanners take care of one another."

"Don't make me do something I'll regret."

"If something happened to Jack and I didn't try to protect him, I couldn't live with myself."

As much as he wanted to wring her pretty little neck, he envied the family loyalty that drove her to put her life on the line. No one except his own soldiers had ever done that for him. How would it feel to have a woman on his side that fiercely? He'd never know—and neither would Jack. Kane knew her brother would applaud any means he took to stop her and save her from herself.

"You leave me no choice. I'm sorry to have to do this, Cady."

"What do you mean?" Her eyes widened in alarm.

"I'm putting you in protective custody." He took her upper arm.

She tried to pull free but he tightened his grip and headed for the door, taking her along.

"What are you doing? Where are we going?"

"The guardhouse."

"How dare you!" Outrage wrapped around every word. She started to struggle.

When yanking her arm didn't free her from his grip, she tried to pry his fingers loose, one by one. He took no satisfaction in using his superior strength to control her. Soon she was breathing hard from her efforts.

Kane felt like the town bully. She had forced him to do this, he reminded himself. If she was one of his soldiers and he could trust her to follow orders, she could go about her business. She would be safe as long as she stayed under military protection within the perimeter of the fort.

But Cady Tanner acted first and thought about it later. When he had met her two years ago, she had run away from her fancy eastern boarding school and showed up without warning in Arizona. This time she wouldn't get her way.

When he tried to move her toward the door, Cady dug her heels in. "Wait, Kane."

He stopped, wondering what she had on her mind. Her voice was too calm, too controlled. But the tight set of her mouth told him what she was feeling and he couldn't help thinking that she was planning some trick.

"What?"

Anger grew in her eyes. "You can't put me in prison."

"It's not prison."

"You're evading the issue."

He kept trying, but she wouldn't let him get away with it. "Unless you have something to say that will change my mind—"

"If you lock me up, who will warn Jack?"

"I've already told you, I'll do what I can."

"Don't you see that's not good enough? Let me go!"

"I can't. You'll die out there by yourself as surely as if someone put a gun to your head and pulled the trigger. I'd never forgive myself if I let you go off on this fool's mission and something happened to you."

"So no matter what I say, you're going to put me in prison?"

Equal parts of guilt and irritation warred within him. "It doesn't matter what you call it. I'd put you anywhere there was a lock on the door as long as I had the key."

"Why won't you let me help my brother?"

"I can't. I'm damn well going to lock you up, and I'll damn well keep you there for as long as it takes for you to calm down and come to your senses.

"Any more questions?" he asked. When she didn't say anything but just stood there simmering, he said, "All right. Let's go."

She tried digging her heels in again, but one firm tug had her jumping forward. He opened the door and pulled her out into the cool night air.

Cady couldn't believe this was happening to her. Kane pulled her down the steps and into the sand. Maybe here she could get a grip and slow him down. She tried to make herself dead weight. He glared down at her. "Pick your feet up and march or you won't like the alternative."

"I am not one of your soldiers. I don't have to do what you say. I don't have to follow orders."

"You do while you're under my protection."

"You call this protection? This is an outrage!" She used all her strength to try to pull her arm away from him. "You're the one I need protection from."

He stopped and scowled down at her. "I don't have time for this. Just remember, you were warned."

He slid his hand down to her wrist, bent at the waist, and hoisted her over his shoulder. When he straightened, his shoulder dug into her abdomen, driving the air from her lungs. The ground suddenly looked very far away, and she realized he truly meant to lock her up. She should have kept her intentions to herself.

She wanted to order him to put her down, but if

angry words had had any effect, he would have released her arm after the fuss she'd made. She had to try another way.

She lifted her upper body a little and tried to see his face. She only managed to get a better view of his broad back. The muscles beneath his uniform shirt flexed from his struggle to hold onto her. His sheer strength and size convinced her that words were her only weapon.

"Stop, Kane. You win."

"What?" he asked.

"I said you win. Obviously you feel very strongly about this. I'll do as you say."

Kane stepped up onto a plank walkway and came to a stop in front of a door with wooden bars where the top part should have been. He bent at the knees until her toes touched the ground and then grabbed her upper arms to steady her on her feet.

He stared down at her, assessing her. His look was skeptical. "You'll do as I say?"

"Yes. You're right, of course, about the danger. I can't imagine what I was thinking even to consider going off into the desert by myself."

He raised one brow doubtfully. "Is that right?"

She nodded vigorously. Her hair, done up so neatly for the literary society meeting, was coming down around her face. She brushed it out of the way impatiently. "That's right." She smoothed her skirt and checked to make sure her blouse was neatly tucked into her waistband. "Now if you'll excuse me, I'm late for my meeting."

She had started to walk down the step when she felt his hand on her upper arm.

"What do you take me for, a bloody idiot?" His tone was irritated, but she could swear beneath the surface he was laughing, or at least smiling a little. If she didn't know differently, she might have noticed a touch of admiration there too.

"Of course I don't think you're an idiot."

He opened the door to the guardhouse, put her inside, and shut it, sliding the latch into place before she could say fiddlesticks.

"If you think for one minute that I believe a word you're saying, think again, Cady. I'm nobody's fool."

She looked at him through the bars. He'd done it! He'd really done it! He'd locked her up!

"You let me out of here!" In frustration, she stamped her foot so hard she felt the jolt all the way up her leg. "What about Jack? You can't do this to me!"

"I think I already have. I'll see you later." He turned and walked down the steps.

"Kane Carrington, you come back here this minute or you'll regret this," she called. "You can't leave me here. I'm not in the army. You have no right." She took a breath. "What about my meeting?"

"Don't worry. I'll take care of it." He motioned to a passing soldier to approach him.

The young man, hardly old enough to draw a straight-edge across his face, saluted. "Yes, sir?"

"Private Duncan?"

"Yes, sir. What can I do for you?"

"I'm putting you in charge of the prisoner."

"But, sir, I'm off duty. I was on my way to the literary society meeting the schoolteacher is puttin' on."

"There's not going to be a meeting, private." He cocked his thumb over his shoulder and indicated Cady.

She glared daggers at Kane, then waved and smiled sweetly at the young soldier. He started to wave back and his eyes widened. He looked at Kane and instantly dropped his hand to his side. She could see a thousand questions racing through the private's mind as his gaze shifted from her to Kane and back to her.

"What's she done, sir?"

"Nothing, yet. I plan to keep it that way."

"But, captain—"

Cady could see Kane's profile. His jaw clenched, and the muscle in his cheek moved rapidly.

"Guard the prisoner, Duncan!" The man backed up a step. "And if you've ever believed anything in your life, believe this: If she gets out of there, you'll have an easier time with the Apaches than you'll have with me!"

"Yes, sir." The private started to move toward her, then stopped. "Should I get my rifle, sir?"

"I don't think you'll need it." Kane sent her a dark look. "Will he, Cady?"

"Private Duncan, I learned rule number one about guns today. Don't ever point one at anyone or anything you don't plan to shoot. So do *you* think you'll need your gun?"

"No, ma'am." His boots rang on the planks as he took up guard position next to her door. "That don't mean I won't follow orders, though."

"I understand," she said.

Kane looked her straight in the eye. She wondered if he might change his mind and let her out, but there was something hard and unbending in his expression. Then he turned away. She watched him walk toward the mess hall, and from the way he stomped his feet she knew he was angry.

He wasn't the only one.

She whispered to herself, "If I get out of here, you'll be sorry, Kane Carrington. That's a promise. And Tanners always make good on their promises."

10

When R. J. heard the men's angry voices just around the corner, he pressed his back against the outside wall of the mess hall. If he was paint on wood, he couldn't have been closer. He wanted to hear why Kane had come storming into the literary society meeting looking mad enough to kick his own dog. R. J. knew it had something to do with the schoolmarm. Until she showed up, Kane had never got so mad and now it was happening regular. He wanted to know what in blazes was going on.

It had stirred R. J.'s curiosity more than a little when Kane motioned Mac Thorne outside. R. J. had sneaked out the back door and around the side of the building to hear what he had to say.

"Why the hell did you tell her that her brother was in trouble?" Kane demanded. R. J. let out a breath, glad he wasn't on the other end of the conversation.

"Thought she had a right to know."

The sound of boots shuffling on the boardwalk carried to R. J. "Well, now she knows," Kane said. "And she demanded I send a patrol out to warn him."

"You can't do that." Now Mac sounded mad too.

"That's what I told her. She said she'd go by herself."

"Shit."

"She won't."

"How can you be so sure?" Mac asked.

"Because she's in the guardhouse."

R. J. covered his mouth with his hand to keep from laughing out loud. He'd give almost anything to have seen the look on her face when Kane did that. Bet it took the starch right out of her.

"Guess one of us has to go in there and tell all those men there's not going to be a meeting." It was Mac's voice.

"I'll do it." Kane didn't sound sorry at all. Fact was, he sounded eager to call it off.

It was quiet for a minute, and R. J. took a chance and peeked around the corner of the building. The two men stood practically nose to nose. He could only see their faces from the side; even so, Kane was staring at the other man, mad as all get out. Mac looked like it didn't bother him none, just stood there loose as you please.

Mac grinned. "You didn't lock her up to keep her away from me, did you?"

"Why the hell would I do that?"

Yeah, why would he want Mac to stay away from her? R. J. wondered. He liked Mac almost as much as he did Kane, and he'd swear Mac was trying to make Kane mad. But why? On account of Miss Tanner? R. J. scratched his head. For the life of him, he couldn't figure what either of 'em saw in that old schoolteacher.

"How long are you going to keep her locked up?" Mac asked.

"Overnight. I have no cause to keep her there longer than that."

R. J. wanted to ask why not; he almost blurted it out. If she stayed in the guardhouse, there wouldn't be any school tomorrow.

"What are you going to do if she still wants to go find her brother?" Mac wanted to know.

Kane let out a long breath. When he did that, R. J. knew he was just about as mad as he could get. "I'll watch her like a hawk and make sure she doesn't do something stupid."

Well, isn't that just dandy! R. J. thought. Kane had already been spending his free time with her, teaching her how to shoot, riding with her. And to make matters worse, she was still riding Prince! If Kane started watching her all the time, he'd never have time for anyone else.

Why in tarnation didn't Kane let her do what she dang well pleased and go find her brother?

R. J. froze. Now there was an idea, one of the best he'd ever had. He turned away, moving carefully so the two men on the boardwalk couldn't hear him.

Cady paced the floor of her prison. She felt as if she'd been locked up for days, but she knew it hadn't been more than a couple of hours. With every minute that went by, she grew angrier, more frustrated—and frightened for Jack.

She kicked the wall beside the door, and pain shot through her foot.

"You all right in there, Miss Tanner, ma'am?" Her guard peeked through the bars.

"Yes, private, I'm just *fine*," she said, through gritted teeth.

"Just checkin'. Heard something."

"What could possibly happen to me with you so vigilant outside?"

"Sorry, ma'am. Don't rightly know what vijeelant means. Only know I gotta stand here till the captain says different. Orders is orders."

"Yes. I can see that."

He yawned, then quickly slapped his hand over his mouth. "Sorry, ma'am. Been a long day. Ain't you sleepy?"

"No. What time is it?"

He looked up at the evening sky. "I'd say somewheres around ten."

"Is that all? Feels like midnight."

"Don't it, though?"

"Why don't you get some sleep?" She put her hands around the bars in her door and shook it. There was no give. "I'm not going anywhere."

He grinned at her. "Nice try, ma'am. But orders—"

"Is orders. So you said." She sighed. "Well, I believe I'll lie down. It appears there's nothing else to do."

"Night, ma'am. Don't let the bedbugs—" He glanced sideways at her. "Just an expression. I'm sure that there bed's just fine."

If she hadn't been so furious, she would have laughed at his obvious discomfort. "I'm certain it is. Thank you, private."

Cady backed away from the door and flopped disgustedly on the hard cot, the only piece of furniture, if one could call it that, in the small room. Above the bed there was a barred window, and a cool breeze drifted through it, giving her some air. The walls were thick adobe. Even if she had some instrument to use to dig her way out, it would take weeks.

Her mind raced, trying to come up with a plan. She thought about playing sick to get Private Duncan inside. Then what? He was thin but looked to be over six feet tall. For all his shy manner, she sensed a wiry

strength in him and knew she couldn't overpower him.
Orders were orders. He'd keep her there, no matter
what. She thought about the trick her brothers had
shown her to use against a persistent suitor, but even
the length of time it would take him to recover
wouldn't be enough for her to get away. When he did
get his wits back, he'd put out the alarm.

Nor was she about to go off into the desert without
proper preparation. She needed a horse, a gun and
ammunition, supplies, a map—she had no idea how to
get to the Superstition Mountains. Resting her elbows on
her knees, she put her chin in her hands. Her heart sank
as she let out a long breath. She was very much afraid
she couldn't help Jack unless someone helped her first.

"Psst."

Cady sat up straight. Half turning, she looked at the
window behind her. R. J. Wexler stood there, red hair
hanging in his eyes.

He put a finger to his lips, to show she should be
quiet. She nodded, letting him know she understood
and he handed a note through the bars.

She opened it and angled it so that the moonlight
shining inside illuminated the words.

be reddy, i'll git you owt, i'll git you to yer bruther.

She looked at the paper, biting her tongue to keep
her teacher's comments about spelling and punctuation
to herself. Then she knelt on her cot and leaned toward
the window, their faces only inches apart. After glancing over her shoulder to be sure Private Duncan wasn't
checking in on her, she looked at R. J. and mouthed one
word: "Why?"

His only response was a sullen shrug. Cady knew
this had more to do with getting rid of her than with his
desire to help her get to Jack. Although she suspected
Kane wanted nothing to do with her, R. J. had flat out

told her he wished she was gone so the captain would have time for him. The boy was lonely. In spite of the way he'd treated her, Cady's heart went out to him. She knew she might get him in a lot of trouble, but there was no other option. When she came back with Jack, Kane would be more likely to go easy on the boy.

Through the barred window she whispered, "Can you get me a gun and the supplies I'll need?"

He nodded.

She glanced over her shoulder to see if she'd been overheard. When she knew all was quiet, she looked back. If she had had any choice, she would have refused to cooperate with the boy, no matter what his motive for helping her. The truth was, without him she was stuck.

She leaned close to the bars and whispered, "Do what you can. I'll be waiting."

He nodded and slipped away. Cady sighed and sat down on her cot and prayed that R. J. could do what he said. He had managed to put an entire fort on alert. Getting her out of prison should be a piece of cake.

She was counting on him.

R. J. climbed back into his bedroom after getting the schoolteacher past the perimeter and into the desert beyond without getting caught. He was real proud of himself and wished he could share his cleverness with Kane. But he knew that was impossible.

Just as he was pulling his shirt over his head, he heard someone tapping on his window. He opened it, surprised and pleased to see John Eagle. Then he reminded himself that they weren't friends anymore. That empty feeling opened up inside him again, making him miss their friendship more than he ever had before.

John climbed in and folded his arms over his chest. "I saw what you did."

"What d'you mean?" R. J. asked.

"You helped Miss Tanner get out of the guardhouse and gave her supplies to leave the fort."

No point in denying it. R. J. nodded. "What's it to ya?"

"It's too dangerous out there for her. That's why the captain locked her up in the first place."

"She was set on goin'. Even Kane said he couldn't keep her prisoner more than overnight. Come morning, she was gonna hightail it outa there anyways."

John was frowning at him. "At least when the captain let her out he would have been able to watch her." John shook his head as worry slid into his black eyes.

Nervous now, R. J. narrowed his gaze at the other boy. "You tell anyone about this?"

John shook his head.

"Good. There's nothin' to fret about. I fixed her up with everything she needs. Gave her a map a blind man could follow. She'll hook up with her brother. Nothin's gonna happen to her. And she'll be outa our hair. No more school."

No more keeping Kane all to herself either.

"What if Cuchillo finds her? You know what renegades do to women captives."

R. J.'s eyes widened. He hadn't thought about that. He didn't want any harm to come to her; he just meant to get her out of his hair. "She's got a gun."

"That wouldn't do her any good against one warrior, let alone a raiding party."

"Dang it, John. If you're on her side, why didn't you try to stop me from helpin' her?"

"She wouldn't have listened, and I didn't want the guards to catch you. But if anything happens to her, you'll be in real trouble. I think you should tell Captain Carrington right now, before she gets too far from the fort."

R. J. shook his head. "He'll tan my hide good."

"If you won't tell the captain—"

"You gonna tell him what I done?"

The other boy shook his head. "You're my blood brother. But you have to find her and bring her back. I'll go with you."

That big empty feeling inside him closed up quick. In its place, excitement grabbed him, and sheer pleasure at the idea of once again sharing an adventure with his friend. R. J. grinned and nodded.

John Eagle flashed a smile that said he felt the same way. "We'll wait until almost dawn, even though rain's coming."

R. J. poked his head out the open window and looked up at the sky. Stars twinkled brightly; there wasn't a cloud in sight. "How do you know there'll be rain?"

"I can smell it."

R. J. knew John told the truth. He looked at his friend and was mighty glad to have him back. "Not that I ain't got faith in you, John. You could track a whisper in the wind. But in the rain—"

The other boy grinned again, his white teeth gleaming against his copper-colored skin. It was the best thing R. J. had seen in a month of Sundays. He'd go through hell and back to have his friend again. If it meant they had to find that ol' schoolteacher and convince her to come back, he'd do it.

"Do you really think we should wait? That'll give her a pretty good head start."

"Only two hours. She'll go slowly, even with the moon and stars to light her way. By morning the clouds will be here. It would be best to find her before the rain.

But I think we can move faster in the light." John looked out into the desert. "If this storm is as bad as I think, we need to get her back to the fort before the river rises."

"I'd never have thought about that." R. J. clapped a hand on John's shoulder and gave him a shake. "Jumpin' Jehoshaphat, I'm glad we're friends again!"

When the other boy grinned back, R. J. knew he was happy too. John didn't show what he was feeling much, so three smiles in as many minutes said a mouthful.

The sky lightened to gray, and that was the only way Cady could tell it was dawn. She figured she had traveled two or three hours by now. But even if she was experienced enough to determine the time by the position of the sun, she couldn't because of the thick black clouds. It didn't matter. She had to keep moving, because she wanted to put as much distance as possible between her and the fort. When Kane discovered her gone, she didn't want to be close enough for him to be able to bring her back.

R. J. had managed to distract the guard, unlock the door with the key hanging outside, and then replace it so no one would be the wiser. She was rather proud of her contribution to the escape. Her idea to plump up her blanket on the cot to make it look like she was sleeping was sheer genius. He had brought her a horse that she'd never ridden before, a big bay. The animal was high-strung and hard to control. Her arms ached and her inner thighs were chafed from her efforts, her muscles quivered from the exertion. She'd have to stop soon. The horse needed rest as much as she did.

She'd been a little frightened when she first started out. The desert seemed so big and lonely. But she thought about Jack and forced herself to keep going. R. J.'s map was a good one. The boy had a real talent for drawing, and she had no trouble following the route he'd marked.

After she crossed the Verde River—she smiled a little because it was hardly more than a trickle—the terrain was flat for miles, with only sand and cactus, junipers, and formations of boulders to mark the landscape. It was growing cooler. The wind picked up, and she shivered and turned the collar of her coat against her neck. Holding her floppy black hat on her head, she tilted back to look at the sky. It had been clear during the night, but now the clouds looked like they would open up any minute. Maybe she should try to find some shelter.

She could build a fire to keep warm. She'd proven that. The thought brought an image of Kane, the moment before he'd kissed her. His eyes had turned as stormy as the clouds moving over her now. She just didn't understand him. One minute he was tender and concerned and she was sure he must care about her. The next, he threw her in the guardhouse.

She winced a little, picturing how mad he would be when he found her gone. She didn't think it would take him long to decide how she got out. She wasn't sorry she wouldn't be there to face his wrath, but she felt guilty that R. J. would have to take the blame alone.

How R. J. had gotten the supplies together without being caught was something she'd never understand. The whole time she'd led her horse into the desert, until she was far enough away to mount up and move faster, she'd expected to hear a bugle blow. Since she'd been at the fort, she heard the signals for getting up in the morning, going to bed at night, and impending Indian attack. Surely the bugler would blow something for a prisoner on the loose. But all had been quiet. She wondered if Kane had discovered her absence yet.

Her horse nickered and snorted. She rubbed her gloved hand over his neck to settle him down. "I'll find Jack and bring him back to the fort. When I do, Kane will see that his concern was completely unnecessary."

The bay tossed his head and snorted. He danced sideways, nervous and restless.

Cady spoke soothingly. "Easy, there. We'll stop soon. I know you're tired."

Her calm tone and comforting words didn't have any effect. He continued to balk at moving forward, the metal in his bridle clinking as he shook his head. Leaning forward, she tried one more time to reassure him. From the bushes to her right she heard a rattling sound. Suddenly, the horse reared, his front legs pawing the air.

Taken by surprise, Cady didn't have time to grab onto anything. She tumbled backward. When she hit the ground, a blinding pain exploded in her head and then everything went black.

"What do you mean she escaped?" Kane folded his arms over his chest. R. J. looked up at him and fiddled with the reins of his horse.

"As soon as we found out Miss Tanner was gone, me and John thought we should go find her and bring her back. John said the Apaches might get her."

"You were going by yourselves?"

"Heck, no. We were coming to get you."

"With your mounts already saddled?" he demanded.

On his way to check on the prisoner, Kane had discovered R. J. and John Eagle slinking out of the stable with two horses. He had a sneaking suspicion that their furtive behavior had something to do with Cady.

He didn't wait for an answer. "How did you know she was gone?"

R. J. shuffled his feet. "Well, that's a real good question. And if you'll give me a minute, I'll tell you."

"You've got thirty seconds to tell me what's going on."

R. J. looked scared. "I'm real sure she's fine. She had supplies for a week. I gave her a map. She said it was a good 'un. She wanted to find her brother and—"

"She's out there alone? Dammit!" He glared at both boys. "You're confined to quarters until further notice."

R. J. looked up. "It's not John's fault. He didn't get her out of the guardhouse, I did."

"It's my fault as much as yours," John said. "I should have gone to the captain as soon as I found out."

"Why? Why the hell did you both go off half-cocked?" Kane demanded. "Why did you break her out of the guardhouse?"

R. J. hung his head. "I didn't want her here."

"Why?"

"'Cause she's dumb. She makes me read, she gets me in trouble. She—" He glanced up from beneath the brim of his hat.

Kane's eyes narrowed. "She what?"

Resentment and betrayal flashed in R. J.'s eyes. "Since she came you haven't played Sunday-night checkers. Not even once."

Kane was furious with the boy but also with himself. He should have seen this coming, and he hadn't. He'd been distracted by a pair of beautiful green eyes and a smile that was nothing but trouble.

"So you sent her off into the desert because I didn't have time for a game?"

"You didn't have time for *me.*" His voice cracked as it rose in outrage. "Just like my pa. You didn't have time for nothin' but her."

"If anything happens to her," Kane ground out, "you'll wish you never laid eyes on me."

"I didn't want nothin' bad to happen to her. I just wanted her to go away." Defiance darkened his gaze, but apprehension lurked around the edges. "It's not John's fault, none of it. He said we should go after her. He wanted to get you right off."

"How long has she been gone?"

"'Bout two or three hours is all."

"I'll leave now," Kane said. "I should be able to catch up with her pretty quick."

"Me and John are comin' with ya. We want to help."

"No. You're confined to quarters. But tell your father what's going on."

There was a splat as a raindrop hit the ground. R. J. looked at the sky. "What about the storm?"

Kane glanced up. "I can't leave her out there. I don't care how good the map is or how many supplies she has, she'll never survive on her own in the desert."

R. J. looked worried. "Ya *can* find her, can'tcha?"

Kane saw the concern in the youngster's face and knew he was looking for consolation and forgiveness for a stupid, selfish, dangerous stunt. If Kane found her and no harm had been done, he might be able to relent. But not now.

"I'll have her back before lunch."

"Good luck, Kane," R. J. said.

John Eagle stared at him solemnly. "Her trail will be easy to see." He looked up as more drops of rain fell. "If you hurry."

Kane nodded and headed for the stable. He quickly saddled Soldier Boy and notified the perimeter guard on his way out of the fort. He would have to square this with the major later.

The rain was falling a little harder as he crossed the Verde River, and he prayed he'd find Cady soon. If this storm was as bad as he thought it would be, the river would be impassable within hours. How could she do something so foolish?

Kane stoked his anger. He thought about what he would do to her and the two boys after he brought her back to the fort. Those thoughts kept him from the other emotion that had been building inside him, the one he'd been fighting off since he discovered Cady was gone. He didn't want to name it; he didn't want to acknowledge it.

He just had to find her alive and well. Anything else was unthinkable.

11

Cady shivered. Why was her bed so hard and cold and why was someone pouring water on her? She opened her eyes and sat up, then winced as pain shot through her head. It took a few seconds for her to remember where she was and what had happened. Then she looked around for the big bay horse and found he was nowhere in sight.

She was in big trouble. She was on foot, without supplies, and lost.

She wished she was back in the guardhouse at the fort. Kane had been right about everything, though if she lived to see him she would never admit it. But she wasn't sorry she'd done it. For Jack. Well, maybe a little sorry.

Tears pricked her eyes and a sob caught in her throat. She blinked and gritted her teeth to keep the sound trapped. She was afraid if she started crying, she would never stop. She wasn't sure how she was going to get out of this mess, but she couldn't do it if she lost her head. It was a matter of survival.

She thought of Kane and the fact that she might never see him again. She would welcome a chance to show him how much she cared about him. Now she knew how swiftly opportunity could be snatched away in this land.

A small sob tore from her throat. She clamped a hand over her mouth and took several deep breaths until she was under control. Then she stood up, a little unsteadily.

"Chin up. Shoulders back. Keep your wits. Tanners don't quit. You're going to be just fine." She said it out loud, and the words continued to echo in her head, a litany of determination. Every once in a while, another thought crept in, but she pushed it away.

She wouldn't die. That's all there was to it. God helps those who help themselves. She looked up at the gray clouds between her and heaven and blinked her eyes at the steady rain coming down.

"Please, God, let me live to see Kane again."

She had to get busy and find shelter. There were huge rock formations scattered all over the desert. Surely there was somewhere she could curl up until the rain ended.

As near as he could tell, Kane had been riding for an hour. The rain had increased in intensity and had obliterated any signs that Cady had come this way. He was counting on the fact that she would stick to the route R. J. had given her. He kept up a steady pace, confident that he could cover the same ground she had in half the time.

He cantered Soldier Boy over a small rise, and up ahead he thought he saw a horse. He blinked, focusing through the rain dripping from his hat, and his heart fell. It was indeed a horse—a riderless horse. He came alongside the animal and grabbed the bridle. It was the big bay from the fort, and he was carrying a bulging saddlebag. This had to be the mount R. J. had given Cady, with all the supplies she'd need.

She was on foot, in a downpour, and she had nothing. Even if she knew her way, it was difficult to see more than four feet ahead. Lord, he might never find her!

Then another thought crept in. If her horse had thrown her, she could be hurt—or worse.

The feeling he'd been fighting off took hold of him, and he gave it a name: fear.

He pushed it away. It wouldn't do her any good. He had to think clearly. He'd stick to the trail. If she was hurt, he would find her. If she was afoot, she would take shelter. He would find her. He *had* to find her.

Cold and wet, Cady forced herself to keep moving even though her arms and legs were growing numb. Through the curtain of rain, she thought she saw a group of boulders. Blinking the water from her eyes she looked again, and at the top she thought she saw an opening. If she could get up to it, and if she was very lucky, there might be an overhang, possibly even a small cave.

She climbed halfway to the top and stopped on a flat rock to rest. Below her, she thought she heard a horse whinny. She sat still and listened. All the things Kane had said about Indians came back to her. If they were out there, they would take her alive, because even if she had the nerve to take her own life, her pistol was with her runaway horse.

Maybe she was wrong. Maybe it was just the wind. Before that thought could bring her comfort, she heard the sound again, along with the clink of a horse's bridle. The hair at her nape prickled as fear seized her.

She crouched down behind a rock and pressed her back to it, shaking like a leaf in the wind. She wrapped her arms around drawn-up knees and made herself as small as she could.

It was quiet, except for the whistle of the wind and the splatter of raindrops on the rocks. Then she heard the creak of saddle leather as the rider dismounted. She knew it was a man, and she knew he was hunting her. She could feel it. Just below her rocks slid, rattling downhill.

He was climbing. And he was getting closer by the second. There was nowhere to hide.

In a flash, she made up her mind. If the man below meant to harm her, he wouldn't have an easy time of it. She picked up a good-sized rock and hefted it in her hand to judge its weight. Satisfied, she stood up, every muscle tensed, waiting. Lowering her arm to her side, she nestled the rock against her thigh, into the folds of her split riding skirt. When she got the chance, she'd bash him in the head as hard as she could and run.

The climber continued relentlessly. He was so near she could hear his heavy breathing. Shivers started in her upper body and spread to her arms and legs. She tensed her muscles; she made her body rigid. If she collapsed, she would be a sitting duck. Tanners never gave up, she told herself. Her best chance, maybe her only one, was to strike when he was unaware.

From a small opening between the rocks, she glimpsed him searching. In the downpour, she could only tell that he was big and dark. Then instinct took over. Taking a deep breath, she moved from her hiding place and lunged at him with her arm held high and the rock ready.

He threw up an arm to block her and grabbed her wrist. In a flash, his other fist stopped barely an inch from her chin.

"Cady?" The deep voice sounded blessedly, wonderfully, familiar.

"Kane? Is that you?"

"Yes." He took a deep, shuddering breath, then dropped her wrist and pushed his water-soaked hat back on his head.

Through the rain blurring her vision, she made out his dark hair plastered to his forehead, his eyes narrowed angrily, the strong jaw tightened so tensely the muscle in his cheek moved. He was angry. He was the most beautiful sight she had ever seen.

She threw her arms around him. "I've never been so happy to see anyone in my whole life!"

He hesitated for a second. Then his arms came around her in a hug so fierce she could hardly draw breath. Cady thought he touched his lips to her hair, but she was so wet and cold she couldn't be sure. All she knew was that he was here and she was safe.

"What the hell were you thinking of to come out here?"

"What were you thinking of to come after me?"

"I was thinking to save your hide." His voice vibrated with fury, but she only burrowed closer.

For the rest of her life, she could have stayed within his embrace, pressed to that wide chest which made her feel protected, made her feel nothing could harm her. He could yell at her, but compared to the dangers all around, it would be like a Sunday picnic. She sighed and pushed away from him. It would be best to get the lecture over with.

"You know why I had to do this." She ran splayed fingers through her wet hair, lifting it away from her face. When her palm grazed the knot on her forehead, she winced. "Ouch."

His eyes narrowed. "What's wrong? Are you hurt?"

She touched the tender spot carefully. "Just a bump. Nothing serious."

"I was afraid—"

Something flashed into his eyes as he assessed her. His gaze seemed to dart over every part of her face as if taking inventory, assuring himself that she was all right.

Unexpectedly, a slow smile turned up the corners of his mouth. "I notice you tried to crack my skull with a rock this time instead of running me through with a hatpin."

"It was all I had." What if she'd had her gun? She shivered at the thought. "Oh, my God. I could have shot you."

His smile faded and a frown took its place. "Why the hell didn't you stay put? That redheaded little scoundrel—" There was a note of exasperation in his voice. "I can't believe the two of you pulled this off. But apparently John Eagle convinced R. J. that he'd made a mistake. I caught them sneaking out after you."

"Really?" That surprised her. "How sweet of them!"

"Sweet? It was stupid, irresponsible, and foolhardy. And that's just them. I haven't even started on you yet."

"You have no right to tell me—"

"I have every right. But not now. We have more important things to think about."

He was right about one thing: now wasn't the time to talk. She was miserably wet and getting more chilled by the second. The temperature in the mountains was a lot cooler than the desert, and it was dropping steadily.

"You can yell at me all you want, but would you mind if we found someplace to get warm first?" She pointed to the rocks above them. "I think there's a cave up there. I was climbing up to see when I heard you. If it's not deep, at least the overhang will give us some protection."

"I saw it too. I was hoping you'd had enough sense to get out of the rain."

Kane was so angry he'd hardly felt the rain, but now he could see her teeth were beginning to chatter. A flash of admiration sliced through him. She had to have been half out of her mind with fear, but she hadn't lost her head. She'd been thinking, looking for shelter. But what kind of chance would she have stood without supplies? He pushed the thought away. It brought up things he didn't want to think about.

He knew the storm would have made the Verde River impassable by now, so he had no choice but to see if there was a place to get warm and dry.

He moved in front of her. "I'll go first."

He climbed up over the slippery stones, stopping frequently to check on her over his shoulder. At the top, they found a cave about twelve feet deep. Even if the wind picked up, they could stay reasonably dry. In the dim light, he could see pieces of wood scattered around the pebble-strewn dirt floor. Branches of surrounding bushes and trees must have blown in. At least he could start a small fire, and there was enough kindling to keep it going through the night. He looked at Cady. Maybe he should let her do it.

He pulled a match wrapped in oilskin from his pants pocket and held it out to her. "Make yourself useful. Start a fire."

"With one match?" She took it and gave him a doubtful look.

"More than that is a waste. This is the frontier. Sometimes one chance is all you get." He took off his wet hat, set it on a rock, and ran his fingers through his hair.

She started gathering kindling. "What are you going to do?"

"I have to take care of the horses."

"You found mine?"

He nodded. "Then I'll bring some supplies up here."

"By the time you get back, I'll have a nice fire going."

"Be careful, Cady. Don't use your clothes this time."

She met his gaze and grinned. "Even if I wanted to, they're too wet to burn."

He couldn't help smiling as he left her. Down below, Kane concealed Soldier Boy and Cady's bay in a group of rocks and spread branches from a paloverde tree to keep them enclosed. He made sure the animals had feed. Then he grabbed the two canteens, threw saddlebags and blankets over his shoulder, and climbed back up to the cave. If there were renegades nearby, they would have taken shelter too. Revenge could wait for dry weather.

He handed her one of the canteens. "You must be thirsty."

"I am," she said. She took the container from him and began to gulp eagerly.

"Just a little at first. You'll make yourself sick." He took it back.

"Thank you." She wiped the back of her hand across her mouth and pointed to the flames, dancing and casting shadows on the cave walls.

"I didn't set myself on fire," Cady said. "Kane, for goodness' sake, you're soaked. Come over by the fire right away and get warm."

He shook his head, flinging droplets of water from his hair. "There's more to do."

"How can I help?" she asked.

He unrolled the blankets and, finding they were pretty dry, laid them over the rocks to get warm. Then he handed her the saddlebags. "Go through these and see what we need."

As he worked, he glanced at her, then forced his gaze away. A few minutes later, he looked at her again as she knelt by the fire. The flames highlighted her fine cheekbones. Her delicate skin was red and chapped from wind and cold. Wet hair cascaded around her face. She was the most beautiful thing he'd ever seen. There weren't many women who could have gone through what she had today and still look so damned appealing.

In spite of the fire, she was shivering. She had taken off her wet jacket. Beneath it, her blouse was soaked with water. The material molded to her breasts, showing him the soft curves in more detail than he wanted to handle.

His gut tensed, but this time it wasn't from fear for her. It was fear for himself. He knew they had to get warm and dry quickly; he knew what they had to do. He wasn't sure he could survive it.

He was alone with her, and it was about to get worse.

He cleared his throat. "Cady, we have to get out of these wet clothes." He unbuttoned his shirt and slipped it off. Heat radiating from the fire warmed his skin.

She glanced up and her gaze lowered to his chest. She swallowed hard before glancing up at his face again. "It wouldn't be proper."

"There are times when you're settling the frontier that circumstances force you to put aside certain rules. You can't afford to get sick. We may be stuck here for a while. A rain like this will flood the riverbed between us and the fort. We may not be able to cross for a couple of days." Even as he explained the reality of their situation to her, he prayed for the strength to keep his distance.

Why in God's name hadn't he put in for a transfer the moment he knew she planned to stay in the West? Because he was arrogant enough to believe he had the situation under control. What a joke. He had about as much command over his feelings for her as he did over the heavens pouring water down on them right this minute.

She sighed. "You're right. I know that. But it's hard to disregard my upbringing."

"Just pretend it's an order. It's not hard for you to disregard those." He turned his back. "Take off everything and wrap up in a blanket."

She sighed. "All right."

Behind him, he heard her drag a blanket to the farthest corner of the cave. It wasn't nearly far enough, not by a long shot.

She dropped first one and then the other boot. He didn't know about her, but he was getting warmer by the second.

"Kane?"

"Hmm?" Good, he thought. Talk to me. Distract me. He couldn't afford to think about what she was doing.

"I'm going to find Jack tomorrow."

That distracted him, all right. "Like hell you are. I'm taking you back to the fort."

"But you just said we may not be able to get across the river."

"We're damn well going to try."

"So you can lock me in the guardhouse again?"

"If I have to."

"I'll get out."

"I'll keep the only key and stand guard myself." He heard the slap of her wet skirt as it slid against her legs on the way down. His breathing grew faster. He wasn't sure if it was because he was mad as hell or because he wanted to kiss her senseless. Or both.

"Kane, just give me a day or two. You could help me. We could look for my brother and warn him. Then I'll go back with you. I swear I won't give you another minute of trouble."

"Your middle name is trouble."

"No, it's Elizabeth." She grunted. "Damn these buttons."

He couldn't help smiling. She was a lady even when she was swearing. He started to turn toward her, and the grin instantly disappeared as he stopped himself. He had to be on guard even when she wasn't locked up. Especially when she wasn't locked up.

"What's the matter?" he asked.

"I can't get my blouse off." Her voice was muffled, as if she was twisting in her struggle to unfasten it.

"Why not?"

She sighed impatiently. "It's sopping wet, my hands are ice cold, and the buttons are impossible. Will you please help me?"

She had no idea what she was asking. Knowing she was undressing right behind him and listening to her clothes fall was bad enough. Now she wanted him to help. He had to look at her to do that. It was more than he could handle.

"Just rip the thing," he said harshly.

"I will not rip a perfectly good piece of clothing." She sniffed. "I have no way to repair it and nothing else to put on. You keep quoting the rules of survival to me. It's only common sense that one should protect one's few possessions."

He gritted his teeth and turned around. "Let me have a look."

She moved by the fire and presented her back to him. Smoke curled up and burned his nostrils. The ventilation wasn't great but enough smoke escaped that they could get by. In her pantalettes, high-necked blouse, and bare feet, she was probably the most appealing sight he'd seen since—since he'd made her lift her skirts to make sure she wasn't burned.

"Why in hell are you always wet and half undressed when we're together?"

She stiffened. "You're exaggerating."

He stared at the row of tiny buttons that marched up her back. She had managed the ones at the neck and shoulder blades and the ones at her waist, but not the six or seven in the middle.

The seductive curve of her backside, covered only by her pantalettes, made him ache to fit his hands there. Just below her neck, silky exposed skin beckoned to him. He wanted to taste the spot right in the middle of her back and feel the shiver he knew he could arouse.

He shook his head to clear it. "Why in tarnation would you wear something like this?" he asked angrily.

"I know you think I don't have a brain in my head, but I'll have you know I gave careful consideration to my clothing for this trip. This blouse is a dark color so as not to draw attention to me, and it's a heavyweight material because temperatures drop in the mountains."

"You should have worn something with big buttons down the front."

"I didn't know it was going to rain. Would you please stop shilly-shallying and help me undo this before I catch my death?" A shudder from the cold ran through her from shoulder to knee.

She was right again. He had to get her out of her clothes before she caught a chill. He lifted his hands to the buttons and cursed inwardly because he was shaking badly.

He got the first one, but the second was stuck in the wet material. Between that and the fact that every time his fingers grazed her soft skin they wouldn't work right, he was having a devil of a time. It didn't help either that his eyes kept straying to the seductive swell of her backside.

"I told you it was hard," she said, turning her head to peek over her shoulder.

"Hold still." He took a deep breath and finished the job as fast as he could. When it was done, the sides of the garment drifted apart and the back of her chemise was freed to his gaze.

The blatant femininity of that small piece of material slammed him hard. Sweat broke out again on his forehead.

He took a step back. "It's done. Finish up and put a blanket around you."

Instead, Cady turned around. She was awed by his stark masculinity. He stood by the fire, and the light from the flames highlighted his magnificence, stealing her breath. She clutched the blouse to her front with trembling hands.

"Thank you, Kane," she whispered. She continued to stare at him, unable to tear her gaze away.

His hair was wet, dark and wavy from the rain. Wide, powerful shoulders and broad bare chest tapered to a flat midsection, and his wet trousers molded to his muscular legs.

His eyes darkened and their intensity grew until she felt she could reach out and touch it. She swayed toward him.

"No." He shook his head and took a step back. "Cady, don't you dare look at me like that."

"Like what?"

"Like the sun rises and sets on me," he said. "I've made so many mistakes in my life. I won't let you be another." He sighed. "Don't tempt me. I'm not the right man for you. You can't depend—"

She lifted her chin. "I can so depend on you. Don't tell me I can't. Who came after me to see that I was all right?"

"You have no idea what kind of danger you're in, now that I've found you."

"You would never hurt me."

"I can hurt you in ways you can't even imagine."

She shook her head. "You're wrong, Kane. Why are you so hard on yourself? I trust you."

She wanted to be with him and love him, more than she'd ever thought possible. This was right. She knew it in her heart; she felt it in her soul. She had come back to the Territory because of him. Fate had stepped in and crossed their paths.

"If you truly trust me, Cady, you're a fool."

"I've done some foolish things in my life. Who hasn't? But this isn't one of them."

She tugged first one cuff and then the other free of her hands and dropped her blouse to the dirt floor of the cave. Standing before him in chemise and pantalettes, she felt her cheeks grow warm. Her embarrassment melted away when she saw a spark light his eyes as he looked at her. His gaze lowered to her breasts, then fell to her waist and, finally, to the place where her thighs joined, covered only by her soaked pantalettes. His lips parted slightly and he groaned.

She moved nearer, not quite touching him but close enough to feel the warmth from his body. Looking up at him, she knew her face reflected the need inside her that refused to be denied.

His chest rose with a quick intake of breath. "Don't, Cady. I'm no good for you. Don't start something you can't finish. Isn't that what your father said?"

She didn't understand why he was convinced that loving him would harm her. Today she had been alone in the wilderness and had faced the fact that her life could end at any time. What if it happened tomorrow and she never experienced the joy of showing him how much she loved him? She couldn't bear the thought.

"I don't care what my father said." She closed her eyes for a split second, pulling her emotions together so she could fill her words with what was in her heart. Somehow she had to make him understand that he was a good man. "You told me that sometimes a person only gets one chance. I want it, with you. I want to be with you. I want to love you." She put a hand on his chest and felt the shudder that rippled through him. "Please, Kane."

"God, Cady. You shouldn't be doing this."

Easier said than done. She had never felt anything more wonderful than his lips pressed to hers. Today she had learned at first hand how cruel this land was. What if the Apaches found them tomorrow? What if they never made it back to the fort? What if Kane was the only man she ever met who made her want to kiss him?

"You're right, of course." She looked up at him. "Kane? Would you do something for me?"

"Sure."

"Will you kiss me?" He started to shake his head. "It doesn't have to mean anything. I know you don't feel the same way about me that I do about you. But I liked it so much when you kissed me before."

"Cady—"

"I was so afraid today." With an effort, she kept her voice steady. "I thought I'd never see you again. And it's just that—"

Memories of today's pain, terror, isolation, and regret mixed together and pressed against her heart. Her vision blurred as the moisture gathered. Angrily she brushed a knuckle to the corner of her eye to catch the single teardrop that escaped. She didn't want his pity. She started to turn away from him.

"It's just that you're the only man I've ever wanted to kiss me."

He groaned, and the anguish in the sound didn't escape her. Unexpectedly, he reached out and wrapped his strong fingers around her, turning her. "All right, Cady. You win. One kiss."

He curved his other arm around her waist and nestled her against his long, lean form. Then he lowered his head. She slowly closed her eyes. His soft lips pressed to her own and her sigh was muffled by his mouth. She moaned at the sweetness of it and her breathing quickened; then his arms tensed and tightened, pulling her closer.

When he lifted his head and stared at her, his own breathing was ragged, his eyes full of fire. "You were right. I do want you, Cady. I can't fight it anymore."

"Then don't. Love me, Kane. And let me love you."

He nodded, and together they drifted down to sit together beside the flames.

12

Kane stared into Cady's passion-glazed eyes and knew he was lost. But he couldn't find it in him to care. The storm outside created a dull roar. Surprisingly, a sense of peace settled over him. He felt as if he and Cady were the only two people in the world. Since the first time he had seen her, whatever had sparked between them had been so strong, he knew this moment was inevitable.

Face-to-face in the golden interior of the cave, they held hands loosely. Cady's were ice cold. Her hair, like a curtain of light brown silk, cascaded around her face and spilled over her breasts. Her green eyes were large and apprehensive. Her mouth trembled until she took the corner of her bottom lip between her teeth.

He squeezed her fingers reassuringly. "Don't be afraid."

"I'm not." She spoke too quickly, too breathlessly.

"We can stop right now, if you want. We can pretend—"

She shook her head and the movement caught the

fire's light, turning the blond streaks in her hair to burnished gold. "I can't pretend. Not anymore. I have a confession to make."

"A confession?" His gut clenched.

"I came to Arizona for three reasons. The first, as I told you, was to teach and prove I could take care of myself."

He sat back on his heels. "I remember."

"Second, I left home to get away from all the gossip after I broke off my engagement."

"Why didn't you go through with it?" He held his breath, waiting for her answer.

"There's more I didn't tell you. I couldn't even kiss another man after you. How could I marry him?"

He couldn't have been more stunned if she had told him she'd bedded another man. At the same time, a primal satisfaction swelled inside him.

Cady had saved herself for him.

She hadn't so much as kissed another man. Kane knew he didn't deserve a woman like her. That kind of loyalty should belong to a better man than he. He almost backed away from her. But the mixture of passion and promise in her eyes stopped him. It would take a stronger man than he to walk away from her now.

"What was the third reason you came out here?" He asked the question, but he knew what she was going to say.

"Because of you."

He shook his head slowly. "Cady, I—"

She lifted one hand from her lap and touched a finger to his lips to silence him. "It's all right. I'm not asking for promises you can't give. After today, I believe what you were trying to tell me. This land is too wild and uncertain to make vows lightly." She cupped his cheek in her palm, and he moved slightly to place a soft kiss in the center of it. She shivered and closed her eyes for a moment. "I want to be with you as a woman. I've never been more sure of anything in my life."

"All right. I won't question you again." One corner of his mouth lifted slightly. "But you're still afraid." She started to shake her head, and he took her face in his hands. "You're not a good liar, Cady."

"I am, a little. But not of you. Or—or this, at least not much. It's because I don't know what to do. I'm afraid you'll be disappointed."

He smiled, a big joyful grin. The past and the future didn't matter. There was just the present. The scents of smoke, rain, damp earth, man, and woman wove a sensuous spell around them. At this moment, nothing mattered to him but Cady and making her happy.

"You couldn't disappoint me."

"How can you be so sure?" The whispered question and the uncertainty in her eyes betrayed the agony of her inexperience.

He lifted her heavy hair away from her face and settled it over her shoulders. "Because I'm going to teach you how to please me."

She smiled a little. "So I'm the student and you're the teacher?"

"For now."

"What does that mean?"

"You'll find out." He took her hands and pulled her to a kneeling position. They were close, barely touching, and he could feel the warmth from her body. The lace from her chemise tickled his chest. He took her face in his hands again. Her breathing increased, sweetly washing over him, and he nodded with satisfaction. "Something tells me you'll pick this up as fast as you learned to shoot and start fires."

"But, Kane, what if—"

"The first lesson is not to talk so much." He lowered

his mouth to hers, slid his hands into the lush mass of her hair, and closed his hands around the silky strands. Slowly, he tugged her head back. The long slender column of her neck was bared to him, and he kissed her just beneath her ear. He trailed kisses down to her collarbone and, with his tongue, caressed the rapidly beating pulse there.

He had known passion before, but that was nothing compared to the hunger inside him now. Only sheer effort of will kept him from tumbling her to the ground and taking her right away.

She moaned. "Oh, Kane. That feels so—so—"

He smiled against her skin. "I can't believe you're speechless."

"I thought you were going to show me what you like."

"I am showing you."

"But I—you—" She blinked at him, her eyes puzzled yet full of fire.

"I like to touch you. I like to kiss you. I like it that I put that expression in your eyes and made you look at me the way you do now."

"How am I looking at you?" she asked breathlessly.

"As if you want me."

He slid his hands down to her small waist, to the bottom of her chemise. Taking hold, he lifted slightly, waiting for her to stop him if she was frightened. She hesitated several moments, reminding him of her innocence; then she raised her arms. The movement nearly drove him out of his mind.

He pulled the garment over her head. Bare from the waist up, with her hair tangled and wild about her face, Cady was the most beautiful thing he'd ever seen. He pulled her into his arms, against his chest, skin to skin, soft curves to firm muscle, tender to rough. The hard ache in his groin told him how desperately he needed to bury himself in her softness. Concern for her held him back.

Cady closed her eyes. In spite of Kane's gentle manner and reassuring words, she was a little frightened. She reminded herself this was Kane, the man she had waited so long for. She looked at him, and the admiration in his eyes chased away any lingering doubt or self-consciousness. This was right. She wrapped her arms around his neck and pressed herself to him. Against her naked breasts, his skin was cool and damp from the rain. The hair on his chest tickled, making her nipples erect. He curved his arms around her and held her tight for several moments, as they savored the sweetness of being close.

Then he lowered her to the scratchy wool blanket. Beneath it, the hard ground pressed into her back. He touched his mouth to hers, and the day's stubble on his cheek and jaw scraped a little. Then he moved, slowly at first, until he deepened the kiss, creating sparks that set her whole body on fire.

She touched her tongue to his upper lip and he sucked in his breath. He opened his mouth, letting her inside, and the kiss grew more intense, more hungry. It was as if he was starving for her. She knew the feeling and kissed him back with everything she'd been saving over the last two years.

He lifted up, taking his weight on his elbows, and looked at her. "You learn fast, lady."

"You're a good teacher." Her voice was a whisper.

A slow smile turned up the corners of his mouth and sent the blood racing through her veins. Her heart pounded against her ribs. Then he lowered his head to her breast and took the peak in his mouth. The warmth created by his lips swept over her skin like wildfire. He stroked the sensitive tip with his tongue and she almost came up off the ground, the sensation was so powerful.

Never in her life had she felt anything as wonderful. She writhed against him, searching for a way to release the tight core of need coiled low in her belly.

"Kane." His name was nothing more than a sigh of pleasure on her lips.

"What, love?"

"I don't know how much more of your teaching I can stand."

"Am I hurting you?"

"No. I just feel like I'm coming apart inside and I-I don't know what to do."

"There's a lot more to learn."

"Then teach me—fast," she said breathlessly.

"Is that an order?"

"Oh, yes!"

"Consider this a salute." He kissed her again.

He worked loose the knotted ties at the waist of her pantalettes and pushed them down her legs and away. He swept his hand up her thigh, caressed her belly, then slid his fingers lower until they touched her woman's place.

She started at the contact and pressed her legs together. He froze, then pulled his hand away.

"Do you want me to stop?" he asked gently.

"No!" She reached up a hand and cupped his cheek tenderly. Stubbly whiskers brushed her palm. Doubt darkened his light brown eyes. "I'm sorry, Kane. It's just that—I told you—it's not easy for me."

"I'm glad this isn't easy for you."

Her eyes widened. "You are?"

He nodded. "It makes me proud that you chose me, that you trust me." He stopped and swallowed hard. "God knows why, love, but you do. I'll do my best not to let you down."

"I know." She smiled as she caressed his face, then traced his ear with her finger.

He sucked in his breath. Then he grinned down at her. "Are you sure you've never done this before?"

"As God is my witness, I swear."

"But you always swear like a lady," he said, nuzzling the sensitive spot just below her ear.

Then he kissed her on the lips, and the sound she made was part sigh, part moan, pure pleasure. He rolled away from her, and she missed the warmth of his body as he slipped off the rest of his clothes. When he was beside her again, he slid one arm beneath her and pulled her close, so that they lay on their sides facing each other. She felt his hardness pressing into her. His blatant maleness both shocked and excited her.

She watched him as his gaze traveled up and down her body. As the firelight flickered over his face, outlining the hard angles and planes, she could see the desire glowing in his eyes.

This time when he touched her at the juncture of her thighs, she didn't shy away. He slipped a finger inside her and the movement was like a bolt of lightning crackling through her body, leaving every part of her tingling.

As a need she didn't quite understand grew inside her, Cady arched against him. Her chest rose and fell rapidly as her breathing increased.

"Teach me now, Kane. I can't wait."

"Yes, ma'am," he said. "Your wish is my command."

He parted her thighs and levered himself above her, then settled between her legs. Slowly and carefully, he nudged his hardness against her soft, unyielding female core. He approached her warmth slowly, letting her become accustomed to the feel of him.

"I'm sorry," he whispered. "I have to hurt you. Just once. I'll make it up to you."

With a swift thrust, he buried himself inside her. There was one sharp stab of pain. Cady closed her eyes tightly and bit her lip until it passed. Kane held her close without moving.

"Are you all right?" he asked.

She looked at him, and his expression of misery and concern tugged at her heart, making her love him more.

She smiled reassuringly. "I'm fine. There's no pain now."

She began to move her hips, to prove it to him. To her surprise, the sensation was wonderful. This intimacy with a man was so exquisite, it brought tears to her eyes. She wanted to give something back to him, to show him how she felt.

Sensing that he was holding himself in check to keep from hurting her, Cady arched toward him to meet his tentative lunges. Her movements inflamed him. He groaned and placed his hands, palm down, on either side of her head. His breathing labored, he moved in a steady rhythm that created a coil of tension low in her belly.

As his thrusts came faster, the knot of need inside her expanded. It grew until she went still. Pulsations of pleasure radiated from where their bodies joined, outward to her arms and legs. With her eyes tightly closed, she saw only flashes of gold and orange and red as sensation took over her body. She couldn't tell if it lasted moments or a lifetime. She only knew it was the most extraordinary feeling she'd ever experienced.

She opened her eyes and wondered at the look of intensity in his just before he lowered his mouth to hers. He began to move within her again until his body tensed and he threw his head back. Cady gripped his wide forearms as he called out his release and spilled his seed inside her. He took the majority of his weight on his arms and rested his forehead to hers. She held him as he shuddered. When he was still and spent, he rolled away from her and rested on his back. He slid an arm beneath her shoulders and pulled her close, then drew the extra blanket over them.

She snuggled against his warmth. "If all lessons were that pleasurable, I'd still be in school."

He laughed, and she felt the vibration of the deep sound in his chest. He touched his lips to her forehead. "You're not the only one who learned something. Behind that refined exterior beats the heart of a passionate lady."

She smiled, then sighed, and her eyelids fluttered sleepily. Her weariness was bone deep and she couldn't seem to keep her eyes open.

Outside the cave rain still poured down, resounding, relentless. The noise somehow made her feel safe and secure. Within seconds, she was sound asleep.

Kane wasn't as fortunate.

He looked down at her and smiled tenderly as he brushed the hair away from her face. "Cady, love," he whispered.

She mumbled and her lids fluttered as she squirmed against his side, instinctively burrowing into the warmth of his body until she was more comfortable. Her small movement made him distinctly uncomfortable. He wanted her again. God help him. Would this one time with her be enough?

Some part of his soul said no. Another part told him it would have to be.

Taking her was wrong. He wouldn't let her be a part of his life. He couldn't take her again. He hadn't sunk so low that he could forget two wrongs never made a right. If he walked away from her now, all she'd lost was her innocence; if he asked her to stay, she would lose her life.

Maybe not right away. But eventually this desert land, being uprooted, moving from post to post, the boredom, the isolation, all would take a toll. It would suck the joy out of Cady's sweet soul. Annie had paid the ultimate price. He wouldn't let that happen to Cady.

He gently traced her delicate jaw with his finger. "No matter what you said, you'll feel bad about giving yourself to me without benefit of vows. You'll want me to make an honest woman of you, Cady Tanner." She sighed in her sleep, and he touched his lips to her forehead. "I hope in time you'll understand what I have to do. For your own good, I can't marry you."

When Cady awoke, the first thing she heard was the quiet. It took her a moment to realize the rain had stopped. There was sunlight beyond the cave opening. Kane stood there with his back to her, leaning a shoulder against the rock. Her heart pounded at the sight of him.

She stretched and groaned as every muscle in her body ached. Between her legs, a very different sort of discomfort reminded her of what they had done. She tried to shrug off the knot of guilt that tightened in her stomach, but she couldn't. The fact was, she would never be the same again.

She didn't regret her night with Kane. She had never felt more alive in her life. It was just difficult to forget twenty-one years of rules, regulations, and moral teaching. But she would. She'd told Kane she didn't want promises he couldn't freely make. And she had meant it.

She sat and pulled up the blanket to cover her naked breasts. "Kane?"

He was dressed, with the tail of his uniform shirt hanging over the waistband of his pants. He glanced over but didn't move to touch her. "Morning."

His gaze slid away. The line of his shoulders was tense, and she wondered if he had regrets.

"It stopped raining," she said, trying to make conversation.

He nodded. "Looks like another storm's coming, though." His voice was tight, clipped.

She stood up, wrapped the blanket around her, and moved to stand beside him. Fragments of rock on the cave floor bit into the tender soles of her bare feet. Outside, drops of water glistened in the branches of the junipers. The air was crisp and cool, the sky above blue. But Kane was right. As she stood beside him, she saw the clouds of an approaching thunderhead gathered, black and billowing in the distance.

"What are we going to do?" She clutched the blanket tightly at her neck.

His eyes mirrored the approaching storm. "Get dressed, Cady."

Each word was like a knife pricking her heart. He was angry at her. What right did he have? She had given herself to him without asking for anything in return. Because she loved him.

"Blast you, Kane Carrington, what do you have to be angry about?"

"You're imagining things," he said, his tone cool.

"How dare you treat me like a stranger after we—after what we—well, you know what I mean."

He slapped the boulder with the flat of his hand; the sound made her jump. "I thought you understood that I wasn't making any promises," he said furiously. His indifference was gone in a heartbeat.

She took a step back, then lifted her chin and glared at him. "May I remind you that I'm the one who's ruined."

"I can't marry you."

"Who asked you to?"

"That's what you're getting at, isn't it? Why are you so fired up about marriage all of a sudden?"

"Me? You're the one who brought it up."

"I told you right off that I was married once before and I'd never subject another woman to army life."

"Why, Kane? Because she was unfaithful?"

"I don't blame her for that."

"You should. But if you don't, it doesn't make sense. Why are you so set against sharing your life with someone?"

A look of soul-wrenching pain leaped into his eyes before he could shutter them. But he didn't say anything.

Cady sighed. "I once told you I wouldn't ask any questions about your wife. But now I think I have a right to know. You're not married, but she still has a claim on you? Where is she?"

"She's dead. Murdered by Apaches."

"Dead?" Cady's eyes grew round. "What—" She took a deep breath. "It's obvious you blame yourself. You must tell me why."

"When her infidelity was discovered, her lover was court-martialed. None of the other women would speak to her. She finally left the fort in disgrace."

"You mustn't blame yourself for that." She reached an arm through her blanket and touched his arm. "Everyone suffers the consequences of their actions. She made her own choices."

He shook his head. "Don't you see? Because of my job I was away on patrol a good part of the time. She was alone and going out of her mind from boredom. I drove her into the arms of another man."

"There are other ways to relieve monotony besides— that. And as for the Indians—you had nothing to do with her death."

He looked down at her with an intensity she could almost feel. "If she hadn't married me, she'd be alive today. This land is not for the faint of heart. I told you from the beginning you didn't belong here. You should have taken a safe teaching job back east."

Teaching! Her eyes grew round. Who would let her near their children now? Had he realized that before he—before they—?

"Did you bed me so you could have me fired from my teaching post?" As soon as the words left her lips his expression turned hard, as if she had betrayed him in the worst possible way, and she wished she could take back what she'd said.

"I did everything I could to talk you out of what we did last night."

She hated that he was right and wanted to apologize for accusing him. The most humiliating part was that she had practically begged him to take her. Practically, nothing. She *had* begged.

"You're right. But that doesn't change the fact that I'm ruined."

"Would you quit saying that? You're not ruined."

"Yes, I am." She did her best to control it, but her lips trembled. She was afraid. She was taking it out on him. She knew it and she couldn't seem to stop. "Not that I mind," she added quickly. "Not really."

Pain—deep, dark, desperate—flashed across his face, sharpening the angles, forging more shadows. "You're better off without me, Cady." His voice was hard.

She lifted her chin. "You're damm right. I *am* better off. I wouldn't marry you if you were the last man on earth."

It was nearing sundown when they returned from the Verde River after confirming what Kane already knew: After the rain it was too deep and dangerous to cross. He couldn't leave Cady alone, so she had gone with him. And the devil of it was that another storm had moved in and they were soaked all over again. At this rate, they'd be stuck here half naked forever.

He built a fire while she huddled in a blanket. Still in his wet clothes, he scattered hers over the rocks to dry.

She had been quiet all day, upset about their fight that morning. Kane knew he should have been glad she wouldn't have him, but somewhere deep inside a part of him died. He started to say something to her when he heard the sound of rocks sliding below them.

He looked at Cady, her wide eyes telling him she hadn't missed the noise.

"Get back," he said, pointing to the rear of the cave. "Behind that rock."

"Give me a gun."

Admiring her courage, he grabbed the Colt from her saddlebag. Quickly, he flipped open the chamber, spun the cylinder to check the load, then held it out to her.

"There's six bullets. Make sure you save one."

Fear swirled in her eyes, but she nodded, walked behind the boulder, and huddled down in her blanket.

Kane grabbed his own revolver and moved to the cave opening, careful to keep himself hidden from whoever was out there. Sliding rocks and dirt told him the man made no attempt to hide his approach. Then a long shadow crept across the ledge in front of him. In spite of the brisk air, sweat beaded on his forehead.

The shadow stopped and Kane cocked his gun.

"I know someone's in there." The voice sounded familiar to Kane, but he stayed under cover.

Cady gasped and stood up. "Jack!"

"Cady, stay down," Kane called out.

She moved from behind her rock, tripping slightly over her blanket. "But it's Jack!"

"Cady? That you in there?"

"Yes, Jack."

With his thumb, Kane eased the hammer forward and lowered his gun to his side. Tanner had grown a beard since they'd last seen each other, or he'd have recognized him. Cady had known him instantly from his voice.

She moved forward, through the small arc of the cave opening, and stopped in front of her brother. "I'm so happy to see you, Jack!" She started to lift her arms and hug him, but she couldn't and maintain her modesty.

Jack hefted a rifle in his right hand, and Kane noticed the disapproval on the other man's face when he took in his sister's state of undress. He could imagine what Tanner was thinking, seeing her clad only in a blanket.

"I'm so happy to see you, Jack." Cady said again. "I'm so glad you're all right."

"'Course I am."

"How did you find us?"

"I was headed back to the fort and looking for shelter from the rain. Smelled the smoke from your fire and found the horses down below. I saw the army brand on them and knew it was safe to come up."

He looked down at her, then glared hard at Kane. "You're supposed to be looking after my sister, Carrington. There are renegade Indians on the loose. What are you doing out here with her, in the middle of nowhere?"

Kane saw the frown on her face when Cady looked up at her brother. "Jack, listen."

Jack never glanced at her. "Carrington, this is a dangerous place for a wedding trip, and pretty irresponsible if you ask me. But if you aren't married to my sister, you're in a hell of a lot of trouble."

13

Cady watched the two men eye each other like warring wildcats. She had to do something before her brother really lost his temper.

"For pity's sake, Jack, calm down," she said.

"I'm not talking to you." Jack narrowed his gaze on Kane. "You didn't answer my question, Carrington. You married? Or is my sister standing there, wearing practically nothing, in front of a man who's not her husband?"

"You had *better* start talking to me," Cady said, even as she self-consciously tightened her grip on her blanket. "And the answer is no."

"No what? I can see that you're wearing only—"

"No, we're not married. But you don't need to get so excited."

Kane set his gun down on a rock, then stood up straight, tall and strong, not backing down in the face of her brother's displeasure. Cady's heart swelled with pride and love. It didn't matter that all day she had wanted to throttle him with her bare hands.

Kane stood a foot away from Jack. "Stay out of this, Cady. This is between your brother and me."

"There's no way I'm staying out of this," she said.

"So you're taking the blame, Carrington?" Jack said, completely ignoring her. He cradled his rifle in his arms like a newborn baby.

"If there's any blame to be had, it's mine," Cady said, looking at first one man and then the other. "I came out here on my own to find you. None of this is Kane's fault."

"I take full responsibility." Kane met the other man's gaze squarely, also disregarding her.

"My father always said a man who apologizes when there's no need knows something you don't." Jack's eyes were black as coal.

Kane calmly met his look. "That was no apology, Tanner. It's a fact."

Cady moved forward and gripped a handful of her brother's linen shirt. "*Listen* to me, Jack!"

He looked down at her, and she knew she finally had his attention. She shivered as a chill wind found its way inside her blanket to her bare skin.

"Let's go inside by the fire. Are you hungry? I know I am. I was just about to make some coffee."

"You plan to put some clothes on first?"

She looked down. "About my clothes. You see, Jack, this is what happened. I came to look for you because Cuchillo has sworn to kill you, to get even with you for taking his brother's life."

Jack's jaw looked hard as the rock ledge they stood on. He took a step toward Kane. "You brought her out here knowing there's Indian trouble? I ought to break your neck."

Cady pressed her hand against her brother's chest. "For pity sake, Jack! That's not the way it happened. Will you please calm down and listen?"

Jack shot Kane a deadly look. "I'm all ears."

"Kane didn't bring me out here. In fact, he locked me in the guardhouse to keep me from leaving the fort. I came by myself. You were in trouble and I came to warn you. He followed after me because he was worried about me."

"That's the truth?" He studied her carefully, to see if she was lying.

"I swear it. I love you, Jack. You're my brother. I couldn't stand by and do nothing, knowing there was an Indian somewhere who's sworn to kill you. I was afraid for you." Her voice caught and she bit her lip.

"Sounds like my little sister," Jack said, and his expression softened. It lasted until he looked at Kane. "If you locked her up, how'd she get out?"

Cady released his shirt. "R. J. helped me. You know him, don't you? Major Wexler's son." She sucked air between her teeth as she shivered again. "It's chilly up here in the mountains. I thought I'd never be cold again."

"So why are you standing there in a blanket?"

Cady looked down at her bare feet. Jack had always been able to read her easily, and the last thing she wanted was for him to know what had happened the night before. She turned away from him as she felt the flush that crept into her cheeks.

"What's wrong, Cady?" Jack's voice was hard.

"Not a blessed thing. I'm wearing a blanket because my clothes are soaked. Last night it took hours just for my underthings to dry."

She heard the words and too late wished to have them back. She whirled around, and even in the deepening shadows she could see Jack eyeing Kane with nothing short of murder in his expression.

"What were you wearing during the night?" Jack asked. If his tone was hard before, this time it was like steel.

"A blanket. My clothes were soaked from the rain.

I'd have caught my death if I didn't get out of them and let everything dry. It was a matter of survival, Jack."

The story was true as far as it went. Her brother didn't have to know the rest. He wouldn't understand.

Jack ran a knuckle gently over her cheekbone. His eyes smoldered with an emotion she didn't understand. It was especially puzzling when a hint of a tender smile lifted one corner of his mouth. "What happened last night, Cady?" he asked softly.

"Nothing much." Her gaze rose to the top of his shirt, just below his bearded chin. She couldn't quite look him in the eye. "I started a fire so we could get warm. Then we went to sleep."

"You never were a very good liar." He rested his rifle against a rock, took her upper arms, and kissed her forehead softly. "I'm sorry," he said gruffly.

Then he moved her out of the way, stood in front of Kane, and punched him in the eye. Cady was horrified.

Kane staggered back, then caught himself and raised his fists. "I don't want to fight you, Tanner. Let it go. What's done is done."

"So you admit you bedded my sister."

"I never denied it."

Jack moved forward as swiftly and gracefully as a cat. He grabbed the front of Kane's shirt with one hand and brought his fist back and punched him again.

"Jack, stop it!" Cady screamed, shocked at his violence.

Kane lowered his head and grabbed Jack around the waist so he couldn't land another blow. The two men struggled, each trying to get the upper hand.

"Stop it!" She was shouting at both of them and they ignored her, as usual. She moved forward and pulled on Jack's arm. The distraction made him drop his hold, allowing Kane to pull free.

Jack stood there for a moment with his boots braced

wide apart, breathing hard. He brushed his forearm across his forehead and glared at Kane. Then he leaped at the other man again and hit him in the mouth. Kane grabbed him again, and even to Cady it was obvious that he wasn't throwing punches. He was merely trying to contain the other man, to keep him from inflicting damage.

Once again she was proud of Kane. At the same time, she couldn't help feeling that if he hauled off and knocked Jack's teeth down his throat, she wouldn't have blamed him. But he didn't. The muscles in his arms bulged and strained against the material of his uniform as he exerted every ounce of energy trying to immobilize a man of his own size and strength. Their grunts and panting mingled together and echoed through the rocks.

Cady couldn't stand by and do nothing. She moved forward and grabbed Jack's ear, pulling as hard as she could.

"Ow!" he cried, reaching up to cover it. "Let go, Sis. What the hell are you doing?"

"There's a foolish boy sleeping in many a grown man you'd call sensible." Cady hung on and pulled until he went still. "That's something else Father used to say. But *I'm* telling you this: If you're going to act like a schoolboy, I'll treat you like a schoolboy. And I've had my share of practice with this sort of thing."

"Ow!" he cried when she yanked again. "Dammit, Sis, you made your point. You can let go now."

She glared at him. "Can I? Before I do, I want to make it quite clear that I don't need you to fight for my honor. Whatever happened or didn't happen between myself and Captain Carrington is my business. I will take care of it. I don't need you to behave like a ruffian on my behalf. I will not permit it."

"I get the message," he said, his head tilted to the side as she held his earlobe.

Kane watched brother and sister and admired the

hell out of Cady. Jack Tanner was over six feet tall. The top of her head barely reached the underside of his jaw, yet she had him at her mercy. He couldn't help smiling.

"At ease, Cady. Let him go. It's over. Right, Tanner? We'll handle it."

Jack nodded, then winced when she pinched his ear tighter.

"You haven't heard a word I've said, either of you." Cady glared from one man to the other. "What makes you think I want you to handle anything? There's nothing to handle. I want you to stop fighting, that's all."

"I won't lay another hand on him," Jack said, trying to ease out of her grasp.

"Do you swear?" Cady asked.

Jack nodded, then grimaced. "Let me go."

Cady released him and he backed away, standing beside Kane as he rubbed his ear.

She looked at both of them. Kane's split and bleeding lip made her wince and his eye was beginning to swell. She was partly to blame for what had happened and she felt guilty. But she pushed the feeling away. Second-guessing was a waste of time.

"Now then," she said. "I did what I set out to do. I found Jack and I warned him. I don't much care what the two of you do. But I'm going inside by the fire and make some coffee."

Kane watched the other man massage his sore ear and thought it prudent not to point out that her brother had found her, not the other way around. He met Tanner's gaze and knew, in spite of what Cady had said about taking care of herself, that her brother wasn't to be discouraged so easily.

Jack picked up his rifle and pointed the barrel at Kane's chest.

Cady gasped. "What in the world are you doing?"

"Sorry, Sis. If Father were here he'd be doing this instead of me. But it's got to be done." He looked at Kane. "Choose right, Carrington, and we'll have a wedding. Choose wrong and we'll have a funeral. Doesn't make much difference to me."

"You can't be serious, Jack!" Cady cried.

"Dead serious."

Cady stepped in front of Kane. "Then you'll have to shoot me first."

"You don't understand, Cady. Let me talk to Jack man to man." Kane settled his hands on her arms and tried to move her out of the way. She wouldn't budge.

"My future is at stake too. I will not have it decided without putting in my two cents." She glared at her brother. "The truth is, Jack, I refuse to marry him. You're going to have to shoot me. But heaven knows how you'll explain that to Mother."

Jack nodded thoughtfully. "Can't argue with that. But have you considered your reputation? You just spent the night alone with him. Everyone at the fort will know it. If you don't marry him, do you really think anyone will let you teach their children?"

She trembled and Kane squeezed her arms in a reassuring gesture. "The parents at the fort are glad to have me there to teach and they're happy with my performance. They wouldn't stop me."

"Are you sure?"

"Don't threaten her, Tanner."

"It's not a threat." Jack lifted his steely-eyed gaze to Kane. "And what do you suppose will happen to your career when Major Wexler hears about this?"

"The major knows I followed Cady to bring her back safely."

"Does he know you planned to bed her while you were at it?"

Kane's hands went still. "That's not the way it was."

"Doesn't matter. The major will see to it that you do the right thing by my sister, especially if my brother calls in some favors from his Washington contacts."

Cady went rigid. "I can't believe you'd do this to me. You're my brother, Jack. Don't you care about what I want? Don't you care what's best for me? Doesn't it matter to you that Kane and I don't love each other?"

"Some things are more important. Come hell or high water, there's going to be a wedding when we get back to the fort."

Kane sat behind his desk and looked up from his paperwork. His eye was not swollen so much, but now it was turning every shade of purple. He wished for the hundredth time that he'd put in for a transfer the day Cady had arrived. If it came through now, it would be too late.

Someone rapped sharply on his office door. "Come in," he said.

As if his thoughts had produced her, Cady stepped inside, slammed the door, and marched across the room and stopped in front of him. This was the first time he'd seen her since they'd returned the day before.

His gut clenched and his pulse quickened at the sight of her beautiful flushed face.

"Hello, Kane," she said.

"Cady. What are you doing here?"

"You have to put a stop to this wedding."

Stunned, Kane put down his pen.

"Why?"

She looked him straight in the eye. "Because you don't love me. And I"—her gaze lowered to just about the level of the button at the neck of his uniform"—I don't love you."

Jack was right. She was a lousy liar. She loved him, all right. She just wished she didn't.

An odd sense of loss came over him. She was a beautiful, spirited woman. She had risked her life to protect Jack, and Kane knew she would do the same for any other man she loved. If only he could be that man!

The fact remained, they were stuck with each other.

"There's more to consider besides love," he said.

"Like what?" She lifted her chin slightly.

"Like what you want more than anything else in the world. Do you know what that is, Cady?"

She hesitated, then said, "To teach."

"Then you have two choices. You can leave Fort McDowell and try to find another position without references. If you're asked why you left here, you'll have to tell them what happened."

"And my second choice is to marry you."

He nodded. "To protect your reputation."

"What if I don't?"

"Then none of the women on this post will give you the time of day, let alone allow you near their children."

She began to pace restlessly. She stopped, looked out the window, then turned back to him. "I can't believe this is happening. I came to the Territory to have a say in my own life, and now look."

"You said yourself that everyone suffers the consequences of their actions."

Her skirts swished as she walked over to his desk and placed her palms down on the wood. "So this is my fault?"

"Not entirely."

She stepped back and folded her arms. "What do *you* want more than anything, Kane?"

"To be a soldier," he replied without hesitation. "The army is like family to me. You risked your life to save

Jack. I'll do what I have to do for my career. A scandal would ruin it."

"So it seems we're both suffering the consequences of our choices. Had I known the outcome would be so costly, I'd never have done what I did."

He stood up. "If you had followed orders, none of this would have happened."

"You're absolutely right, captain. I wish I could argue with you but I can't. I'll tell you this: I won't make the same mistake again."

"Neither will I."

"Jack left with a patrol for Fort Apache. He plans to bring the army chaplain back with him to marry us."

"I know."

"And you won't stop it?"

In spite of what he said about his career, he could refuse to go through with the ceremony. His transfer would come through and eventually the gossip would die out and do him little damage. But it was different for Cady. She needed the protection of his name or her life would be ruined. After they were married, he would figure out how to get her out of the Territory. In the meantime, their fate was sealed.

"I can't stop it."

She nodded grimly and walked over to the door, where she stopped and looked back at him. "I'm sorry about this, Kane. I truly wish my mistake didn't affect you. I'm sorry Jack found us, and I'm sorry he hit you. And I'm sorry—"

"Forget it," he said, rubbing a knuckle above his colorful eye. "I guess I'll see you at the wedding."

"I guess. Too bad you don't have a uniform to match that purple shiner." Then she was gone.

Kane wasn't sorry. He was angry, at himself and at her. She didn't want to be married to him. He would do his best to make it seem as little like a marriage as possible.

* * *

Two days after her conversation with Kane, Cady paced in her quarters. Jack had wired that he'd be arriving later that day, and the wedding ceremony was scheduled to start as soon as the chaplain had time to freshen up.

Rays from the setting sun shining through the window blinded her and she turned away. She sighed. In a few hours, she would be sharing this room with Kane. She would be Mrs. Kane Carrington.

How had all her hopes and dreams and ambitions gone so wrong?

For a short time, she had thought about running away, but her last excursion had gone so badly she decided it wasn't a viable solution to her problem. If she wanted to be a teacher, she was out of options.

A knock on the door startled her and made her heart race. It must be Jack, coming to escort her to the ceremony.

"Come in," she called out.

The door opened, but instead of her brother it was R. J. Wexler. She hadn't spoken to him since the night he had helped her escape from the guardhouse. Irritation tightened in her belly. If not for him, she wouldn't be marrying Kane.

"What is it, R. J.?"

"Ma sent me over. She's gettin' ever'thing ready over at our quarters for the weddin'. But she wanted you to have these."

He pulled some things from his pocket: a blue ribbon, a brooch, and a white lace handkerchief.

"She said it was tradition. Something old, something new—"

"Something borrowed, something blue," she finished. "That was very considerate of your mother."

"Yes'm. The handkerchief is something new. Ma said you should keep that as a gift from her, and the blue ribbon too. The brooch is the borrowed part. It's Grandmother Wexler's, and she'd like to have it back."

"Of course. Tell her I'll take good care of it."

"She figured you'd have something old," he said, handing her the things.

Cady nodded. "This dress."

It was the long-sleeved high-necked white cotton with pink rosettes at the collar and wrists she'd worn to her welcome reception.

"You look real nice, Miss Tanner." Now that his hands were free, he whipped his hat off and curled the brim nervously.

Cady stared at him suspiciously. If she didn't know better, she would think he was being nice.

"Are you feeling all right, R. J.?" she asked.

"Yes'm, just fine. Why?"

"Because you're not looking at me as if you wish I'd fall in a prairie-dog hole."

"About the way I been actin', ma'am. You'll be pleased to know that Pa tanned me good for what I done." His voice cracked and he cleared his throat. "I'm glad Kane found you and you're all right after bein' up in the mountains. I want to apologize for sendin' you into danger. I didn't mean you no harm. I'da come and said it sooner, but I figured you'd best have a couple days t'simmer down before I did."

Cady wanted to give the boy a piece of her mind. After all, if it hadn't been for him, she wouldn't be forced into this marriage. Then she reminded herself that this mess was really her fault. A sudden warmth crept into her cheeks as she remembered that night and the pleasure she'd found in Kane's arms.

"I appreciate your apology, R. J. It takes a big person

to do that." She placed the brooch and handkerchief on her pine table and pulled the ribbon beneath the heavy length of her hair. She fixed the bow at her crown and turned to the boy. "How does it look?"

"Right pretty, ma'am." He frowned at her. "Is everything all right now?"

"Yes, why do you ask?"

"Ya seem sorta jumpy. Are ya sure about marryin' Kane?"

It surprised her that the boy was so perceptive. If she hadn't been so nervous, she never would have said anything, but the need to say out loud what she felt was too strong.

"I don't think he likes me very much, R. J."

"You're wrong about that, ma'am. He's sweet on you."

"What makes you think so?" He was wrong, of course, but she was curious about why he would say that.

He squeezed his hat brim until his knuckles turned white. "After I busted you out of the guardhouse, I never saw Kane look like that before. He was mad and scared too. He lit right out lookin' for you. I ain't never seen him ride that way, especially through the desert."

"Like what?"

"Like the devil was after him." He paused for a second, then went on. "Ma says he's sweet on you too."

"Really?"

He nodded. "She told Pa the first time she saw Kane and you together that there would be a weddin', although she didn't think it would be this soon."

"Give your mother my thanks for the things," she said, touching the brooch she had just pinned on her bodice. "And for all her help with the wedding preparations."

"Yes, ma'am." He put his hat on and left.

Cady stared at the door for a moment. Her anger had passed after she'd tried to get Kane to call off the wedding. Now she was merely sad. In spite of what R. J. said, she didn't believe Kane cared about her at all. She had lost her innocent conviction that she could have a say in what happened to her, but not her belief that she could make a difference in settling the West. She was resigned to the fact that being loved was not something she could hope for. Her fulfillment would have to come from her work.

Kane stood in his office with his hands clasped behind his back and looked at the scratches on his desk. Soon he would marry Cady Tanner, and she'd made it clear that she was not happy about being tied to him.

He wondered how he had messed everything up so badly. From the day he'd first met her, he had tried to prevent this.

There was a knock on the door. It must be the sentry notifying him that the chaplain had arrived.

"Come in, private."

The door creaked open and he turned around. R. J. stood there. "Howdy, captain," he said, removing his hat.

Kane frowned as he looked at the kid. That lanky, redheaded, freckle-faced hellion was why everything had gotten messed up so badly. If he had just minded his own damn business. "What do you want, R. J.?"

"Wanted to see how you were doin'. How's the eye?"

"Feels all right. How does it look?"

"Not too bad. Still a mite purple. The lip's down now, though. Except for the cut, you're as good as new." R. J. looked curious. "You never said how that happened, captain."

"No, I never did."

R. J. grinned. "Can't blame a fella for askin'."

"Guess not. But I can blame you for other things."

R. J. looked down at the hat in his hands, then back up. "I'm here t'say I'm sorry for what I did. I never should have helped Miss Tanner get away."

"You got that right."

Still, he couldn't blame the kid for what went on when he found her. The truth was, if he hadn't bedded Cady, nothing Jack Tanner said or did could have forced him to marry her. The fault was his alone.

"Forget it, R. J."

"Miss Tanner's sweet on you," he blurted out. "Ma says so," he added. Kane had the feeling that it was supposed to make him feel better. It didn't.

"How does your ma know?"

"Got me," he answered, looking confused. "She just said she knew the first time she saw the two of you together. Guess I'll be diggin' outhouses for a long time t'come."

Kane looked up at the kid and couldn't help smiling. "No, I think you've learned your lesson."

R. J. grinned back as he rubbed his backside. "Pa walloped me good."

Kane nodded approvingly. The major's attention was all the boy had ever wanted. He'd probably gotten more than he bargained for, but in a strange way Kane felt this whole incident had brought father and son closer.

"So you think Miss Tanner's sweet on me?" Kane asked.

"Yup. Why would she marry you if she wasn't?"

"Why indeed," Kane said, remembering his conversation with the lady two days before in this room. It was too complicated to go into, and R. J. was far too young.

They heard the sound of horses in the compound outside, and R. J. went to the window and looked out. "Mr. Tanner's here with the chaplain."

"Then I guess it's time for me to get married." Kane stood up and took his hat from the desk. "Want to walk me to your place?"

The boy's eyes grew bright as he nodded eagerly.

Kane put his hand on R. J.'s shoulder as they left his office. He was glad the boy stopped by. For some reason he felt a little better.

Cady stood in the doorway to the Wexlers' home clutching Jack's arm. Due to the speed with which the wedding had come together, they had decided to have only a few people. A reception would be held in the mess hall afterward.

Cady saw Lieutenant Brewster, as well as R. J., the Hallecks, the Chases, the Stantons, John Eagle, his father, and Mac. The small room was filled, but she found Kane almost immediately, standing head and shoulders above almost every other man. In his spotless dress blue uniform, he was so handsome he took her breath away. His thick brown hair was neatly parted and combed. He was so tall and strong. If only he could have been there because he wanted to and not because Jack had forced him.

When he had first seen her, Cady thought there had been approval in his eyes: then his expression became unreadable and she wasn't sure if she had only imagined it because she wanted so badly for it to be true.

Next to Kane stood a gray-haired man in uniform who held a book in his hands: the chaplain, no doubt. Beside him, Major Wexler held his wife's arm while she dabbed at her eyes.

Cady felt like crying too, but not from happiness.

The people parted and Jack walked her through their midst, stopping beside Kane. The two men exchanged a look, and then the minister cleared his throat.

"Miss Tanner, I'm Chaplain Barnes," he said, nodding at Cady. Then he looked around at everyone. "We are gathered to unite this man and this woman in holy matrimony. If anyone present can show just cause why these two should not be joined, let him speak now or forever hold his peace."

Cady started to lift her hand from Jack's forearm to get the man's attention. This was her last chance. Her brother instantly covered her fingers with his own and whispered in her ear, "I wouldn't advise it."

She pressed her lips together and glared at him.

Finally, when no one spoke up, Jack smiled tightly. "Guess it's time to get on with it."

He held her hand out to Kane, who took it and tucked her palm in the bend of his elbow, then stood beside her as they faced the chaplain.

"Captain Carrington, Miss Tanner, is there a ring?"

"No," Cady said.

"Yes," Kane said at the same time.

She looked up at him.

He smiled at her. "I'm not sure it will fit, but I'd like you to accept my mother's ring. Will you?" He pulled it from his pocket and handed it to the chaplain.

She swallowed the lump forming in her throat. "Of course I'll wear it."

"With the matter of the ring settled, do I have your permission to begin?" When they both nodded, he continued. "Do you, Kane, take Cady to be your lawfully wedded wife, in sickness and in health, until death do you part?"

Kane looked down at her. "I do," he said in a clear, deep voice.

"Do you, Cady, take Kane to be your lawfully wedded husband, to have and to hold, for richer, for
poorer, until death do you part?"

She couldn't look at Kane. He would see the tears
gathering in her eyes and she couldn't bear that. When
she trusted herself to answer she replied in a voice as
loud and clear as Kane's, "I do."

"Kane, will you love and honor your wife and keep
her safe to the best of your ability as long as you live?"

"I will," he said.

"Cady, will you love, honor, and obey your husband?
And forsaking all others keep him only unto yourself
for as long as you live?"

Cady thought about what she was being asked to do.
"Sir, may I ask you a question?" she whispered.

She felt all eyes in the room on her, and Kane's arm
tensed beneath her fingers.

The minister looked down at her with a hint of surprise. "What is it?"

"Do I have to promise to obey my husband? I mean
I'll do my best with everything else, and forsaking all
others is easy as pie, but I'm not sure I can vow to obey
blindly without at least some discussion. Especially if I
think he's wrong. I know that's how it is in the army,
but I have to tell the truth here in the eyes of God, and
the truth is that I'm not sure I can do it."

The minister cleared his throat. "What if we insert
that you promise to obey if, after discussion, you agree
with your husband? Can you promise that?"

"Yes, I will," she said.

The chaplain nodded and handed the ring back to
Kane, and he slipped it on her finger. It was too large,
and he held it in place while he took her other hand in
his and turned her to face him. There was something in
his eyes, an intense look that Cady didn't understand.

"With a ring given and solemn promises from Cady and Kane expressed before God and witnesses present, I now pronounce them man and wife. May I present Captain and Mrs. Kane Carrington."

Quiet applause rose from the gathering. Then Chaplain Barnes said, "You may kiss your bride."

Cady saw Kane's eyes smolder with an emotion she couldn't name. His right arm encircled her waist and he pulled her against him. With his left, he cupped her cheek, then slowly lowered his mouth to hers. At the first contact, cheers went up from the gathering. When Kane slipped his fingers in her hair and gently pressed the back of her head to force their lips closer and deepen the kiss, Cady didn't hear anything but the pounding of her heart. Everything and everyone disappeared except Kane.

She was married now. And the heated way her new husband kissed her was a hopeful promise for their life together as well as for the wedding night to come.

14

Kane escorted Cady across the acequia and hesitated beneath the ramada outside the quarters they would now be sharing. In the cool breeze blowing off the desert, the scent of mesquite and juniper mixed together and surrounded them. As soon as the sun went down, gentle teasing from the people gathered at their reception had compelled him to take her home. Betsy Wexler's eyes had twinkled when she had said everything was ready for them.

As much as he'd wanted to, he couldn't put this moment off any longer. It was important that everyone thought they were a typical couple in love. After all, isn't that why they had gotten married in the first place, to preserve their respective reputations?

Cady waited beside him, nervously clasping her fingers as she waited for him to open the door. The fragrance of flowers drifted from her and the sweet smell took him back to that night in the cave and the moments of heaven he'd spent in her arms. Had it been worth what had happened afterwards?

He looked down at her, bathed in moonlight. Her long golden-brown hair was tied back from her face with a blue satin ribbon and flowed free down her back to her waist. Her lips were full and soft, her eyes big, bright, trusting, hopeful. His breath caught as he realized she was the most beautiful woman he'd ever seen.

Kane opened the door and let her precede him inside.

"Oh!" she said, looking around.

He closed the door and stood behind her. Another iron cot stood beside the one Cady had been using. Candles had been lighted and placed around the room, bathing everything in a flickering golden glow. As he looked closer, he noticed that his belongings were there, his uniforms hanging beside Cady's dresses on pegs in the corner, his shaving things on the dresser beside her brush and comb. On the table, a bottle of champagne stood in an olla, its coolness preserved by the clay container. Someone had taken the liberty of preparing the place for their wedding night.

Someone had gone to a lot of trouble for nothing.

"Who did this?" Cady asked, turning to look up at him with the trusting expression that always twisted his gut inside out.

"My guess is Betsy Wexler. I can't even imagine how she got her hands on a bottle of champagne."

"That was very sweet of her."

"Cady, I—" He stopped, noticing that his mother's ring was suspended from a piece of string resting against Cady's breast.

"It was a little too big. Betsy helped me tie it on because I was afraid I'd lose it. Why did you give this to me?" She glanced down, then back up at him shyly. "Didn't your first wife—"

"Annie never saw it." He blurted it out and wasn't sure why, anymore than he knew why he'd put a ring on Cady's finger that he had never considered giving to another woman.

Cady stiffened a little at his sharp tone. Then she said, "Tell me about your mother. You've never told me anything about your family."

"They're all dead. My father was killed in the war, fighting for the Union at Gettysburg."

"How old were you?"

"Twelve." He saw the sympathy in her eyes, but she said nothing. "My mother never got over it. She died a year later."

"A broken heart?"

His jaw clenched for a moment. "A foolish romantic notion."

"I'm a foolish person, as you've pointed out once or twice."

"Cady, I didn't mean it like that."

"It doesn't matter," she said.

But he could tell by her tone that it did matter. He hated himself more for what he still had to say. He was stalling and he knew it.

She walked over to the table, running one finger through the moisture collected on the side of the champagne bottle. "What did you do after your mother died?"

"I joined the army."

She looked up sharply. "But you were only thirteen. That's just a little older than R. J. is now."

"I lied about my age and got away with it because I looked older. The army fed me, put clothes on my back, and gave me a place to sleep. It's the only family I've known for a long time."

"Did the army always come first? What about Annie?" She absently toyed with the ring hanging around her neck.

He didn't know how to answer that. She probably had

another romantic notion about him and Annie, but all he felt for his first wife was guilt and regret. She had shared his life and now she was dead and he was partly to blame.

"Annie never understood how I felt about the army."

"How did you meet?"

He sighed. "Five years ago I was at Fort Huachuca. Annie's family had a ranch nearby. She was born and raised in the Arizona Territory and still didn't understand what it takes to keep the peace. She wanted more of my time than I could give her."

"I see."

Kane wondered if she really did. But it was useless to worry about it now. They were married. Although he suspected Cady had almost put a stop to it.

"Why didn't you stop the wedding today? You lifted your hand to get the chaplain's attention. Why didn't you say something?"

"Jack wouldn't let me."

"So you'll obey your brother, but your husband first has to convince you he's right?"

She looked up quickly. "I'm sorry, Kane. I didn't mean to embarrass you. It's just that I wanted you to know how I felt. I've told you before that I can't do something I don't understand and believe in with all my heart."

At least she believed that marrying him was the right thing to do, or she would have spoken up at the ceremony in spite of her brother's disapproval. She did what she felt was right, no matter what. It was one of the things he admired most about her.

He was the first to admit that he didn't understand much about women, and this one baffled him completely. But one thing he'd learned about her: Always expect the unexpected. He wished things could be different between them, because she was a hell of a woman.

She was looking at him now with expectation

sparkling in her eyes. How was he going to order her not to share his bed and persuade her it was for the best? How was he going to persuade himself? Especially when she stood there bathed in candlelight and looking so damn beautiful?

He just couldn't take the chance of loving her. His concern wasn't today, or tomorrow, or even the day after that. But sooner or later the time would come when she would leave, and that didn't bear thinking about. The only way to protect them both was to keep his distance until he could figure out a solution to this mess.

And if he was going to try to think, there was no way he could stay with her tonight.

"Do you want to open this?" she asked, indicating the bottle on the table.

"Would you like some?"

"Yes, I believe I would."

He opened the bottle with a loud pop. Some of the liquid bubbled over the top and splattered on the canvas floor at Cady's feet.

"Sorry." He picked up one of the glasses that had been left for them.

"That's all right." She took the glass he offered, raised it to her lips, and then stopped as he put the bottle down. "Aren't you having any?"

He shook his head. "I have to be on duty soon."

"Tonight?" she asked, incredulous. "It's our wedding night. Surely no one expects you to—"

"No one *expects* me to do anything."

"They can't get along without you for one night?"

"There are hostile Apaches out there just waiting for us to let our guard down. The watch has been doubled since Cuchillo escaped from the reservation. Every man on this post has been doing extra duty, including me. Tonight is no exception."

Cady opened her mouth to say something, then closed it again. He was sure she was remembering what he'd told her about Annie not understanding his commitment to the army. The difference was, this time he was hiding behind his duty to protect Cady.

"I understand, Kane. You have a job to do."

"It's important for me to set an example. It's also important to keep things around here as normal as possible. So if you want to take your afternoon ride it's all right as long as you stay within sight of the fort." He stopped and thought for a moment. "It would be best if one of the troopers accompanied you."

She set her full glass down beside his empty one. "All right."

"I have to go now."

"Should I wait up for you?"

The image of her, sweet and soft in bed waiting for him was damned appealing, but it wasn't something he would let himself get used to.

"No. And we might as well get something straight here and now."

"What's that?"

"You said the cost of what we did in the mountains was too high, and we agreed we wouldn't make the same mistake again."

"Yes, I did, but—"

"Under the circumstances we'll never have a conventional marriage; it's clear that's not what you want. I see no reason to complicate the situation. For appearances, I will move in here with you, but I won't touch you again. You have my word as an officer."

"Is this—" Her voice caught, and she cleared her throat before speaking again. "Is this what you want?"

"Yes. Isn't it what you want?"

She hesitated, then said, "Yes."

"So we're agreed." It was one of the few times they had agreed about anything, and it felt like hell. "I'd better go."

She nodded, then walked over to him and put her hand on his arm. "Be careful, Kane."

Where her fingers touched, his skin burned, and he pulled away abruptly. He saw the light go out of her eyes and despised himself.

How much longer could he go on protecting her? The sooner he got her out of this marriage *and* the Territory, the better for both of them.

Cady walked into the mess hall the following morning with her lessons, papers, and books. She was late. It had been almost dawn before she had fallen asleep. She couldn't get Kane's words or the look on his face out of her mind. He had hurt her before, but that slight two years ago was nothing compared to his rejection last night.

She had tossed and turned and refused to cry. He wouldn't break her.

She looked around and was surprised at the small number of children there. She was thirty minutes late, and only Martha Halleck, Bart Grimes, Polly Chase, R. J. Wexler, and John Eagle were sitting in their seats.

Cady walked to the head of the table and set her things down. "Where is everyone else this morning?"

Bart Grimes tossed his head to get his straight brown hair out of his hazel eyes. When he could see her, she noticed a twinkle. "Guess they figured there wouldn't be no school today, what with you gettin' married 'n' all, ma'am."

"Any school, Bart. And why wouldn't there be?"

"Well, now." The boy shifted uncomfortably. "I ain't sure I should repeat it, Miss Tanner."

"It's Mrs. Carrington now," Martha Halleck chimed in. Black ringlets danced around her shoulders as she shifted excitedly on the hard bench. "Isn't that right, ma'am?"

"Yes, Martha, I am Mrs. Carrington now." How strange that sounded: Mrs. Kane Carrington. She had his name, but as far as he was concerned that's all she would ever have of him. "But I'm still waiting to hear why Bart thinks there wouldn't be any school today."

Bart's face flushed bright red as he shifted on the bench. Good Lord, what had the boy heard?

Cady put her hands on the table and stared at the blushing thirteen-year-old. "Out with it, Bart. I want you to repeat what you heard."

He looked down at his hands. "Ma and Pa was talkin' about what a nice weddin' you had. Ma was goin' on and on 'bout how romantic it all was, him lovin' you so much he lit out after ya and saved your life. Then Pa said 'Hell, won't be romantic when she can't even walk into school this mornin'.'"

Cady felt her own cheeks flood with heat. It had never occurred to her that the whole fort would be interested in what she and Kane should have been doing on their wedding night. That was humiliating enough. That it hadn't happened was downright mortifying. That their marriage was a fake made her heartsick.

She cleared her throat. "As you can see I have no difficulty walking and I think I can manage to conduct lessons this morning. Those who didn't show up today will have a lot of work to make up. Is that clear?"

A chorus of murmured assents filled the room.

"Good. Take out your slates and we will start with multiplication tables. If I'm not mistaken, we were on the sixes last time?"

The children nodded, and a clatter of activity followed as they did what she asked.

R. J. had been uncharacteristically quiet. He stood up, walked over to her, and held out a book. She took it from him and saw that it was *The Adventures of Tom Sawyer,* the volume she had given him the day she arrived.

"Is there something wrong, R. J.?"

"No, ma'am, I'm just returning this."

"I meant for you to keep it. Did you finish reading it?"

"Yes'm. It was good."

She lifted one brow skeptically. "You don't have to say that if you don't really think so. You're allowed to have your own opinion."

"No'm. I mean yes'm, I really liked it. I had some trouble in the beginning. You might not've noticed, readin' is a mite hard for me."

She had noticed. "But you persevered?"

He looked at her blankly.

Cady suppressed a grin. "You kept on going until you finished?"

"It got easier."

She smiled warmly. "See what happens when you don't give up? Perseverance pays off."

"I guess so." He held out the book. "I thought you might've changed your mind about givin' this to me after what I done."

"What I did. And no, I still want you to have it. Although you might like to donate it to the literary society or loan it to someone else."

"Can I let John Eagle borrow it?"

"Of course. Now take your seat and start on your numbers."

"You're not gonna let me out of it on account of I persevered on the book?"

"Arithmetic is important too. There's more to life than words, R. J."

She wandered around as the children scratched on their slates with chalk. Outside, she could hear sounds from the parade ground. From time to time, a blue uniform would pass on the boardwalk, and her heart would start to pound when she thought it might be Kane. But every time she was disappointed.

She loved him. Could she live with herself if she didn't do everything in her power to make their marriage work? She had just told R. J. to never stop trying. Could she do any less?

Cady recalled telling Kane that Tanners never gave up. She was a Carrington now, but she couldn't turn her back on who and what she was and what she wanted more than anything. She had told him she wanted to teach and that was true. But she had come to the Territory for the man who had haunted her dreams and her heart since the first time she had seen him. If Cady could prove to him that she could be a good soldier's wife and follow orders, maybe he would learn to love her just a little.

Bart Grimes sighed loudly. "Miss Ta—I mean Mrs. Carrington, I just can't do this stuff." He put his slate down with a sharp sound on the wooden table.

She stood behind him. "This is just like addition, Bart. If you can't remember, just add six. Look, six times six is thirty-six. Add six to that and you get forty-two. So, six times seven is what?"

"Forty-two?" he asked.

"Right. It's slower, but until you have them memorized, it's an easy way to remember. Don't give up. There's always something you can do to get where you want to go."

She nodded emphatically. Bart would never know the words were more for herself than him. She made up her mind that she would immediately start her campaign to win Kane's heart.

*   *   *

Kane stood up and walked from his desk to the window. He stared at the soldiers moving around inside the fort. At the perimeter, he saw the guard had been doubled as he'd ordered. So far everything had been quiet. He hoped it stayed that way.

Just beyond the buildings that comprised the fort, Cady and a soldier were riding side by side. She had come to Kane's office after school and asked if he would accompany her on her afternoon ride. Although it was one of the hardest things he'd ever done, he'd begged off, claiming he had too much work to do. Her look of disappointment had both surprised and flattered him. He'd quickly suppressed the feeling. When the couple appeared a few minutes later, he saw it was Mac Thorne who rode beside her.

Now he took a deep breath, counted to ten, and by the time he was finished, they had ridden out of sight. Kane stayed where he was. The surge of emotions inside him told him if he moved, he would go out there and do something he'd regret. Minutes later they showed up again. Now they were riding so close to the perimeter they were in danger of trampling the guards.

Kane wondered how it was possible to be curious and angry at the same time. Mac would never endanger Cady, but he knew it wasn't necessary to stay so near that the guards choked on the dust their horses kicked up. So it must be Cady's idea.

He remembered telling her to stay within sight of the fort, but she was carrying it to an extreme. For a woman who had altered the obey part of their wedding vows to the point where she could practically do as she pleased, this was curiously out of character.

Why had Mac agreed to go with her? He hated

riding. Cavalry officers spent so much time in the saddle, you couldn't pay them to ride when it wasn't part
of their job. Mac had assured him he had no interest in
Cady. Then Kane remembered their conversation more
clearly. Mac had said he wouldn't horn in on another
man's territory. Kane had told him that Cady was free
to see whoever she wished. But that was before yesterday, before they were married.

When they rode by again, he saw that Cady was
laughing at something Mac said. The knot of anger in
his gut tightened.

"That does it!" He yanked open the door and strode
quickly to the perimeter, waiting as the pair came into
view around the corner of the stable.

Cady waved when she saw him and said something
to Mac before pressing her knees to the horse's flanks
to increase the animal's pace. When she came close, she
pulled back on the reins. Mac was right beside her.

Her cheeks were a becoming shade of pink. She
smiled brightly and looked a little too happy. She never
looked that way when she was with him. Maybe she
found Thorne's company preferable to his own. The irritation he'd recognized before sliced him more sharply
this time. In one fluid motion, the other man swung his
leg over the animal's rump and stepped down, then
moved beside Cady and raised his arms to assist her.

Kane stood alongside Mac, staring at his junior officer. "At ease, lieutenant. She's my wife. I'll help her
down."

Mac's brows lifted slightly. Then he touched the brim
of his hat and backed away. "Anything you say, captain."

"No one needs to help me. I'm not finished with my
ride yet," Cady said. Then she frowned. "Forgive me,
Mac. You probably have more important things to do
than act as nursemaid. I'll stop now."

"Ma'am, there's nothing going on that could keep me from riding with you." Mac slanted Kane a questioning look. "Unless your husband has some objection?"

"I have no objection," he said. "But since I'm free, I'll accompany Cady."

"I'd like that," she said. "But I thought you were too busy."

He frowned. "I can spare a little time."

"You're sure?" Mac asked. "I don't mind escorting this pretty lady."

Kane glared at him. "Mac, do us both a favor. Stay away from my wife."

"Just trying to be neighborly."

Mac Thorne's attitude was beginning to wear on his nerves like a persistent toothache. It was high time he was set straight.

"Don't be neighborly. And don't go near Cady. Is that clear?"

Cady looked down at him, shocked. "What's wrong with you? I asked him to ride with me because you ordered me not to ride alone."

Kane knew he was making a fool of himself and couldn't seem to stop. He knew if Mac had ulterior motives where Cady was concerned, he sure as hell wouldn't do anything about them in front of the whole fort. But Kane was acting on pure emotion now, beyond caring why he was behaving like a jackass.

Kane looked up at her. "Cady, listen—"

"No. I don't think my temper can stand it right now." She wheeled her horse away and cantered toward the open desert.

"Cady, come back!" he hollered.

Mac handed him the reins of his own horse. "Better go after her, captain."

Kane took the leather strips the other man handed

him, swung quickly into the saddle, and kneed the horse, urging it into motion. He had no difficulty catching up, and his horse fell into an easy pace beside hers. They rode for a while without speaking. He could feel her annoyance. The funny thing was, he didn't blame her but he didn't know what to do about it.

Finally he broke the silence. "Cady—"

"Am I too far from the fort?" Her tone was clipped and taut with irritation.

"No."

She glanced at him and her eyes flashed green fire. "You're sure?"

"We're not right on top of it, but yes, this is within sight of the sentries."

"You're positive? I wouldn't want to disobey orders."

"Since when?"

"Since—" She looked at him, then straight ahead, and he could see the tension in her profile. "Never mind."

"Cady, listen to me. I didn't mean to—"

"I'm not Annie," she said, still not looking at him.

Kane's whole body tensed. His mount grew restive and difficult to control. He pulled back on the reins. Cady halted beside him and patted her mount's neck.

"What did you say?" he asked.

"I said I'm not Annie. I won't betray you with another man."

"What are you talking about?"

"You behaved like a complete ninny with Mac, and I can only conclude it's because you're jealous."

"That's ridiculous." But he knew she was right. Since he'd already crossed the line, he decided he couldn't do more damage. He had to know something. "Why did Mac Thorne ride with you?"

She shrugged. "I asked him."

"But why Mac?"

"You seem to have a lot of faith in him. I thought he'd be good to have along if the Indians showed up."

"Cady, you were practically on top of the perimeter guards. You didn't need Mac Thorne or anyone else."

"I was merely following your orders."

"And I have to ask again, since when?"

"Since our wedding yesterday. I took a vow to obey you as long as the orders made sense. It makes perfect sense to stay as close to the fort as possible since there are hostile Indians on the loose. It makes even better sense to have an experienced Indian soldier with me. Mac was telling me about some of his experiences. He certainly has seen his share of adventure. I chose him because—"

"Be careful of Mac," he said through gritted teeth.

"Why?"

"He's a womanizer."

"Mac?" She laughed. "The few times I've seen him, he's been a perfect gentleman."

"Don't argue, just trust me on this. Stay away from Mac Thorne."

He'd never experienced jealousy before. He had never felt this possessive of a woman, not even Annie. While he'd been married to her, he'd heard rumors about her and other men, but he had dismissed them as gossip. He hadn't cared enough to check them out.

But Cady was wrong about one thing. He wasn't comparing her to his first wife. He'd never met a woman more loyal than Cady, and it never crossed his mind that she would be unfaithful to him. He just didn't trust other men around her.

"So you want me to keep my distance from Lieutenant Thorne. Is that an order?" There was just a hint of teasing in her words.

"Yes, if that's what it takes."

"Then I'll do my best to avoid him."

"As easy as that?" he asked, surprised that she had agreed.

"According to the letter of my vow, I'm entitled to a bit more discussion about *why* I should avoid him, but I'm willing to give you a break. Just this once." Now he knew she was joking.

He let out a long breath, relieved that things between them were back to normal, whatever that was. He looked at her, then grinned when he caught the twinkle in her green eyes.

"I owe you one," he said.

"Yes, you do. And I think I'll collect tonight."

"Tonight?" he asked. He hoped she wasn't asking what he thought. They had both vowed not to make that mistake again.

"I'm having the first official meeting of the Fort McDowell Literary Society and I'd like you to be there." She held up a gloved hand. "Before you say anything, the last time was not a real meeting. If you recall, I wound up in the guardhouse."

"I remember." How could he forget? If he had been more vigilant in keeping her there, they wouldn't be married now. "Will Mac Thorne be there?"

"I can hardly keep him away." Kane watched her eyes grow pleading as she looked at him. "It would make me very happy if you'd come, Kane. Will you? Please?"

He wanted to say no. But he couldn't resist the appealing look on her face and the fact that it seemed important to her that he attend. "I wouldn't miss it."

She smiled brightly and said, "Thank you."

Kane cursed himself for a damn fool. He knew if he didn't do something soon, it would be impossible to let her go.

15

Cady had eaten a quick dinner alone in their quarters while Kane finished up the work he'd set aside to ride with her. She arrived at the mess hall early, just as the kitchen detail was clearing the evening meal, so that she could set up for the literary society meeting. The lingering odors of beans, onions, and salt pork drifted to her as she worked.

Kane had ordered two of the enlisted men to carry her trunk for her, and now she pulled each book out and set it, spine out, on a table that had been moved against the wall. Just like everything else in the desert, her volumes had gotten dusty even packed away in her trunk. She brushed her hands together to dislodge the dirt, then looked down and noticed that her green wool skirt was streaked. Absorbed with shaking it out, she didn't hear the footsteps behind her.

"Evening, ma'am."

She whirled around. "Mac! You scared the life out of me."

"Sorry, didn't mean to." His easy grin coaxed a similar response from her.

"You might give a body some warning," she said, taking a deep calming breath.

"I'll do that next time."

Cady studied the man with an objective eye. She had to admit that Mac Thorne was a very attractive man and would make many a female heart flutter outrageously. But she was not moved by his charm. Kane had stolen her heart, and she knew he would have it forever.

In spite of his denial, she knew Kane was afraid she would be like Annie and turn to another man if life on an army post proved to be more than she could cope with. Cady would rather be alone than be with any other man. But if it would prove to her husband that she could follow orders and be a good army wife, she'd do her best to avoid the dashing lieutenant.

"Mac, I was just on my way back to my quarters to pick up more books. Would you mind watching these in case anyone comes early?"

"Sorry, Mrs. Carrington. You did that to me the last time, and you never came back."

"That wasn't my fault."

"Doesn't matter whether it was or not. I can't stay. I'm on my way to relieve the guard and I can't be here this evening. I just wanted to know if you'd hold on to that copy of *A Tale of Two Cities* for me."

"I'd be happy to. Or better yet." She glanced toward the door to make sure Kane wasn't standing there. Satisfied, she looked back at Mac. "Why don't you take it with you now?"

"Got my hands full of Winchester," he said, hefting his rifle. "Besides, even if I had time to read it, the light isn't real good out there. That moon is only good for kissing under."

Cady's cheeks flooded with color. She'd never have thought anything of the remark if Kane hadn't warned her about Mac. She believed he was nothing more than a harmless flirt, but now she was highly sensitive to anything he said.

"Lieutenant, it's not proper for you to talk that way in front of me. I'm a married woman."

"Yes, ma'am, I know. And no disrespect intended, but if I were you I'd get that husband of yours out under that big old moon and do some sparking." His eyebrows rose suggestively.

"Why do you say that?"

Did he know that Kane didn't want her as a wife? Did everyone know their marriage was a sham?

"There's a problem when a man stands guard duty on his wedding night who's got a woman like you waiting for him."

So he did know, or he'd guessed.

"Oh, Mac. I don't know what to do. He was married before."

"I know all about Annie. That's over and done with. He's got you now."

"That's the problem. He doesn't want me. I'm doing my best to make this marriage work, but—" She covered her mouth with her hand and glanced at the door. "That reminds me, you'll have to go. I'll hold the book for you, but Kane can't see us talking together."

He frowned. "Why not?"

"He warned me to stay away from you."

A wide grin turned up the corners of his mouth. "That's a real good sign."

"It is?"

"Yes, ma'am. He's jealous."

"I told him that earlier, after he was so rude to you, but he denied it. All I know for sure is that I have my orders and I'm trying to show him I can be a good wife."

"Take my advice, a good wife would get him out there under that moon. He won't give a tinker's damn about orders or anything else if you're there."

"That's kind of you to say so, Mac." She flashed a quick look at the door again. "Now don't take this the wrong way, but please go."

"Good thing I'm not the sensitive type." He smiled again, then politely touched the brim of his hat before he left her.

"Good evening, Major Wexler. I'm very glad you could join us," Cady said, smiling at the fort commander.

"It's my pleasure, Cady. Or should I say Mrs. Carrington?"

"You can call me whatever you'd like, sir. I'm still not used to being Mrs. Carrington. Marriage certainly is an adjustment."

"That it is." He rubbed his jaw as a puzzled look crossed his face. "I have to admit I was a little surprised when Kane stood guard duty on his wedding night."

Oh, Lord, even the major knew something was wrong.

She smiled thinly. "That's Kane. I knew when I agreed to marry him that he was dedicated to his career."

"He's a fine officer. The army is lucky to have him. And he's lucky to have you."

"That's very kind of you, sir." Now she wanted to change the subject. She indicated the table beside her. "Is there anything here you'd care to read, major?"

"Let me take a look."

"Be my guest."

Kane walked in the door and scanned the room. Cady's gaze was drawn to him like a bee to honey. He was so tall, so handsome. When he looked in her direction, her heart pounded until she was sure it could be heard over the sound of voices.

He walked across the room, greeting people as he moved through the crowd. Some of them had already picked out books to read; most used the evening as an opportunity merely to visit. Either way, Cady was pleased with the way it had gone so far. Her aim was to break the monotony of army life. She felt she had done that.

"Good evening, Major Wexler." Kane nodded to his commanding officer.

"Captain. I was just chatting with your lovely bride. Now I'm going to have a look at these books."

"Yes, sir." Kane looked at her, and his mouth lifted in the little smile that always made her knees weak.

Cady glanced at Major Wexler, but he had moved to the far end of the table.

Kane stood beside her, close enough that their arms brushed.

"I didn't expect to see so many people here," he said.

She smiled warmly. "I wasn't sure what to expect, but the turnout has been encouraging. I told you people were looking for something to do."

"You did, didn't you?" he said, a teasing note in his voice.

The major came up on her other side, and she stood between the two men. He held a book up for her to see. "I believe I'd like to try this one."

Cady saw the title and frowned. "I am sorry, Major Wexler, but I already promised to hold that one for Lieutenant Thorne. He's on guard duty and couldn't be here tonight. Is there something else you'd be interested in?"

Cady felt Kane go rigid beside her. She knew he was displeased, but she *had* promised the book.

The major browsed a little more through the volumes on the table. "I'll take this, then."

Cady glanced at the title and smiled. "I'm sure you'll enjoy that one, sir."

"I'll try and bring it back for the next meeting."

"Keep it as long as you like, major."

"Thank you, Mrs. Carrington. I believe I'll go find Betsy and see what she's up to."

Cady gestured across the room. "She's over there with Mrs. Grimes. Please give her my regards, will you?"

"My pleasure." He looked at her, then nodded at Kane. "Captain, Mrs. Carrington, good evening," he said and walked across the room to his wife.

Cady didn't like the frown on Kane's face. "What's wrong?" she asked him.

His eyes grew dark. "Let's go outside."

She thought about her earlier conversation with Mac and his advice to get Kane out in the moonlight. Somehow she thought this was not precisely what he had meant.

"Is that an order?"

"Yes," he said tightly.

She nodded. "As you wish, captain."

He took her elbow and guided her through the gathering in the mess hall, outside, and down the steps. The street was awash in moonlight. There was a chill in the breeze that pushed the wisps of hair from her face. After the crush of bodies inside the mess hall, the isolation was a relief and the air on her hot cheeks was heaven. He stopped by a grouping of rocks and glared down at her, but he still held her arm. His features looked harsh in the moon's eerie light.

"What did you think you were doing in there?" he asked.

"I was loaning books."

"Then why did you turn down the major?"

"Because I had already promised to hold that book for Mac."

"After I asked you to stay away from him?"

"You knew he planned to stop in. I couldn't very well ignore him. That would be rude."

"But it wasn't rude for you to refuse a request made by the commanding officer of this fort?" He frowned.

"I was polite. The major didn't seem upset at all. I don't understand why you're making an issue of this."

"Because in the army, when the commanding officer asks for something, it's considered an order. On a military post, his word is law for everyone—including you. You need to understand the rules, for as long as you're married to a soldier."

"What does that mean?"

"You know—rules, a code of laws that guides the way you live."

"I know what rules are. I meant the part about for as long as we're married. That doesn't sound like it's going to be very long."

"You're impulsive, Cady, and you've pretty much done what you wanted when you wanted. You can't do that in the army."

"We're not talking about law and order, we're talking about borrowing a book that someone else asked for first. Whatever happened to the rules of polite society?"

"That's what I've been trying to tell you since the first day you got here. That way of life doesn't work here. The fort commander is in charge and he gets what he wants."

"What about you? You're the second-in-command. What do you want?"

The moon glowed over his thick brown hair and the curl that drifted onto his forehead. His strong jaw was tightly clenched, drawing her attention to his mouth. The way it turned up at the corners made him look like he was smiling. She knew he wasn't. His moods were as clear to her now as a cloudless sky.

But something was going on inside him. Cady would give up her last book if it wasn't the same thing she wanted—the touch of his lips against her own. The yearning stretched and grew in her chest until she almost couldn't breathe.

This was what Mac had meant about getting him outside. The moonlight, the mysterious desert surrounding them, cast a spell. The danger lurking behind every hill and cactus heightened the sense of urgency between them. She had experienced candlelight suppers and Sunday picnics, but she had never felt the magic of a place as much as she did in this Arizona desert.

Cady searched his face and saw the effort he exerted to keep his distance from her. If she was going to get through to him, she had to do something and she had to do it now.

He was still holding her arm. She placed her free hand on his chest and saw the small intake of breath he couldn't quite hide.

"Kane, I don't think you're as angry that I refused the major as you are that I did a favor for Mac."

"That's ridiculous. I'm a soldier, a by-the-book officer. You don't spend as much time in the army as I have without learning the man in charge calls the shots—"

She lifted her hand and covered his mouth with her fingers. "I don't give a fig for this mysterious book all you soldiers talk about. I said it before and I'll say it again: You're jealous of Mac Thorne."

"Bull—!"

"Deny it all you want. If it will help, I don't mind if you say some of those words men are so fond of. I won't faint. I've got two brothers; I've heard some of them before. But it won't change the fact that you're jealous and you have no reason to be."

"Have you been out in the sun without your hat?"

"No. But I've been thinking a lot about this."

Cady slid her arm from his cheek and rested it around his neck, then stood on tiptoe and softly touched her lips to his. His body went rigid and he started to pull away.

"Don't, Kane. Please."

She kissed him again, and there was only a slight hesitation before his arms went around her and crushed her to his chest. He pressed his mouth against hers hungrily, and his breathing grew shallow and rapid.

Cady's heart pounded against her ribs as she was swept away by the sweetness of being in his arms once again. She slipped her hand from his neck and threaded her fingers through the thickness of his hair and heard him moan low in his throat.

He pressed his fingers to the back of her head and squeezed a fistful of her hair, not hurtful but with an eagerness that thrilled her. He made the contact of their mouths more firm. His tongue teased her closed lips and instantly she opened to him. He stroked the inside of her mouth and shivers rippled through her body, starting in her breasts and ending at her toes.

Cady pulled her mouth from his and stared into the smoky depths of his eyes. "You are a devil," she whispered. "You've stolen every last ounce of my strength. If you weren't holding me like this, I'd be in a heap at your feet."

He sat down on the rock beside them and pulled her onto his lap. His arms came around her waist and she crossed her wrists loosely behind his neck. Their faces were so close she could feel his breath stir the wisps of hair framing her face, smell the fragrance of his shaving soap, breathe in his masculine scent.

He smiled, a slow, self-satisfied, all-male smile that made her heart race. When he looked at her that way, she knew she would follow him to the ends of the earth.

"If I'm a devil, you're a witch, Cady Carrington. You make me forget everything but you—your silken hair, your tempting body." His hand slipped up and, with his thumb, he stroked a feather-light touch across the side of her breast. "You're so beautiful. Do you have any idea how lovely you are?"

Slowly, she shook her head.

His eyes narrowed. "So beautiful that every man on this post can't help but want you. Most of them wouldn't do anything about it, but you're right: I'm jealous as hell and I don't trust Mac as far as I can throw him."

"You have no reason to be jealous. I don't want anyone but you, Kane. There's never been anyone but you."

His mouth came down on hers then, hard and demanding. His tongue invaded her mouth and caressed the sensitive interior until a soft moan escaped her.

He slid his hand over her chest. He stopped suddenly, pulling away as he lifted her wedding band from where it rested against her breasts. In his palm, the circle of gold gleamed as the moon's light reflected from it.

"You're still wearing this?" He stared at her, and it was as if he was trying to see clear into her heart.

"Of course. Why wouldn't I?"

"I don't know."

"This ring is special because it came from you. It's

precious, not because it's gold but because it was your mother's. I'll never take it off."

She leaned forward and placed a kiss on the ring in his hand.

He sucked in a breath as he let the golden circle slide from his fingers to fall against her bosom. Then he covered her breast with his palm. She leaned into the caress. The sensation slammed through her even though her cotton blouse kept the contact from being skin to skin. She arched forward, wanting to increase the pleasure his touch gave her, wishing there was no barrier to the warmth of his fingers, the strength of his hand.

He shuddered at her eager response. As if he could read her mind, he undid the buttons down her front and pushed the material aside, then slipped her chemise down, freeing her sensitized flesh. His fingers slowly and exquisitely explored the peak of her breast. His breathing quickened, growing more wild. But his arms trembled, straining to control his power. He could break her in two if he chose, and his restraint, the care he took to be gentle with her, touched her to her very soul.

Cady kissed him back with all the heat she'd learned from him, trying to return some of the wonder he'd given to her. Finally, he pulled away and looked at her, the tension in the angles and planes of his face etched in moonlight. His chest rose and fell heavily.

"You are a witch, Cady. You make me forget every promise I ever made, to myself or anyone else."

She kissed his neck and spoke against the warm skin there. "What did you promise, Kane?"

"That I wouldn't hurt you. That I'd protect you."

"And you have."

"No. You married me because you had to. How is that protecting you?"

"You're wrong, Kane, about why I married you. I didn't have to, not really."

She gloried in the feel of him, the power of his possession, the passion he created inside her. The sensation filled her to near bursting. The words had rushed out before she could stop them.

"What do you mean, you didn't have to?"

If she hadn't been so light-headed from his touch, she would have heard the edge in his voice. But before it registered she blurted out, "No one could have forced me to marry you if I didn't love you, Kane."

As soon as she said the words, she wanted to call them back. But it was too late. He went still and she pulled back to look at him. The expression on his face told her it was the last thing he wanted to hear.

"You don't mean that," he said harshly.

Cady had never hated her impulsiveness more than she did at that moment. But she couldn't lie either. "I do mean it. I've loved you since the day we met. I tried not to, but it was no use. I was engaged but I had to end it because I couldn't marry anyone else."

"Don't say any more." He put his hands on her waist and stood her up, then took a deep shuddering breath. As she straightened her clothes, he rose to his full height and stared down at her, a look of betrayal in his dark eyes. "I don't want to hear any more."

"Not even if it's the truth?"

"Especially if it's the truth." He tilted his head back and raked a hand through his hair as he stared at the moon. When he looked at her again, it was as if a cold stranger had taken the place of the warm, tender, responsive man she had just kissed. "I'll walk you back now. Everyone will be wondering where you are."

"You don't want to talk about this, do you?"

"No."

She tamped down her anger and frustration and took a deep breath. "All right, Kane. We won't talk about it. But that won't change the way I feel."

She turned away and started down the hill. Behind her, she heard the rocks and sand beneath his boots as he followed without a word. She had said more than enough tonight. She knew he would think about it. This wasn't over. Not as far as she was concerned.

The following day, Cady was in the classroom when she saw Jack in the doorway. He motioned for her to join him.

She looked at her students, fifteen in all now, busily working the sums she had given them. She glanced at R. J.'s red head, bent to his task. Even he came on a regular basis. More important, he was learning. That small miracle gave her great pride.

"Children?" The scratching on their slates stopped and all eyes lifted to hers. "We have a visitor. Continue with your work until I've finished speaking with him."

"Yes, Mrs. Carrington," they all said together.

Cady pulled her shawl around her shoulders and walked to where Jack lounged in the doorway.

He grinned, and she couldn't help smiling back. The beard he'd grown during his time in the Superstitions was still there, but neatly trimmed. She thought it still gave him an evil, forbidding look, but he didn't frighten her. She knew him too well. One good tug on his ear and she could bring him to his knees.

"Hello, Jack." She stepped onto the boardwalk and rested her back against the adobe wall.

"Cady," he said, nodding.

"Why didn't you come to the literary society meeting last night?"

"I was busy getting supplies together. I'm here now to say good-bye."

She stood up straight, hand against her heart. "You're leaving? I thought you planned to stay until the army caught Cuchillo."

"That could take months, or it may never happen. I can't wait that long."

"Why, Jack?"

He took off his black hat and spun it as he looked at her. "Same reason as always."

"You don't have anything to prove."

He smiled without humor, but his hand was gentle when he cupped her cheek. "Maybe not to you, little sister. You always thought I walked on water."

"You're a very special man, Jackson Tanner. When are you going to realize that?"

He shrugged. "When hell freezes over."

"Or when you find that special woman who thinks you walk on water too.

He shook his head. "You *are* a dreamer, aren't you?"

"No." A tight feeling in her throat stopped her. At the same time, tears burned her eyes and she looked past him, down the street to where soldiers were standing at attention on the parade ground. When she had her emotions under control, she looked up again. "I suppose it would be a waste of time to try to talk you into staying?"

"It would." He took a deep breath.

"What's on your mind, Jack?"

"I'm sorry about the wedding," he blurted out. "I know it wasn't what you probably always dreamed of. I did what I thought was right. Are you still mad?"

"No."

"You're not?"

"I stopped being mad when Kane put his mother's ring on my finger."

"That was his mother's?"

"It's all he has of hers. He cares about me, Jack, I know he does. I just have to figure out how to convince him."

"So you do love him?" Jack looked relieved.

She nodded. "The pigheaded soldier doesn't know it yet, but he loves me too. At least I think he does. And I'll get him to say it out loud or die trying."

At her last words, his eyes narrowed sternly. "Speaking of that, don't do anything stupid, like taking off alone again."

"Believe me, I learned my lesson. I intend to prove that I can follow orders."

"Good. Because I just heard from Kane and Mac Thorne that Cuchillo's band struck again, close by."

"What happened?"

"They ambushed a family on the road from town."

"Was anyone hurt?" she asked anxiously.

"You don't really want to know, Cady."

"You can't protect me, Jack. I'm going to hear anyway. This is my life now."

"The parents, Mike and Laura Carberry, were killed. The children, a girl and a boy, are missing, presumed captured."

She gasped. "Oh, Lord, no."

"That's why I'm telling you: Listen to that stubborn husband of yours. He knows what he's talking about."

"I will."

"Promise me, Cady. If anything happened to you—"

"I promise. Nothing is going to happen to me."

He smiled, a slight lifting of his mouth, but she knew that for Jack it meant a lot. "Do you know how proud I am of you, Cady Tanner—I mean, Carrington?"

She grinned at his slip. She kept forgetting her married name too. "Yes, I know, because I'm just as proud of you."

He looked down at the hat in his hands, then back up at her, and the haunted expression was back in his eyes. "Maybe someday I'll do something to justify the way you feel about me."

"Maybe someday you'll remember my name is Carrington."

She started to say something more, but Jack touched a finger to her lips. "I have to go. Just say good-bye."

"Good-bye." Her voice caught on a sob.

"Don't you cry, now."

She nodded, even as two tears trickled over her lower eyelid and slid down her right cheek. He brushed them away with his thumb, then wrapped his arms around her in a fierce hug.

After he let her go, Cady swallowed the lump in her throat as her brother took the lead on his pack mule and mounted his horse. She watched until he passed the last building of the fort, crossed the perimeter, and headed into the desert. She hoped Jack would find what he was looking for and discover whatever his restless spirit needed in order to know peace. She might say the same for herself.

She had spoken brave words when she'd vowed to make Kane admit he loved her. Time would tell whether or not she could do it.

16

Several days after saying her farewells to Jack, Cady walked into the stable. She craved the relaxation of a ride. She figured it would be all right since, as always when she rode, she would keep the perimeter well within sight. Still, she had brought the pistol Kane had given her and felt its reassuring weight pulling at the pocket of her split riding skirt.

She breathed in the scents of hay and horses and sighed with satisfaction. It had been a trying day. The children were all on edge with the rumors of Indian trouble, and it hadn't been easy to maintain order in her classroom. More disturbing, she hadn't seen much of Kane.

He was still doing double duty and invariably came into their quarters late. The first time she had tried to talk to him, he'd pleaded exhaustion. After that, he just slipped into bed and turned away from her. When she awoke in the morning, he was always gone.

She hoped the Indians would be back on the reservation soon, not only for the safety of soldiers and settlers but for her sake as well. How could she get her husband to admit he loved her if she never saw him? If she ever came face to face with Cuchillo, she would give him a piece of her mind!

The whinny of a horse and a responding nicker pulled her back to the business at hand—her afternoon ride.

"Hello?" she called out, for the soldier on duty in the stable. As she turned from side to side looking for him, she felt Jack's old black hat trailing down her back, held on by the leather strings at her neck.

"Isn't anyone here?" She glanced around, surprised that no one appeared to be on duty. "I guess I'll just have to saddle Prince myself."

It wasn't easy, but she managed to lift the heavy saddle onto the horse's back. Fortunately the animal was docile and cooperative. When she was finished, she mounted up and rode down the street, past Kane's office, to the perimeter of the fort.

"Hello, sergeant," she said, waving to a burly guard with a bushy mustache.

"Ma'am." With two fingers, he respectfully touched the bill of his forage cap. "Nice day, ain't it?"

"Yes. Is everything quiet?"

"Yes, ma'am. But me and the boys'll watch real close while you ride," he said, indicating another guard about ten feet away.

"Thank you, sergeant. I won't be too long."

Cady kneed her horse into a walk and rode a short way into the desert, then glanced around her in every direction to make sure she saw nothing out of the ordinary. Satisfied, she nudged the horse into a brisk canter. His instant response told her that he was as eager for exercise as she was.

* * *

Kane stared at the duty roster on his desk and rubbed the back of his neck. No matter how hard he tried or moved his men around, there was just no way to overcome the shortage of manpower. With Major Wexler at the Indian reservation keeping things quiet there, Kane was in charge of the fort. The soldiers were pushing themselves to the limit in patrolling the area, to see if there was any trace of the captured children. Every time he thought about Cuchillo attacking right under his nose, his gut tightened with anger.

As if he didn't have enough to worry about, Cady was never very far from his thoughts. Going to bed with her beside him and not being able to touch her was about to tear him apart. Sometimes he wondered why he didn't just give in. After all, she'd said she loved him. She was his wife. Why didn't he take her again and try to get her out of his system? It made sense but he just couldn't do it, because every time he touched her he lost another piece of himself. He was sure if he bedded her again, she would take his soul.

Kane looked out the window and watched Cady ride by on Prince. Surely with all the trouble they had she wasn't taking her afternoon ride.

He walked over to the door, just in time to see her pass the perimeter, talk briefly with Sergeant Harrison, and canter Prince into the desert.

"Dammit to hell!"

He grabbed his hat and went to the stable, readied Soldier Boy, and swung up into the saddle. As he passed the guard, he pointed to Cady and shouted, "She's not to ride until further notice. If she gets past you, I'll bust you down to private."

"Yes, sir!"

With the slightest pressure from his knees, his mount shot forward after Cady. As he drew closer, he realized she wasn't trying to outrun him, in fact she was constantly watching her surroundings. He caught her easily. Or, more precisely, she looked over her shoulder and pulled up when she recognized him.

He wheeled his horse to a stop beside her. "What the hell do you think you're doing?"

His angry words and tone destroyed the gladness that had sparkled in her eyes at the sight of him.

"We're up to our necks in an Indian uprising," he continued, when she didn't respond.

"I'm aware of that. I brought my gun with me, and I've kept the fort in sight. I've been keeping my eyes open, watching for anything amiss. I followed all your orders. So, captain, if that's all, I'd like to continue my exercise. It's been several days since I've had any, and I do miss it."

"Your exercise is finished now."

"Why?"

"Because the Apaches attacked right under our nose and two children are missing. I don't want you outside the fort."

"If anything happens, I'll ride immediately for shelter."

He shook his head. "Like I said, your ride is over."

"Is that an order?"

"Damn right."

"Would it make any difference if I told you I'm not about to let the Apaches or anyone else intimidate me and keep me from doing something I enjoy?"

"No."

"I don't understand, Kane. I thought that if I followed all the rules, it would be enough."

For anyone else it would be enough. But he couldn't take any chances with her safety. He couldn't do his job the way it should be done if he was worried about her.

"Out here the rules change from day to day, minute to minute. You have to think about everything you do and—when you're sure you've got it figured out—think again. It might save your life."

Just then a shot rang out. It came from the fort.

"What is it?" Cady asked, alarm stripping the color from her cheeks.

Kane whipped around and saw the guard pointing in the distance. There was a cloud of dust on the horizon. "Riders."

"Who are they?"

"From here I can't tell if it's a returning patrol or renegade Indians."

Common sense told him Apaches wouldn't be foolish enough to show their faces within rifle distance of an army post in broad daylight, but he couldn't take any chances. They weren't going to sit there like clay ducks in a shooting gallery.

"Get back to the fort," he said.

Kane turned and saw that Cady was already wheeling her horse around. When she did, he smacked it sharply on the rump, and the animal leaped forward. Behind them, several shots rang out and he knew that was not a returning patrol. He glanced over his shoulder. The cloud of dust had dissipated, the wind carrying it away in a long trail that just barely touched the mesquite bushes and paloverde trees. He could make out ten or twelve Indians sitting on horseback.

He urged his horse after Cady. When he pulled up beside her she glanced at him questioningly.

"Apaches!" he shouted.

That one word bent her over the saddle, urging her horse into a faster gait. When they were inside the fort, she continued on to the stable while Kane slowed his mount.

He stopped beside the perimeter guard, who was down on one knee, rifle raised and ready. "Sound the call to arms and then mount a patrol, sergeant."

"Yes, sir!" The man raced to the parade ground, where soldiers were already assembling, weapons in hand.

Kane followed Cady to the stable and swung down from his saddle. Already dismounted, she stood holding her reins, eyes wide. Outside, the bugle sounded the call to arms.

When Cady spoke, her voice belied the unmistakable traces of fear on her face. "What are you doing here?"

"I wanted to make sure you're all right."

"I'm fine. But you should be with your men."

She was right and Kane knew it. He had gone after her, once again thinking with his heart instead of his head.

"What happens now?" she asked.

"I plan to chase Cuchillo until I catch him."

Cady watched him and saw the exact moment when the gleam of excitement stole into his eyes. It was the same instant her blood turned cold at the thought of what might happen to him when he caught up with the Apaches.

He walked over to her and lifted her chin with his knuckle. "We don't know what the Apaches are up to. Until we do, I want you to stay inside." He sent her a slow smile that she knew was meant to be reassuring. "Consider that an order."

She tried to return his smile, but bit the corner of her lip when hers wavered. "Yes, sir."

"Will you be all right? Stay with Betsy Wexler."

"Don't worry about me. I'll be fine. Go do your job."

He gave her an all-out grin; then he was gone. He'd left before she could tell him to be careful—before she could say she loved him.

Cady paced the length of her quarters for what she thought was the hundredth time. The sun had gone down long ago, and still there was no word from Kane.

By itself, that didn't worry her, but occasional spurts of gunfire made her heart go cold. She didn't know if it was nervous guards firing at shadows or an all-out attack.

If he hadn't ordered her to stay inside, she would have flown out of there. But where? How she wished Kane would get back.

A burst of anger shot through her as she recalled the look in his eyes when he told her he was going after Cuchillo. He was enjoying this. He loved the excitement, the danger. It made him feel really alive.

No woman could compete with that and win.

She was beginning to see what Annie had faced, what any woman faced who fell in love with a soldier. There was a lot more to being a military wife than following orders. He thought she was afraid, and he was partly right. Her fear was for him. Any woman who shared this life had to be willing to accept the fact that her husband was in constant danger. Then she had to find the strength to let him go while she stayed behind, waiting and worrying. She had to let him know she could take care of herself, with or without him. Anything less than that was another burden and distraction that a soldier didn't need.

Cady stifled the sob that jumped into her throat. She loved Kane, and the thought of losing him was terrifying. All she could do was make his home a place he longed to come back to, try to give him something that made him feel as alive as the army. God willing, he would return to her tonight. He didn't want to hear that she loved him. But with every ounce of energy she had, she would show him how she felt.

She would show him everything but her fear for him.

*   *   *

Kane walked through the maze of the fort buildings, making his way on sheer memory in the pitch blackness that had forced his patrol back to the fort. The Apaches had disappeared into the desert, and it was suicide to continue the pursuit. In the morning he would lead a troop out to see if there was a trail to pick up. For now, he'd grab a few hours of sleep.

The thought of saying good-bye to Cady tore at him, but she had sent him away with her blessing.

As he walked in the darkness, he couldn't help thinking of Annie and her petulant behavior during their brief marriage. He realized now that short of giving her his undivided attention, she would never have been content. Even then, it wouldn't have been enough to make her happy.

Cady was so different. Her exuberance and sheer joy in being alive seemed to radiate to those around her, and her laughter touched everyone she met.

An image of her green eyes and long golden-brown hair flashed into his mind. A sense of yearning swept over him, so strong it nearly doubled him over. Even as he instinctively increased his pace, he remembered that he had sent her to wait out the situation with Betsy Wexler. That was just as well. The sense of urgency for her was strong within him, and he knew he would never be able to keep his hands off her.

Kane crossed the board covering the acequia in front of his dark quarters. He let himself inside and realized he needed to light a candle. Cady had moved the furniture in making a home for them. He'd kill himself on something if he didn't have some light.

He made certain the curtains were pulled, then struck a match to the candle on the table by the door. He took off his uniform jacket and hung it on a wall peg. Then he pulled his white cotton shirt over his head and yanked off his boots. He picked up the candle and crossed the room to the dresser and poured some water from the pitcher into the basin beside it. After washing up, he picked up the candle and turned. The light spilled over a figure half on and half off the bed.

He moved closer. It was Cady, sound asleep. She was sitting in a chair but had fallen face forward on the mattress of the nearer iron cot, with her cheek resting against the blanket and the handle grip of a pistol loosely clutched in her fingers.

He couldn't help smiling, and the swelling of tenderness that filled his chest was almost painful. When had he started loving her? Had it been when she was ready to fight him with her hatpin? The time she had caught her dress on fire? Or when she'd gone to warn Jack of the danger he was in, regardless of any harm that might come to herself? He didn't know when his feelings had crystallized into love, he only knew they had.

He wondered why she hadn't gone to wait out the Indian trouble with Betsy Wexler. For a woman who suddenly was bent on following his smallest order to the letter, this seemed a little odd.

But he was glad she was here waiting for him, the way other army wives did. He didn't usually let himself think of Cady as his wife, at least not if he could help it. Tonight he couldn't help it. He was dead tired and she was a sight for sore eyes, so beautiful and sweet. The room smelled like a field of flowers. After the stench of horses and sweat and gunpowder that had filled his head for hours, she was like a small bit of heaven.

Soundlessly, he set the flickering light on the table in the center of the room and moved to where Cady lay. With thumb and forefinger, he carefully lifted the gun from her limp fingers. He didn't want to startle her and have the thing go off. Setting the weapon on the table beside the candle, he turned back to her.

She stirred and stretched and sighed. Her unconsciously seductive movements aroused him instantly. The need in him pulled tight, then blazed through him like a spark to dry grass. He wanted her, more than he had ever wanted any woman in his life.

She yawned, then sat up, and when she looked at him in the shadows a gasp escaped her.

"It's me, Cady. Don't be afraid."

"Kane," she said softly, her voice husky from sleep.

She let out a long breath, then relaxed and rubbed her eyes like a sleepy child. She pushed her loose, heavy hair behind her shoulders and stood up.

"Is everything all right? Are you all right?"

"Fine."

"What happened?"

"Nothing much. We gave chase but couldn't find any trace of them. I suspect it was just an Apache show, a gesture of defiance to let us know they're still out there."

"Will they come back?"

He shrugged. "There's no way to tell. I'll send out a patrol when it gets light."

She nodded as she let out a shuddering breath.

"The danger's over for now. Don't be scared, Cady."

"I'm not." She answered a little too quickly, a shade too confidently.

"You're not a very good liar." With one step, Kane stood in front of her and gently lifted her chin with his knuckle. She was forced to meet his gaze, and he saw the remnants of fear that clouded her eyes and took the color from her normally rosy cheeks.

"Why would I lie?" she asked.

"That's a good question."

He just wasn't sure whether she was hoping to deceive herself or him. The real question was why she would even try to hide her feelings from him. Only a fool wouldn't be afraid.

"Let's just say I'm glad you're back," she said.

"I'm sorry I woke you."

"I was tired." Her lashes lowered as she looked down sheepishly.

"Tell me why you didn't stay with the Wexlers."

She glanced up quickly. "I know that was an order, but I-I wanted to be here, close to my things. And if anything happened, if you were hurt or—" Her voice caught, forcing her to stop.

She whirled around then, but not before the candle caught the gleam of tears in her eyes.

"Cady, what is it?" He turned her gently to face him. "Were you afraid for me?" he asked softly.

She started to shake her head, then hesitated and nodded. Her eyes were huge in her pale face.

He let out a deep, shuddering breath. It had been a long time since someone had cared whether he lived or died. Whether he came home in one piece—or didn't come home at all.

The tenderness swirling inside him refused to be contained any longer. He couldn't hold back the flood of feelings that had rained down on him since he had walked through the door and seen her, his beautiful brave Cady, waiting for him.

Kane lowered his mouth to hers. Anticipation made his breathing quicken, the exquisite fullness of her lips set him on fire. Her soft moan of contentment put him over the edge of rational thought.

He needed to feel her naked against him, he wanted to hold her and kiss her and make the ugliness go away, he wanted her with a desire he had never known before.

With shaky fingers, he worked at the buttons on her blouse even as he kept his mouth on hers. He couldn't bear to pull away, not even long enough to expose her satin skin to his touch.

She reached behind to undo the fastenings of her split skirt and let it drop to the floor. He pushed the blouse from her shoulders as she stepped from the pool of material at her feet. In seconds, her chemise and pantalettes were gone and she stood before him naked.

He stared at her, branding her loveliness in his mind. She held herself proudly before him.

"You're so beautiful I can hardly believe you're real, and you're here, with me."

"I'm very real, and there's nowhere else on earth I'd rather be than here, with you."

Nestled between her breasts was the ring he'd given her, suspended from a string around her neck. He lifted the gold circle and started to pull it over her head, but she stopped him with a light touch.

She placed her hand on his. "Don't take it off."

He smiled at her and placed a kiss in her palm. When he heard her draw in a sharp breath, he glanced up at her, noticing her rapid breathing and the smoky look of passion in her eyes.

She rested her hands on his chest. The feeling was so soft and delicate, Kane thought he'd go out of his mind. He could barely draw enough air into his lungs. When she slipped her hands up around his neck, he wrapped his arms around her, hungrily holding her close as he enjoyed the sensation of her bare skin against his.

Kane had survived a lot in his life and had cheated death more than once, but one thing he knew: If he didn't have Cady soon, he would die.

He bent slightly and placed an arm behind her knees and lifted her, walked the few steps to his cot, and placed her gently on the blanket. Before joining her, he quickly shrugged out of his wool uniform pants, stretched out beside her, and pulled her close.

Cady wondered if this was all a dream. She'd had so many, and she always awakened alone and full of longing. She curved a hand around his strong neck, then pulled him to her for a kiss filled with all her pent-up yearning. His moan of pleasure sounded real enough. She nudged his lips apart and stroked the inside of his mouth. His arms tightened with restrained passion, even as the hard ridge of his desire pressed against the juncture of her thighs.

Kane looked at her with such hungry intensity that she knew this was real. He lowered his lips to her breast. A bolt of pleasure shot through her, clear down to her toes, and she knew she was wide awake, held in the arms of the man she loved. Unbridled happiness filled her until she thought she couldn't possibly hold any more. She gave herself up to the tingles of pleasure as he laved her nipple with his tongue until she thought she'd go mad. Then he lifted his mouth, but only long enough to move to her other breast and suckle it the same way.

Cady was frantic from the pressure building within her. When he slid his hand down her belly to nestle between her thighs, she opened for him gladly. He slipped a finger into her moistness and she gasped.

"Kane, I want you," she whispered fiercely.

"Is that an order?" He smiled at her.

"Oh, yes!"

"This will be one order it will be my pleasure to carry out."

He raised up and positioned himself between her legs. When he looked into her eyes, all traces of humor were gone. Cady saw only a haunted expression and a hunger so intense she knew it matched her own.

"Please, captain," she whispered as he slid into her waiting warmth.

Sheer contentment welled inside her, creating a tender ache. When he began to move slowly, something else took root and started to build. A heat that surpassed anything she'd experienced in the desert glowed in her belly and radiated outward.

He increased his pace, and the embers within her burst into flame. But still there was no freedom from the tension he nurtured. With exquisite caring, he kissed her, then lifted himself up and took his weight on his arms as he thrust into her harder and faster. The blaze he'd created inside her burned brighter and hotter until finally she cried out his name.

Her release came in a flare of brilliant white light, a fireball as hot as the Arizona sun.

Above her, Kane tensed, the tendons in his arms corded as he braced himself. He threw his head back and groaned as he shuddered from the force of his pleasure. Tears filled Cady's eyes at the joy she felt, for she was the one who had given him this powerful release.

Kane lowered himself, resting his weight on his forearms as he kissed her nose. Then he rolled to the side and gathered her against him.

Cady snuggled into his warmth, loving the smell of his skin and the feeling of closeness being in his arms brought her. As she rested her cheek on his chest, his hair tickled her cheek. She suppressed a smile as she waited for him to say something.

But within minutes, she heard and felt his even breathing that told her he'd fallen asleep. Disappointment flooded her. With an effort, she pushed it away, for she knew he must be exhausted after everything that had happened today.

She'd try to be patient. After all, she knew he cared for her. He had just proved it to her with the tenderness of his possession.

Tomorrow was time enough to hear him say he loved her.

17

The next morning when Cady awoke, Kane was gone. She tried not to let it bother her. After all, he was preoccupied with renegade Apaches, and the welfare of every man, woman, and child in the fort depended on him. Still, a part of her had expected him to hold her in the dawning light the way he had in the darkness the night before.

"Patience, Cady," she scolded. "Give the man time." But patience was not one of her strengths.

She picked up her hand mirror from the dresser and checked her appearance before school. She wasn't sure if the children should gather for lessons, considering the scare with the Apaches the previous day, but she would be ready if Kane said it was all right.

Looking at her reflection, she said, "A good soldier's wife does not act without thought. A good soldier's wife follows orders and restrains herself."

Cady wrinkled her nose and sighed. She was trying very hard, but she wasn't sure she had the makings of a good soldier's wife. All she had in her favor was her love for Kane and her determination to be the best wife she could be.

She left her quarters to look for him. After searching in vain everywhere in the fort she could think of, Cady finally went into the mess hall. Betsy Wexler was there, trying to get the upper hand over a rowdy group of children. "Excuse me, Bart," Betsy was saying, with a barely controlled edge of anger in her voice. "Please don't jump off the table. You'll hurt yourself."

"No, ma'am," he said stoutly. "I can jump from higher'n that there table."

"Still, I must ask you not to do it. What if everyone here jumped off the table?"

A lively sparkle gleamed in Bart's hazel eyes. "We could have us more fun than a flea in a doghouse."

Cady walked over to the other woman, who looked ready to throttle the boy, and put a comforting hand on her shoulder. Betsy heaved a relieved sigh.

Then Cady frowned at Bart. "You know better than to behave like a ruffian in my schoolroom. Please take a seat."

"Yes'm," Bart said. He pulled out the bench closest to him and sat.

She glanced at the rest of the group, who hadn't noticed her entrance. Martha Halleck, reddish-brown braids flying behind her, ran after Polly Chase and, when she caught the younger girl, squealed, "You're it!" Emily Stanton smiled coyly at John Eagle as she blinked her dark blue eyes and twirled a black curl around her finger. R. J. glared at the two of them, then slapped John on the back, whereupon a wrestling match ensued.

Cady clapped her hands and said in a loud voice, "Children, please take your seats. On the double!"

She might not be the best army wife there ever was, but she was picking up the language and she had learned how to use it in her classroom.

The children stopped their shenanigans and sat down immediately.

Betsy brushed a loose strand of graying hair away from her flushed face. "I'd like to know what magic you use to do that. I've been trying to get them to listen to me for fifteen minutes."

"It's not magic, it's the voice. Takes time to develop just the right tone."

"I don't plan to be here long enough to acquire the skill."

Cady smiled sympathetically. "Sorry I'm late. I was looking for Kane to see if it was safe to have school today. I never found him."

"He took a patrol out first thing this morning to see what those devil Indians are up to, if anything."

Cady stifled first a stab of fear and then the envy she felt that this woman knew more about her husband's comings and goings than she did. "I see. Then I suppose I'd better check with the officer in charge to see if we should have school or not."

"Oh, I'm sure it's all right," Betsy said quickly. "If anything happens, there will be plenty of warning. Besides, the children are better off following their normal routine. It will take their minds off what's going on."

Cady agreed but still felt she should get permission. Just before she could voice the thought, Bart Grimes toppled off the end of the bench, as the three children beside him shifted suddenly and shoved him. A chorus of giggles followed his undignified thump. Then the flush of embarrassment on his face gave way to anger and he jumped up and yanked on Martha's pigtail.

From then on, all Cady's thoughts focused on restoring and keeping order. She never noticed when Betsy Wexler slipped away, but after she had separated Bart and Martha and calmed the shrieking girl down, the major's wife was gone. Cady proceeded to keep the restless group busy.

When she had everyone back in their seats and all eyes were upon her, she said, "You all remember we were talking about the events in history that led up to America's War of Independence?" When the majority of heads bobbed up and down in assent she continued, "Today I want to tell you about the Boston Tea Party."

Emily Stanton stared at her. "They had tea before they had the war?"

Cady shook her head and told the children about the incident.

When she finished, R. J. asked, "What did the colonists do about those ships in the harbor?"

On the bench to Cady's left, Polly Chase pinched little Bobby Armstrong, who sat beside her. The youngster yelled "Ow!" and pushed her.

Before Polly could retaliate, Cady moved behind them and placed a firm hand on each of their shoulders. "That's quite enough."

Obviously the children were too keyed up just to sit and listen, and a tedious writing assignment was also out of the question. Cady had to think of something that would keep them occupied or she'd have Bart jumping off the table again. That gave her an idea. Maybe if she gave them a lesson that involved activity, she might be able to capture their attention.

She looked at R. J. and glanced at the rest of the children. "You want to know what the colonists did next?" When they nodded, she said, "You're going to show me."

"But how? We don't know." R. J. looked skeptical.

"I'll tell you, then we're going to reenact the Boston Tea Party. Who wants to be a colonist and who wants to be a loyalist?"

"What did the colonists do?" R. J. asked again.

"They dressed up as Indians and dumped a whole shipload of tea into Boston Harbor."

R. J.'s eyes lit up. "I'll be a colonist. I can use these," he said, pulling a wad of firecrackers from his pocket.

"Haven't you learned your lesson yet?" Cady asked, holding out her hand for the explosives.

He shook his head as he gave them to her, and a wide grin split his features. "You can have these. Don't matter much to me. I've got a whole pile of 'em in my saddlebags."

"See that they stay in your saddlebags," Cady said sternly. "Now, I think Martha and Bart and R. J. should play the colonists. And Emily and Polly and John can be the loyalists."

"What do I get to be?" Bobby Armstrong asked.

Cady thought for a minute. "You can be King George the Third."

"Oh, boy!"

Cady organized her troops and marshaled her forces in their respective places, all the while spouting snippets of history to them. She was completely absorbed in her task when her husband walked into the room.

Kane studied the scene of complete chaos before him.

"What's going on here?" he asked.

Cady whirled around and touched a hand to her chest, clearly startled. "Kane! You're back!"

The children stopped to welcome him and he returned the greeting. "Go on with what you're doing while I talk to the captain," Cady said to her students.

Then she turned and crossed the room to Kane. He'd bet his captain's bars that she planned to throw her arms around him—Cady wasn't the type to hold anything back—but he couldn't deal with that. If she touched him, he'd be lost.

He frowned and folded his arms over his chest. She stopped and hesitated before clasping her hands together in front of her.

"I asked you what was going on here," he said.

"What are you doing back from patrol so soon?" she countered.

"We caught up with the Apaches in Horseshoe Canyon. They had Jason and Sarah Carberry with them, so I brought them back here. Mac and the rest of the men are escorting the renegades back to the reservation."

"That's wonderful!" Cady cried. "Are the children all right?"

"Just scratched and bruised. But their parents were butchered right in front of them, so who knows what scars they have on the inside."

Cady sobered instantly, and the expression on her face was pure compassion. "The poor things. What will happen to them now?"

"They're being looked after. Sergeant Armstrong and his wife have offered to take them in until next of kin can be notified."

Cady looked thoughtful. "When they're strong enough, I think they should come to school with the other children. It will help take their minds off their loss."

There was a loud thump behind them, followed by a wail. Bart Grimes was sitting on the floor at the end of the table as he rubbed his ankle.

"I told you not to jump from there, Bart," Cady said sternly as she started toward him.

"Ain't broke, ma'am," he said, in a voice that carried across the room. "Just hurts a little."

She stopped and nodded. "I believe it's time to write standards. Twenty-five times: 'I will obey my teacher.'"

"Yes'm," he said.

Kane admired her way with the children. With a combination of control and warmth, she had them practically eating out of her hand. She had tamed R. J., and that was saying something. She was a beautiful, capable woman and he couldn't help loving her. But he felt himself being drawn so completely under her spell the power of his feelings scared him. He had to do something to stop it.

"What's going on here, Cady?"

"I'm conducting school."

"Even though there was a very real threat of Indian attack?"

"I tried to find you. When I couldn't, I came here and the children had already arrived. Betsy said to hold school."

He nodded at the whooping and hollering behind her. "You could have dispersed them."

"We agreed that it was better for them to go about their normal routine."

"This is their normal routine?" he asked when a loud argument erupted among the children.

She glanced over her shoulder, then back at him. "They couldn't sit still, so we decided to act out the Boston Tea Party."

"You want to bring two fragile children into this chaos? You call that teaching?" Kane knew he was being a bastard, but he couldn't stop himself.

Cady's chin snapped up and her green eyes blazed. "Since when does the army train officers to deal with children? How dare you come into my classroom and criticize my methods?"

"I'm in charge of the post."

"Does that give you the right to stick your nose into something you know nothing about? Do I tell you how to run your fort?"

"It's not the same thing."

"It most certainly is." Cady stopped and took a breath as she glared up at him. "If the Indian threat is over, there's no reason on earth why I shouldn't conduct lessons."

"You should never have started class in the first place."

Kane knew he was splitting hairs. He knew he was wrong and he knew he should apologize and beat a hasty retreat, but instinct was driving him and he'd learned to do whatever he had to for survival.

He stood his ground. "For all you knew, the Indians could have been massing out there for a major assault, and here you'd have been with a room full of children and no way to protect them."

"You told me they'd never get past the perimeter."

"I didn't want you to be frightened."

She put her hands on her hips. "So in addition to being an inadequate teacher, I'm also a coward? Please leave now, captain, before you upset my students more than they already are."

"You're throwing me out?"

"I am."

He stared at her for a few moments, then realized the children had stopped their activity to watch the two adults. Kane didn't take kindly to being ordered out, but he had enough sense left to hold his tongue. "We'll discuss this later, when we're alone."

"We've said everything there is to say."

She turned away, her spine ramrod stiff, her shoulders back, as tall and straight as any good soldier he'd ever seen. She was walking away, but he felt as if he'd been dismissed. And her final words made him uneasy. They would talk later whether she wanted to or not. That was an order.

Cady walked into the stable after school that day, carrying a saddlebag, and proceeded to saddle Prince. In an effort to make amends, R. J. had told her to ride the horse any time she wanted. Since the boy's apology on her wedding day, everything had been fine between them.

If only she could say the same for her husband. In her mind, the list of "if onlys" started ticking like the seconds on a clock.

If only R. J. hadn't helped her out of the guardhouse, if only the rain had waited, if only the river had been passable, if only Jack had arrived sooner. If only Kane loved her.

She shook her head. She would go mad if she kept this up. The fact was, all of it had happened, and she was married to a man who had little or no respect for her: as a teacher, as a wife, as a woman.

She heard footsteps rustle in the hay behind her and whirled around. She felt tremendous relief that it was R. J. walking toward her from the far end of the stable.

"Howdy, ma'am," he said, his grin friendly.

"Hello, R. J. What are you doing here?"

"I was goin' ridin'. How 'bout you?"

"Me too."

He eyed the saddlebag she had just settled behind the saddle near the horse's rump. "You usually take all that with you for an afternoon ride?"

She wanted to evade questions, but what was the point? "I'm going to my brother Jack's cabin."

The boy nodded thoughtfully. "Yes'm, I know where it is. Ain't far, but it's out of sight of the fort."

"I know, but Captain Carrington said the Apaches were no longer a threat"—she turned away from him and put her left hand on the saddlehorn and her foot in the stirrup and hoisted herself onto the horse's back—"and I need some time alone."

R. J. moved beside the horse and patted its nose. "Hi, Prince. How ya doin'?" Then he looked up at her, a suspicious look in his bright blue eyes. "Does Kane know you're goin'?"

"No." She had a little guilty feeling but pushed it away with a reminder of how ill-mannered and judgmental he'd been in her classroom earlier. She could stand almost anything, but when he criticized her teaching and was unreasonable to boot, he'd gone too far.

"You gonna tell him you're leavin'?"

"There's nothing to worry about, R. J. I'll be back tomorrow, in time for school." She laughed when he made a face, and at the sudden sound the horse shifted beneath her. At least she could count on one thing staying the same: R. J. disliked schoolwork as much as he had the day she'd arrived at the fort.

"Kane might be worried if he doesn't know where you are," the boy persisted.

"I doubt it." Cady told herself he'd probably find some excuse not to share her quarters that night, so how would he even know she'd gone? "I'm sure he won't miss me."

"Whatever you say. I reckon you know what you're doin'."

"I do." She knew she wanted to be alone, and Kane had developed a bad habit of coming after her. This time she had to make sure that didn't happen. "R. J., I'd appreciate it if you'd keep this under your hat."

"Ain't wearin' one, ma'am."

"It's just an expression. If you see Kane, don't say anything to him about where I've gone."

"You want me to tell him a falsehood?" he asked, exaggerating his shock at her suggestion.

"Of course not. Just—don't bring it up if you happen to see him."

"Whatever you say."

"Thank you, R. J. I'll see you tomorrow morning. And R. J.?"

"Yes'm?"

"If you're going to go out riding, put on a hat."

When he grinned and nodded, she exerted gentle pressure on Prince's flanks and the horse moved forward.

Cady rode over the rise and reined in her horse when she saw Jack's cabin. The sight of the small structure reminded her of her brother. A rush of loneliness tightened her chest and slipped upward into her throat. She missed Jack even more than the day she'd told him good-bye. If only he were there to talk to. But it was a foolish fantasy, almost as foolish as thinking that she might have a future with the man she loved.

When Prince snorted and pranced restlessly, she patted his neck. "Easy, boy."

Normally, the sound of her voice and a gentle touch were all she needed to calm the animal down. Today, he was uneasy. He tossed his head and whinnied.

"What is it, Prince?" She looked around, but in every direction the desert was quiet and peaceful. "I don't see anything. What's got you so on edge?"

He'd probably eaten something that didn't agree with him.

"Let's go, boy," she said, urging him forward. "I've got some oats for you, and I'll give you some water. That will make you feel better."

When Cady stopped in front of the small cabin, Prince pawed the ground. She tied his reins securely to the rail out front. She tried the front door and found it unlocked, the same as the first time she'd come here.

Pushing the door wide, Cady stepped into the single room. Everything was just as she remembered: the wooden table and one chair stood in the center of the room, a few pots and pans were stacked on the shelf beside the window, and a trunk rested at the foot of the cot against the wall.

There was wood piled beside the fireplace, and since she'd brought a few provisions from the fort, she figured once she hauled in water from the well she'd have everything she needed.

Everything except Kane.

She pushed the thought away. She left the cabin and unsaddled Prince, turning him loose in the corral that Jack had fashioned from the trunks of cottonwood trees. After making sure there was water and feed for the animal, she filled a bucket and carried it inside.

The sun would set soon, and when it did a chill would descend over the desert. The last time she'd been here, she recalled how hot it had been. Now she needed to build a fire.

She smiled sadly as she remembered how excited she'd been to see Jack, after several years' separation, and her own eager anticipation to start a new life. How could she have been so wrong about everything?

She lit a match, and when she had a popping, crackling blaze going, she put two logs on. They caught, and she sighed with satisfaction. At least that skill was something Kane couldn't take away from her.

"This is a fine kettle of fish," she scolded herself. "You came all this way to be by yourself, to get away from that pigheaded man, and all you've done is think about him."

From outside, she heard Prince whinny and then the sound of his hooves as he galloped around the corral. Cady looked out the window and wondered why, after their ride out here, he wasn't standing contentedly like he did in the stable at the fort.

The door suddenly flew open. Heart pounding, Cady turned to see an Indian there. He was tall, not as tall as Kane but an arrogant, imposing figure nonetheless. His skin was the color of copper and as smooth as leather. He wore a long-sleeved cotton shirt belted at the waist by braided leather thongs, trousers, and knee-high moccasins. His blue-black hair fell straight to his shoulders, and he had a bandanna tied around his forehead to hold back its length.

When she saw the pistol in his left hand pointing at her, Cady knew bone-chilling fear. Did Indians aim a gun at anyone they didn't plan to shoot? She realized she hadn't brought a weapon, not even the gun Kane had given her; she'd left it in her quarters. She was alone, with nothing to defend her but her wits.

The man was silent. Finally, Cady couldn't stand it.

"Who are you?" she asked.

He didn't answer. She wondered if he spoke English.

Her knees shook and her heart pounded painfully against her ribs. Still she decided to ask him something else.

"Wh—" Her throat was dry and she swallowed, then tried again. "What do you want?"

He didn't respond except to let his gaze wander over the interior of the cabin. Was he looking to see what he could steal? Kane had told her the Apaches usually raided for guns and ammunition. If that was so, he'd be sorely disappointed here. Would he be angry enough to kill her? If he tried, could she do anything to stop him?

Kane had told her just that morning that the Indians had surrendered to the reservation. Was this man part of that band? Had he escaped or refused to give himself up? Was there a patrol out looking for him?

"Since you won't tell me your name, I'll tell you mine. I'm Cady Tanner—I mean Carrington. I keep forgetting. I haven't been married long, you see. My husband is Captain Carrington of Fort McDowell."

The Indian barely moved, but the way he looked at her frightened her terribly. His muscles were stretched as tight as a fiddle string, and a look burned in his eyes that she could only describe as loathing. What had she said to make him despise her so?

The hand holding the pistol flexed and when he gripped it again, his knuckles went white. "So you are the wife of the army officer."

She gasped. "You do understand me."

"Better than you know. You are the sister of Jack Tanner?"

Cady nodded. "Do you know him?" she asked eagerly. Maybe things weren't as bad as she had thought. After all, Nathan Eagle was an army scout and John Eagle was her student. They were Indians, but more importantly they were her friends. "Are you a friend of Jack's?"

"No." He smiled, but instead of reassuring her, the malevolence that radiated from that baring of white teeth sent chills down her spine. "I am Cuchillo."

Cady gasped, feeling cold and hot at the same time.

"But I thought you went back to the reservation."

"No. The soldiers will not take me alive. Before that happens, I have something to do."

"You're going to kill my brother."

He said nothing. What would he do to her? With a sinking heart, she realized no one knew where she was except R. J., and she'd made him promise not to tell. No one was likely to happen by to help her.

She met Cuchillo's smoldering hate-filled stare and realized she was looking into the face of death.

18

Kane tried to concentrate on the supply order in his hands but, instead of words, all he could see was the look of betrayal on Cady's face in the mess hall that morning. He knew he'd hurt her terribly. He hadn't meant to. As soon as he thought it, the lie rang hollow through his head. He ran his hand through his hair. He had been unreasonable and judgmental, and he had done it to push her away, because he was afraid he wouldn't have the strength to let her go when the time came.

He felt lower than a scorpion's tail. He couldn't live with himself if he didn't try to explain to her why he had acted that way. If he was lucky, he would find the words to make her understand and forgive him.

He grabbed his hat from the chair by the door as he walked out. On the boardwalk, he ran into Mac Thorne, covered with dust and showing two days' worth of stubble on his face.

Kane knew there was trouble by the look on his face. "Don't you ever bring good news when you come back from patrol?"

Mac went straight to the heart of the matter. "Cuchillo wasn't with the Apaches who surrendered."

"Dammit! How did you let him get away?"

"Me?" Anger blazed across Mac's tanned face. "You were there when we caught up with them. How did he get away from *you*?"

"I brought the children back to the fort. You had orders to return the Apaches to the reservation."

"And I did that."

"All but Cuchillo."

"Look, captain, neither one of us knows what he looks like. You didn't know he wasn't with that band of renegades anymore than I did. You've been riding me real hard lately, and I want to know why." Mac's eyes narrowed. "This is about Cady, isn't it?"

"She's got nothing to do with this." But Kane couldn't stifle the wave of jealousy that sliced through him when the other man mentioned her name.

"She's not Annie."

"Don't you think I know that?"

"Hell, no, I don't think you do. You treat Cady like your sister, not your wife, even though you're crazy in love with her. You keep trying to push her away because you're afraid of getting hurt. Damn right she's paying for what Annie did."

"Butt out, Mac. This is none of your concern," Kane said angrily.

"Someone has to make you see reason."

"It sure as hell isn't you."

Mac glared at him. "She deserves better. When you're through with her, you let me know."

"Thorne, you go near her and I'll—" Kane saw red at the thought. "Hell, I'll do it now."

He punched the other man so hard, Mac staggered

backward, hit the wall, and slid down the side of the adobe.

Mac wiped the trickle of blood from his mouth and, amazingly, he grinned. "That's what I thought. You're in love with her."

Kane stared at him, unbelieving. "You did that on purpose? You dumb son of a bitch."

"How else could I get through that hard head of yours?"

Kane knew he was right. He also knew there was a time to stand and fight and a time to surrender. He decided to wave the white flag and stop acting like a damn fool.

Kane held his hand out, and when Mac took it he pulled the other man to his feet.

"You knew how I felt about her the first time you saw her in my office, didn't you? You tried to make me jealous then," Kane said.

"Let's just say I was testing the waters."

"Did you ever have any intentions toward Cady?"

Mac shook his head. "She's the marryin' kind. Although she does tempt even a confirmed bachelor like myself." Mac held his hands up in a conciliatory gesture as Kane felt his own face tighten with anger again. "Hold on, captain. I just meant that she's got more heart and more spunk than any woman I ever saw. You're a lucky man."

"Sorry, Mac." Kane held out his hand. "You're a good friend. No hard feelings?"

"None as far as I'm concerned," he said, gripping Kane's palm in a hearty handshake.

"I'm on my way to look for Cady. I've got some explaining to do if it's not too late."

"It's not," Mac said.

"How do you know?"

"Truth is, I'd never have had a chance with the lady. She's crazy in love with you too."

"I hope you're right. I'll see you later." Kane hurried down the steps and called back over his shoulder. "Put the word out that Cuchillo is still on the loose."

An hour later, Kane was feeling damned uneasy. He had searched everywhere inside the fort and couldn't find Cady. No one had seen her. His last hope was the stable; she usually came back from her afternoon ride around this time. As he walked inside, Kane was disappointed. The place looked empty.

Then he heard someone talking. Kane walked past several stalls, and as he neared the rear of the building he recognized the voice.

"R. J.? Is that you?"

"Back here, captain."

When he came to the last stall, Kane saw the boy inside, brushing down a small pinto.

"Where's Prince?" Kane asked.

"He's not here?" The boy quickly looked away.

"I didn't see him when I passed. Did Cady take him this afternoon?"

"Might've."

Kane frowned, disturbed by the kid's guilty tone. He pushed his hat back and leaned his arms on the rail. "Has she come back from her afternoon ride yet?"

"Ain't seen her back here." R. J. started brushing as if the pinto's shiny coat was the most important thing in the world.

"But you saw her earlier?"

"You saw her too, remember?" He stopped currying the animal and turned around. "Today when we was actin' out the Boston Tea Party. Remember when Bart

Grimes jumped off the table and Miz Carrington told him they threw tea in the harbor, not themselves?"

"No."

"Sure you saw her. The two of you were squawkin' about somethin'."

"Yes, I saw Cady. No, I didn't hear her tell him—never mind." R. J. was using a flanking maneuver, which told him something was going on that concerned his wife.

"Today was the most fun I've ever had in school," R. J. said.

"So you and Cady have worked out your differences?"

"Yes, sir."

"Did you see her after school?"

"Yes," he said, lowering his gaze just before he went back to brushing.

"When did you see her?"

He scratched his head. "Don't know exactly."

"Was it about the same time she normally rides?"

"I reckon it mighta been."

"And you haven't seen her return?"

"No."

Kane knew he was holding something back and was about ready to throttle the kid. At the same time, a small seed of worry took root in his gut and was growing by the minute. As it got bigger, the level of his patience dropped.

"Look, R. J., I need to talk to her. If you know where she is you'd better tell me."

"What makes ya think I know anything?"

"Because you're the first one I've asked who's seen her."

"Hmm. That a fact?"

"Look, you little—" Kane took a deep breath. The

more time that passed without a sign of Cady, the more uneasy he got. And if the kid could shed some light on where she was, he'd damn well better do it.

But since he was getting nowhere fast, Kane decided to try a different strategy. "Mac Thorne just told me that Cuchillo didn't give himself up with the other Apaches."

R. J. whirled around. "Ain't he the one who swore to kill Miz Carrington's brother?"

Kane nodded. "If she's out there somewhere, she could be in real trouble."

It was a long shot that the Indian was still in these parts. No doubt he'd followed Jack to the Superstitions. But if R. J. thought she was in danger, Kane might get the information he was convinced the boy had.

R. J. shuffled his feet in the hay, jammed his hands on his hips, curry brush and all, and turned away. When he circled around to face Kane again, there was an uncertain look in his eyes.

"She made me promise not to say anything."

"So you know where she's gone?" Kane moved forward. Thank the Lord he was finally getting somewhere.

"Yes, sir. But she made me promise not to tell you."

Anger, frustration, and guilt boiled up inside him and spilled over. "Damn it! You tell me now, boy, or I swear I'll tan you good."

"She's at her brother's cabin," he said, his eyes wide. "She said she'd be back in time for school in the morning."

"I'm going to get her and bring her back now."

"If Cuchillo is out there, you might need some help, sir. I'm comin' with you."

"No. Stay here. Tell Lieutenant Thorne where I've gone."

"But, sir—"

"That's an order, R. J."

"Dang it." He kicked at the floor of the stall and hay flew into the air.

Kane walked over to him and ruffled his hair. "Telling me was the right thing. I owe you."

"How about we play some checkers Sunday night? Miz Carrington could play the winner."

Kane nodded. "I'd like that. And I'm sure Cady would too."

If he could convince her that he loved her. If not, he figured he'd have a lifetime to learn the finer points of checkers.

Cady sat on the chair by the table where Cuchillo had ordered her and nervously clutched her gold wedding ring. It seemed she had been held prisoner for a lifetime, but in reality it hadn't been very long. Funny, she thought, how fear distorted one's concept of time.

She had watched the Apache go through every square inch of Jack's cabin, looking for God knows what. Kane had told her repeatedly that she should have returned to the East where she belonged. If she had listened, she wouldn't be in this fix now. But then she would never have known the joy of being in Kane's arms and loving him. Her only regret was that she would probably never see him again. And, dear Lord, if she had a last wish, it would be to see him one more time.

A sob rose in her throat but she swallowed it. If she could help it, she would never betray to Cuchillo by look or sound how very afraid she was of him.

Now the Apache was going through the trunk at the foot of the bed. When he finished, he dumped out the saddlebag she'd brought. She pulled herself together, trying to think of a way out of this.

Since she couldn't overpower him physically, her only chance was to run. She couldn't ride Prince bareback and there wouldn't be time to saddle him, so she'd have to make it to the gully behind the cabin and find a place to hide. It was pretty thin as far as plans went, but it was all she had. And there was no time like the present while Cuchillo was occupied with his scavenging.

Glancing out the window in front of her, she mentally marked her escape route. When she had it set in her mind, she surged out of the chair and headed for the door. Her limbs were stiff from sitting and she reached it the exact moment Cuchillo did. Before she could even yank it open, his palm slapped against the wood.

He was behind her, his body pressing against hers. The smell of smoke and sweat mingled together and surrounded her along with the heat of his body. She went cold all over. For the first time she realized that death wasn't the only thing he could do to harm her. And she remembered Kane's warning not to let the Apaches take her alive.

Fear sliced through her as Cuchillo pushed her heavy hair aside and lowered his head so that his mouth was close to her ear. She felt his hot breath on her cheek. "That was a foolish thing to do, Mrs. Carrington. What did you hope to gain?"

"My freedom," she said, in a voice that she hoped was even and calm, if not quite as defiant as she wished.

He took her upper arms and turned her around. "You see how far you got."

"In my position would you have done any less?" she asked.

A glint flashed in his eyes, and for a moment she thought it might be admiration. Then it disappeared and his expression was blank again. That was more unnerving than the hatred. At least she could understand that.

He dragged her back to the chair and thrust her into it, hard. "Do that again, and I will slit your throat."

His eyes smoldered with hatred again and Cady knew he'd do what he said. She didn't trust her voice to stay steady, so she nodded once to show him she understood.

With his back to the window, Cuchillo stood about a foot away from her and crossed his arms over his chest. "What are you doing here? Are you meeting your brother?"

"No, I haven't heard from Jack since—" She had started to say *since he left the fort*. This was no time to be impulsive. *Think, Cady,* she said to herself. *Don't tell him more than you have to.*

"Since when, Mrs. Carrington? Where is your brother now?"

"I don't know."

"You expect me to believe that he just left without telling you where he was going?"

"It's the truth."

He stared at her for a long time and Cady held her breath. He could slit her throat at any moment just because she was the enemy. But common sense told her that he wanted Jack, and if he believed there was any chance she could help him, he would keep her alive. But what would he do to her while she was his prisoner?

"Why should I believe that Jack Tanner's flesh and blood would tell me the truth?"

"If you expected me to lie, why did you ask me in the first place?" she demanded.

To her surprise, he threw back his head and laughed. When he stopped and looked at her, she saw that flash of respect again. "You have spirit. I like that."

"I don't care what you like," she said defiantly.

He made no response.

Cady thought she heard something outside and she glanced beyond Cuchillo's shoulder out the window. Then she chided herself for being a fool.

A moment later, she saw a rider in an army uniform. Kane. She knew it was him. Even with just a glance, she could tell by the straight, proud way he sat a horse. Had the Apache heard his approach too? Her heart raced, thumping hard against her ribs. When he pulled the pistol from the band of material at his waist and pointed it at her heart, she knew he had heard Kane. And she knew that somehow she had to warn her husband.

He glanced out the window and then back to her. "If you make a sound, you will be dead and so will the captain."

"What makes you think that's my husband?" she asked, trying to distract him.

He lifted one shoulder nonchalantly. "You are a beautiful woman. He would follow you."

"You're wrong. He doesn't like me very much. He'll be glad I'm gone."

"You are not a good liar. A man would be a fool to turn aside a spirited woman like you. One thing I know of this Captain Carrington: He is no fool."

Cuchillo went to the window and cautiously looked out. Cady knew this might be her only chance to warn Kane. Before the Indian turned around, she jumped to her feet and raced to the door, screaming as she went, "Kane! Don't come in! Go for help—"

Cuchillo pulled her away from the door. The movement swung her around. His hand connected with her cheek, and Cady felt sharp, hot pain radiate through her head as she fell to the floor.

The door burst open and Kane stood there, pistol in hand. He glanced at Cady, then at the Apache, and said one word, "Cuchillo."

"Yes, captain. And you'd better drop the gun or I'll shoot her."

"Don't do it, Kane," she screamed.

Panic welled up inside Cady, not fear for herself but for Kane. He couldn't defend himself without a gun.

"Silence!" Cuchillo took a threatening step toward her.

"You lay a hand on her again, and I'll break you in half," Kane said through clenched teeth.

"Your gun, captain. Drop it," he said, pulling back the hammer of his own pistol aimed at Cady's chest.

Kane hesitated in the doorway, legs bent slightly, every muscle tensed for action. He had no choice. If he didn't put his gun down, Cady would be dead.

Slowly, he bent and placed the pistol on the canvas floor, then straightened.

"Kick it to me," Cuchillo said.

Kane did as he was ordered. The Indian grabbed it and stuck the barrel in his waistband without breaking eye contact.

"Cady, are you all right?" Kane glanced at her and saw her push herself to a sitting position. Then he saw the red imprint of a palm on her cheek. A murderous rage swept through him. He'd never before wanted to kill a man in cold blood, but he did now.

Kane took a step toward him and Cuchillo raised the gun, aiming it at his heart. "I wouldn't advise it, captain."

Kane knew if he didn't keep a cool head he would be no help to Cady. He pushed the anger aside, clearing his mind of everything except the enemy. What was Cuchillo's weakness?

"I'm going to help my wife. Shoot me if you have to."

In two strides, Kane was beside her and dropped to one knee. She touched his arm and her hand trembled. When she looked at him, her eyes were frightened but clear.

"Are you all right?" he asked again.

"Yes. Don't worry about me." She smiled slightly, a small expression meant to reassure him, but considering what she'd been through and what they still faced, it was the most courageous thing he'd ever seen.

He didn't know if they would live to see the sun rise tomorrow, but he prayed that he'd have the opportunity to tell her how proud he was of her and, more important, how much he loved her.

"Your wife has much spirit," Cuchillo said, almost as if he could read Kane's mind.

"Yes, she does."

Kane stood up and helped Cady. When she staggered slightly, he put his arm around her and pulled her against his side.

She rested her uninjured cheek against his chest and sighed. "I'm sorry you're mixed up in this too, but I can't help being glad you're here."

Kane squeezed her waist reassuringly. When he knew she was steady on her feet, he dropped his hands and looked at the Apache. "I don't know what you want, Cuchillo, but Cady's not part of this. Let her go."

"She is the sister of my sworn enemy." An evil light glowed in his black eyes. "If I kill her, Jack Tanner will know the same sorrow I have felt."

Frustration and fear coiled together in Kane's gut and he flexed his fingers, wishing he had his gun. When he fixed his gaze on the other man's throat, he was shocked at how much he wanted to put his hands there and press, squeezing the breath from him. Then Cady would be safe.

The only thing stopping him was the knowledge that if he tried, he'd probably wind up with a bullet through the heart and Cady would be left alone with Cuchillo. The thought turned his blood to ice and cleared the haze of fury from his mind. Their only chance was to stall long enough for him to force a break in their favor and get her out of this in one piece.

"You son of a bitch. You harm one hair on her head and I won't rest until you're dead."

"Brave words, captain. But I have the guns. Do you think I would let you live? Jack Tanner is the one I want. To avenge his sister he will search for *me*. When he finds me, I will kill him."

"No," Cady cried. "My brother was only protecting his friend. He didn't mean to harm anyone."

As she spoke, Cady clutched the ring around her neck as if it gave her protection.

When she let it go, Cuchillo lowered his gaze to her chest and his eyes narrowed. "So, there is something of value here after all. How many guns do you think this will buy for my people?" Swift as a cat he reached out, grabbed the gold ring, and yanked on it, ripping the string.

Cady gasped and her hand came up to her chest. "No! You can't have that. It's mine. It's all I have of Kane's."

With a sudden movement that startled Kane and the Indian too, Cady rushed him. She got in so close, so fast, he didn't have time to squeeze off a shot. She started clawing at the hand that held her ring.

"Give it to me! It's mine!"

Before Kane could help her, she bit the Indian's hand. He hissed loudly at the pain, then opened his fingers, and she grabbed the ring. Cuchillo raised his gun hand high in the air. Kane knew he meant to hit her. He jumped forward, gripping the Apache's wrist with both hands. With every ounce of strength he had, Kane brought Cuchillo's hand down on the edge of the table, trying to dislodge the weapon. The Indian hung on. Both of them were breathing hard from the struggle.

The next thing Kane knew, Cady had jumped on Cuchillo's back and grabbed him around the neck.

"Get away!" Kane yelled. "Get the hell out of here!"

"No, I won't leave you," she cried. She gripped the Indian's ear and pulled on it with enough strength to force a grunt from him.

With catlike swiftness, he seized a handful of Cady's hair and yanked until she cried out and let go. He pulled her off him and backhanded her, so hard the blow knocked her several feet. As she fell, she hit her head with a dull thump on the wooden footboard of the bed.

Deadly fury roared through Kane. He delivered a vicious blow to the Apache's nose and smiled a cold grim smile of satisfaction when he saw blood. With fierce single-mindedness, he lashed out, hitting the other man again and again. He landed a blow in Cuchillo's midsection and another to his chin. Rage gave him a strength he'd never known. He kept raining blows, delivering as much punishment as he could. Still, Cuchillo stood there, blocking punches, landing a harmless blow here and there, curving a leg behind Kane to trip him, but he wouldn't go down.

Then Cuchillo lowered his head like a charging bull and grabbed Kane around the waist, trying to bring him to his knees.

As they struggled, there was a noise outside, a series of pops. Kane felt Cuchillo tense and hesitate. Then, from a different direction, came another series of small blasts, not quite like rifle fire or even pistol reports.

Kane had heard the same sound before, at the fort. It was like . . . firecrackers. Dammit! R. J. had followed him!

The momentary distraction loosened Kane's grip on the other man and Cuchillo didn't hesitate. He delivered a bruising punch to Kane's cheek that knocked him off balance, long enough for the Apache to race out the door.

Kane shook his head to clear it and had started to follow when he heard Cady moan. He looked at the empty doorway where the Indian had disappeared. Then he looked down at Cady's fragile form and knew he couldn't leave.

Kane knelt beside her. "Cady?" he said, brushing the hair from her face.

"Kane?" she whispered, without opening her eyes.

"I'm here." He lifted Cady into his arms.

Just then he heard footsteps on the front porch and R. J. stuck his head in the door. "Kane! He had a pony hidden in the gully behind the cabin. Cuchillo's gettin' away!"

"Forget him. Cady's hurt." She was the most important person in the world to him. "I've given my life to the army. I won't give Cady's too."

"But, Kane—"

"Get me some water!" he ordered. "On the double!"

"Yes, sir," the kid said, and disappeared.

Kane carried his wife to the cot by the wall. Her belongings and the saddlebag she'd brought them in were scattered over the blanket from the Apache's search. If anything happened to Cady, there was nowhere Cuchillo could hide that Kane wouldn't find him and kill him. Damn the army or anyone else who tried to stop him from doing it.

19

"Tell me again what happened when them firecrackers went off."

"Those firecrackers," Cady corrected automatically.

She smiled at R. J., who sat cross-legged on the end of her cot in her quarters at the fort. After she had regained consciousness, Kane had brought her here, insisting that she ride with him. He wouldn't take the risk of her falling off Prince. She had to admit that his strong arms around her were heaven after what seemed like an eternity of hell. The tender way he held her made her feel cherished after a lifetime of longing.

When they arrived, he had bullied her to stay in bed. Then he brought the post surgeon to examine her. The man had told Kane the same thing she had been trying to tell him, which was that she was perfectly fine.

Kane had always been bossy, but now there was an edge to him, a tension that even she wouldn't test. Except to fetch the doctor, he hadn't left her for a minute since they'd come back. Then, when R. J. had come to see how she was, Kane had ordered the boy to stay with her until he returned from bathing in the river.

She sensed a shift in her husband but was afraid to trust that it meant his feelings for her had changed. Besides, she hadn't the strength to question or fight this different Kane.

She would just enjoy his fussing over her and his attention, for as long as it lasted. Which would probably be until he questioned her about why she had gone to Jack's cabin in the first place.

The youngster at the end of her bed shifted restlessly. "Quit thinkin' about Kane and tell me again about the firecrackers."

"How did you know I was thinking about Kane?" She bit back a smile.

"Don't take much. You get that gooey, sugary-sweet look in your eyes, and it's clear as a new mirror."

That surprised and disturbed her. If she was that obvious, everyone must know. They'd all pity her when they found out Kane didn't really love her.

"Kane already told you the firecrackers fooled Cuchillo into thinking he was surrounded by the army," Cady replied patiently. "So he ran."

"How many times do you want to hear that you saved our behinds?" Kane stood in the doorway with a towel draped around his neck. Dark wet hair fell onto his forehead and drops of water glistened on his bare chest. He hadn't even taken the time to dry off completely before coming back to her. In his hand was the damp cloth he had insisted on holding to the side of her face. He had cooled it off in the river.

R. J. grinned. "I wouldn't mind hearin' it again."

"You also disobeyed orders," Kane said seriously. "Didn't I tell you to stay at the fort and not follow me?"

The boy nodded, but there was a twinkle in his blue eyes that told Cady he wasn't in the least sorry for what he'd done.

Kane fixed her with a hard look. "What you did was just as foolish and reckless. Didn't I tell you always to stay within sight of the fort when you ride?"

"Yes." Cady met R. J.'s eyes and winked at him.

Kane saw her expression and scowled at them both. "Doesn't anyone around here follow orders?"

"Of course they do." Cady leaned forward and plumped up the pillows behind her back, then rested against them with a tired sigh.

Kane frowned at her, then glanced at R. J. "Cady needs to rest now, son."

"Before I go, can I ask you somethin', Miz Carrington?" When she nodded, he continued. "You ain't mad at me for tellin' where you were, are ya? I mean, I tried not to, but the captain wouldn't take no for an answer."

"Of course I'm not angry with you, R. J. If you hadn't told him where I'd gone, I probably wouldn't be here now. How can I ever repay you?"

"Don't owe me. Just glad I could help."

"I bet Cady would like it if you'd come back for a visit tomorrow," Kane said.

"That won't be necessary," Cady answered, glancing up at him beside her. "I'll see you in the morning for school."

"Yes'm." R. J. unfolded his long legs and rolled off the bed. "I'll be there. 'Night, Miz Carrington. Captain."

"Good night, R. J." The door closed, leaving the two of them alone. Kane looked sternly at her, an expression that was getting far too familiar for her liking.

Cady had a feeling she knew what was coming and decided to change the subject. "That was really sweet of

you to let him believe he saved our lives with the firecrackers. The truth is, you'd have overpowered
Cuchillo if you hadn't been distracted when they went
off. Isn't that right?"

Kane shrugged. "We'll never know. I just wish I'd
been able to hang on to him. I'd feel a whole lot better
if he was in custody." He crossed the room and looked
down at her with just the hint of a twinkle in his eye.
"Did you think you could distract me that easily?
You're not going to have class tomorrow. You're going
to stay in bed and rest."

She grinned. "It was worth a try. Besides, I feel fine."

He sat down beside her, and the mattress dipped
from his weight, letting his thigh brush hers. He leaned
one hand on her other side and looked into her eyes.
His comforting warmth and familiar masculine smell
surrounded her and made her feel safe and protected.
His thick hair was dark and wet and disheveled. There
were lines in his handsome face that she'd never
noticed before, and an ugly bruise darkened his jaw.
Cuchillo must have done that. Her chest tightened
painfully at the thought that she could have lost him.
She wanted to reach out and touch his cheek.

Clasping her hands in her lap, she held back, unwill-
ing to risk any physical contact that would reveal her
feelings. Her body had survived a brutal and frightening
experience. Her heart wouldn't hold up to another blow
from Kane.

Kane frowned when he looked at the injury to her
face. "Next time you pull on someone's ear, make sure
they're not likely to hit you back."

"It worked with R. J. and Jack," she grumbled.

"See what I mean?"

She pointed to his bruised jaw. "You're a fine one to
talk."

"Bravely sustained saving your backside, which I might add wouldn't have been necessary if you had followed orders in the first place."

"I'm sorry."

When Kane tenderly placed the damp cloth on her face, she winced; then the treasured coolness eased the ache. He didn't take his hand away, but very gently held it there, looking at her as if she might disappear at any moment.

A vision of Cuchillo flashed into her mind. She had been told what had happened after she'd hit her head, but she still didn't understand why Kane had let the Indian get away. She thought she'd heard Kane say something, but in her semiconscious state, she couldn't be sure.

"What's that look for?" he asked.

"I was just thinking about Cuchillo. He's out there looking for Jack. He won't stop until my brother is dead."

"Jack can take care of himself. I'm worried about you. That renegade threatened to kill you. So don't get any ideas about going to warn your brother again. Haven't you learned your lesson?"

"I don't plan to look for Jack. I was just wondering why you didn't go after Cuchillo when you had the chance."

"You were unconscious and needed help. I couldn't leave you."

If that was true, it meant he cared about her. In spite of her resolution to hide her love, Cady couldn't stop the tiny spurt of hope that rose within her. If he had feelings for her, why had he done everything possible to push her away from the moment he had stopped her runaway wagon?

"I don't understand you," she said, shaking her head.

"That makes two of us. At least I didn't until Mac Thorne straightened me out."

"What does Mac have to do with anything?" she asked, her forehead wrinkling with confusion.

"For one thing, I was jealous as hell of him." He laughed without humor. "Not just him. I wanted to strangle any man who looked at you. I was against your literary society meetings because I didn't want the men near you."

Her eyes widened in surprise. "I don't believe it. There was no reason for you to be jealous. I just wanted to lend books to ease their boredom."

"You certainly did that," he said wryly.

"I never did anything improper—"

His finger on her lips cut off her words. "That was not a criticism."

"What was it?"

"A confession, I guess. Mac made me see that I'd deliberately pushed you away. And I did a damn fine job of it too, right into Cuchillo's arms. If R. J. hadn't told me where you'd gone—"

He clamped his jaw shut as if trying to keep some emotion locked inside. But he couldn't seem to keep it contained.

"If I had lost you, Cady, I don't know how I could go on. I don't know how I'd be: as a soldier, as a man. I don't know. . . I don't know. . ." His voice trailed off and he looked down.

When he lifted his gaze to hers, she saw fear in his eyes. "What is it, Kane? What are you saying?"

"It scares me how much I need you."

She did reach out then, to cup his cheek in her palm. He turned his lips into her hand and kissed it. This time she couldn't stop the surge of joy and hope that filled her. She needed to hear it all but was almost afraid to say anything and break the spell. He was quiet for so long, she finally had to.

"Go on," she whispered. "What did Mac say?"

"He said you weren't Annie." He took her two hands in both of his. "You see, Cady, I needed you to be as selfish and shallow as she was. It was safer that way."

"Safer?"

"If you were like her, I wouldn't care about you, and when you left—"

"It wouldn't hurt."

He nodded.

"Did you love her, Kane?" Cady knew whatever he said would prick her heart. She'd never be the first woman in his life, but she vowed she'd be the last.

"I thought I did. But I guess the fact that I couldn't give her my mother's ring says everything. I never questioned giving it to you. It just seemed right." He gazed at her intensely. "When I met Annie, I was tired of being alone. I know now I never loved her. Because of that she felt isolated and bored and finally turned to another man. It was her decision to leave the fort. Because of the scandal she was an outcast. But no one deserves to die like that. I felt guilty."

She wanted to tell him not to—Annie had made her choices and paid the price for them—but she knew it wouldn't do any good. If he didn't take things to heart the way he did, he wouldn't be the man she loved.

"Mac is right. I'm not Annie. In case you hadn't noticed, I manage to keep myself too busy to be bored." What she didn't say was that she could never turn to another man. She loved Kane and only him. She always would.

"The more I saw that you were nothing like Annie, the harder I tried to push you away." He glanced at her, and she read self-derision in his expression. "Everything you did was unselfish. Teaching the kids, trying to warn Jack; even today, you risked your life for me." He swallowed and went on. "I've never met a more courageous, committed woman, be it to your work or your family. The man who has your love is one lucky son of a gun."

"You have my love, Kane. You've always had it." She blurted it out without thinking. She had told him before, but maybe he didn't believe her then. Annie had stood between them. Now was the time to get everything out in the open. He was revealing himself to her in a way he never had before.

"I never meant to hurt you, Cady. I'm sorry for what I said to you today. You're a fine teacher, and the kids are lucky to have you."

"Thank you for saying so."

There was a question she needed to ask him, a clarification of something she'd heard when she was semiconscious. She'd been afraid of Kane's answer before, afraid to let her heart hope. But now she had to know.

Shyly, she looked down at their clasped hands. "When R. J. told you Cuchillo was getting away, I thought I heard you say that you'd given your whole life to the army and you wouldn't give mine too."

"I did."

She blinked. "What did you mean?"

He took a deep breath and released it.

"The army has always come first because I felt indebted. It was the only family I had for a long time—until now," he said. "Now you're my family, Cady."

Her heart beat so hard she thought he must be able to hear it. Her joy was so big she could hardly contain it. He did care about her and had told her in every way but one. "Are you ever going to say it?"

"What?" he asked. "I think I've said a mouthful already. More than I've probably ever said in my whole life."

"You left out three small but very important words."

"I have?" Lines creased his forehead, but a teasing glint in his eyes told her he only pretended deep thought. He knew what she wanted to hear. He finally shook his head. "Nope, I can't think of anything else I need to say."

She pulled her hands from his. "Kane Carrington, I have a gun and I know how to use it."

He grinned, then turned serious. Such powerful longing radiated from him that she couldn't doubt his sincerity.

When they came, the words were the sweetest she'd ever heard.

"I love you, Cady Tanner Carrington, more than I thought it possible to love a woman. I love you with my body, my heart, my soul. I love you with—"

She touched his mouth with her finger. "You don't do anything halfway, do you? Kiss me," she said, taking his face between her hands, loving the way his day's growth of beard tickled her palms.

"You are one reckless woman," he said, his mouth a mere inch from her own. "Do you know what you're asking?"

"I do indeed."

"Is that an order?"

"Most definitely," she said, sighing as he eased himself into the bed beside her, pulling her into his arms.

"It would be my pleasure to kiss you senseless, Mrs. Carrington. Unlike you, I always follow orders."

"I told you before, if an order makes sense to me, I'll obey without question. This one definitely makes sense."

"You talk too much." He covered her mouth with his own and kissed her until she was breathless and wanting.

He loved her. Her heart sang the words over and over. From the first moment they met, Cady had somehow felt their destiny was linked. If she had known the ecstasy she would find in his arms, no power on earth could have made her leave him two years ago. They had lost so much time and there was no way to get it back. But what they had gone through would make them cherish the precious gift they had. She vowed to spend every moment of every day showing him how much she loved him. Although she would never tell him so, his reckless wife would even follow orders, if it would make him happy.

Not every order, of course.

Let HarperMonogram
Sweep You Away!

Touched by Angels by Debbie Macomber
From the bestselling author of *A Season of Angels* and *The Trouble with Angels*. The much-loved angelic trio—Shirley, Goodness, and Mercy—are spending this Christmas in New York City. And three deserving souls are about to have their wishes granted by this dizzy, though divinely inspired, crew.

Till the End of Time by Suzanne Elizabeth
The latest sizzling time-travel romance from the award-winning author of *Destiny's Embrace*. Scott Ramsey has a taste for adventure and a way with the ladies. When his time-travel experiment transports him back to Civil War Georgia, he meets his match in Rachel Ann Warren, a beautiful Union spy posing as a Southern belle.

A Taste of Honey by Stephanie Mittman
After raising her five siblings, marrying the local minister is a chance for Annie Morrow to get away from the farm. When she loses her heart to widower Noah Eastman, however, Annie must choose between a life of ease and a love no money can buy.

A Delicate Condition by Angie Ray
Golden Heart Winner. A marriage of convenience weds innocent Miranda Rembert to the icy Lord Huntsley. But beneath his lordship's stern exterior, fires of passion linger—along with a burning desire for the marital pleasures only Miranda can provide.

Reckless Destiny by Teresa Southwick
Believing that Arizona Territory is no place for a lady, Captain Kane Carrington sent proper easterner Cady Tanner packing. Now the winsome schoolteacher is back, and ready to teach Captain Carrington a lesson in love.

And in case you missed last month's selections . . .

Liberty Blue by Robin Lee Hatcher
Libby headed west, running from her ruthless father and her privileged life. Remington Walker will do anything to locate her, as long as her father keeps paying him. But when Remington does he realizes she's worth more than money can buy.

Shadows in the Mirror by Roslynn Griffith
Iphigenia Wentworth is determined to find her missing baby in West Texas. She never expected to find love with a local rancher along the way.

Yesterday's Tomorrows by Margaret Lane
Montana rancher Abby De Coux is magically transported back to the year 1875 in order to save her family's ranch. There she meets ruggedly handsome Elan, who will gamble his future to make her his forever.

The Covenant by Modean Moon
From the author of the acclaimed *Evermore*, a spellbinding present-day romance expertly interwoven with a nineteenth-century love story.

Brimstone by Sonia Simone
After being cheated at the gaming tables by seasoned sharper Katie Starr, the Earl of Brynston decides to teach the silly American girl a lesson. But soon the two are caught in a high stakes game in which they both risk losing their hearts.